J. Passavant

Raphael of Urbino and His Father Giovanni Santi

Anatiposi

J. Passavant

Raphael of Urbino and His Father Giovanni Santi

Reprint of the original, first published in 1872.

1st Edition 2023 | ISBN: 978-3-38213-339-9

Anatiposi Verlag is an imprint of Outlook Verlagsgesellschaft mbH.

Verlag (Publisher): Outlook Verlag GmbH, Zeilweg 44, 60439 Frankfurt, Deutschland
Vertretungsberechtigt (Authorized to represent): E. Roepke, Zeilweg 44, 60439 Frankfurt, Deutschland
Druck (Print): Books on Demand GmbH, In de Tarpen 42, 22848 Norderstedt, Deutschland

RAPHAEL OF URBINO.

"*TU SOLO IL PITTOR SEI DE' PITTORI*"

RAPHAEL OF URBINO

AND HIS FATHER

GIOVANNI SANTI

BY J. D. PASSAVANT

FORMERLY DIRECTOR OF THE MUSEUM AT FRANKFORT

ILLUSTRATED

London and New York

MACMILLAN AND CO.

1872

THE MADONNA WITH THE DIADEM.

In the Louvre.

CHISWICK PRESS:—PRINTED BY WHITTINGHAM AND WILKINS,
TOOKS COURT, CHANCERY LANE.

PREFACE.

SO long ago as the year 1839 Herr Passavant, Director of the Museum at Frankfort, published a work in two volumes entitled "Rafael von Urbino und sein Vater Giovanni Santi," which was without doubt the most comprehensive life of Raphael that had at that time appeared. A third volume, containing many additional particulars, was published in 1858.

For many years Passavant's work was known only to German scholars; till, in 1860, a new Edition, corrected and much enlarged by the author, was translated into French by M. Jules Lunteschutz, and, with many valuable annotations by M. Paul Lacroix, published in Paris in two closely printed volumes containing upwards of twelve hundred pages. To this elaborate book, on which it is evident that both Author and Editor must have bestowed much labour, Raphael's admirers have turned whenever they have sought for information; and it will doubtless remain for many years the best book of reference on all questions pertaining to the great painter.

The present work consists of a translation of those parts of Passavant's volumes which are most likely to interest the general reader: occasionally a section has been abridged, reference, however, in most cases being made to the French edition. An Essay on the Genius of Raphael; a Dissertation on the Works of his Pupils; a History of the Family of Santi; as well as a Catalogue of Raphael's Sketches and Drawings, have been omitted; but the valuable descriptions of all the known Paintings of Raphael, and the Chronological Index, which is of so much service to amateurs who wish to study the progressive character of his works, have been preserved.

The Illustrations, by one of the new permanent processes of photography (Mr. Woodbury's), are from the finest engravings that could be procured, and have been chosen with the intention of giving examples of Raphael's various styles of painting.

TABLE OF CONTENTS.

CATALOGUE OF RAPHAEL'S PAINTINGS.

THE ILLUSTRATIONS.

PREFACE TO THE GERMAN EDITION.[1]

RAPHAEL is now universally acknowledged to be the greatest genius of modern painting, and the history of his life is important even to the history of art.

And yet, the numerous biographies of Raphael that have been written since the time of Vasari, are far from satisfying the wants of the present time. They bear no trace of profound study or of that judicious and independent criticism which alone are able to make us realise the past. There have been no deep researches, no fresh discoveries, and a complete and truthful biography of this extraordinary man is still wanting.

A rapid examination of the works published on Raphael will show how insufficient they are.

The most ancient of these is that written in Latin by Paolo Giovio. It appeared for the first time in the "Storia della Letteratura Italiana," of Girolamo Tiraboschi. It contains but few facts, and the author, for want of artistic knowledge, has fallen into many errors.[2] Paolo Giovio deserves, however, the gratitude of all friends of art, for it was he who induced Vasari to write his "Lives of Italian Artists."

Giorgio Vasari, in his important work ("Vite de' più eccellenti Archi-

---

[1] "Rafael von Urbino und sein Vater Giovanni Santi." Leipzig, 1839, in 8vo, with atlas in fol.

[2] This was no doubt intended to be included in the work of P. Giovio, entitled "Illustrium virorum vitæ," published at Florence in 1549. (Note by Lacroix.)

tetti, Pittori e Scultori,"[1] &c.) has treated the life of Raphael with peculiar care; but there were several circumstances in the early life of the painter which he was not acquainted with; he had only confused notions as to the works in the first "Camera" of the Vatican, and he has entirely omitted notices of many easel-pictures, which had been already dispersed.

It must be acknowledged, however, that he indicates with sufficient clearness the chronological order of paintings; that his opinions are generally very correct, although rather too uniformly enthusiastic, and that he foresaw the great influence Raphael would exercise on the history of art. Without the treasures of information to be found in his work, our present task would be almost impossible.

In 1790, there appeared at Rome the "Vita inedita di Raffaello da Urbino," illustrated with notes by Angelo Comolli.[2] An endeavour has been made to prove that this biography was anterior to all the other biographies of Raphael. Comolli even believes that it was drawn up almost immediately after the death of Raphael by Giovanni della Casa. And yet it is merely a meagre extract from Vasari, with the addition of a few fresh documents. This was perceived by Lanzi. And indeed the anonymous authors and Vasari are so much alike that one must certainly have copied from the other. This *other* must be Vasari, for the anonymous writer gives information about the portraits of Tibaldeo and Carondelet, and of the "Child" in marble, works which were unknown in the time of Vasari, and were only discovered in the last century. The anonymous writer commits certain errors, which a contemporary of Raphael could not have done. For example, he states (p. 22) that Raphael painted the Holy Family, for Dom. Canigiani, in 1516; (p. 24) that on his arrival at Rome he met Pietro della Francesca and Bramante da Milano (both having been long dead); (p. 53) that he had painted the portrait of Donna Beatrice d'Este (although there was at that time no princess of that name in the family of Este; Vasari merely names Beatrice Ferrarese); (p. 63) that he had been named, by Leo X., superintendent of the works of art at the Vatican (whilst the brief of the 27th

---

[1] Firenze, 1550, 2nd edition, enlarged and improved, in 1568. The life of Raphael also appeared separately, under the title "Vita di Raffaelle da Urbino, Pittore ed Architetto, tratta da quelle de' Pittori, Scultori ed Architetti, di Giorgio Vasari. In Roma, 1751."

[2] Second edition, corrected, in 1791.

August, 1515, had merely authorized him to collect stone and antique marbles for the building at St. Peter's, and to prevent the destruction of the ancient inscriptions).

But what is sufficient proof that the "Vita inedita," is quite fallacious and of modern composition, is the passage in which the statue of Jonah is spoken of as being in the Church of Santa Maria del Popola. The "Jonah" was only placed in this church in 1554. It was still in the studio of Lorenzetto when the first edition of Vasari was published, in 1550, and it is only the edition of 1568 which mentions its having been removed to the Chigi Chapel.

According to appearances, the learned editor Comolli, the author of the notes, was the first to be deceived by this fraud.

For more than two centuries it has been considered sufficient to make compilations from Vasari's "Life of Raphael," or else to reprint Vasari himself, adding, either indications drawn from ancient authors, or modern discoveries.[1] Amongst the biographies taken from Vasari, we must place those contained in the works of Carl van Mander, Joachim von Sandrart, Filippo Baldinucci, Isaac Bullard, d'Argenville, Lairesse, Gault de Saint Germain, Andrea Lazzari, Pellegrino Orlandi and others; several separate lives, as "Abrégé de la Vie de Raphaël Sanzio d'Urbin," by Pierre Daret, Paris, 1607, in 12mo, and 1651, in 16mo; "Recherche curieuse de la Vie de Sanzio d'Urbin, de des œuvres, peintures et stampes (*sic*), gravées par Marc Antoine," &c., by Jean de Bombourg;[2] Lyons, 1675, in 12mo, and 1709, in 12mo; and even the English work of Duppa, "Life of Raffaello Sanzio," London, 1816.

A number of other authors have written on the life and works of Raphael, for example—Dolce, Armenini, Lomazzo, Borghini, Scanelli, Boschini, Malvasia (the anonymous writer of Morelli), Francesconi, Bellori, Montagnani, Fea, Conca, Lanzi, Orsini, Reynolds, Richardson, Webb, Father Dan, Félibien, Lépicié, Mariette, Seroux d'Agincourt,

---

[1] Such, in particular, as the editions of Geo. Bottari, Roma, 1759; of Guglielmo della Valle, Siena, 1791-94; and the German edition of Ludwig, Schorn, Stuttgart, 1832.

[2] This work, which is only a free translation of Vasari's "Life of Raphael," is in reality merely a reproduction, under another title, of the translation, published by P. Daret in 1651. J. de Bombourg has only suppressed the dedication, enlarged the preface, and added at the close one page with a description of the pictures at Lyons. This little volume is extremely rare. (Note by Lacroix.)

Mengs, Goethe, Fernow, Fiorillo, von Quandt, Platner, &c. Whatever they may have said of any importance will be found in the course of this work.

Some original biographies, the result of particular views on Raphael or of long researches on his works, deserve, however, a special examination.

H. H. Fuessli, in the appendix to his work entitled "Allgemeines Künstlerlexicon" (General Dictionary of Artists), Zurich, 1814, has given, in twenty-four sheets, a life of Raphael, published separately in 1815, in 4to. This indefatigable compiler, although taking the greater part of his work from Vasari, has added much information on the pictures not described by the Italian author, and even engravings of his works. But the councillor Meyer and the other amateurs and artists of Weimar, who, at that time, blindly followed the opinions and tastes of Mengs, have frequently misled him in his judgments. Fuessli's work then was not equal to its subject, and is only remarkable as a compilation.

"Raphel Sanzio's Leben und Werke," by G. Chr. Braun (Wiesbaden, 1815; second edition, 1819, in 8vo.) is also a compilation in which there is not much artistic knowledge or enlightened judgment. It contains fewer facts, too, than that of Fuessli.

"Rafael aus Urbino," by Friedrich Rehberg, Munich, 1824, 2 vols., with thirty-eight lithographed plates, in 4to. The author, who was a painter, brings forward his own ideas on the progress of art in Italy from Cimabue to Raphael, the highest representative of that glorious epoch. His ideas have nothing very remarkable in them, and the fresh documents he produces have either very little foundation, or else are completely erroneous.

Quatremère de Quincy: "Histoire de la vie et des ouvrages de Raphaël," Paris, 1814, in 8vo.; second edition, 1835. This is the first really important work on the subject. Drawn up with great skill and rich in ingenious observations, it had great and legitimate success at its first appearance. But yet it contains nothing really new, and even presents known facts in a very incomplete and almost superficial manner. He wrote besides, under the influence of the school of Louis David, which was unfavourable for a healthy appreciation of the works of the great Italian master.

"Istoria della vita e delle opere di Raffaello Sanzio da Urbino," del Signor Quatremère de Quincy, &c., Milano, 1829, in 8vo. Francesco

Longhena, in the enlarged and annotated edition, endeavours to complete the French work with fresh information; but the dupe of picture-dealers, interested in falsifying facts, he received and accepted on every side numbers of apocryphal stories. The number of notes render the reading of the text difficult, and interrupt the historical series of the works of Raphael, which M. Quatremère de Quincy himself had not grouped in strict chronological order.

But yet, in spite of all its faults, the book of Longhena contains nearly all the information which was then possessed about Raphael, and even throws some fresh light on his works.

There is also a German translation of Quatremère de Quincy from the second edition. Quedlinburg, 1836, in 8vo.

The celebrated engraver, Baron Boucher Desnoyers, published in 1852 an Appendix to Quatremère de Quincy. This Appendix, which was afterwards enlarged, has gone through a second edition.

"Elogio Storico di Giovanni Santi, pittore e poeta, padre del gran Raffaello da Urbino," 1822; a pamphlet in 8vo. "Elogio storico di Raffaello Santi da Urbino." Urbino, 1829 and 1831; two pamphlets in 8vo., by Luigi Pungileoni. We owe to him our knowledge of the ancestors of Raphael, and of his early life, as well as of the works of his father, Giovanni Santi; for Pungileoni examined all the archives of Urbino, where he made some valuable discoveries. He gives also several documents of greater or less antiquity which had never before been published.

C. F. von Rumohr, "Uber Raphael von Urbino und dessen Nähere Zeitgenossen" (on Raphael and his nearest contemporaries), Berlin, 1831, in 8vo. First published in the third part of the "Italienischen Forschungen," and afterwards separately. The learned author studies the development of the genius of Raphael, and the exterior circumstances which influenced it. His book is very attractive, and even instructive, although he produces but few fresh facts. The two first volumes of the "Researches on Italy" promised more. But if the views of the writer are sometimes very abstract, his style is always serious, and worthy of history: his facts are well supported; he is well acquainted with the works of which he speaks; he usually judges with great clearness, and draws delicately defined deductions. Nevertheless, he too frequently accepts statements which are not quite exact, especially about the earlier paintings of Raphael. In the catalogue of his works we have drawn attention to some of these errors, passing over others in silence when the facts themselves suffice to point them out.

G. K. Nagler, "Raphael als Mensch und Künstler" (Raphael as a Man and as an Artist). Munich, 1836, in 8vo. A large compilation of all that was then known of Raphael, but without any enlightened criticism, without original views or novelty in the facts—a mixture of false and true which the author, having none of the special knowledge required for such a publication, has too frequently confounded together.

Dr. Franz Kugler, "Handbuch der Geschichte der Malerei in Italien" (Handbook of the History of Painting in Italy). Berlin, 1837, in 8vo. The documents relating to the life of Raphael are intelligently chosen, but they are not sufficient to form a biography. The description of the works is tolerably complete.

It results clearly, from this rapid examination, that no reliable critical work on the life of Raphael yet exists. A singular circumstance has led us to undertake this difficult task.

The late Professor Braun, of Mainz, wishing to remodel his little work on Raphael, asked our advice. He soon acquired the conviction that, to attain a satisfactory result, it would be indispensable to have an intimate knowledge of the works of Raphael, of his country, and of his times. He then endeavoured to persuade us to write a biography of the great Italian master. We did not then feel capable of undertaking it, but different circumstances afterwards contributed to decide us.

In order to see for ourselves as many as possible of the works of Raphael, we passed another year in Italy, where we had already resided for seven consecutive years; we took a journey to England, and another to Paris, where in our youth we had admired the treasures of the Napoleon Museum: and, in 1816, in the house of M. Bonnemaison, the Raphaels which now adorn the Museum of Madrid.

All the collections in Germany were already familiar to us, with the exception, however, of those in Vienna, which we went to examine.

We may say, then, that we have examined for ourselves nearly the whole of the works of Raphael.

We have visited Urbino, the birthplace of Raphael, and all the places where he lived and worked. We have searched through all the libraries of Italy, Germany, England, and France, to collect materials. The archives of Rome, and those of the Medici at Florence, are the only ones that have remained closed to us, as to so many others.

These persevering researches have not merely given us a succinct understanding of the subject in general, but have brought out such precise and numerous documents that they enable us to bring the whole of the life of Raphael into full daylight.

As the social position and personal surroundings are very important, especially in the biography of an artist, we have carefully collected all that relates to the family of Raphael: his father, Giovanni Santi, whose artistic qualities have unjustly fallen into forgetfulness; the Court of Urbino, then celebrated among all the courts of Italy for its military glory, its private virtues, and the protection it accorded to learned men.

Raphael's father, received with benevolence and sympathy at that court, has left us a "Chronicle in Rhyme," in honour of Federico de Montefeltro, Duke of Urbino. This chronicle, far from brilliant in a poetical point of view, reveals, at all events, the noble sentiments of Giovanni Santi, and contains some valuable details about the artists of the time. This is the reason why we shall give fragments from it which refer to art.

All the earlier histories have been far from exact as to the early life of Raphael. Our researches have enabled us to fix with exactness the dates of the arrival of Raphael at the house of Perugino, of his relations with him and with other painters of Umbria and Florence, and of his different journeys to Urbino, Florence, and elsewhere, during this first period.

On his existence and labours at Rome there were, indeed, few omissions to make up; but yet we have cleared up many facts that were confused or ill interpreted.

The most difficult part of our task has been the catalogue of pictures. Such an undertaking required a thorough examination of everything that has been attributed to Raphael. We have devoted six years to verifying the pictures of Raphael to be found in different countries. The difficulty with the drawings was much greater. However, our technical knowledge as a painter, and our long habit of looking at works of art from a critical and historical point of view, lead us to hope that we have not committed any serious errors. We have corrected many in the earlier catalogues; we have set aside many drawings falsely ascribed to Raphael, and have added a number of others after having proved their authenticity.

The same difficulty was felt with the engravings of the works of Raphael. The enumeration of these engravings is very incomplete and faulty in the otherwise good works of Carl Heinr. von Heinecken, "Nachrichten von Künstlern und Kunstsachen," Leipzig, 1769, 2 vols. in 8vo.; of Landon, "Vie et Œuvres de Raphaël," Paris, 1805-9, 8 vols. in 4to.; and of the Count von Lepel, "Catalogue des Estampes gravées d'après Rafael," by Tauriscus Eubœus, Frankfort-on-the-Maine, 1819, in 8vo.

These writers attribute to Raphael many works which are not his; Lepel frequently confuses into one article several different subjects, or else, he divides one subject into several articles.

Had the work of Zani, "Enciclopedia metodica critico-ragionata delle Belle Arti," Parma, 1820, been terminated, it would have contained, perhaps, the most exact information on the engravings from Raphael.

But, except in some rare exceptions, which we shall take care to mention, our statements all rest on the results of our own examinations. We have enumerated the second-class engravings as well as the rest, excluding, however, the worst productions of our own time.

Frankfort on the Maine.

CHAPTER I.

GIOVANNI SANTI,

THE FATHER OF RAPHAEL.

GIOVANNI SANTI was born at Colbordolo, a small town, formerly fortified, on the summit of a mountain, in the ancient duchy of Urbino. The remains of a castle may still be seen there. From this height there is a magnificent view over hills, planted with vines and olives, between which the rivers Pisauro and Apsa flow down towards the plain of Pescara and the Adriatic Sea.

At Colbordolo there lived, in the beginning of the fourteenth century, a man named Sante.[1] His descendants received from him the surname of Sante or Santi. At a later period, in the time of Vasari, the Latin name *Santi* or Sanctius was translated according to the Italian custom into *Sanzio*, as we usually find it written now.

Of this elder Sante, we merely know that he had a son—Piero or Pietro. The sons of Pietro were named Luča—who died about 1436, and Peruzzolo—who married, about 1418, Gentilina, the daughter of Antonio Urbinelli.

Peruzzolo had, by this marriage, one son, to whom he gave the name of Sante, and two daughters, Jacopa and Francesca. He was not without a fortune, for there are documents still in existence which prove that he purchased, in 1438, a house in the Castle square, and that he also possessed some fields. But he suffered great losses, in 1446, when

[1] The baptismal name Sante is still used in that part of the country.

Sigismondo Malatesta, passing through the duchy of Urbino with the troops of the pope, laid waste Urbino with fire and sword.[1] Troubled by these disasters, and knowing they would probably be renewed,[2] he made up his mind, in 1450, to leave his home, although his house was still standing, and to go with his wife and children to settle in the town of Urbino, which offered at the same time greater security and greater resources. He died there in 1457, and his wife Gentilina eight years later.

His son Sante had married Elisabetta, and had two sons and two daughters, Giovanni and Bartolomeo, Margherita and Santa. He lived in a house in the Market-place,[3] belonging for a long time to the brotherhood of Santa Maria della Misericordia, which had let it to him for the sum of thirteen ducats a year.

By engaging in business and trading in corn, Sante had improved his fortune. On the 28th October, 1457, he was able, conjointly with one of his nephews, to pay two hundred and forty ducats for some property belonging to Pierantonio Paltroni, secretary and councillor in the duchy of Urbino. On the 30th April, 1461, he acquired more land, and a good meadow, with a stream of water flowing through it. Two years after he bought for the sum of two hundred and forty ducats, in the street named the Contrada del Monte, two adjacent houses, which still form one of the most remarkable constructions of that quarter. It was there that Raphael was to be born.

The new residence of the Santi family produced the happiest effect on the intelligent nature of the young Giovanni.

The town of Urbino is very healthy, and in a beautiful situation, near the highest point of the Apennine which separates the Marches of Ancona from Tuscany and Umbria. The cones and zigzags of the mountains which surround it stand out in sharp relief against the

---

[1] This is the reason why Giovanni Santi, the grandson of Peruzzolo, exclaims dolefully in the dedication to the Duke Guidubaldo of the Chronicle in rhyme, of which we shall speak hereafter—"Fate has reduced my paternal roof to ashes, and destroyed all our goods. Much time would be required to relate one after another all the miseries and afflictions of my existence!"

[2] We read in Clementini (Storia di Rimino, lib. ix. p. 343—"1462. October 3. Colbordolo, having dared to resist, was abandoned to pillage and the flames; the men were made prisoners. . . . . Belenzone, the general of the infantry of Count Federico, and Commandant of Talacchio (the fortress of Colbordolo), surrendered by capitulation, but only after the destruction of half of its walls."

[3] This house may still be seen at Urbino.

sky as far as the Adriatic, looking like the upheaving waves of a tempestuous sea. From the south to the west these peaks crown the horizon. First comes the Fùrlo, a barrier which seems to close in the view; then the magnificent masses of the Monte Nerone; to the east the picturesque rocks of the Monte San Simone, which overlook the whole country, and further on the rock from whence the Tiber flows out, hastening onwards to the Mediterranean. To the north, on a steep point, rises the little republic of San Marino, which is protected by its poverty from the covetousness of wealthy neighbours. To the right of San Marino the Adriatic may be seen, between the cuttings of wooded hills richly stored with game, whilst the plain and small hills are covered with rich cereals, vines, and olives.

The mountaineers of this part of the country, an active and courageous race, were at this time governed by Count Federico, of the family of Montefeltro, bearing the title of duke, which he had only obtained from the Pope Sixtus IV. in 1474. Federico, who was the favourite pupil of Vittorino da Feltro, a statesman and warrior, well skilled in military statistics and in the science of fortification, as well as in Greek and Latin literature, was also the friend and protector of artists and learned men. He possessed a valuable collection of paintings and antiquities, and a library, in which the manuscripts, well bound and furnished with gold and silver clasps, showed his esteem for the works of genius. One of his treasures in painting was the Jan van Eyck, representing a "Bath for Women," a picture which Facius, in 1456, described as a marvel, and which Vasari was also able to admire at Urbino.

When, after having won the victory on the battle-field, the captain-prince returned to the town, he undertook, with indefatigable and praiseworthy energy, to erect some magnificent edifices; a noble occupation for a time of peace, and one which will ever ensure durable glory for princes.

About this time, it was his greatest wish to transform the small castle of Urbino, two towers of which still remain, into a vast palace. He intended this building to surpass all the palaces of Italy in magnificence. With this purpose he sent for several artists, and chose as chief architect the excellent master Luciano Lauranna,[1] who drew up the plan and commenced the work in 1447.

---

[1] Clementini ("Storia di Rimino"), et Rinaldo Riposati ("Della Zecca di Gubbio," Bologna, 1772, p. 262).

In order to obtain the necessary site for so large a building, they were obliged to unite two rocks by filling up the space which separated them. It was on these two rocks then, that the palace (named *la Corte*) was built with its two interior courts. The larger of these, intended for games, is of the form of an amphitheatre, although quite simple; the other, one of the principal ornaments of the palace, is a long quadrilateral. The walls rest on a colonnade of composite order, with arcades; graceful pilasters with cornices surround the windows, and in the upper frieze, which surrounds it, may be read the name of the Duke Federico, accompanied with inscriptions which recall his dignities, actions, and virtues.[1]

Turning towards the grand staircase we find a bas-relief containing the portrait of the noble founder, whose name is indicated by the letters FE. C. (Federicus Comes) in the lower part, and by the letters F. D. (Federicus Dux) in the upper part. The magnificent staircase, covered by an arched roof with golden rose work, leads to a gallery which passes round the court. The Cardinal Stoppani decorated this gallery with seventy-two slabs of marble, on which, according to Vasari, Francesco di Giorgio[2] executed the trophies, which formerly adorned the façade of the palace. In the same gallery may be found the interesting ancient inscriptions, which the same cardinal collected at a great expense. But the six bas-reliefs in bronze, the subjects of which were taken from the life of the Duke Federico, and a seventh bas-relief, representing a "Descent from the Cross," the works of the celebrated iron-founder, Clemente, have disappeared.

The principal wall is vaulted. There are two fire-places, richly ornamented, and several large painted escutcheons, bearing the arms of the princes allied to the family of Montefeltro, often joined to the Lion of St. Mark of the Venetian republic. This emblem and the letters F. C., repeated on the ceiling, prove that this part of the palace was

---

[1] FEDERICUS . VRBINI . DVX . MONTISFERETRI . AC . DVRANTIS . COMES . SANCTÆ . RO . ECCLESIÆ . CONFALONIERIVS . ATQVE . ITALICÆ . CONFŒDERATIONIS . IMPERATOR . HANC . DOMVM . A . FUNDAMENTIS . ERECTAM . GLORIÆ . ET . POSTERITATI . SVÆ . EXÆDIFICAVIT . And in the lower frieze, above the arcade—QVI . BELLO . PLVRIES . DEPVGNAVIT . SEXIES . SIGNA . CONTVLIT . OCTIES . HOSTEM . PROFLIGAVIT . OMNIUMQUE . PRÆLIORVM . VICTOR . DITIONEM . AVXIT . EIVSDEM . IVSTITIA . CLEMENTIA . LIBERALITAS . ET . RELIGIO . PACE . VICTORIAS . ÆQVARVNT . ORNARVNTQVE .

[2] Ambrogio Barocchio, son of Antonio da Milano, according to Pungileoni.

completed before 1474, when Federico was still only a count. The frames of the windows and doors are, as well as the chimney pieces, of whitish marble, and the ornaments on them are of gold on a blue ground.

In the library,[1] besides a number of valuable folios, there was a Hebrew Bible, placed on one side on a metal desk, in the form of an eagle with outstretched wings. Adjoining the library an apartment, furnished with carved wooden benches, served as a study. On the walls hung the portraits of the most celebrated ancient[2] or contemporary authors, with short inscriptions in their honour.

According to Baldi,[3] another room had been decorated by Timoteo Viti with paintings, now destroyed, which represented Pallas armed, Apollo and the Muses. Rich pictures in mosaic, probably executed by Jacomo of Florence, then residing at Urbino, represent various religious and military emblems, and also the portrait of the duke, with this inscription: FEDERICO · DUX · MCCCCLXXVI. The soffit of wood work divided into square and octagon cases, and relieved with gold, adds still further to the splendour of this room.

At the side of the palace, and at the foot of the rock, are the barracks and the stables, with an arched reservoir, of such extent that horses might be watered there, quite sheltered from the attack of an enemy. These stables were not built by Luciano, but, after 1475, by Francesco di Giorgio Martini, of Siena,[4] one of the most celebrated engineers of the time. Martini was very useful to the duke in the fortifications; it was he who built the citadels of Cagli, of Sasso di Monte Feltro, of Tavoletto, Alaserra, Mondavi and Mondosi. He appears to have also executed some works of art for the palace, as Vasari mentions a portrait of the duke painted in a medallion by Martini.

Federico also built another palace at Gubbio, a pretty little town situated on the western slope of the Apennines. He doubtless employed

---

[1] This library is now empty. The collection of manuscripts was removed to Rome in 1657. It forms one of the most important parts of the Vatican library. See Blume, "Iter italicum," iii. p. 53.

[2] In his sketch book Raphael seems to have drawn from the portraits of the ancient authors in this study.

[3] Baldi, abate di Guastalla: "Descriptione del Palazzo Ducale d'Urbino," 1587; and "Versi e Prose," del Baldi, p. 527. Vasari only mentions an Apollo with two Muses, half clothed.

[4] Riposati, "Della Zecca di Gubbio," Bologna, 1772, i. p. 263.

Luciano Lauranna on it; for the architecture is of the same character as the castle of Urbino, although the proportions are finer and the details more elegant, especially in the windows and the decorations of the pilasters.

In the palace of Gubbio, as in that of Urbino, the interior court is marked out, but only on three sides, by a colonnade of composite order, with arcades. The frames of the windows, doors and chimneys, are all executed with the same richness. Some traces of colour on the walls of the principal hall show that they were formerly covered with paintings.[1]

One small room still possesses its ancient splendour. It is encrusted with pictures in mosaic, representing cases filled with books and instruments of music, or the order of the garter and various other objects. The soffit, richly ornamented, has compartments coloured white, blue and red, with very elegant gilded rose work. The inscriptions FE · DUX and G. BALDO · DX. in the wood work show that these decorations were only terminated under the Duke Guidubaldo, after 1482.[2]

Constantly occupied with these great enterprises, Federico, according to Giovanni Santi, often visited the buildings in course of construction, and conversed with the artists on the state of the works. The young Giovanni also watched with curiosity the gradual development of these, and, we must suppose, they contributed in no slight degree to inspire him with a taste for art.

Speaking of himself, in his dedication to the Duke Guidubaldo, he says that having arrived at an age when he might have chosen a career

---

[1] This palace, formerly so magnificent, now serves as a silk factory!

[2] According to a note of Giuseppe Piacenza, added to the first volume of the works of Baldinucci (p. 567, Turin, 1740), it was Federico himself who made the plan of this palace. Piacenza refers for his authority to a manuscript of the Magliabecchiana of Florence; but his supposition is contradicted by the passage in a patent granted to Luciano Lauranna, and dated from Castello di Pavia, June 10th, 1468, in which Federico, showing the admiration he felt for the art of architecture, adds that "grave occupations prevent him from devoting his own time to it." The resemblance that the palaces of Gubbio and Urbino, in the parts copied from the antique, bears to the architecture of Leo Battista Alberti, especially to the façade of the church of St. Andrew at Mantua, which he built in 1472, has also given rise to the supposition, that Alberti assisted in making the plans. But this opinion is not supported by any historical proof, and, on the contrary, is very improbable, from the fact that Alberti was from 1447, in the service of Sigismondo Malatesta, the most bitter enemy of Federico.

which would have insured his future welfare, he had preferred choosing "the admirable art of painting:" that this resolution much increased the cares of his family; and he adds in a grandiloquent manner: "These cares never weigh so cruelly as on a man already laden with the magnificent burden of art, a burden which would be heavy even for the shoulders of Atlas."

These words show how much Giovanni was in earnest with his work; but, unhappily, the manuscript does not mention what master guided his early studies.

We will consult then some indications in chap. xci. when he passes all the artists he knew in review; then by examining his own manner, we may perhaps, discover what painter particularly influenced him.

Giovanni had not the good fortune to be formed in one of those learned schools, where, as under Squarcione and Verocchio, solid instruction might be obtained. Some painter of his own town must have given him his earliest instruction; the works of the old masters preserved at Urbino must also have served him as models.

It is even possible that the frescoes in the oratory of the order of St. John the Baptist, painted in 1416, by the brothers Lorenzo and Jacopo di San Severino, may have especially struck his notice.

However, this cannot be proved either of these paintings, or of any other in the environs of Urbino. Besides, in general, ancient works have less influence on artists than the works of their contemporaries, especially when the arts, as at this period, are being restored.

Giovanni also, does not mention in his verses any of those painters who before him, or during his early life, executed various works at Urbino which have now disappeared: Ottaviano Martini Nelli, Antonio di Matteo, Antonio di Guido, Alberti da Ferrara, Francesco di Antonio Prioris, Pietro da Reggio, Fra Jacomo da Venezia, the Dominican Bartolomeo Coradini, named Fra Carnavale, and many others.

It is astonishing too that he does not mention in any manner the excellent master, Justus of Ghent, who, in 1474, painted at Urbino the remarkable picture of the "Last Supper," whilst he speaks with the highest praise of Jan Van Eyck and of Rogier of Bruges. We must conclude from this that he was not intimate with Justus. In all probability this Flemish master must have made a great mystery in Italy of the art of painting in oil, and for this reason, avoided holding much communication with the artists of the country.

It is at all events certain that, until the close of the fifteenth century, neither Giovanni Santi, nor any other painter in Italy, understood the process of oil-painting.[1] Urbino only possesses two pictures of this period, in which the influence of the school of the low countries may be seen on the Italian painting in distemper.

On the other hand, Giovanni mentions in his poem the greater part of the best painters, who then rendered Tuscany, Venice, Lombardy and the Marches of Ancona famous. He appears even to have been acquainted with their works. There is no doubt that he saw the celebrated altar-piece, which Gentile da Fabriano painted for the Romita di Val di Sasso, and the beautiful Madonna of Fra Angelico da Fiesole at Forano near Osimo; for he must certainly have visited those places. Paolo Uccelli, of Florence, painted at Urbino in 1468 for the brotherhood of Corpus Domini, and the master, Pietro della Francesca di Borgo di San Sepolcro, was living in 1469 in Giovanni's very house, at the expense of that community, which had ordered an altar-piece of him; this picture was never executed, though it is not known why. Pietro, however, painted, at Urbino, the portraits of Federico, then merely a count, and of his wife Battista Sforza. Both these portraits are preserved in the gallery of Florence.

Giovanni only grants a very brief notice to all these painters, but bestows the highest praises on Andrea Mantegna; he delights in extolling the learning and good qualities of this master, and even says that Heaven had opened to him the gates of painting!

Further on, he states that Melozzo de Forli, who caused a great improvement in perspective, "was particularly dear to him," from whence we may perhaps gather that he was one of his fellow-disciples.

Melozzo had been a pupil of Pietro della Francesca, but completed his studies under Mantegna, as is stated by Lucca Pacciolo in his "Divina Proportione." The pictures of Giovanni, however, offer no resemblance to those of Pietro: the slender proportions of his figures, his grey shadows, his dark, hard outlines, and his whole style of painting are all diametrically opposed to the practice and style of Pietro. Notwithstand-

---

[1] Recently the question has been raised, *apropos* to the publication of the "Treatise on Painting," by Cennino Cennini, whether the brothers Van Eyck were really the inventors of the improved process of oil painting. To this doubt we oppose the statement of Vasari that this discovery dates from 1410. Hubert Van Eyck, who also painted in oil, died in 1426, whilst the "Treatise" of Cennino was not written till 1437.

ing this, the later works of Giovanni, very possibly influenced by his friend Melozzo, show a certain imitation of Mantegna.

Several Madonnas, which were formerly either at Urbino, or in its immediate vicinity, may be considered as his first productions; no traces are now left of them.

Unhappily, also, the rest of his earlier works—at least those at Urbino—have also disappeared, either because they were not estimated at their true value, or because they were carried away during the wars of the Revolution. We have but little positive information about them.

This is why we shall pass on to an authentic and important picture, which may be ranked among his first works, and which was painted for the church of Santa Maria Nuova at Fano in the Marches of Ancona. This picture, representing a Visitation, was a short time ago still nailed against the wall above the organ. The complaints of some friends of art have caused it to be placed over the high altar on the left side of the church.

In this meeting of the holy women, the head of the Virgin expresses angelic modesty; Elizabeth is greeting her joyfully. Near them is St. Joseph and several women, whose attitudes are very graceful. In the foreground, a strip of paper bears the following inscription: "JOHANNES SANTIS . DI . VRBINO . PINXIT."

The figures are rather too slender, the hands and feet too narrow; but the drawing, although rather stiff, is not incorrect. The drapery, which is well executed, is not in the style of Mantegna. In short, the execution of this picture still shows the strugglings of an early school, and its endeavours after something higher.[1]

Another altar-piece, much more perfect and of a later time, is also to be seen at Fano. This was painted by Giovanni for the church of the Hospital of Santa Croce, and represents the Virgin seated on a throne, with the infant Jesus giving a benediction. Near the Virgin are the Empress Helena and the venerable Zachariah, patriarch of Constantinople; on the other side, St. Roch showing his wounds, and, behind him, St. Sebastian, whose wonderful beauty of profile gives us a foretaste of something of the future beauties of Raphael. It is signed, JOHANES. SANTIS . VRBI . F .

---

[1] Rossini has given an engraving of this in his "Storia della Pittura Italiana," plate 206.

The church of San Bartolo, outside the walls of Pesaro, possesses a St. Jerome, seated in the attitude of inspiration, on a splendidly decorated seat; two angels in an attitude of adoration hover above him in the air. This picture, painted in paste on canvas, is likewise signed by Giovanni.

Whilst still in this neighbourhood, Giovanni Santi received an order for a "Madonna della Misericordia" for the oratory of the Hospital of Montefiore. The Virgin, standing in a niche, carries in her arms the infant Jesus, who is giving a blessing with one hand, while with the other he holds the terrestrial globe. Two angels are raising the edge of the Virgin's mantle. Below this group kneel seven brothers of the order, and a young and beautiful woman, who is teaching her little child to worship. The faces, which are all portraits, have much animation and show with great justness, a simple and rather narrow faith. The apostles St. Peter, St. Paul, St. John and St. Francis, are grouped around. Above there are two little angels kneeling in the clouds.

In 1484 Giovanni executed for Domenico de' Domenici, the vicar of the church of Gradara, a neighbouring village to Pescaro, an altar-piece representing the Virgin and four saints. She is seated on a throne, holding the infant Jesus on her knees, and lovingly pressing his hand. He, with childish joy, is looking at a goldfinch, which he holds in his left hand. This subject, borrowed from domestic life is rendered with simple grace; but the rest of the composition is in a higher style. On one side is St. Stephen and St. Sophia, the patron saint of Gradara; on the other, St. John the Baptist, pointing to the Saviour, and the archangel St. Michael, with a sword in his hand. In the background are seraphims supporting some drapery. On the steps of the throne is an inscription in the following terms:—

GRADARIE SPECTANDA FVIT IMPENSA ET INDVSTRIA VIRI D. DOMENICI DE DOMINICIS VICARII ANNO D. MCCCCLXXXIIII DIE X APRILIS ET PER DVOS PRIVS TEMPORE D. IO CANOCI RECTORIS ECCLIE SVPHIE.

JOANNES . SAN . VRB . PINXIT.

Giovanni also painted for the church of the Magdalen at Sinigaglia, in the marches of Ancona, an "Annunciation," which also bears his signature, and which is now in the Brera gallery at Milan. Pungileoni supposes this picture to have been ordered by Giovanna Feltria, the wife of Giovanni della Rovere, signor of Sinigaglia and prefect of Rome; perhaps on the occasion of the birth of their son

Francesco Maria (afterwards Duke of Urbino), on the feast of the Annunciation, 1490.

We must now return to Urbino with our artist. In his studio in the Strada del Monte, we shall find him occupied in executing orders for painting and gilding, a union of arts still sometimes practised, and which, doubtless, dates from the period when painting was principally on a gold background.

This work bringing him in a sufficient revenue, he began to think about seeking a wife.

He was fortunate enough to meet in Magia, the daughter of Battista Ciarla, a merchant at Urbino, with a wife who made his life happy, and who on April 6, 1483,[1] presented him with a son, who was to be the greatest ornament of the arts.

---

[1] Vasari says that Raphael died on Good Friday (1520), "which had also been the day of his birth." According to this assertion of Vasari, the date of Raphael's birth has been fixed for Good Friday of the year 1483, which, according to the astronomical tables, occurred on the 26th March; and according to the Julian calendar on the 28th March. But Pietro Bembo in his inscription on the tomb of Raphael, says that Raphael died April 6th, 1520, on his thirty-seventh birthday, day for day. *Vixit annos* xxxvii. *integer integros.* Muzio Oddi, in the inscriptive tablet placed on the front of the house in which Raphael was born, also gives April 6th, 1483, as the day of Raphael's birth. It is clear, then, that the anniversary does not relate to the Good Friday, but to the day of the month.*

---

* Notwithstanding these decisive remarks of M. Passavant, M. Villot, in the twelve editions of his fine catalogue of the schools of Italy and Spain in the Louvre, places Raphael's birth on March 28th, 1483. Mr. Wornum, in the Catalogue of the National Gallery, gives the 6th April as the date, which appears to us unexceptionable. He gives very nearly the same reasons as M. Passavant—"The inscription by Cardinal Bembo on Raphael's tomb in the Pantheon is perfectly clear on this point. The concluding lines are—

> "Vixit An. XXXVII., Integer Integros.
> Quo die natus est, eo esse Desiit
> VIII. Id. Aprilis, MDXX."

That is, he lived *exactly* thirty-seven years; he died on the same day (of the year) on which he was born, April 6. From the circumstance that April 6, 1520, was Good Friday, Vasari and others after him were led into the erroneous notion that Raphael, as he died on Good Friday, was also born on Good Friday, overlooking the fact of this day being a moveable feast. Schorn and others, following the vague assertion of Vasari, have inferred an error in the very particular description of the Cardinal, who was the painter's intimate friend, and doubtless well aware of the real facts of the case. See a communication on this subject by Mr. J. Dennistoun, in the "Art Union Journal" of January, 1842. (Note by Lacroix.)

Giovanni as if he had had a presentiment of the position the child was to attain, baptized him Raphael, a name which had no precedent in the family. According to Vasari, Giovanni did not allow Raphael to have a wet nurse, as he wished the mother herself to nurse the child.

The "Madonna" which Giovanni painted on fresco in the court of his garden seems to be another proof of his extreme tenderness for Magia and Raphael. The Virgin's profile has an indescribable charm; the expression is evidently taken from nature. There is no doubt that the artist must have had some one very dear to him in his mind, and it is very probable that whilst making an offering to the Virgin he desired at the same time to perpetuate the features of his wife.

Nothing is known of the early years of the childhood of Raphael, but the affection of Giovanni and Magia must have centred more exclusively on him from their having lost another child, September 20, 1485. This death was preceded by that of Giovanni's father, the old Sante, so devoted to the welfare of the house. In the convent San Girolamo, he had made a will, by which, Giovanni as residuary legatee, became the proprietor of the house in the Strada del Monte, and of some land. To his other children Sante left the following legacies:

To Bartolomeo Santi, who had entered the church and who was at a later time dean of the diocese of San Donato, a small field and seventy florins;

To Margherita, married to Antonio di Bartolomeo Vagnini, 100 florins as dowry.

Margherita was the mother of Girolamo Vagnini, who afterwards, when chaplain of the chapel, founded by Raphael in the Pantheon, placed an inscription in remembrance of Maria Dovizia da Bibiena, the affianced bride of Raphael, opposite to the inscription of the great painter.

Santa, with the same dowry as her sister Margherita, was married to the master tailor Bartolomeo di Marino. But, having become a widow in 1490, she returned to live with her brother Giovanni, without, however being a burden on him, for she had preserved all the fortune of her husband.

We will now see what were the works executed by Giovanni at Urbino, and in the neighbourhood, the greater part of which, however, as we have already said, no longer exist.

One of the oldest pictures by him, is the altar-piece that he painted for the chapel of the family of the Count Matarozzi at Castel Durante (now Urbania), and which may be seen in the Museum at Berlin. The Virgin and Child appear to be portraits, as they differ from the usual types of Giovanni, and are treated with the feeling of a strong individuality. It is to be regretted, however, that the artist had not more beautiful models to copy from. Around the Virgin are grouped St. Thomas, St. Jerome, St. Thomas Aquinas and St. Catherine; near them the young Count Matarozzi is kneeling.

A picture, which has been almost entirely repainted, but is still interesting, is the "St. Sebastian," executed for the brotherhood of that name at Urbino. The saint, delivered up to the executioners, is surrounded by Christian men and women. What is especially remarkable in this picture is the foreshortening of the archers and of the angel, who is descending with a crown. This peculiarity shows that here Giovanni endeavoured to imitate his friend Melozzo, and in some parts, especially in the archers, he has succeeded very well. The portraits of the men and women, as in the altar-piece of Montefiore, are very natural and true.

Giovanni Francesco Oliva Pianani also ordered an altar-piece of Giovanni for the sepulchral chapel of his family in the church of the Franciscans in the convent of Monte Fiorentino.

This spacious church is to the right of Urbania, on the further side of the river Metauro, on a little hill at the foot of an arid rock of the Apennines. After the death of Count Carlo, in 1478, his relation, Oliva Pianini, had the chapel rebuilt; he erected a splendid tomb for the count and his wife, Maria Sibilla, who died in 1485, and he decorated the altar with a large "Madonna" by Giovanni Santi.

The Virgin is seated on a throne in a niche; she holds the infant Saviour on her knees. On the right stands the young Crescentius, in complete armour; a rich gold chain, set with precious stones, hangs on his breast; at his feet is his helmet, with the peacock's feather, a sign of the Ghibeline party, to which doubtless the Count Oliva belonged. St. Francis, in fervent contemplation of the child, makes a fine contrast to the figure of the knight. Behind the balustrade stand two angels; one of these resembles Raphael very much, but yet it cannot be his portrait, as he was only six years old at the time, whilst the angel is much older; but it may easily be conceived how Giovanni, having always his son's features in his thoughts, should have brought them into his pictures. We have already remarked, while speaking of the earlier pictures of Giovanni, that his children's heads have, in type and expression, a striking analogy with the more perfect and life-like ones that we admire in the works of Raphael.

To the right of the Virgin, before St. Jerome and St. Antony, who are standing, is the Count Oliva on his knees, covered with steel armour; we cannot help seeing that this fine figure is a portrait. Behind the saints are two angels; behind the marble balustrade of the throne, we catch a glimpse of eight angels playing music. Lastly, six heads of cherubim hovering above, complete the composition.

The following inscription is traced on a strip of parchment at the bottom of the picture—

CAROLVS OLIVVS PLANIANI (*sic*) COMES DIVÆ VIRGINI AC RELIQVIS CELESTIBVS . JOANNE SANCTO PICTORE DEDICAVIT .

MCCCCLXXXVIIII.

In this same year, 1489, Giovanni also completed the great altarpiece for the chapel of the Buffi family, in the church of the Franciscans at Urbino. This is also of a Virgin seated on the throne, bearing the infant Jesus, who is giving a blessing. On one side is St. Francis, looking at Jesus, and St. John the Baptist pointing to him; on the other side, near St. Sebastian and St. Jerome, are the Buffi family, the husband, wife, and child kneeling in prayer with clasped hands. Above is the Almighty and two little angels, who hold a crown over the head of the Virgin.

Two pictures, which were formerly placed beside this Madonna—the Archangel Raphael leading the young Tobit, and a St. Roch, both very fine and expressive works, are now placed at the entrance to the choir.

We should remember that Giovanni also painted portraits. We only know two, however. One, at the Colonna palace at Rome, is thought to represent the young Duke Guidubaldo when about twelve years of age. It is in profile, and the head is covered with a cap adorned with a precious stone and a large pearl; his princely costume is completed by a gold chain hanging from his breast. The other, also in profile, belongs to M. Dennistoun. At the bottom of the picture an inscription informs us that it was the portrait of Raphael when six years of age, painted by his father. But the fair hair, the rich clothing, and the suspicious character of the inscription awaken doubts as to this fact.

Whilst Giovanni was accomplishing so many undertakings, many events had taken place in the princely family of Urbino. The Duke

Federico had died in 1482, leaving his son Guidubaldo, still a minor, under the guardianship of the Count Ottaviano Ubaldini della Carda.

Ottaviano exercised an almost absolute authority over the young duke, until the day that his ward attained his majority, when only fourteen years old, sword in hand, by fighting victoriously for the Pope against Boccalino. This valiant action obtained general admiration for him on his return to Urbino, which was heightened still more by his good sense and the beauty of his person. The satisfaction of his subjects was at its height, when, three years later, he presented to them his young wife Elisabetta Gongaza, the daughter of the Marquis Federico of Mantua, a princess of incomparable grace and beauty.

On this occasion all the towns in the duchy organized public rejoicings, each in its own fashion. The inhabitants of Urbino played at a game very common in that part of the country and named the *aita*, in the court of the castle called the Mercatale, which the Duke Federico had prepared for such purposes.

This game of aita was played as follows. Some young men, dressed in tight-fitting clothes, which allowed the movement of the muscles to appear, divided themselves into two camps, and marched against each other; they provoked each other, struggled, and on each side brought back the vanquished as prisoners. After these expeditions and struggles, in which those on the same side lent mutual aid to each other (from whence the name *aita*), the side which had the greater number of prisoners was declared conqueror. The young combatants, who had distinguished themselves by their skill, received costly presents from the generous prince, and the acclamations of the crowd.

The little Raphael, six years of age, was doubtless present at these joyous pastimes, and his young fancy must have been much struck by the animated spectacle. His father, too, was probably not an inactive spectator, as the inhabitants of Urbino had raised triumphal arches, and had entrusted the care of raising them to artists. Urbino in this was emulating Pescara, where at the same moment Giovanni Sforza was marrying Maddalena, the other daughter of the Duke of Mantua, and where similar feasts were also celebrated.

But these passing demonstrations of attachment and love were not sufficient for Giovanni. He wished to show, by a durable monument, and one within his power, the sympathy he felt with his prince's family. The most natural idea to have occurred to him would have been to undertake some allegorical picture to the glory of his sovereign. But, no; he became an author, and wrote that Chronicle in rhyme, already mentioned several times, in which he extols the exploits and virtues of the late Duke Federico.

In order to obtain full and certain information about his hero, he formed an intimacy with Pier Antonio Paltroni, formerly secretary and private councillor to the Duke of Urbino; this appears in the ninth chapter of the Chronicle, in which he mentions that he had often visited Paltroni, the author of a History of the Duke, whose information was very useful to him in his own poem.

This Chronicle in rhyme, by Giovanni Santi, or rather, this biography in triplets, is preserved under the number 1305 in the Vatican library, among the manuscripts of Ottoboniani. It is written on 224 leaves large in-folio, in fine letters of the fifteenth century, except for a few corrections, in a very irregular writing, apparently by the hand of the author. It is preceded by a dedicatory epistle to the Duke of Guidubaldo. "Being an enthusiast about the qualities and military glory of the late duke," says Giovanni in this dedication, "the bitter thought occurred to him that learned men alone possessed the privilege of immortalizing great men in their exceptional language (Latin). Why, then, should it not be permitted to a man without erudition to acquire some glory by illustrating in his native tongue a subject which, like the one of which he spoke, *had nothing superior to it amongst the greatest facts of history!* He then has dared to attempt, though not without great difficulty, to sing the noble actions of the glorious father of Guidubaldo, by rejecting the thought that *such a coarse vase was unworthy to draw water at so pure a spring.* With God's help he had completed his work; and in order to leave behind him a proof of sincere and faithful devotion, he earnestly begs the duke to be pleased to be satisfied with the good intention, and to accept the fruit of his labours as the work of a humble servant."

In the midst of this discourse he breaks off to speak of himself and his unhappy fate, which passage we have already quoted.

The first nine chapters serve as an introduction; they contain a vision which, in the commencement, reminds us of the "Divina Comedia" of Dante. Giovanni, like Dante, loses his way in a dark forest filled with unruly men; but he passes through without yielding to the temptations placed in his way by these wicked men. Afterwards, invoking Apollo and the Muses, he is conducted to the Temple of Immortality, perfectly radiant with celestial splendour. Here he entreats the shade of Plutarch to guide him, and to instruct him about the Greek and Roman heroes whose ghosts surround him. After having talked with some of these, he interrogates the most illustrious warriors of the middle ages, and lastly converses with the ancestors of the Duke Federico da Montefeltro.

The twenty-three following books, divided into three times thirty-three chapters, are filled with a long narration of the actions of the Duke Federico. Those which concern his military glory, and several other circumstances of his life, have already been stated in other biographies. One fact, however, which is more to the duke's honour than many battles gained, has been passed over. It is related in Book XX., when speaking of the quarrels between the Venetians and the Duke of Ferrara, Ercole I.

The Duke of Ferrara, an ally of the Duke of Milan, had appealed to the Duke Federico to join in alliance with them. He hoped in this way to strengthen himself against the Duke of Milan, who was more powerful than he, to conciliate the rival interests of the Milanese and Ferrarese by the intervention of the Duke of Urbino, and even to induce him to accept the command of their united troops against the republic of Venice. The Venetians, knowing the value of Federico, employed every means to induce him to refuse this alliance, and offered him a pension of 3,000 ducats, if he would, on the contrary, command their own troops.

But like a loyal gentleman, the Duke replied: "That neither the attraction of so great a reward, nor the fear of irritating a powerful adversary, could ever induce him to betray a friendly prince; that he was firmly resolved to take the part of the Dukes of Ferrara and Milan, who had appointed him their general in chief."

There are also curious documents in the ninth chapter, containing an account of a visit of Federico to Milan, in 1468. The Duke of Urbino having been present at the wedding of the Duke of Galeazzo and the Princess Bona of Savoy, had seen, whilst at Milan, many pictures by celebrated masters. Giovanni seized this opportunity to pass in a sort of review all the artists known to himself, long after this journey of Federico, and even down to 1490; for he gives special mention of Leonardo da Vinci and Pietro Perugino.[1] He scarcely gives more than

[1] Da Vinci, having been born in 1452, was in fact only sixteen years old at the time of this journey of Federico to Milan in 1648, and Perugino, born in 1446, was only twenty-two. (Note by Lacroix.)

the names, but his list lets out many valuable facts with respect to himself. What he says of perspective is also well worthy of remark, as a proof of the great interest the science then excited. It would be going too far, however, to conclude that he wrote a treatise on perspective.[1] The anonymous work that Lucca Pacciolo saw in the library of the Duke of Urbino was certainly nothing but the Treatise of Pietro della Francesca, now belonging to M. Mazini, at Borgo San Sepolcro.

In this chronicle we meet with lively historical sentences and really poetical passages, as, for example, the account of the death of the Countess Battista, the second wife of Federico. Possibly Giovanni's hero did not quite come up to the requirements of an epic poem, Certainly the style leaves much to be desired. But the Italian poets of that time are neither more correct nor more brilliant themselves.

However, whether the chronicle be judged with severity or indulgence, it does not the less insure for its author an honourable place amongst those painters who have left us books as well as pictures. And there is something touching, too, in his disinterested attachment to two princes of such high qualities. Whilst endeavouring to celebrate the praises of the duke whom he loved, Giovanni has erected for himself a monument worthy of the sympathy of all those with whom the glory of the son will not cause the father to be forgotten.

We must now return to Giovanni's house. He lived happily with Magia, his little son Raphael, his mother Elisabetta, and his sister Santa. This happy family life, however, was not destined to last long.

Elisabetta died, October 3rd, 1491. Four days after, Giovanni had the misfortune to lose his wife Magia, and a few days afterwards his only daughter, still an infant. Thus one grief after another destroyed his domestic happiness.

The isolation soon became insupportable to the affectionate heart of Giovanni; besides, a woman's care was wanted for his dear Raphael. It was, then, with fresh hopes of happiness that he contracted his second marriage, May 25, 1492, at the church of Santa Agata, with Bernardina, a daughter of the goldsmith Pietro di Parte. Bernardina brought him in dowry two hundred florins. He lived happily with her, although her character does not seem to have had the gentleness of that of Magia, as

---

[1] Luigi Pungileoni: "Elogio Storico di Giovanni Santi," p. 36.

we shall see by the annoyances she inflicted on the young Raphael after the death of Giovanni.

We will now speak of the latest works of Giovanni which are known to us. The patrician Pietro Tiranni commissioned him to decorate with frescoes his family chapel in the old church of St. John, which has become the church of the Dominicans, at Cagli. Giovanni then went to that town,[1] with his wife and son, in order to execute the commission; and not only did he realize the expectation of the patrician, but must certainly have far surpassed it, for these pictures at Cagli are the finest he ever produced.

This chapel—the second altar to the left, has an arch in the fore part, supported by two graceful columns. The largest fresco covers the wall at the end. It represents in the lower part, the Virgin on a throne of the form of a niche, and holding on her knees the infant Jesus standing. This manner of placing the Virgin, is often seen in the works of Perugino, and Raphael himself used it in one of his earliest works, now in the possession of the Countess Alfani, at Perugia. An angel stands on each side of the throne. That on the left, like the angel of Montefiorentino, reminds us of the features of Raphael, and this time we may really believe that Giovanni has represented his son, then nine years of age. Near the angel, St. Francis is contemplating with ecstatic ardour a crucifix, which he holds in his hand. The head of St. Francis is admirable, but without a beard, although the oldest portraits of this saint always show him with a very long one. But in this Giovanni and the other painters of Umbria have frequently left the tradition. The apostle St. Peter is near St. Francis; on the other side, St. Dominic and St. John are pointing to the Saviour, which figures are in the same style as the altar-piece for the Buffi family at Urbino. The background represents a slab of marble behind the throne.

In the distance rises a mountain on which the Resurrection is depicted in small figures. Christ in the act of blessing, stands at the entrance to the tomb; six sleeping soldiers lie around in different positions, presenting boldly drawn foreshortenings.

In the midst of the architecture above, in a medallion, the Almighty is introduced resembling the consecrated type of Christ. On the sides

---

[1] Pungileoni relates this fact.

of the supports of the frieze charming little angels, always two together, are either adoring or playing music.

On the two exterior angles of the arch of the chapel the Annunciation is represented by the Virgin and the angel in half-length figures in medallions.

This fine work reveals a well-skilled fresco painter, from which we may conclude that Giovanni executed many frescoes now, unfortunately, destroyed. The drawing is more lively, freer, and less hard, the colouring fresher and lighter than in his distemper paintings. The colouring of the flesh is brownish in the shadows, but in children's faces it is sometimes grey and sometimes of a light brown with transitions to a luminous red with touches of white.

To add still more to the brilliancy of this picture the master has given a variable colour to the garments of the angels, red and green, with gold lights. The expression of the heads is also more animated than usual, and the faces of the Virgin, the child, and the angels give us a foretaste of Raphaelesque beauty.

By the side of the family chapel is also the funeral monument of Battista, the wife of Pietro Tiranni. Above the sarcophagus in a recess in the shape of a niche, Giovanni painted a Pieta in fresco: the Christ is only seen in half-length, being partly in the tomb; on one side is St. Jerome, on the other St. Bonaventura. This little fresco seems to have been executed rapidly. The head of the Christ is the only part on which greater pains were bestowed, it is animated by a noble expression of grief. Above is written with abbreviations "BAPTISTÆ CONIVGI PIENTISSIMÆ (*sic.*) PETRVS CALLIENSIS SALVTEM DEPRECATVR . ANNO M CCCC LXXXI."

On his return to Urbino, Giovanni gilded several candelabras and angels in wood for the brotherhood of Corpus Domini. The expenses of this work, which we mention, in order to omit nothing of the scanty information which has come down to us of this master, are stated in the account books of the order, of the years 1486 to 1493.

Amongst the last works of Giovanni is another Christ supported and wept over by angels, a picture of small dimensions, but very well arranged, painted on the pulpit of San Bernardino, formerly San Donato near Urbino.

At this period, the young Raphael began to show a great inclination for art. Whilst still quite young he assisted his father with some paintings in which indications were given of his extraordinary talent. It is very much to be lamented that none of these early attempts have been saved.

The documents preserved at Urbino are very unsatisfactory with respect to this. A manuscript in the Biancalana library states that Raphael when a child painted in the chapel of the Galli family, at the church of San Francesco of Urbino; this chapel was destroyed at the time of the restoration of the church. It also attributes to Raphael the four pictures of the four Franciscans which formerly adorned the doors of the organ of the same church, and which have also disappeared. All these pictures might indeed have been by the hand of Giovanni. And what proves that we must not receive blindly all that the manuscript states is, that it ascribes to the young Raphael the two pictures still in existence painted by Giovanni for the chapel of the Buffi family.

The information given by Michele Dolci, in his unpublished work entitled, "Ragguaglio delle pitture che si trovano in Urbino" (1775), has no more foundation. He, very arbitrarily, attributes to Raphael a "St. Sebastian," which adorns the sacristy of the cathedral of Urbino, a picture which is neither signed by Raphael nor his father.

According to the same writer, and also according to the book of the Visitation of the churches of Urbino in 1739, by the Archbishop Marelli, a "Holy Family" in the sacristy of the church of St. Andrew is also by Raphael in his earliest style. This is a round picture, which Silvio Rossi bequeathed in 1709 to this church. The principal figures, the Virgin, the child, and St. Joseph, are taken from the Holy Family that Raphael painted in 1518, for King Francis I., and which was ordered by Lorenzo de Medici. This fact only shows the error of Dolci and Marelli, repeated however quite recently by distinguished writers.[1]

Lastly, amongst the earliest paintings by Raphael is placed a charming little picture in distemper, which is at Santa Chiara of Urbino, and which is mentioned by a chronicle of 1500 A.D. as being in the convent. It is added that in spite of considerable offers, neither Algarotti on the part of the King of Prussia, nor a certain Willi were able to obtain it.[2]

---

[1] Luigi Pungileoni, "Elogio Storico di Raffaello Santi," p. 8; and C. von Rumohr, "Italienische Forschungen," iii. p. 23.

[2] Pungileoni, "Elogio Storico di Giovanni Santi," p. 131, and "Elogio Storico di

A Virgin, only in half-length, is standing holding in her arms the Child, who is giving a blessing. In the background is a landscape on a gold ground. At the back of the panel, a note indicates that this painting was bought in 1548, of *Isabeta da Gobio,* the mother of Raphael for twenty-five florins.[1]

It is, in the first place, a flagrant error to call Raphael's mother *Isabeta* or Elizabeth of Gubbio. It is, besides, certain that this picture is by the same master who painted the frescoes on the gate of San Giacomo at Assisi; the "Madonna" in the palace of the capitol, and the "St. Michael" belonging to the Marquis Gualtieri, at Orvieto, all pictures which have been recognised as the work of Andrea Luigi, of Assisi, called the Ingegno, whose works were so long sought for.

The uncertainty is as great about the education of Raphael as about his earliest works. In all probability he must have grown up under the paternal protection, and have imitated the style of Giovanni in painting. It is also possible that he admired the works of Fra Angelico da Fiesole at Forano, near Osimo, and those of Gentile da Fabriano, at the Hermitage of Val di Sasso.[2] This is, however, only a guess hazarded by the Canon Claudio Serafini, in a letter addressed to Lanzi.

The Marquis Maffei, also makes an entirely gratuitous supposition, when he imagines that Venturini, then living at Urbino, taught Latin to the young Raphael. Venturini was the first in modern times who wrote a complete Latin grammar,[3] and at Florence he had already given lessons in it to Michael Angelo. If the opinion of Maffei is well founded, Raphael must often have heard of the genius of his future rival.[4]

Giovanni now felt his end approaching, although he was still in the full vigour of life. He resigned himself as a Christian, and arranged his

---

Raffaello Santi," p. 8. In this he followed the book of the "Visitation of the Churches of Urbino, 1739," which is in the episcopal chancery.

[1] "Fu comprato da Isabeta da Gobio, matre di Raffaello Sante da Urbino, fiorini 25, 1548.

[2] A description of this altar-piece may be found in the work of Ricci, "Memorie storiche della Arti, &c., della Marca d'Ancona," 1834, vol. i. p. 152.

[3] Venturini had his Latin grammar printed at Urbino, in 1494, at the press of Heinrich of Cologne. At the end we read: "Impressus Urbini per magistrum Henricum de Coloniâ, imperante duce Guidubaldo cum III^{mo} D. Octaviano Ubaldino, anno salutiferæ Incarnationis MCCCCXCIIII."

[4] Michael Angelo, having been born in 1474, was not yet twenty.

family affairs by a will, some articles in which were altered, July 29, 1494, two days before his death. He appointed his brother, Don Bartolomeo, guardian to Raphael, and his father-in-law, Pier Parte, guardian to the child whom Bernardina was soon to bring into the world. He stipulated that she should dwell in his house so long as she remained a widow. This clause afterwards gave rise to many quarrels.

Giovanni Santi died August 1st, 1494.

According to his last wish, he was buried by his family, and his pupil, Evangelista da Pian di Meleto,[1] in the church of the Franciscans, now decorated with so many works by his hand, which show of what he was capable.

We must now say a few words on the artistic merit of Giovanni, and on his technical qualities.

His drawing, without being especially fine, is conscientiously studied, and often has a peculiar grace, especially in children's faces. Taking his ideas from the figures of the mountaineers who surrounded him, he often made his personages tall and thin to exaggeration; the extremities too are always tapering. His draperies, which at first were rather confused, assume more simplicity and elegance towards the middle of his career, and still later betray an imitation of Mantegna. We have already noticed, that at one period he rather affected bold foreshortenings in the style of his friend Melozzo da Forli.

The outlines of his pictures in distemper, are always a black line. This makes the scene stand out better at a distance, but gives an appearance of hardness when it is looked at more closely.

His colouring in the simple manner of the fifteenth century is, usually, luminous in the great masses of drapery, and frequently also in the flesh tints, especially when he employs brownish shadows, the transitions are of a light red, and the lights are placed on afterwards. This is a process which Raphael also employed, usually at least. But frequently the shadows of Giovanni have a greyish tone, and are heavy and opaque.

The ground in the front of his pictures is uniformly light brown, and strewn with small plants.

His "Madonnas" generally have a serious countenance, which is

---

[1] We read in the "Bastardello" of Matteo Geri: "1483, Oct. 16. Evangelista Ser Andreæ di Castro Plani Meleti, famulus Joannis Sanctis, pictoris de Urbino," &c. Giovanni's will was opened in presence of Meleto and Ambrosio, an excellent goldsmith and sculptor. See Pungileoni, "Elogio Storico di Giovanni Santi," p. 136.

almost carried to stiffness. Usually they are raising one arm so as to display the interior of the hand. Giovanni, doubtless, attached some mystic significance to this gesture.

We have already remarked that his personages were much more life-like when he took them direct from nature, and that his Cagli fresco is much superior to his pictures in distemper. Unhappily his frescoes are nearly all destroyed, and this is the more to be regretted, as they alone would enable us to appreciate him justly.

If we now throw a glance on the whole of his work in order to assign him his rank amongst his contemporaries, Giovanni appears at once to us as an artist firmly attached to traditional symmetry, such as was taught by the school of Giotto, but, nevertheless, seeking for nature with more fidelity and precision, and aspiring to render every figure more individual and characteristic. He has frequently succeeded in serious expression, and even sometimes in making his children's faces very charming.

He certainly did not possess the science of drawing and perspective to the same extent as Mantegna, whom he so much praised, nor the gracefulness of Francia or Perugino, nor the masculine energy of Luca Signorelli, nor the boldness of his friend Melozzo; he cannot then be exactly classed amongst the most distinguished painters of his time, who made a fresh pathway for themselves in art; but he is one of those conscientious and skilful artists, who make their own whatever good they find, and whose works will be esteemed as long as a love of simple beauty is preserved among men.

Let us then revive the remembrance of Giovanni; it is just to do so, because of his excellent works and personal merit, and not merely because he was the father of the greatest of painters.

CHAPTER II.

RAPHAEL UNDER PERUGINO,

AND HIS VISITS TO FLORENCE AND URBINO (1495-1508).

AFTER the death of his father, Raphael was left to the care of Bernardina, his step-mother, and of the priest, Don Bartolomeo, his guardian.

Bernardina, who had become the mother of a daughter, named Elisabetta, and Bartolomeo, whose character was far from being disinterested, often troubled the household by their quarrels, in which the law was frequently obliged to interfere. They were quite unable to gain the confidence of the young Raphael; but his uncle on the maternal side, Simone di Battista Ciarla, better understood the noble and delicate nature, the ardour and the budding genius of the young artist.

At the height of his glory, Raphael never forgot the kindness of this uncle, and during his whole life showed him the most touching and filial affection.

Nothing is known of the first art-teaching given to the young Raphael, who had now scarcely entered his twelfth year. Both Luca Signorelli[1]

---

[1] Wicar, in order to prove that Raphael received lessons from Signorelli mentions the small Holy Family, "The Virgin with the Infant Saviour standing, and St. Joseph," half-length, in the gallery of Cardinal Fesch, at Rome. This picture, boldly painted in distemper, reminds one vaguely of Signorelli in the position of the Child; but it is too weak to be attributed to that master: it might be however by one of his pupils, for example, Girolamo Genga. But it is the more inexplicable that Wicar should have attributed it to Raphael, as Signorelli had already left Urbino before the death of Giovanni. See Pungileoni "Elogio storico di Raffaello Santi," p. 13.

and Timoteo Viti are said to have been his masters. Signorelli painted at Urbino in 1494, and Timoteo, a native of that town, having returned to it in 1495,[1] after studying in the school of Francia in Bologna, had obtained work in the churches.

Many learned artists and mathematicians are said to have taught Raphael perspective during this time; amongst others, Baccio Pintelli, Bramante, and Fra Luca Pacciolo, whose "Summa de arithmeticâ, geometricâ," etc., printed at Venice, 1494, is preceded by a dedication to the Duke Guidubaldo, of Urbino.[2]. But all these conjectures have little foundation, and are even scarcely probable, when we remember that Raphael was still only twelve years old.

About this time, the family dissensions, aroused by Bernardina, arrived at such a pitch, that she would no longer live in the house, requiring, however, a pecuniary compensation; but her brother-in-law, the priest Don Bartolomeo, would not even consent to grant her what was hers by right, and it became necessary to refer the matter to the clerical tribunal.

In these sad circumstances, the uncle, Simone Ciarla, was obliged to come to an understanding with the guardian, Bartolomeo, in order to place Raphael under some eminent painter, with whom he might pursue his studies.

Urbino being then, on account of the consideration enjoyed by its prince, in communication with all the large towns in Italy, there must have been much debate as to both the town and master to be chosen. Andrea Mantegna had been much thought of by Giovanni; Francesco Francia, of Bologna, was recommended by Timoteo Viti; at Venice, Giovanni Bellini had founded a flourishing school; from Milan, wonders

---

[1] See Malvasia, "Felsina Pittrice," ii. p. 45, extract from the family chronicles of Francesco Francia: "1495, a di 4 Aprile, partito il mio caro Timoteo, che Dio li dia ogni bene e fortuna." In the Borghese gallery at Rome we admire the portrait of a child of about twelve years of age with a sweet and serious countenance; it bears some resemblance to Raphael. It is believed to be the work of Timoteo Viti. It is painted in oil, reveals a certain amount of experience, and, in the colour of the flesh resembles the manner of Francia. Possibly Timoteo who became, at a later time, the friend and in some degree the pupil of Raphael, from affection for the child of twelve years, had taken his portrait.

[2] Pungileoni gives some information about this *savant*, in the "Giornale Arcadico," 1835, vol. lxii. and lxiv. See also an article of Dr. Gaye in the "Kunstblatt" of the 30th August, 1836.

were heard of the great Leonardo.[1] But, in the neighbourhood of Perugia, there was also an artist who had been praised by Raphael's father,[2] and who delighted every one by the celestial beauty of his creations. This was Pietro Vannucci, of Citta della Pieve, near Perugia.

He had the good fortune to be chosen as the guide of this child, who was destined to catch the inspiration of his master, transform it, and raise it to a height that the master himself had never dreamt of. If we possessed a journal of Pietro Perugino's, similar to that of Francia, in which both his family affairs and the coming and leaving of his pupils are chronicled, we should know with certainty the year in which Raphael went to his master. Most probably it was in 1495.

Perugino was then at the height of his glory, acquired principally by the works executed at this time; for his studies at Florence had added fresh qualities to his profound feeling and warm and vigorous colouring.[3]

---

[1] At this time when it was necessary to choose from amongst all those illustrious painters a master for Raphael, somewhere about the year 1495, Mantegna and Giovanni Bellini were already old, the one being 64 years old, and the other 69; Francia was about 45, and Leonardo da Vinci 43.—*Lacroix.*

[2] In the following passage of the Chronicle in rhyme—

> "Due giovin' par d'etate e par d'amori
> Lionardo da Vinci e'l Perusino
> Pier della Pieve, che son' divin pittori."

It follows from this passage that Pietro was already settled at Perugia before 1495. Annibale Mariotti and others choose that year as the date of his establishment in that town, because he was commissioned March 8, 1495, to paint an altar-piece for the church of the Benedictines there—an "Ascension," and that in the preceding years he had been occupied, in 1493, at the church of San Domenico de Fiesole, and in 1494 at the church of the Augustines at Cremona. But could he not have sent these pictures from Perugia, as he sometimes did his other pictures?

[3] Amongst the principal works of Perugino may be noticed the beautiful "Madonna" in a round frame, with saints and angels, bought at the sale of King William of the Netherlands for the Louvre (*); the altar piece now in the church of San Giovanni la Calza at Florence, representing a Crucifixion, with the Magdalen kneeling, St. Jerome, St. Francis, St. John the Baptist, and Giovanni Colombini; a picture no less precious, dated 1495, and quite in the original manner of the master; the "Dead Christ," wept by his disciples and the holy women; this has recently passed from the Florence Academy to the Pitti palace; the magnificent altar-piece (of the same date) of the "Ascension," formerly at San Pietro Maggiore at Perugia, at present in the museum

---

* No. 442 of the Catalogue of the Italian Schools in the Louvre. It had passed in 1825, into the Laperière sale. At the sale of the King of Holland in August, 1850, it was bought for the sum of 23,500 florins (£2140).—*Lacroix.*

As long as he allied severe correctness with this expression of mystic ecstacy—that peculiar characteristic of the Umbrian school, which the old Niccolo Alumno had been one of the first to introduce, he preserved his reputation; but as soon as his productions and those of his school betrayed a pretentious, degenerated and hasty style, they were roughly attacked by Michael Angelo.

The fine qualities of Perugino in his earliest manner, had procured him one of the largest schools in Italy; and when Raphael entered his studio, he was surrounded by companions, several of whom were destined to become celebrated. It was here he made the acquaintance of Andrea di Luigi, of Assisi, surnamed the Ingegno, an artist who had already acquired a reputation, and who had executed remarkable frescoes at Rome, Orvieto, and in his native town, and also of Bernardino di Betto, of Perugia, surnamed Pinturicchio, who had worked much with Perugino in his youth. Pinturicchio attached Raphael to himself, and frequently made use of him.

Amongst his fellow pupils, born at Perugia, were Giambattista Caporali, Sinibaldo Ibi, and Usebio di San Giorgio, who, in his later works endeavoured to follow the progressive march of art, and advance with Raphael and da Vinci, as is shown in his altar-piece, of 1512, in the church of the Franciscans, at Matelica. Gian Niccolò Manni, who painted the pictures on the ceiling of the chapel of the Cappella del Cambio, at Perugia, was a native of Città della Pieve, the birth-place of Perugino. Rocco Zoppo, Baccio Uberti, and his brother Francesco, surnamed Il Bacchiacca, had come from Florence.

Amongst the lowest in talent, may be classed Gerino da Pistoja, who worked a great deal with Pinturicchio, Pietro da Monte Varchi, Tiberio of Assisi, and others. But as if to make up for these inferior artists, there was also the Spaniard Giovanni di Pietro, surnamed Lo Spagna, whose works in the church of the Franciscans, at Assisi and Spoleto, which he had chosen as his place of abode, will always excite admira-

---

of Lyons; Vasari calls it the finest oil-painting by this master. The Belvedera Gallery at Vienna also possesses two very remarkable Madonnas, the largest dated 1493. The king of Bavaria has also acquired a splendid "Perugino," from the Nasi Chapel in the church of San Spirito at Florence, which represents the Virgin appearing to St. Bernard. Lastly we must mention another altar-piece of the same merit in the church of Santa Maria Nuova at Fano. It is dated 1497, and represents a Virgin surrounded by six saints.

tion. A particular friend of Raphael's, and of the same age as himself, was Domenico di Paris Alfani, of Perugia. Domenico endeavoured to follow the progress of Raphael, and even borrowed ideas from him for his own pictures. This may be seen in the "Holy Family," in the church of the Carmelites at Perugia, and the admirable "Madonna with two Saints," dated 1518, in the church of San Gregorio della Sapienza Vecchia, also at Perugia.

Raphael also made acquaintance about 1502, with Gaudenzio Ferrari of Valduggia. Their friendship became so close, that Gaudenzio accompanied Raphael to Rome, and except at rare intervals, remained his inseparable companion.

It is not certain whether Lattanzio Pagani della Marca began to imitate Raphael at this time; but Girolamo Genga, of Urbino, after having worked under Luca Signorelli, in the cathedral of Orvieto, having come to pass three years under the instruction of Perugino, conceived an unbounded love and devotion to Raphael.

One of the earliest works of Raphael in the school of Perugino, was the "Infant Jesus with St. John the Baptist," a composition taken from a larger work representing the "Family of St. Anne," which his master had painted for an altar-piece of the church of Santa Maria de' Fossi, at Perugia. Perugino's picture, now in the museum of Marseilles, shows the Virgin seated on the knees of St. Anne, surrounded by St. Joseph, St. Joachim, St. Cleopha, and St. Salome, and by six children of the holy family.[1] The small partial copy in which Raphael imitated the style of Perugino wonderfully, is painted in distemper on a gold background, and was doubtless done for the sake of practice. It is now in the sacristy of the church of San Pietro Maggiore, at Perugia.

Other studies by Raphael, after his master, drawings in pen and ink, from the pictures of the prophets David and Isaiah, and a St. Sebastian, are preserved in the sketch-book in the academy at Venice.

One of his first original drawings represents St. Martin on horseback. At a later period, Perugino drew in pen and ink on the reverse of this leaf, a "Baptism of Christ," which had been ordered in 1502, for the church of the Augustines at Perugia.[2]

---

[1] The beautiful original sketch by Perugino for these children, carefully drawn in pen and ink is in the collection of drawings at Florence.

[2] This interesting drawing, which was brought from the house of the Baglioni family is now in the Staedelsche Institut at Frankfort-on-the-Maine.

Raphael had soon acquired a wonderful facility of execution, and he showed such great talent that Perugino began to employ him in his own works. The assistance of Raphael is especially to be noticed in a "Resurrection of Christ," intended for the church of the Franciscans at Perugia, and which is now in the Vatican. It is even probable that Perugino intrusted the whole execution of it to him. The studies for the two sleeping soldiers, and for the other two who are running away, by the hand of Raphael himself, are in the Oxford collection. The Christ in the picture, although drawn with much delicacy, is yet wanting in true anatomical science, and shows less of the master's hand than of the pupil's as it was then. The elder of the soldiers has the features of Perugino, the younger those of Raphael. This is, in our opinion, the most ancient proof of the intimacy which united the master and the pupil.

Raphael seems also to have worked at the altar-piece, composed of six parts, which Perugino executed for the house of the Carthusians near Pavia. In the central picture the Virgin is kneeling in adoration before Jesus, whom an angel is presenting to her; above is a choir of three angels singing.

Under the French rule this central picture, and the Archangels Michael and Raphael, with the young Tobit, forming the two sides, passed to the house of the Duke of Melzi at Milan.[1] But the upper part, representing the Father surrounded by cherubims, still adorns the old altar of the Carthusians. We do not know what has become of the two other smaller pieces which together represent the Annunciation.

The Raphaelesque spirit is perceivable in the whole work, and a study of nature is felt throughout it. It has been wished to prove that Raphael assisted much in it, especially as a drawing by him, from nature, of the Archangel Raphael with the young Tobit, forms a part of the Oxford collection. Nevertheless, these paintings are so beautiful, that if Raphael did assist in them, it could only have been about 1503; for his pictures at Cittá di Castello, anterior to that date, are much inferior to the pictures of the Carthusian church.

Fresh dissensions in his family disturbed him in the midst of his active and profitable studies. He was obliged to return to Urbino in

---

[1] The Duke of Melzi sold them in 1857, to the National Gallery.

1499,[1] in order himself to make up these differences, and he fortunately succeeded. He granted his step-mother, for the little Elisabetta, the expenses of living for two years, and twenty-six florins besides in money.

There is nothing to prove that, during his stay at Urbino, he received any orders. However, at that time the court and inhabitants were much impoverished, owing to the enormous ransom they had had to pay to deliver the captive prince.[2]

But, according to Lanzi, Raphael had, in 1500, the pleasure of obtaining some orders at Città di Castello, where he went from Perugia, in company with some of his fellow disciples, their master then being at Florence on business.[3] Whatever may be true about these details, it is certain that the banner executed for the church of the Trinità, of Città di Castello, and the "Crucifixion," in the ancient gallery of the Cardinal Fesch, were the first works of Raphael.

The banner is painted on two sheets of canvas without preparation. The subject is not the same on both sides; they are disjointed, and are actually hung separately. One represents the "Trinity," the other the "Creation of Man."

The "Trinity" is treated quite in the traditional manner, in use in the studio of Perugino: the Almighty, seated on a cloud in the centre of a glory, holds a crucifix before him; and the Holy Spirit, symbolized by a dove, hovers between the two figures. At the foot of the cross kneel, in conformance to the requirements of the commission, St. Sebastian, clothed, holding an arrow, and St. Roch, both raising their eyes towards God, to entreat Him to deliver the country from the plague. All these figures remind us of the style of Perugino, whilst two little heads of angels, in the upper part, and the landscape in the background, recall the style of Giovanni.

---

[1] In the settlement of 1499, it is said that "Bernardina agreed with *dom Bartolomeo and Raphael*, &c." whilst the definitive agreement of 1500 states that "Do. Bartolomeo stipulanti pro se et *nomine Raphaelis*, fil. dicti Joannis, &c." These documents authorize us to conclude with Pungileoni, that Raphael went to Urbino in 1499.

[2] See B. Baldi, "Della vita e de fatti di Guidubaldo I da Montefeltro duca d'Urbino," Milano, 1821.

[3] This information of Lanzi's might however refer to Raphael's second journey to Città di Castello, when he painted the "Sposalizio," for Vasari, names this picture at the same time as the others we have mentioned here, although certainly it must have been painted several years later.

In the "Creation of Man," Raphael shows himself more original. Adam is asleep on the ground, near a rock which projects a mysterious shadow. Over this shadow the Father stands out in light, approaching the man to form Eve. Two angels, in adoration, scarcely touch with their feet the clouds which bear them. These figures of angels are quite in the style of Perugino—in conception, colour, and execution.

Every subject is gracefully framed, with ornaments of meanders and palm-leaves, on an azure background. In the border of the mantle of the Almighty is an R very visible.

The "Crucifixion" was executed for the chapel of the Gavri or Gavari family, in the church of the Dominicans. Around the Christ are the Virgin, St. John, St. Mary Magdalen, and St. Jerome. At the first glance it might be taken for a picture of Perugino's, and yet the colour and the drawing are weaker than with that master, whilst the expression of the heads is more delicate and spiritual. Signed "RAPHAEL. URBINAS. P."[1]

These paintings having attracted attention, obtained for Raphael an order for a more important picture for the church of the Augustines in the same town: "The Coronation of the Holy Hermit, Nicholas of Tolentino," celebrated for his miracles. According to Lanzi, and the sketch in the Wicar collection at Lille,[2] the Almighty was represented in the upper part, surrounded by heads of seraphim ; at his side are the Virgin and St. Augustine, all half-length figures in the clouds, and together holding a crown over the head of the hermit. He, a crucifix in his hand, is trampling a demon under his feet ; four angels, in two groups, surround him, bearing strips of parchment on which his praises are inscribed.

During nearly three centuries this picture adorned the church of the Augustines ; but, the church having been almost destroyed by an earth-

---

[1] This picture was bought by Cardinal Fesch at Rome ;* it is now in Earl Dudley's collection.

[2] Wicar who was a painter of the school of David, lived for a long time in Italy and collected a large quantity of drawings by the Italian masters. He died in 1834, and bequeathed them to Lille, his native town.—*Lacroix*.

---

* This picture sold for 10,000 Roman crowns, at the cardinal's sale, in 1845, about £2500.—*Lacroix*. It was established at the Manchester Exhibition in 1857, and again in the Royal Academy Exhibition in London, January, 1871.

quake, the monks, desirous of restoring it, sold their Raphael, which had been much injured, to Pope Pius VI., in 1789, for a considerable sum. The picture was cut into several pieces, which were hung up in a room at the Vatican; they disappeared at the time of the French invasion.

These labours terminated, the young artist returned to Perugia, and there painted several pictures of large and small size. All bear the impress of the school of Perugino, and sometimes contain whole figures from that master's works, probably because they were executed for him. Even when Raphael at this time painted his own compositions, they differed little from those of Perugino, except by a more spiritual sentiment, a more delicate observation of nature, and a slight tinge of his own individuality, which was beginning to be visible.

In the number of the small pictures of this kind, we count two wings for a Madonna of Perugino's, now lost. They represent a St. Catherine and a St. Mary Magdalene. They are now united in a single frame, and form a part of the rich collection of the Chevalier V. Camuccini at Rome.

It was certainly, too, under the influence of his master, that he executed the "Madonna" belonging to the Countess Anna Allani, at Perugia. He added, however, according to his father's custom, two charming cherubim heads in the upper corners. The delicacy of the touch, and the sentiment which animates the heads, also betray the hand of Raphael, whose initial letters, "R. D. V.," are found on the breast of the Virgin's garments.

The museum of Berlin also possesses a Madonna of the same period, and for which Raphael must undoubtedly have made use of a sketch of Perugino's, preserved in the Albertine collection at Vienna. This valuable little picture, of very careful execution, shows the Virgin contemplating the Child who is seated on a cushion on her lap. On either side are St. Jerome and St. Francis, standing in adoration. The figures are half length.

Another small Madonna, also in the Berlin Museum, appears to us to belong to the same time as the "Crucifixion," for the church of the Dominicans at Città di Castello. This came from the Solly Collection.

According to Canali, a letter of Raphael's, written at this time, and addressed to a friend, must have been found among the manuscripts of Cardinal Borgia. The young painter of Urbino expresses in it his joy at an order he had received from Madonna Maddalena degli Oddi, and at that lady, who possessed great influence, having procured him several other commissions.

This passage of the letter doubtless refers to the large altar-piece, of the "Coronation of the Virgin," formerly in the Franciscan church at Perugia. For we must believe that this order took place before the reigning family degli Oddi, at Perugia, was dispossessed by Giovanni Paolo Baglione, which happened immediately after the death of Pope Alexander VI., August 17, 1503.[1]

The "Coronation of the Virgin" is also composed and executed in the traditional style of the Umbrian school, so much so, in fact, that it is difficult to distinguish it from the works of Perugino.

Vasari has made the same remark, saying that it needed "a well-practised eye" not to be mistaken. The twelve Apostles, however, who surround the Virgin's tomb, which is filled with flowers, are in more life-like attitudes, and express greater movement than the usual figures of Perugino. The four angels playing on instruments of music near Christ and the Virgin, especially show the Raphaelesque character. The progress of his genius is evident.

From the Napoleon Museum this picture returned to Italy, and was placed in the Vatican, with its *predella*,[2] which represents, in three scenes, the "Annunciation," the "Presentation in the Temple," and the "Adoration of the Magi." They are graceful little compositions, separated by fantastic grottos, which are red on a black background.

At the same time as the "Coronation of the Virgin," Raphael painted for Count Staffa an exquisite little Madonna, which is in the house of the Constable della Staffa, at Perugia. The mother of the Saviour, a figure of virginal sweetness, is walking in the country in early spring, when the trees are still bare, and the distant mountains are covered with snow. She is walking along pensively, reading in a little book, in which the child in her arms also looks attentively. Nothing could be found more exquisite. Everything in it shows that Raphael must have devoted himself to it with especial ardour.

Another little picture of the same period, not less attractive, and treated with equal solicitude, represents a young knight lying asleep at the foot of a laurel tree. Two women, allegorical figures of noble

---

[1] See B. Baldi, "Della Vita ede' fatti di Guidobaldo I da Montefeltro, duca d'Urbino," ii. p. 120.

[2] The Italians called *predella* the smaller compositions which, at that time, usually accompanied the principal subject, and were placed around the large picture.—*Lacroix.*

THE CORONATION OF THE VIRGIN.

ambition and of the joys of life, appear to him, and offer him—one glory, the other pleasure. This reminds us of Raphael himself. Certainly this subject must have been suggested to him by the struggles which, at this period of his noble existence, must have distracted his soul.

At the right hand of the knight, one of the two women, of a gentle and serious expression, clothed in violet and purple garments, is presenting him with a book and sword, as if to invite him either to study or to warfare; behind her rises a steep rock. But, on the left, the other woman, clothed in dazzling raiment and precious stones, is offering him a flower, as if to invite him to taste the pleasures of life; behind her, in a rich landscape, is a town on the banks of a river. He, however, lying on his shield, seems much moved at the dream, and is doubtless deciding in favour of true glory, as the laurel shadowing his head seems to imply. This charming picture, formerly in the Borghese Gallery at Rome, has now passed to the National Gallery of London, with the original pen and ink sketch.

To the same period belongs the portrait of a young man,[1] front face. On the metal clasp fastening the cloak, near the neck, may be seen the name of Raphael.

It was also about this time that Raphael painted a *predella* with several small subjects, for an altar-piece, representing the "Birth of the Virgin," which Pinturicchio executed for the Piccolomini chapel in the church of the Franciscans at Siena. These pictures were destroyed when the church was burnt down in 1655.[2]

When Pinturicchio[3] was commissioned to paint for the library of the cathedral of Siena, ten subjects drawn from the life of Æneas Sylvius Piccolomini,[4] who became pope under the title of Pius II., Raphael was

---

[1] Now in her Majesty's collection.

[2] "Lettere sulla pitt., scul. et arch.," vi. p. 393. The picture in the Piccolomini chapel was discovered November 8, 1504, according to Tizio. See "Vasari," edit. of Siena, iv. p. 259.

[3] It was the Cardinal Francesco Piccolomini, afterwards Pius III., who ordered these pictures of Pinturicchio, for the library he had built near the cathedral in 1494.

[4] The following are the ten subjects: 1st, The "Departure of the young Æneas Sylvius, with Cardinal Domenico da Capranica for the council of Basle." 2nd, "Æneas Sylvius pronouncing his discourse before James I. King of Scotland." 3rd, "The Emperor Frederick III. crowning him with laurel." 4th, "Pope Eugenius IV. naming him legate." 5th, "The Marriage of the Emperor Frederick III. with Leonora of Portugal." 6th, "The Pope Calixtus III. making him cardinal." 7th, "His eleva-

of great assistance to him. Pinturicchio, feeling himself deficient in invention and power of composition, persuaded his young friend to make him sketches for his frescoes. Two of these designs of Raphael's have come down to us.[1] The costumes, treated with much grandeur and good taste, are, of course, those of the close of the fifteenth century.

The pictures are not exact copies of the drawings; in some parts, alterations for the worse may be noticed: a superabundance of ornaments, and several figures quite useless to the action; which fact demonstrates clearly that Raphael had nothing to do with the cartoons, nor with the execution of the picture. He never, besides, executed works of any importance at Siena, and the manuscript of Sigismondo Tizio on the History of Siena, written between 1527 and 1550, in which there is particular mention of the painters who had formerly worked in that town, says nothing of any co-operation of Raphael's in the picture of Pinturicchio.[2]

Raphael, however, remained some time at Siena, and in the valuable

---

tion to the tiara." 8th, "Pius II. at the Council of Mantua." 9th, "The beatification of Catherine of Siena." 10th, "Preparations for the departure of the fleet at Ancona against the Turks.

All these subjects were engraved by Raimondo Faucci, 1770-1771, folio. They were afterwards better engraved from the drawings of Luigi Boschi, by Lasinio his son, in his work, "Raccolta delle più celebri pitture esistenti nella città di Siena." Firenze, per Nicolò Pagni, 1825, large folio.

[1] The first drawing of this series, "Æneas starting for Basle," &c., with an inscription by the hand of Raphael, is in the Florence Gallery. The other, the fifth of the series, "Meeting of Frederick IV. and Leonora," &c. also with an inscription by Raphael, is in the Baldeschi House at Perugia. When Vasari speaks of drawings and cartoons made by Raphael for these pictures, he must refer to the large drawings and small sketches, some of which are still in existence.

[2] This silence of Tizio and also the stiffness of the fresco of the "Coronation of Pius III. at the cathedral of Siena," are sufficient refutation of the writers who have advanced that Raphael took part in this picture. In reference to the date we must mention that the recent discovery of the contract between Cardinal Francesco Piccolomini and Pinturicchio (June 29, 1502) and the bill given to the painter, January 18th, 1509, by the heirs of Andrea Piccolomini, remove all doubts as to the period of the execution of the celebrated pictures in the Siena library.

The will of Pope Pius III. when he was still a cardinal, also contains an article which relates to these pictures; the following is an extract from it: "Item, quia magistro, Bernardino pictori perusino, vocato il Pinturicchio, locavimus depingendam historiam sanctæ memoriæ Domini Pii in libreriâ nostrâ cum pactis et conditionibus, ut in quâdam cedulâ manu nostrâ et suâ subscriptâ continetur et voluimus, quod si, nobis decedentibus, non fuerit perfecta, hœredes nostri curam perficiendi et satisfaciendi

sketch-book (at the Academy at Venice), there is a drawing of the antique group of the "Three Graces," decorating the *libreria* of the cathedral.

Having quitted the studio of Perugino, in the beginning of 1504, Raphael painted the "Marriage of the Virgin," known under the name of the *Sposalizio* (now at Milan), for the church of the Franciscans at Città di Castello. It may be supposed that the monks, imitating the example of the ancient Greeks, who consecrated the masterpieces of art in invariable types of their gods, asked Raphael for a picture similar to the celebrated "Sposalizio" of Perugino, painted in 1495 for the cathedral of Perugia. Or else Raphael, induced by the beauty of that work, thought it right to imitate it. However this may be, Raphael certainly borrowed much of the general ordering of his picture from his masters,[1] though with several changes; thus, he places the groups of men and women on opposite sides of the picture, and the man breaking the reed, whom Perugino places in the background, Raphael brings to the front; he also improves the architecture of the temple. Vasari rightly praises the perspective; for Raphael, during his residence with Perugino, had

---

suscipiant juxtâ nostram voluntatem in dictâ cedulâ expressam." Pius III. who became Pope, September 22nd, 1503, died on the 18th October following.

We must also mention here an ancient tradition according to which the portrait of Raphael would be found in these paintings. It is singular that his portrait has always been recognised when every probability is against the supposition. For a long time his portrait has been seen in the young Æneas Sylvius of the first picture, as if a painter would venture to draw himself as the principal figure. The translator of "Quatremère de Quincy," F. Longhena, fancies he recognizes Raphael, then at least twenty years of age, in the little page, of about twelve, who is holding the cap of the Doge Christoforo Moro. There is nothing besides sufficiently characteristic in this page to authorise us to conclude that it is a portrait at all. Others such as Rohberg and Pungileoni, have endeavoured to discover Raphael amongst the numerous portraits of celebrated men at the coronation of Pius III. But all these suppositions are destitute of truth. The Baron of Rumohr is the first who has with any reason pointed out, as the portrait of Raphael, the youthful face by the side of Pinturicchio himself, in the picture of the "Canonization of St. Catherine of Siena." Pinturicchio is standing a little on one side, behind this young man, and seems to be looking at him with admiration; this shows plainly enough that this group is by him. It is a noble testimony of appreciation and gratitude, publicly given to his fellow disciple, by Pinturicchio, who was older than he.

[1] At the time of the French invasion of Italy, Perugino's picture was taken to Paris, and given in 1804 to the museum at Caen, where it still remains, in spite of the demands of the powerful allies in 1815, thanks to the energetic resistance of the municipal administration. This magnificent picture, one of the master-pieces of Perugino is in the best state of preservation. See in the "Artiste" of 1838, a curious article by M. Thoré on the "Sposalizio" of the Museum of Caen.—*Lacroix.*

studied this science, which he always employed with exquisite taste. In short, the "Sposalizio" of Raphael, far surpasses that of Perugino, in beauty of form and in execution, without however being freed from the school of Perugino. Its date, 1504, furnishes us with a valuable record of the artistic progress of Raphael.

The existence of old copies of this picture, proves that from its first appearance, it was held in the value it deserved.

At Bergamo, the Count of Lecchi possesses a small half-length "St. Sebastian," which evidently belongs to the same period. The saint is clothed, and holds an arrow in his hand. There is a landscape background. This charming picture possesses all the qualities of the "Sposalizio."

In the course of these small excursions, Raphael felt a desire to revisit his birth-place.

The Prince Guidubaldo had just returned to his State after having incurred many sufferings and run many dangers. The natural son of Cæsar Borgia, called Il Valentino, had first, under the mask of friendship, defrauded him of troops and money; then treacherously invading the country, he had endeavoured to kill him, as he had already killed several of his other allies. The Duke of Urbino only owed his safety to a precipitate flight. But, a year after, August 18, 1503, the pope having died of poison, and his son Cæsar having almost died of a similar death, the faithful inhabitants of Urbino rose everywhere, to the cry of *Feltro*, drove out the troops and partisans of Il Valentino, and, in the same month, hailed the return of their legitimate prince.

After the twenty-six days of the government of Pius III., and when Giuliano della Rovere was pope, under the name of Julius II., Guidubaldo was summoned to Rome, and created gonfalonier di Santa Chiesa. But it was stipulated at the same time, that Francesco Maria della Rovere, nephew of the pope and of the duke, should be recognised heir to the Duchy of Urbino. This solemn inauguration of the Prince della Rovere, and the presentation to Guidubaldo of the general's bâton (*bastone del generalato*), in presence of a large number of nobles, took place in the cathedral of Urbino, in 1504, at the very time when Raphael had just placed his altar-piece at Città di Castello.

Sensible to the elevation of his prince, the young artist wished to show by his presence, that he shared in the general joy.

The duke received him kindly; but, notwithstanding his wish to find

THE MARRIAGE OF THE VIRGIN.

In the Brera, Milan.

suitable work for him, his pecuniary means at this time did not allow him to indulge in expenses for works of art. Raphael, however, painted several small pictures for him, and especially one of "Christ in the Garden of Gethsemane,"[1] of which Vasari speaks as being "of such finish, that a miniature could not surpass it. The three apostles are lying asleep in the foreground, at the foot of the hill, on which Jesus is kneeling in prayer, whilst an angel is presenting him with the cup of bitterness.

Here again Raphael has borrowed the composition from one of Perugino's; but, as in the "Sposalizio," he has wonderfully changed it by nobler lines, and has developed in the expression of Christ and the apostles a nobler sentiment than that conveyed by the master. He has succeeded less well in imparting to the other countenances the coarse, wicked character suitable for them. The armed archers in the background, and even Judas himself, are represented as having honest and agreeable countenances, whilst that of the latter in particular bears no trace of treachery. The dark abyss of wickedness was still unpenetrated by the young Raphael, and in his simple mind the world still showed pure reflections.

The small "St. George,"[2] and the "St. Michael" in the Louvre, also date from this visit to Urbino.

St. George, in complete armour, and mounted on a white horse, rushes towards the dragon, against whom he has already broken his lance, and he is now about to pierce it with his sword. In the rocky landscape in the background a small figure of a woman is seen rushing away.[3]

---

[1] This picture, bought by W. Fuller Maitland, Esq. at the Coningham sale in 1849, was exhibited at the Manchester Exhibition, 1857.—*Lacroix.*

[2] Paolo Lomazzo (Book I. chap. 8) mentions this "St. George," and says that it is painted on a draught board, and that in his time it was at Fontainebleau. Lomazzo is confused. It is the pendent of the "St. George" which is painted on a draught-board, of which "St. Michael" also he appears to speak in the same passage, unless indeed he refers to the great "St. Michael" in the same museum.*

[3] This picture as well as its pendent, was executed according to M. Villot, for

---

* M. Villot in his "Catalogue of the Italian Schools," says that "there is now no trace of a draught-board on the panel, but it may have been blackened or effaced, unless indeed Lomazzo confused the "St. George" and the "St. Michael," its pendent, on the reverse of which there were still traces of the draught-board a short time since, before a thick layer of colouring in oil had been laid on the back of the picture. These two pictures now bear the Nos. 380, 382.—*Lacroix.*

The St. Michael also represents the Christian warrior, attacking evil with divine assistance. The archangel, resplendent in youth and beauty, is victoriously fighting the monster, who encircles him in its folds. Other smaller monsters, concealed in cavities of the rocks, are looking on with fury and fear. The subjects in the background, recall different scenes from Dante's Inferno, for example, the description of the town of Dis, (Canto VIII.) Around the symbolical town prowl mysteriously the masked figures of the hypocrites, covered with leaden hoods (Canto XXIII.)[1] On the other side are naked figures representing thieves, tormented and bitten by serpents (Canto XXIV.)[2]

These two little pictures, which are very carefully treated, still have much of the Peruginesque character, and are only distinguished from it by a higher amount of imagination and beauty, by wider and

---

Guidubaldo de Montefeltro, Duke of Urbino, in 1504. However this may be, the "St. George" formed a part of the collection of Francis I. whilst the "St. Michael" only came into the king's collection after the death of Cardinal Mazarin.—*Lacroix.*

[1] There in the depth we saw a painted tribe,
Who paced with tardy steps around, and wept,
Faint in appearance and o'ercome with toil.
Caps had they on with hoods, that fell low down
Before their eyes, in fashion like to those
Worn by the monks in Cologne. Their outside
Was overlaid with gold, dazzling to view,
But leaden all within, and of such weight,
That Frederick's compared to these were straw.
Oh, everlasting wearisome attire!
Cary's Translation of the Inferno.

[2] Amid this dread exuberance of woe
Ran naked spirits wing'd with horrid fear,
Nor hope had they of crevice where to hide,
Or heliotrope to charm them out of view.
With serpents were their hands behind them bound,
Which through the reins infix'd the tail and head,
Twisted in folds before. And lo! on one
Near to our side, darted an adder up,
And, where the neck is on the shoulders tied,
Transpierced him. Far more quickly than e'er pen
Wrote O or I, he kindled, burnt and changed
To ashes all, pour'd out upon the earth,
When thus dissolved he lay, the dust again
Uproll'd spontaneous, and the self-same form
Instant resumed.—*Ibid.*

more spiritual execution, and by the luminous colouring peculiar to Raphael.

The sketch-book, at Venice, also contains a view of the town of Urbino (taken from the Capuchin road, and drawn in pen and ink), including a part of the castle and of the old cathedral. Raphael, no doubt, took this sketch to carry away with him, as a memento of his birth-place.

It was during this residence at Urbino, in 1504, that he drew in the same sketch-book the portraits of ancient philosophers and poets, taken, as it would appear, from those the duke had had painted in the library of his palace.

At the court of Urbino, Raphael made the acquaintance of several persons of high rank. The connection thus formed was very useful to him. Achilles de'Grassi, of Bologna, Bishop of Pesara, gave him a commission for an "Annunciation," which was afterwards executed. This daily intercourse with the *élite* of contemporary society, could not fail to enrich his mind.

He also heard much of what was going on in art in other towns, especially in Florence, where Leonardo da Vinci had just executed his most celebrated works, the wonderful portrait of the beautiful Mona Lisa, the cartoon of the Holy family, and his master-piece of the combat round a banner, at the battle near Anghiari.[1]

What he was now told of the great Florentine painter, of whom he had already heard much, and whom he may have seen at Perugia, where Da Vinci, when in the service of Il Valentino, went to inspect the fortifications in the beginning of 1503, must have inspired Raphael with a great desire to go to Florence. Every one at Urbino encouraged him in this wish, and the sister of the duke, Joanna della Rovere, even gave him a letter for the gonfalonier of Florence, Pietro Soderini. The following is a copy of her letter:

"Most magnificent and powerful lord, whom I must ever honour as a father!

"He, who presents this letter to you, is Raphael, a painter of Urbino, endowed with great talent in art. He has decided to pass some time at

---

[1] The original portrait of Mona Lisa is in the Louvre, and the cartoon for the Holy Family, in the Academy in London; but the cartoon of the "Combat of the Horsemen" was destroyed during the troubles in Florence, and there is no longer any trace of it left in the hall of the old palace.

Florence, in order to improve himself in his studies. As the father, who was dear to me, was full of good qualities, so the son is a modest young man, of distinguished manners, and thus I bear him an affection on every account, and wish that he should attain perfection. This is why I recommend him as earnestly as possible to your highness, with an entreaty that it may please you, for love of me, to show him help and protection on every opportunity. I shall regard as rendered to myself, and as an agreeable proof of friendship to me, all the services and kindness he may receive from your lordship.

"From her who commends herself to you, and is willing to render any good offices in return,

"JOANNA FELTRA DE RUVERE (*sic.*)

"Duchess of Sora and *prefectissa* of Rome."

"Urbino, October 1st, 1504."

This first journey to Florence was to unfold a fresh life before Raphael. The sight of the masterpieces of the ancient Florentine school, and especially an intimacy with artists, whose emulation had been excited by the example of Leonardo da Vinci and Michael Angelo, in fact, every thing in this town contributed to develope his talent.

The young painter of Urbino was very favourably received in several patrician houses, who ordered pictures of him, and, under such happy auspices, he soon felt himself at home in Florence.

Here, the masters he principally studied were Masaccio and Leonardo da Vinci.

Massaccio had been the first at Florence to emancipate himself from the cold imitation of Giotto. By his grand ideas of composition, by the decided contrast of light and shade, and by his love of nature, he had pointed out, more than half a century before, the road that Leonardo was afterwards to follow with more penetration and deeper knowledge.

The works of these two artists, and those of so many others, who ushered in the great century, revealed to Raphael his own wonderful powers, until then almost concealed. Awakened suddenly, and excited with the inspiration that seemed all at once to flow in on him from every side, he pushed forward at once towards the perfection he was so soon to attain.

Vasari relates that Raphael, with his companions Ridolfo Ghirlandajo, Aristotile di San Gallo and others, studied the pictures with which Masaccio decorated the chapel of the Brancacci at the church of the Carmelites at Florence. Several works by Raphael confirm this assertion; for example, the "Expulsion from Paradise," in the Loggie of the Vatican.

The influence that Leonardo exercised on him, however, a little later, is also proved by decisive documents. The collection belonging to the University of Oxford, contains one sheet on which Raphael drew, by the side of the head of a saint in his own peculiar style, another man's head in evident imitation of Da Vinci; and on a corner of the same sheet he sketched very small, the group of horsemen,[1] from the cartoon of the battle of Anghiari.

The sketch book (at the Academy of Venice) also shows some imitations of the great Florentine painters; amongst others, two men's heads in profile, in the style of Leonardo's caricatures.[2] Besides this, the sketch-book contains five sheets of studies of children from life, and several heads, all very carefully drawn on prepared grey paper. Now, this process of execution was introduced by Leonardo, as being particularly adapted for the study of form, and he nearly always made use of it himself, as is proved by several of his studies in the collection at Florence.

That Raphael did not at once abandon completely the style of Perugino, is very easily understood. He could not free himself, suddenly and without any effort from so attractive a style, and one which he had so long cultivated.

Vasari very judiciously makes the following remark: "When Raphael

---

[1] G. Edelinck made an engraving from this group, from a design by Rubens. The "Etruria Pittrici," i. tab. xxix. has published another engraving of it, from a copy attributed to Bronzino, which is at Poggio, or from a drawing in the Buccelai collection. M. Bergeret* of Paris has published, nominally from an original sketch by Leonardo, this same group of horsemen, with additions which appear to be of French manufacture.

[2] See the facsimile of Celotti: "Disegni originale di Raffaello," per la prima volta pubblicati, esistendi nella imperial-regia Accademia delle Arti di Venezias 1829, in fol.

---

* It is well known that M. Bergeret had great skill in copying the sketches of masters, and that dealers often sold them as originals. M. Bergeret was prouder of this talent than of being an historical painter; he liked to recognize in the collections of amateurs, certain drawings which he had copied, or even invented under illustrious names.—*Lacroix.*

saw the works of Da Vinci, he was perfectly astonished. This style pleased him better than any other; he studied it, and left by degrees, and not without difficulty, the style of Perugino."[1]

One of the earliest pictures by Raphael, at Florence, is the "Madonna," usually called *del Gran Duca.* This still resembles the school of Perugino, but the drawing is more studied, and of a higher character. The bold, commanding and luminous style, in which the painting stands out from the background, makes the figure and divine expression of the head still more impressive. Thanks to all these qualities united, this Madonna produces the effect of a supernatural apparition. In short, it is one of the master-pieces of Raphael.

This Madonna long remained unknown, until the day when the late Duke Ferdinand of Tuscany acquired it. He became so attached to it, that he carried it with him in all his migrations, and it was from him that it received its name. This inclination, or rather, this veneration, is still more decided with the present duchess, who, having at last presented the country with an heir-presumptive, attributes the blessing entirely to her prayers to Raphael's "Madonna."

Another beautiful Madonna of this time has been recently purchased for the Berlin Museum, of the Terranuova family, who had possessed it from the time it quitted the hands of Raphael. It is of a round shape. The Virgin is bending forwards towards St. John, who is presenting a scroll, inscribed with the words: *Ecce Agnus Dei,* to Jesus, seated on his mother's lap. On the other side, a third child leaning on Mary's knees is gazing on Christ. A rich landscape adds another beauty to this valuable painting.

Amongst the pictures that Raphael painted during his first residence at Florence, must be included the portrait of a young man, who, to judge from his costume, must have belonged to a patrician family. This

---

[1] According to Piacenza, Bottari must have seen in the house of Benedetto Luti, a portrait of Raphael, which he believed to be by the hand of Da Vinci; from this he drew a proof of the affection that the old master must have felt for the young painter of Urbino. This drawing, which passed from the collection of W. Kent, Esq. to that of General W. Guise, and which is now at Christ Church College, Oxford, probably indeed represents Raphael at about twenty years of age, but has no relation with the execution of Leonardo. It is probably by a friend, or fellow pupil of Raphael's. Bottari is also mistaken, when he concludes the oil-painting, in the Gallery at Florence, attributed to Leonardo, to be intended for the young Raphael, whom in reality it does not at all resemble.

portrait, obtained from the house of Leonardo del Riccio, of Florence, is now in the possession of King Louis of Bavaria.

After Raphael had passed a portion of the years 1504 and 1505, at Florence, occupied either with his studies or his pictures, several commissions obliged him to return to Perugia. It appears that he had already commenced a large altar-piece in that city, for the nuns of St. Antony, of Padua, as very different styles may be noticed in this picture; certain figures, principally St. Peter and St. Paul, reminding us of the "Coronation of the Virgin," the vigorous colouring of some parts recalling the "Sposalizio," whilst St. Catherine and St. Dorothea show the new style acquired at Florence. According to Vasari, the nuns had required that the Infant Saviour blessing St. John should be clothed.

The principal picture, surmounted by an arched panel, with the Almighty and two angels, is now in the palace at Naples.

Five other subjects composed the *predella.* The three largest represented "Christ in the Garden of Gethsemane," "Christ bearing the Cross," and the "Virgin supporting a dead Christ;" the two smaller ones are of St. Francis, and St. Antony of Padua. They are now dispersed in different galleries in England.[1]

The Madonna, that Raphael executed on the order of the heirs of Filippo di Simone Ansidei, who died in 1490, for the chapel of St. Nicholas, which he had founded in the church of San Fiorenzo, of Perugia, has much more unity. It was painted apparently at one time, and betrays the Florentine influence in every part, although the general ordering of the picture is in the style of Perugino. It bears the date MDV.

The Virgin, seated on a throne holds the Infant Jesus on her knees. Both are reading in a book. At the left, St. John the Baptist, at the age of manhood, is pointing to the Saviour and raising his eyes towards him. At the right, the Bishop Nicholas de Bari, is reading in the Scriptures; his venerable features express deep thought. These two saints may be considered as symbols of divine inspiration and profound science.

This altar-piece had also a predella of three little pictures, two of which have been destroyed. The largest, which was in the middle, representing St. John the Baptist preaching in the desert; several of

---

[1] Two of these small pictures formed a part of the Manchester Exhibition. See "Treasures of Art," by W. Burger.—*Lacroix.*

the figures, and especially the drapery, reminds us singularly of the style of Masaccio.

Another little picture, in the same style as the altar-piece, described above, represents in half-length, the risen Christ. From the Mosca de Pesaro house, it came into the possession of the Count Paolo Tosi, who justly regards it as a wonderful treasure of art.

In this same year, 1505, Raphael was commissioned to decorate with frescoes, a lateral chapel of the Carmelite church of San Severo, at Perugia. He painted at this time, as a trial, a child's head in fresco on a brick, which long remained at Perugia, and is now in the possession of King Louis of Bavaria.

The fresco of San Severo has, in the upper part, the Holy Trinity; in the lower, six saints of the order of the Carmelites. The whole of the upper part of the picture resembles certain principles of Fra Angelico da Fiesole and Fra Bartolomeo di San Marco, when they symbolized the holy Hierarchy in their Last Judgment.[1]

Some years afterwards, Raphael repeated the same idea, but with richer developments in the upper part, of the assembly of theologians, called the "Dispute on the Holy Sacrament," which is in the Vatican.

It is frequently asserted, though entirely without foundation, that, when he painted this fresco, Raphael had already conceived the idea of painting the "Dispute on the Holy Sacrament;" but in the fresco, he employed the traditional composition, whilst in the "Dispute" the upper part bears quite a different relation to the lower.

However, in the fresco, as well as in the picture, there may be seen the Almighty in the midst of a glory, holding the book of eternal life; below him the Saviour, in the act of blessing; two angels in adoration are standing at his sides; a little lower, are seated on the left, St. Maur, St. Placidus, and St. Benedict. To the right, St. Romuald, St. Benedict the martyr, and St. John the martyr. The noble countenances of these saints are all of a fine type; but the angels have something of that affectation to be met with in Raphael's first Florentine period. None of his preceding works, however, show such full drapery and an imposing aspect.

---

[1] For example, in the small pictures of Fra Angelico in the Academy of Florence, and in the fresco of "Fra Bartolomeo," in the hospital of Santa Maria Nuova, which fresco was completed by Mariotto Albertinelli.

This noticeable progress may be attributed in the first place to the study of Masaccio, and afterwards to the nature of a fresco, which, requiring a rapid touch, also requires a freer execution.

Whether because the season was far advanced, or because he could not resist the desire of returning to Florence, he deferred the completion of the lower part of his fresco, and, unhappily never returned to finish it. It was only after his death, that his master, Perugino, completed the unfinished half. It would even appear that there was no cartoon by the hand of Raphael left, for the six figures of saints standing, added by Perugino, are of his own invention, and betray only too much the old age of the painter.

In September of the same year, 1505, Raphael received another very honourable commission. The nuns of the convent of Monte Luce, near Perugia, obeying the desire of their late abbess, Chiara da Procia, wished to have an altar-piece painted by the best painter attainable. After a discussion between the priests, their directors, and the magistrates of the town, the task was entrusted to "*Master* Raphael of Urbino." The contract which has been preserved, thus names the young artist of twenty-two years of age.

Raphael, however, did not undertake this picture. Since he had seen Florence, an irresistible force seemed to draw him towards that celebrated city, the queen of the arts. He knew that at Perugia, his talent would be in some degree confined, that instead of enlightened criticism he would only meet with adulation; and that, in short, at his age, his genius required free room and a vast theatre. He started then for Florence, his heart full of hope and animated by the noblest ambition.

The return of Raphael to Florence was joyfully hailed by his friends. They could not have forgotten the young man who was so essentially an artist, the enthusiastic mind in which everything revealed a lofty genius. Their zeal received fresh fuel from him; and, when assembled together before the works of the masters, especially of Leonardo da Vinci, Raphael was expressing eloquently his feelings and thoughts, this new generation of illustrious artists were more filled with enthusiasm than the spectator now in contemplating their works. These artistic discussions were constantly resumed with the greatest animation, in hours of relaxation, in the studio of the architect and sculptor in wood, Baccio d'Agnolo. In his studio assembled Andrea Sansovino, Filippino Lippi, Benedetta da Majana, Il Cronaca, Antonio and Giuliano da San Gallo, Francesco

Granacci, and sometimes even the most intimate friend of Agnolo, the greatest of all these masters, Michael Angelo Buonarroti.

Besides the sympathy of the artists, Raphael also acquired that of many other distinguished personages, learned men, nobles or patricians, frequenting Agnolo's house, whose relations were very widely extended on account of the numerous architectural works which were going on in Florence under his directions.

One of these patricians, Lorenzo Nasi, having given an order for a Madonna, Raphael painted the "Madonna with the goldfinch," which now ornaments the tribune of the Florence gallery; a painting of great simplicity and exquisite grace, which Nasi held in the greatest honour all his life, as a precious souvenir of the young painter he had taken such a fancy to. Taddeo Taddei, a learned Florentine of noble family, in communication with nearly all the scientific men of the time, and very intimate with the celebrated Pietro Bembo,[1] was also a passionate admirer of Raphael's talent.

Taddeo, having a house built by Baccio d'Agnolo, frequently came to visit him, and it was thus he formed an acquaintance with Raphael, to whom he showed consideration and kindness in every way; according to Vasari, he wished to have him constantly at his table.

On his side, Raphael, out of gratitude, painted him two Madonnas: one of these, the "Madonna in the Meadow," is in the Belvedera Gallery, at Vienna; the other, apparently, was the "Holy Family under the Palm tree," which passed from the Orleans Gallery into that of the Duke of Bridgewater, in London.

An examination of these Madonnas confirms the following opinion of Vasari. The two pictures painted by Raphael for Taddeo Taddei, have still something of his earlier Peruginesque manner, but also something of his better style acquired at Florence.

From this stay at Florence, date the portraits of Angelo Doni and of his wife, Maddalena Strozzi. Doni was a rich merchant, a friend and protector of artists. He possessed some excellent pictures of the greatest masters; for instance, the "Holy Family" of Fra Bartolomeo, now in the Corsini Palace, at Rome, and Michael Angelo's "Holy Family," a round picture, placed in the tribune of the Florence Gallery.

---

[1] See the letter of Pietro Bembo to Taddeo Taddei, in the third volume of his "Letters," Venice, 1560.

THE MADONNA WITH THE GOLDFINCH

Notwithstanding all the care he gave to these portraits of Angelo Doni and Maddalena Strozzi, Raphael does not yet show himself a practised portrait painter. His drawing is not very correct; the execution is timid, the attitudes rather embarrassed. They are, nevertheless, interesting works, of striking effect, in the style of Leonardo's pictures. The woman, especially, is painted with peculiar care.

The two portraits remained long in the family, passed afterwards to Avignon, and at last returned to Florence.

The portrait of a Florentine woman, taken for some time for that of Maddalena Doni, before the authentic portrait just mentioned was discovered, is treated with a greater freedom. It is unhappily much injured. It is in the tribune at Florence.

Florence possesses likewise a fourth portrait of a woman, also in the Florentine costume of the period. Without being of regular beauty, this woman has such a pleasant, benevolent countenance, that she attracts us at once. The painting, executed by the hand of a master, is in perfect preservation. This fine portrait was laid aside, it is not known why, among the pictures of the Grand Duke, and it was only a few years ago that it was given its legitimate place in one of the halls of the Pitti Palace.

We will now accompany Raphael to Bologna. He may, perhaps, have gone there at the invitation of Giovanni Bentivoglio, then lord of that town; perhaps he was attracted thither by the reputation of Francesco Francia; perhaps he went simply to visit a celebrated city.

Some writers have altogether doubted this journey to Bologna, which is sufficiently proved by the intimacy of Raphael with Francia,[1] and by the letter he wrote to him in 1508.[2] Both this letter and Baldi inform us that Raphael painted a "Birth of Christ" for Bentivoglio. And as Bentivoglio was driven out of Bologna by the troops of Julius II., during the autumn of 1506, it follows as a matter of necessity that the painting

---

[1] Francia was much older than Raphael; he was born about 1450, and was in consequence at least fifty years old.

M. Villot No. 318 of the "Catalogue of the Italian schools in the Louvre" (1855), attributes to Francia a portrait until then ascribed to Raphael, but which may very possibly belong to neither.—*Lacroix.*

[2] Vasari says nothing of this journey of Raphael's to Bologna. Probably the information he received from this town was very unsatisfactory. This is the more probable, as he does not speak of two important pictures of Raphael's in that town, an "Annunciation" and an "Adoration of the Shepherds."

must have been executed before that period. It is much to be deplored, that no contemporary author has left us any description of it, and that it is not known what became of it.

The same letter of 1508, informs us also of the friendship between Raphael and Francia. We see by it that they had promised each to paint his own portrait, and to exchange them in memory of the happy days they had passed together. Francesco had also promised to his new friend, the drawing for a "Judith," and Raphael, on the contrary, the drawing for an "Adoration of the Shepherds," a work he had painted at Bologna.

These engagements were faithfully performed, as we shall see presently, on transcribing the letter of Raphael and the sonnet in his praise written by Francia.

A picture of the "Marriage of St. Catherine," which is in London[1] will perhaps furnish another proof of the artistic relations between Raphael and Francia; for, in the drawing and general character of the heads, it bears the seal of Raphael, whilst the execution belongs unmistakeably to Francia or to one of his pupils.[2]

It would appear that Raphael likewise formed a friendship with Lorenzo Costa, one of the most eminent pupils of Francia, since, according to what we learn from Mallazzappi,[3] he must have painted in a picture of Costa's, between a St. Ursula and a St. Catherine, the head of a St. Antony of Padua. This altar-piece, in 1580, was still in the church of San Niccolo at Carpi. It now belongs to Count Teodoro Lechi at Brescia, where we saw it in 1835. It is an admirable picture, quite in Francia's style, except this head of St. Antony, which strongly reminds us of the manner of Raphael at that period.

---

[1] In the possession of Mr. Allen Gilmore. It is signed by Raphael's hand. See on this signature, "Kunstreise durch England und Belgien," p. 125, and plate of monograms, No. 1.

[2] A "Madonna," with the Child and St. Joseph in a landscape, at the Pitti palace, proves how closely some of Francia's pupils imitated their master, for there is no connoisseur who would not attribute this "Madonna" to Francia himself, if it were not signed "Jacobus de Boateriis.

[3] In the manuscript chronicle of Gio. Francesco Mallazzappi, which was only terminated in 1580, and which is in possession of the fathers Osservanti at Parma, we read, p. 357: "San Nicolo di Carpi L'ancona o tavola dei Vaschera, di mano di Lorenzo Costa, con S. Catterina et Orsola, et in mezzo S. Antonio di Padova, la testa del quale si ritiena che sia di Raffaello."

These works terminated at Bologna, Raphael went to pay a visit to his native town to see his relations and friends, who had escaped the plague, which had just desolated the country.[1] This time he found Guidubaldo in a more prosperous state, and with a more brilliant court.

This prince had recovered, at the taking of Forli, the valuable library and other treasures of his father. He had sumptuously decorated the apartments in the palace with pictures, gold and silver ornaments, bronzes, and marble. Around him and his charming wife, Elisabetta Gonzaga, were assembled all the wit and valour of Italy.

The heir of his father's military glory, he possessed a still greater degree of general knowledge. Besides being well versed in the principal Greek and Latin authors, he knew the poetry of Homer and Virgil by heart, and could recite long passages from them. An enemy to idleness, he divided his leisure time in peace between study, the chace, and military exercises. He was so affable, that it was said of him, "The Duke renders those happy who serve him."

The court of Urbino, with respect to learning and morals, was accounted the first of the smaller courts in Italy. Count Castiglione[2] has left a lively and agreeable picture of it in his "Libro del Cortigiano." After having praised the noble qualities of the duke, and described the life led at the court, he gives an idea of the tone of charming gaiety and modest liberty which prevailed among the ladies; he praises the duchess particularly, and describes her striking beauty, her gentle rule, and the deep respect she inspired.

Amongst the greatest men then assembled at the court of Urbino, we must mention Giuliano de' Medici, brother of Leo X., and who, like his father Lorenzo, was surnamed the Magnificent; a noble man, full of love to science;—Andrea Doria, the Genoese, whose name is everywhere celebrated; he had passed his youth at the duke's court, and had received from him the investiture of Castello di Sascorbaro;—Ottaviano Fregoso, son of Agostino and Gentile, natural daughter of Duke Federico of Urbino; he subsequently became Duke of Genoa, and was a brave soldier, endowed with great qualities;—Federico Fregoso, his brother,

---

[1] We read in the "Acts of Lodovico Oddi," p. 188: "Non me rogavi propter pestem epidemiæ de mense martii 1506 redivi ad civitatem Urbini cum totâ familiâ . . . . etc."

[2] See Baldassare Castiglione: "Il Libro del Cortigiano," and B. Baldi: "Della vita e de' fatti di Guidobaldo I da Montefeltro, duca d'Urbino." Milano, 1821.

who wrote the account of the death of Guidubaldo to Julius II.; he was named Archbishop of Salerno by that pope, and was raised to the cardinalate by Paul III.;—Count Lodovico da Canossa, who became Bishop of Tricarico, and afterwards, under Francis I., Bishop of Bayeux;—Count Baldassare Castiglione, a writer and diplomatist, frequently charged with political missions by the Dukes of Urbino and Mantua; at a subsequent time he entered the service of Julius II. and Leo X., and became one of the most intimate friends of Raphael;—Pietro Bembo, secretary to Leo X., and a cardinal under Paul III.; one of the most celebrated *savants* and writers of his time; like Castiglione, he has left us a good picture of the court of Urbino,[1] and like him, also, he was very intimate with Raphael;—Bernardo Divizio da Bibiena, a caustic and witty writer, the author of "La Calandra," the first regular comedy in prose that had been written in Italy; he was named Cardinal of Santa Maria in Portico, under Leo X., and, at a later time, felt so much affection for Raphael, that he wished to marry him to one of his nieces;—Cesare Gonzaga, of Mantua, the second of four brothers, both a warrior and a scientific man: he died too early to have achieved great fame;—Gasparo Pallavicino, who also died very early, after having given rise to great hopes;—Lodovico Pio, of the family of Carpi;—Sigismondo de' Riccardi, also named *Morella da Ortona*, who had immense possessions in the Abruzzi near Amalfi, and in Sicily:—the warriors Pietro da Napoli and Roberto da Bari; the latter, an amiable young man of great personal beauty, died in the flower of his age;—Alessandro Trivulzio, the son of Fermo; he subsequently entered the service of Francis I., and was killed under the walls of Reggio;—the learned sculptor Gio. Christoforo Romano, then very celebrated;[2]—Bernardo Accolti, surnamed the Unico Aretino, on account of the magical effect of his improvisations accompanied with music; he was private secretary under Leo X., and invested with the Duchy of Nepi;—Niccolò Frisio (Nicolaus Fries), whom

---

[1] In his work: "De Guido Ubaldo Feretrio deque Elisabetha Gonz., Urb. ducibus, Liber," Veneta, 1530.

[2] See "Lettere pitt.," iii. No. 196, and A. Carlo Fea: "Notizie intorno Raffaello," etc. p. 25, when in a letter from Cesare Tribulzio, of June 1st, 1506, addressed to Pomponio Trivulzio, Christoforo Romano, is mentioned conjointly with Michael Angelo, as one of the best sculptors at Rome, and as having perceived with him that the group of the Laocoon, which had just been discovered in the Baths of Titus, was not made of a single block.

Bembo calls "a German with distinguished Italian manners;" he had been sent to Italy by the Emperor Maximilian, on business connected with the treaty of Cambrai; he afterwards passed into the service of the Cardinal di Santa Croce (Bernardino Carvajal).

At the court there was also a lady of great intelligence and exalted mind, Emilia Pia, the sister of Ercole Pio, Lord of Carpi, wife of Count Antonio da Montefeltro, natural brother to the Duke Guidubaldo. Early left a widow, when she was still in the full charms of youth, she yet refused any fresh alliance, and lived with an unblemished reputation in close friendship with the Duchess of Urbino.

On a medal, which was struck in her honour, are engraved, on one side, her portrait, with the inscription, "*Æmylia Pia Feltria,*" and on the reverse, a pyramid with an urn, and the words, "*Castis cineribus.*"

Amongst the ladies who adorned the court of Urbino, there was also Joanna della Rovere, widow of the Duke of Sora, who, after the death of her husband, likewise took refuge with Guidubaldo her brother.

Sometimes the court became more animated, from the presence of other guests, as when, in May, 1505, the members of the Venetian embassy, sent to Pope Julius II., sojourned there a short time, and were grandly treated by the duchess, in gratitude for the hospitality that Guidubaldo had met with at Venice.

The embassy was composed of Cardinal Bernardo Bembo, Girolamo Donati, Paolo Pisani, Andrea Veniero, Niccolò Foscarino, Leonardo Mocenigo, Andrea Gritti, and Domenico Trevisani, all persons eminent by birth and knowledge; each of them was accompanied by five young nobles, and many servants, so that the number of these strangers amounted to two hundred.

The brilliancy of this court of Urbino must have had a great influence on the young and impressionable Raphael. If at Perugia he had been captivated by the simplicity of a retired life, and had been struck at Florence by the proud and intelligent activity of the citizens, at Urbino he was initiated into the life of the higher classes; he made acquaintance with some of the noblest and most learned men of the time, and even contracted a friendship, which lasted his whole life, with Pietro Bembo and Count Castiglione.

Both these learned men, imbued with the Platonic ideas, then so prevalent, were constantly bringing them forward in enthusiastic discourses, and turning the thoughts of the company to the beautiful. We shall see, presently, that Raphael was deeply penetrated with these fertile theories, and this fact explains why, without having enjoyed a learned education, he yet shows in his works such deep thought, and the exalted mind which has justly caused him to be named the philosophic painter.

To show still more clearly the taste, the spirit and the manners of the circle that surrounded Raphael during this period of his youth, we shall relate the conversation of one evening, as it has been described by Count Castiglione in his "Courtier's Book."

The Duke Guidubaldo, retiring early in the evening on account of his health, the company assembled in the duchess's apartments. One evening, the princess requested Bembo to communicate to her his ideas on love and beauty.[1]

Bembo commenced his discourse by reflections on corporeal beauty and sensual love, peculiar to youth; he explained afterwards how the beauty of the mind is the fundamental cause of physical beauty; how at the age of manhood, mystical spiritual love procures noble enjoyment; how love increases and becomes nobler, when it creates an image of general beauty; which, however, is never entirely realised, but only partially, with some individuals; now, however sublime love may be, it can yet not be called perfect, since it is only produced by the interposition of the senses flowing from imagination.

After this exordium, Castiglione allows his friend to continue thus:[2]

"When our courtier, then, shall have attained this degree of love,—although he may esteem himself a happy lover in comparison of those who are plunged in the misery of sensual love—yet I would not have him remain there, but, on the contrary, he should advance still further in this sublime path, following the guide, who is conducting him to true happiness; and thus, instead of going out of himself in thought, as he who considers corporeal beauty, the courtier must keep his mind free to

---

[1] From the first half of the fifteenth century, in Italy, the study of the Platonic writings brought in by the fugitive Greeks, protected especially by the Medici at Florence, were much in fashion. The *beaux esprits* at the court of Urbino, did not fail to take it up eagerly. In 1505, Pietro Bembo, as an admirer of Plato, had already acquired much fame from his Dialogues on the nature of love ("gli Asolani," from the name of the Castle of Azolo, where he wrote them.) The following reflections are merely an imitation of Plato's "Banquet."

[2] At the end of the fourth book of the work, which appeared for the first time in the month of April, 1528, "Venetia," nelle case d'Aldo Romano, in folio, reprinted the same year at Florence by the Giuntis, 8vo.—*Lacroix*.

contemplate the beauty that is only seen by the eyes of the intellect, those eyes which are never more piercing than when the bodily eyes lose their clear-sightedness.

"For the soul being a stranger to vice, purified by the study of true philosophy, attentive to the philosophy of the mind, well practised in intellectual things, and loving the contemplation of its own substance, as if awakened from a deep sleep, opens the eyes that we all possess, though few know how to use them aright; then she sees in herself a ray of light, the true image of angelic beauty, which is communicated to her, and of which she transmits an uncertain shadow to the body.

"Now, the soul, having become blind to terrestrial things, is far-sighted in regard to celestial objects; sometimes when the motive forces of the body are abstracted by assiduous contemplation, or else are bound in sleep, the soul being no longer obstructed, inhales a certain odour concealed under the true angelic beauty, and soon dazzled by the splendour of the light, she begins to be inflamed, and follows it with such ardour as to appear almost intoxicated and carried out of herself from her desire to attain this light; for she thinks she has found the road which leads to God, in the contemplation of whom she seeks to rest as in a centre of happiness.

"And thus, kindled by a holy flame, she rises to her noblest part—intellect, and there, being no longer blinded by the obscure night of terrestrial objects, she beholds divine beauty. Yet even then she does not enjoy it perfectly, because she contemplates it only through her own intelligence, which is incapable of understanding the immensity of universal beauty.

"Thus love, not satisfied with this benefit, gives a still greater felicity to the soul; for as, from the beauty of one body, it leads to the universal beauty of all bodies in the same manner, in the highest degree of perfection, it leads from a single intelligence to universal intelligence.

"At this point, the soul, smitten with the holy fire of true divine love, bounds forward to acquire the angelic nature, and not only does she abandon her senses, but has even no longer need of her reason, which, transformed into an angel, understands all intelligible things, and, without a cloud, perceives the wide and spacious sea of pure divine beauty, receives it into her being, and enjoys that supreme felicity which is incomprehensible to the senses.

"If the beauties, then, that we see every day with our darkened eyes in corruptible bodies, although only dreams or fugitive shadows of true beauty, if these beauties seem to us so lovely, as frequently to kindle in us an incandescent fire, and give us such pleasure, that we esteem no felicity to be compared with that which we feel, at merely a glance from the charming eyes of a lady, oh! with what overpowering admiration must those souls be filled who obtain a glimpse of divine beauty! What a gentle flame, what sweet ardour must be theirs, who reach the source of this supreme and true beauty, the principle of all other beauty, which never increases, never diminishes, remaining always beautiful and always the same in itself in its simplicity, resembling itself alone and participating in no other, but wholly beautiful, with a beauty which makes everything beautiful, because their beauty merely proceeds from it alone.

"It is beauty, inseparable from sovereign goodness, which, with light, attracts all things to itself, and not only gives intelligence to intellectual beings,—sense and a desire of life to sensible beings,—but also communicates a sort of image of itself to plants and stones, in movement and the natural instinct of their properties.

"This love then is incomparably nobler and happier than any other, inasmuch as the cause which animates it is more excellent and more certain. And yet as material fire refines gold, thus does this sacred fire destroy and consume in the soul all that is mortal, and refreshes and beautifies still more the celestial part which before was mortified and almost buried in the senses.

"This is the pyre, on which the poets say that Hercules burned himself on the summit of Mount Œta, in order by this self-immolation to become after his death divine and immortal.

"It is the burning bush of Moses! the spirit which descends in the tongue of fire! Elijah's chariot of fire, which heightens the joy in the souls of those who are worthy to behold it, when quitting this terrestrial valley, it takes its flight back to heaven!

"Let us, then, turn all our thoughts, and all the desires of our souls, towards that holy light which shows us the way to heaven; and, laying aside the affections, with which we are weighed down in descending, let us ascend the ladder, the lowest step of which is attached to sensual beauty, let us ascend towards the celestial abodes where true beauty is to be found concealed with the deep secrets of God, that profane eyes may not behold. There shall we find the happy end of our desires, the true rest, the certain remedy for our miseries, the wholesome cure for our infirmities, and the surest port against the whirlwinds and waves of the stormy sea of this life.

"Where then, oh love! is the mortal tongue that can worthily praise thee, who art infinitely beautiful, infinitely good, infinitely wise, because thou proceedest from the union of divine beauty, goodness, and wisdom; because thou dwellest in this union, and fliest to it as to thy centre.

"Thou art the link placed between things terrestrial and celestial; by thy beneficent intervention thou inclinest superior virtues to the government of inferior ones, and, by directing the minds of mortals to their principle, thou bindest them to it.

"Thou makest the elements to accord; thou excitest nature to produce all that grows to keep up the succession of life, thou assemblest separate things, thou givest perfection to the imperfect, and similarity to the dissimilar; friendship to enmity; to the earth, fruits; to the sea, calm; and to the sky, vital light.

"Thou art the father of all true pleasures, graces, peace, mansuetude, and benevolence; thou art the enemy of barbarity, of rusticity, and of slothfulness; thou art the commencement and the end of all good.

"And, since thou delightest to dwell in beautiful bodies and beautiful souls, and that from them thou sometimes revealest thyself to the eyes and understanding of those who are worthy to see thee, I believe that thou dost now dwell among us.

"Oh Lord, do thou then deign to listen to our prayers; enter into our hearts, and, by the splendour of thy sacred fire, enlighten our darkness, and, like a faithful guide, show us the right way, in this dark labyrinth; correct, if it please thee, the illusions of our senses, and, after our long errors and vain thoughts, give unto us the true and solid good; make us to inhale those spiritual odours which refresh the virtues of the intelligence; enable us to hear the celestial harmony, so that no agitation from the passions may ever arise in us; assuage our thirst at that fountain of contentment that can never be exhausted, whose waters always delight and can never weary, and of which when we drink, we taste pure happiness; purify by the rays of thy light our eyes darkened by the clouds of ignorance, so that they may no longer attach any value to mere mortal beauty, and may know that the things they thought they saw, do not really exist, whilst those they did not see are actual realities; accept our souls which we offer in sacrifice to thee; burn them in that quick flame which consumes all material ardour, so that being separated from the body, they may be united by a soft and perpetual link to divine beauty, and that, becoming strangers to ourselves, we may, like true lovers, be transformed into the loved object, then raised above the earth, and admitted to the banquet of angels, where being satiated with ambrosia and immortal nectar, we may at last die a happy death, which will begin our true life, like the death of the ancient patriarchs, whose souls through ardent contemplation, were by thee, oh love, separated from their bodies and united to God."[1]

After having spoken thus with extreme enthusiasm, Bembo remained standing motionless, with his eyes turned towards heaven; and he seemed almost petrified, when the Signora Emilia recalled him to earth by saying to him, "Take care, Signor Pietro, that with such thoughts your soul does not quit your body." "Signora," he replied, "it would not be the first miracle that love has wrought in me."

There is no longer a possibility of learning, with any certainty, whether Raphael was present at these philosophic discussions; but it is certain that these mystic tendencies had a great influence on him, leaving, however, uninjured the truer sentiment of nature that the artist always possesses more largely than the philosopher and poet. Some passages in the "Libro del Cortegiano," although relating to posterior facts, give us to understand that Raphael was present at the poetical and literary tournaments at the court of Urbino.

Thus it says: "One day, when Count Lodovico da Canossa was sustaining, against Christoforo Romano, that painting was a more complete art than sculpture, Castiglione interposing, cried out, 'On my honour, Count Lodovico, it seems to me that you are speaking against your own conviction, and in favour of your protégé Raphael. Perhaps you will also say that his works surpass anything that has been executed in marble. But remember that this is the praise of an artist, and not of an art;' on which the Count da Canossa smilingly replied, 'I am not speaking in favour of Raphael, and you must not think me so ignorant as not to appreciate the works of Michael Angelo and other sculptors,'" &c.

During this residence at Urbino Raphael painted for Duke Guidubaldo a "St. George" on a white horse, rushing forward against the

[1] In this mystical pathos, we might almost imagine we are reading a page from St. Theresa; and certainly the Duke de la Rochefoucauld, who never spoke of the work of Baldassare Castiglione, but as a masterpiece, would not have been able to understand this definition of true beauty, but by studying the pictures of Raphael.—*Lacroix*.

dragon, who is transfixed by his lance; in the background, among some rocks, the princess is kneeling in prayer. The young hero wears under his right knee the order of St. George, also called the order of the Garter.

This "St. George of the Garter" was, indeed, intended for Henry VII. of England, who, on the occasion of the embassy to Pope Julius II., had sent to Guidubaldo, by the Abbot of Glastonbury and Gilbert Talbot, the order and insignia of the Garter.[1]

Count Castiglione was commissioned to go to England to receive the accolade in the duke's name. He set out July 10th, 1506, with Francesco di Battista Ceci, of Urbino. He took with him magnificent presents, fine horses, falcons, and a number of precious objects, among which was a small "St. George," by Raphael. Arrived at Dover, October 20, he was received with much pomp, and conducted to the king in London. The ceremony completed, he was gratified with a necklace bearing the arms of Henry VII.; he afterwards visited all the knights of the order, and returned to Urbino in February, 1507.

The small "St. George," after many vicissitudes, is now at St. Petersburg. It has been placed, in the manner of an *ex voto*, with a burning lamp before it, by the side of the great portrait of the Emperor Alexander, in the long gallery of portraits painted by Dawe in the Hermitage.

Vasari mentions two small Madonnas which Raphael must have painted for the duke, and praises their extreme beauty, adding that they belong to the second Florentine manner: they must have been executed during the visit to Urbino in 1506. But Vasari gives no description of them, and old writers give us no information respecting them.[2]

It was probably during this visit that Raphael painted the portrait of Duke Guidubaldo, a portrait alluded to by Pietro Bembo, in a letter of April 19th, 1516, to Cardinal Santa Maria, in Portico.

This portrait has disappeared, but we must conclude that it was painted at this time; for Raphael, when it was done, must already have

---

[1] The Duke Federico had also received them from Edward III.

[2] We suppose that these two pictures may be: one, a small "Holy Family," with St. Joseph without a beard, half-length figures; coming from the house of Angoulême, to the Crozat collection, and now at St. Petersburg;* the other from the Orleans Gallery, and now in the possession of M. Delessert at Paris, after having been in England at several picture dealers'.

---

* M. Viardot (p. 296 of his "Musées d'Angleterre, de Hollande et de Russie,") speaks of two "Holy Families" at the Hermitage, both of which seemed to him very doubtful.—*Lacroix.*

had some reputation, and it is quite impossible that it should have been painted later, since he did not return to Urbino, and he had besides no opportunity of seeing Guidubaldo again, who died April 11th, 1508.

It is to be presumed that Raphael also painted the portrait of the Duchess Elisabetta; indeed, according to Antonio Beffa Negrini, Count Castiglione possessed a portrait, by the hand of Raphael, representing a princess, in whose honour he wrote, in 1517, two sonnets, which were found behind a large mirror belonging to her sister, the Countess Catterina Mondella. Pungileoni goes so far as to suppose that Raphael painted this portrait for the count himself. It is much to be regretted that there is no more precise information on this point.

Raphael also drew at this time the portrait of Pietro Bembo. The anonymous writer edited by Morelli,[1] to whom we owe this information, thus describes the drawing, which was long preserved in the house of Bembo, at Padua, with other works of art: "The small portrait in chalk of the same Signor Pietro Bembo, in his youth, *when he was at the court of Urbino*, by the hand of Raphael." Now, Bembo only went once to Urbino in 1506.

The portrait of Bembo has disappeared, like those of Guidubaldo and the duchess. But one treasure of the same period has been preserved, which apparently he must have executed for his uncle, Simone Ciarla. At all events, this picture long remained at Urbino, after having passed the Academy of St. Luke, at Rome, it came to the Florence Gallery to the collection of artists' portraits, painted by themselves. Raphael, then twenty-three years of age, has taken his own likeness in a close-fitting black dress, with a cap on his head. The eyes and hair are brown; the complexion pale. The head slightly thrown back, possesses a wonderful charm; the countenance expresses gentleness and amiability, and exhibits fully the natural languor of this noble and poetic soul. The simplicity of the attitude and costume, is far removed from pretension. It is a valuable picture painted in an exquisite manner.

The little picture of the "Three Graces," in the antique style, was apparently executed for some one at the court of Urbino. The study[2]

---

[1] "Notizie d'opere di disegno nella prima meta del secolo xvi. etc." scritto da un anonimo di quel tempo, pubblicata e illustrata da D. Jacopo Morelli, etc. Bassano, 1800, p. 18.

[2] Already mentioned, page 45. We said that this fine study was preserved in the Academy of Venice, in the Sketch-book.

that Raphael had made from the antique group in the *libreria* of the castle, served as his model. He merely added a few details, such as the coral necklaces round the necks and in the hair, and the golden apples in the hands.

It is remarkable that the first antique subject treated by Raphael, should have been that of the Three Graces, to whom the painter of Urbino rendered more constant homage than any other artist of Christian times.[1]

We do not know positively if Raphael was still at Urbino when Julius II. stayed there on his way to Bologna to repress an insurrection.

To receive the pope with requisite pomp, great preparations had been made, triumphal arches and columns had been erected, as well as statues, trophies, and other emblems. The cathedral and palace were decorated with carpets and pictures, and all the streets were strewn with flowers.

Julius II. arrived September 25th, 1506, accompanied by twenty-two cardinals and a number of prelates. A hundred horsemen, splendidly equipped, and three hundred halberdiers of the papal guard preceded the Holy Sacrament borne on a palfrey.

Twenty-five of the finest young men in Urbino came to meet the pope, who stopped at the Bernardine convent, one mile out of the town, on a height from whence he might contemplate the magnificent landscape spread around him. In the evening he advanced on horseback, under a dais, to the steps of the cathedral, in which he recited a prayer; he then went on to the court. He remained there, with the greater part of his suite, three whole days, and, being in a good temper, was agreeable and pleasant to every one.

Perhaps he may have seen at the court some work of Raphael's. Perhaps he may at this time have learned something of the great painter, whom he was to have the honour of choosing for the decoration of the Vatican.

On leaving Urbino, Raphael returned to pursue his studies at Florence, where an artistic treat was awaiting him. Michael Angelo had just ter-

---

[1] This charming little picture* was formerly in the Borghese Palace. It is now in the gallery of Earl Dudley. It has been well engraved by F. Forster.

* It formed a part of the Manchester Exhibition. See "Treasures of Art," etc. by W. Burger, p. 56.—*Lacroix*.

minated his celebrated fresco of the "Soldiers bathing," at the battle between the Florentines and Pisans,[1] and this masterpiece had created universal astonishment and enthusiasm. It was, indeed, a marvel of art, even in that memorable period.

Raphael, however, on his way through the mountains, must have stopped a few days at the Convent of Vallombrosa, to paint the portraits of two ecclesiastics there. These portraits, painted in distemper, were religiously preserved there for two centuries. But at the time of the suppression of the church and convent, they were transported, with other works of art, to the Academy of Florence, where they are at present.

One of these, of very gentle expression, is the general of the order, named Blasio; the other, of a more intellectual countenance, is Don Baldassare. Both are in profile, with their eyes turned upwards, which would lead us to suppose that they were formerly placed on each side of a crucifix, or an *ex-voto*. These heads are admirably painted, of severely correct drawing, and full of life and spirit.

On his arrival at Florence, Raphael painted for Domenico Canigiani the beautiful "Holy Family" of pyramidal form. From the Canigiani house it passed to the Grand Duke of Tuscany, then living at Dusseldorf with the Elector Palatine, Johann Wilhelm, as a wedding gift at the time of his marriage to Anna Maria de' Medici, daughter of Cosmo III.; then from the gallery at Dusseldorf to the Pinocothek at Munich.

It was a valuable picture, with quite a Raphaelesque grace; but it has been so spoiled by cleanings and restorations that scarcely any trace can now be seen of its first beauty.

---

[1] According to Vasari's account, Raphael heard at Siena, about 1504, of the two cartoons of Michael Angelo and Leonardo da Vinci, and hastened to Florence in order to see them. But, as the cartoon of Michael Angelo was only completed about the year 1506, (see in Gaye, "Corteggio," vol. ii. p. 92, the letter of the gonfalonier Soderini at Florence, addressed on the 24th November, 1506, to the Cardinal of Volterra), the assertion of Vasari is evidently erroneous. The letter of recommendation of Joanna della Rovere (October, 1504,) and the small pictures executed the same year for the Duke of Urbino, prove clearly that Raphael went then for the first time to Florence in order to see the work of Da Vinci. And it was only towards the close of this year, 1506, during which he had been occupied at Urbino (as for example on the portraits of the Duke, and Bembo, &c.) that he appears to have made his third journey to Florence, where he was to see the cartoon of Buonarroti. A good idea may be formed of this cartoon, which has disappeared, by the copy in oil, preserved at Holkham in England, and of which Schiavone has made a good engraving. See our work "Kunstreise durch England und Belgien," p. 194.

The small "Holy Family" in the museum of Madrid belongs to the same period, and has wonderful finish. The Virgin is standing bending over the Child, who is sitting on a lamb; St. Joseph, leaning on his stick, is watching the scene.

Raphael, when he was still under Perugino, had received from Donna Atalanta Baglioni, when passing through Perugia, after the recapture of the city by Gio. Paolo Baglioni, the order for an "Entombment" for the church of the Franciscans. As he wished to show in this picture of what he was capable, he had waited some time in order to execute the cartoon at Florence, where the advice of masters and friends would be very useful to him.

The cartoon no longer exists, but we still have a number of sketches and studies for this work,[1] all very original.

However fine these preparatory sketches, it seems that Raphael finally made up his mind to adopt the celebrated composition of Andrea Mantegna, which he had already drawn in his sketch-book (in the Academy of Venice). Nevertheless, he did not keep to it strictly, but completed it with that sense of the beautiful which was peculiar to him.

In the present day there would be something very shocking in this appropriation of the inventions of others; but it was not the same in the sixteenth century. An artist might take a traditional composition or

---

[1] We must mention the following:

1. The first pen-and-ink sketch for the principal group, known under the false appellation of the "Death of Adonis."—At Oxford.

2. Another pen-and-ink sketch, for the same group, but in which the Virgin is kneeling in the middle.—Cabinet of Samuel Rogers, Esq., London.*

3. The same part of the composition, drawing in pen and ink.—In the Florence collection.

4. Three naked figures; two men bearing the body of Christ.—At Oxford.

5. A sketch of nine figures; "the Magdalen kissing the hand of Christ."

6, 7. Two slight sketches, each of three figures—Cabinets of Messrs. Forster and Woodburn at London.†

8, 9. Two groups of women; the Madonna and another figure are drawn in the skeleton.—Leembrugge Cabinet, at Amsterdam.

10. The same group, with the figures clothed.—In the Weimar Cabinet.

---

* The collection of the late Mr. Rogers was sold in 1856.—*Lacroix.*

† The Raphaels of M. Woodburn were derived in great part from the collection of Sir Joshua Reynolds. The whole of this collection cost £3000; but Mr. Woodburn, at once sold a small portion of these drawings, for the same price to Lord Ashburton, and the remainder to other amateurs.—*Lacroix.*

types of figures, and reproduce it according to the measure of his own genius.

The cartoon once decided on at Florence, Raphael set out for Perugia, where he executed the picture. Vasari states this expressly, on exact information.

The picture is treated with much care. The body of Christ, very well drawn, is being borne to the tomb by two men; the weeping Magdalen is holding his hand, and gazing on the lifeless form. Near her Joseph of Arimathea is going to the sepulchre. St. John, plunged in deep grief, seems almost unable to believe that his master is really dead. A little way off the Virgin is fainting in the arms of three women. In the distance is Mount Calvary. In the foreground is the name of Raphael and the date, 1507.

Besides the principal picture, Raphael also painted the Almighty, surrounded by angels, all half-length figures, which may still be seen in the Franciscan convent at Perugia.

In the predella he represented, in chiaroscuro, the theological Virtues; three medallions, separated by Genii standing. These little pictures, executed in a rapid and masterly manner, are now in the collection of the Vatican.

When Raphael terminated these pictures, he returned to Florence, whither he was summoned by other labours.

We may also mention, as belonging to this period, the charming "St. Catherine of Alexandria," a half-length figure, the size of life,[1] which adorns the National Gallery of London.

This fine picture, although painted after preparatory studies, and from a cartoon preserved in the Louvre, is yet not so carefully treated as the "Entombment." But it possesses another attraction: the extreme lightness[2] of the execution reveals more of the immense knowledge and divine sentiment of the master. It is one of those works which nothing can describe; neither words, nor a painted copy, nor engravings, for

---

[1] No. 168 in the Catalogue "St. Catherine of Alexandria." "She is represented in the picture looking upwards, with an expression full of resignation, and is leaning with her left arm on the wheel, the intended instrument of her martyrdom; the back-ground is a landscape. Small figure, *three-quarter length*."

[2] The shadows are made by a sort of hatching or strokes of the pencil as in a pencil drawing or an engraving. Some *golden* rays, on which the saint is gazing, descend from above and streak the sky.—*Lacroix*.

SAINT CATHERINE OF ALEXANDRIA.

In the National Gallery.

the fire in it appears living, and is perfectly beyond the reach of imitation.

A small "Madonna," of the same period, and surnamed the "Madonna with the Pink," is only known through the innumerable copies taken of it at the time. It is a pretty work, but far less important than the "St. Catherine."

Another Madonna of extreme beauty, and very spiritual execution, is the "Madonna de la Casa Niccolini," of Florence.[1] It is dated 1508, with the letters "R. V." The Virgin, almost in profile, is holding the Infant Saviour on her knees; she is looking tenderly at him, while he is looking at the spectator. There is a certain expression of affectation in the face of the Child, and he resembles in this the two angels of the fresco of San Severino, as well as the Child in the "Madonna di Casa Colonna."

In the latter picture, now in the Berlin Museum,[2] free play is given to the Raphaelesque fancy. It appears to have been very rapidly executed, without the assistance of models or studies, and is less finished than the "St. Catherine" in London.

We now come to one of the purest and noblest creations of Raphael, to the jewel of the Louvre, known by the name of the "Belle Jardinière."

The Virgin is seated in the midst of a rich landscape, the ground in front being covered with grass and flowers. The Infant Christ, leaning against his mother's knees, is looking up at her with celestial tenderness. On the left the little St. John is kneeling before him. This is the outline of the picture; but how can we attempt a description of the impression it produces? The sublime sentiment of maternity is here depicted in its pure ideal. The mind is as much delighted as the eye.

The "Belle Jardinière" bears the date 1508.[3] It was not completed

---

[1] Now at Lord Cowper's residence at Penshangar.—Exhibited at Manchester.

[2] At the Manchester Exhibition there was a pretended *replica*, which in reality was merely a copy. See "Treasures of Art," by W. Burger, p. 59.—*Lacroix.*

[3] We must mention here that some amateurs declare this "Jardinière," of which there are repetitions in several other museums, to be a copy. The date is not 1508, but M.D.VII. in figures very visible on the edge of the robe. This authentic date proves that the "Belle Jardinière" of the Louvre, could not have been the picture ordered by Sergardi, and completed by Ridolpho Ghirlandajo. All these details related by Vasari, and by several authors who have copied Vasari, applied no doubt to another Madonna. However M. Villot's catalogue has rectified these errors. See No. 375 of the "Italian Schools in the Louvre," and the note pp. 78-79.—*Lacroix.*

when Raphael was summoned to Rome. He entrusted to his friend Bidolfo Ghirlandajo the task of finishing the blue mantle of the Madonna; and, in fact, this drapery does not come up entirely to the simple and beautiful style of the painter of Urbino. The picture had been ordered by a gentleman of Siena, in the service of Leo X., named Filippo Sergardi, who subsequently sold it to Francis I.

In 1508 Raphael also painted the Madonna raising the veil which covers the sleeping Jesus, to show the Divine Child to St. John. It is not known what has become of the original, though there are a number of excellent copies. They are all alike in the principal parts and in the landscape, which prevents the supposition that any of these pictures were taken from the cartoon of Raphael preserved in the Academy of Florence; for, in that cartoon there is no landscape.

At a later period at Rome, Raphael repeated this composition, with a few changes; the young St. John has his hands clasped in adoration, instead of pointing to the Saviour; and the landscape represents some ruins, still seen in the Sacchetti Villa, near St. Peter's. This picture, known under different names—the "Sommeil de Jesus," the "Vierge au Linge," the "Vierge au Diadême"—is in the Louvre.[1]

We have just remarked that the execution of Raphael is by no means equal, especially at this period, when he was beginning to free himself from old ideas. However, he rarely executed a picture without, in the first place, making studies for it from nature, to which he kept as closely as possible. In this manner he could, when painting, give free vent to his inspiration, without being tormented by seeking after good attitudes or correct drawing. This process, besides the confidence it gave to the artist, had also the advantage of facilitating and hastening the execution.

It was during his stay at Florence that Raphael made the acquaintance of Fra Bartolomeo di San Marco, who was four years older than himself. After having left off painting for some time, Fra Bartolomeo had just returned to his old pursuit, and had executed,[2] for the church of

---

[1] See No. 376 of the "Catalogue of the Italian Schools." This picture is also called the "Vierge au Voile." According to Lepicié, it was sometimes called the "Silence de la Vierge." However it is not mentioned by Vasari, and did not form a part of the king's collection before 1742. Waagen criticizes it much and comes near to doubting its originality.—*Lacroix.*

[2] P. Seraphino Razzi, "Istoria degli nomini illustri Domenicani," 1596, p. 366: "L'anno 1500, 26 luglio (Fra Bartolomeo) si vesti frate . . . dopo quattro anni riprese l'arte del dipingere." See also Vasari in his life of this painter.

St. Mark, a large picture of magnificent colouring, which, in 1512, was acquired by the republic of Florence, who made a present of it to the French ambassador. Subsequently this picture passed into the collection of Francis I., and is now in the Louvre.[1]

Raphael admired this great master, and they became intimate friends. This artistic relation was very useful to both. Raphael, already initiated under Perugino into the science of perspective, taught that science to the *frate*, who, in return, taught him the art of disposing draperies, and imparting a luminous tint to the colouring by developing his broad style of painting.

The young painter of Urbino, whose impressionable genius appropriated immediately all that he approved, for a short time imitated to such a degree the style of his new friend, that the picture he painted at this time for the altar of the family Dei at San Spirito, might at a first glance be taken for the work of Fra Bartolomeo.

This picture shows the Virgin on a very high throne, in a niche with columns; she is tenderly pressing the Child to her heart. He, full of simple grace, is looking at St. Peter and St. Bruno, who are standing at one side; at the other side the Apostle St. James the Less, and the Father of the church, St. Augustine, seem to be exhorting the faithful to the worship of the Saviour. Two little angels are singing before the steps of the throne. Above hover two angels, who are drawing aside the curtains of a canopy.

Raphael having left this picture unfinished, his pupils and heirs, Giulio Romano and Francesco Penni, sold it to the President of the pope's Chancery, Baldassare Turini, who placed it in the church of Pescia, his native town. The Grand Duke of Tuscany bought it subsequently, and it is now in the Pitti Palace, under the name of the "Madonna del Baldacchino."

Towards the close of his residence in Florence, Raphael sent to his

---

[1] This is the picture marked "La Vierge, Sainte Catherine de Sienne et plusieurs sainti," No. 65 of the "Italian Schools in the Louvre." But M. Villot's catalogue does not agree with M. Passavant as to this picture. According to M. Villot in the biographical notice of Fra Bartolomeo, it was not in 1508, but in 1506, that Raphael became acquainted with the Florentine painter. "In the month of October, 1506," says M. Villot, "Raphael, being at Florence, became the friend of Fra Bartolomeo, taught him the rules of painting, and received in return, useful lessons on the employment of colours.—*Lacroix*.

old fellow-pupil, Domenico di Paris Alfani, a drawing for a "Holy Family." Alfani had asked for this sketch for an altar-piece that he was commissioned to paint in the church of the Carmelites at Perugia.

This drawing, executed with peculiar care, from a part of the collection was bequeathed by the painter Wicar to Lille, his native place. On the drawing itself, Raphael wrote the following words:

"Do not forget, Menicho (Domenicho); send me the love songs[1] that Ricciardo composed in his transports at the moment of his journey. Remind Cesarino,[2] also, to send me a *Sermone*, and give him my compliments. Do not forget, either, to beg Donna Atalanta[3] to send me my money, and try to receive it in gold pieces.[4] Cesarino might tell her so. If I can do anything else for you, write to me."

Raphael had attained his twenty-fifth year. His reputation had increased, and was beginning to spread all over Italy. A letter, addressed to his uncle, Simone Ciarla, shows that he was hoping at that moment to obtain an important commission for a hall in the old palace of Florence. It was probably the hall that Pietro Luzzi, surnamed Il Morto da Feltro had decorated with pictures and *groteschi*, which were destroyed when this room was being prepared for the habitation of the Duke Cosmo. The following is Raphael's letter:

"To my dear uncle Simone di Battista de'Ciarla da Urbino.

"Dear to me as a father.

"I have received the letter in which you announce the death of the duke; may God receive his soul with mercy. Truly, I was unable to read your letter without tears. But it is all over; nothing can be changed. This is why we must submit to the will of God.

"I have lately written to my uncle, the priest (Bartolomeo Santi), that he send me the small picture serving as a wing to the "Madonna" of our prefect (Giovanna della Rovere). But he has not done so. I pray you then to remind him again, and that he send it me on the first op-

---

[1] "Istrambotti, Strambotti, or Strambottoli," a sort of love song, usually in octaves, which was sung by the lover to his lady-love.

[2] Cesare di Francesco Rossetti, a very skilful worker in metals, at Perugia; he was called Cesarino, on account of his small size.

[3] Donna Atalanta Baglioni, for whom he had painted the "Entombment."

[4] From which it would appear that Raphael was then planning a journey; perhaps that to Rome?

portunity, in order that I may content that lady; for you know that I may presently have need of her. I pray you also, very dear uncle, to tell the priest and Santa (Raphael's aunt, who lived with Bartolomeo, her brother, in the paternal house) that, if the Florentine Taddeo, of whom we have frequently spoken, come to Urbino, they show him every possible honour, without sparing anything; you also, for love of me, render him every service he may require, for truly I am under the greatest obligations to him.

"I have not fixed any price for my picture, and shall not do so even when I am able; for it would be better for me that an estimation should be made of it. This is why I have not written the price, and shall not write it. I have no other news to give you, unless it be that he, who ordered the picture from me, has also promised me works, to the value of 300 ducats, as well for here as for France.[1] After the feasts, I will, perhaps, write you to what price the picture mounts, for which I have already made the cartoon, and after Easter we shall have completed it.

"I should much like to obtain, from the signora prefect, a letter of recommendation to the gonfalonier of Florence. A few days since, I begged my uncle and Giacomo, of Rome, to procure it for me, for it might be very useful to me in procuring some work in a room, which depends on his highness. I beg you then to send me this letter, if possible; and I believe that if it is asked for in my name, he will certainly have it written; recommend me to him as his old servant and friend. Recommend me also to the master, and to Ridolfo,[2] and to all the others.

"This XXI April, MDVIII.[3]

"Your RAFAEL,

"Painter at Florence."

---

[1] This probably refers to Gio. Battista della Palla, who at this period bought many objects of art in Florence to sell them again to Francis I. See Vasari in the lives of "Andrea del Sarto and Fra Bartolomeo."

[2] Doubtless Ridolpho Zaccagna, son of his aunt Lucia, *née* Ciarla.

[3] The date of the original letter has been half effaced; but from the XI. which remains, it follows positively that the letter must have been written on April XXI., since the Duke of Urbino died on the XI. of the same month, as is shewn by the public registers in the Posteria quarter at Urbino: "Die XI mensis Aprilis 1508. Guidubaldos, Urbini dux, et S. R. Ecclesiæ Capitanus generalis, circà horam, quintam noctis decessit, et ab hâc vitâ migravit in civitate Fori Sempronii, sedente Julio II., P.M." P. Baldi relates what follows: "The Duke Guidubaldo, suffering much from gout, had

We have been unable to discover what are the pictures spoken of in this letter. However, the cartoon alluded to, seems to be that for the altar-piece of the Dei family. The sentence, "After Easter *we* shall have completed it," is very remarkable, as the plural number seems to indicate that Raphael had already assistants and pupils.

Did he receive this letter of recommendation so much desired? and if he received it, what use did he make of it? We have no information on this. We only know that about the middle of the year 1508, he quitted Florence to enter the service of Pope Julius II.

This departure was so precipitate, that Raphael was unable to complete the picture for the Dei family, and was even obliged to entrust it to his friend Ridolfo Ghirlandajo, to finish the blue mantle of the Madonna, called "la Belle Jardiniere."[1]

---

been removed to Fossombrone, where the air is milder than at Urbino. But he died there on the 11th April, 1508, in presence of the Duchess Elisabetta, of Francesco Maria della Rovere Ottaviano, Fregoso, Baldassare Castiglione, Pietro Bembo, Emilia Pia, and other persons. The Duchess, when death had taken all hope from her, threw herself on the body and remained as if dead, lying by his side. Recalled to life she complained that she had not been allowed to die with him. She neither ate nor drank for two days, and grief rendered her almost unrecognisable.

"The body of the duke was brought back to Urbino, and exposed in a hall of the palace, under a magnificent catafalco, covered with black cloth embroidered in gold. He was clothed in a doublet of black damask, and red trunk hose, his cap was on his head according to the custom of that time, in the costume in which his portrait had been taken, by a superior hand (Raphael).

"Two days after, April 13th, the priors presented to the new prince, Francesco Maria della Rovere, the keys and standards of the town. When he afterwards went out on horseback, the people surrounded him crying out 'Duke! Duke!' On his return to the palace, pages relieved him of his gold-embroidered mantle, and he went with eleven of the inhabitants of the town to the duchess's apartments. She made a touching speech, begging them to transfer to the prefect the devotion they had always shown for their late lord.

"A large catafalco was erected in the cathedral, from the designs of Girolamo Genga. . . . On May 2nd the funeral was celebrated, during which Ludovico Odazio pronounced the funeral oration which has been preserved by Pietro Bembo" . . . &c.

These ceremonies may have induced Taddeo Taddei to go to Urbino, the more so as he would there meet his friend Pietro Bembo.

[1] "Several critics," says M. Villot in his "Catalogue of the Italian Schools in the Louvre," have thought that this Madonna, in Raphael's second Florentine manner, might be the one ordered according to Vasari by a gentleman of Siena, and which he left on quitting Florence for Rome, in the hands of Ridolfo Ghirlandajo, an order that that painter might complete some blue drapery. Other critics on the contrary, pretend

Amongst the pictures left unfinished, is that of the "Madonna with the Infant Christ and the young St. John" (Esterhazy Gallery at Vienna), of which several copies exist, reproducing the original incomplete, as it was left by Raphael.

We frequently meet with old copies of other pictures, also painted by Raphael during his last residence at Florence. We conclude from this, that at this time his pupils began to make profitable speculations, by thus meeting the wishes of amateurs who could not obtain works by the master himself.

According to Vasari, it was the architect of the pope, Bramante Lazzari, of Castel Durante,[1] a relation of Raphael's, who sent for him to Rome. Guglielmo della Valle and Pungileoni believe that Raphael obtained the intervention of the new duke, Francesco Maria della Rovere, prefect of Rome, to obtain the works in the Vatican. But, as already Giuliano da San Gallo[2] had proposed the sculptor, Michael Angelo, to Pope Julius II. for the execution of his mausoleum, and as it is usual in courts for the architect to present the artists to be employed on the decoration of their buildings, it is quite possible that Bramante hailed the opportunity of opening a wider field to his already celebrated fellow countryman.

We may also suppose that the young duke, who, from his childhood, had known Raphael,[3] thought it better to recommend him to the pope rather than to any foreign prince. It is also possible that Julius II. should have sent for Raphael of his own accord, at the first word of recommendation of the distinguished artist, whose works he had doubt-

---

that the picture mentioned by Vasari is that known by the name of the "Madonna di Casa Colonna," which is now in the Berlin Museum. However this may be, it must be observed that an artist does not sign an incomplete work, and that Raphael's departure from Florence merely taking place in the summer of 1508, Ghirlandajo, in finishing the picture and signing it for Raphael, would have dated it 1508 and not 1507, a period when Raphael was still at Florence. The date 1507 is incontrovertible, and proves that the painting in the Louvre is not that finished by Ghirlandajo."—See note, p. 73.—*Lacroix.*

[1] According to Pungileoni, he was named Donato or Donnino Bramante, and was born in 1444 at Monte Asdrualdo, near Urbino. See "Memorie intorno alla vita ed alle opere di Donato o Donnino Bramante," Roma, 1836.

[2] As is related by his son Francesco. See Carlo Fea, "Notizie intorno Rafaele Sanzio," &c. p. 12, and in his "Miscellania," p. 329.

[3] Raphael's letter (p. 77) also shows that Giovanna della Rovere had already been solicited to procure him larger works.—*Lacroix.*

less seen at Urbino. This is the more probable, as this ambitious pontiff did not merely seek glory in politics, but also in the fine arts. The greatest of architects and sculptors, Bramante and Michael Angelo, were already engaged in executing his projects. He now required a great painter, and had the good fortune to summon Raphael.

Raphael, transported with joy, hastened at once to Rome, the eternal city.

CHAPTER III.

RAPHAEL UNDER JULIUS II.

(1508-1513.)

RAPHAEL was now entering upon a wider sphere in the service of a prince who united great intelligence in temporal things to the most energetic mind. Besides being a great sovereign and an illustrious general, Julius II. also paid much honour to the arts and sciences. He raised the state of morals,[1] so depraved under Alexander VI., and brought back peace, which Rome had not enjoyed for a long time.

His artistic enterprises, especially, were magnificent. He was not permitted to see them completed; but he impressed on them all, by the assistance of the talents which he had recognized and chosen, the stamp of his own governing mind.

It was he who carried out the vast project of Nicholas V., of enlarging the Vatican to the proportions of a sort of pontifical town, where there would not merely be room for the pope and his suite, and for all the high clergy and guests of distinguished rank, but also for all the clerical administrations; and thus, in reality, to make of this palace a centre of Christianity.

He it was, also, who conceived the idea of restoring the old Basilica

---

[1] See the Lectures of Uberto Fogliatta: "Clarorum Ligurum Elogia," p. 28; "Oldoino al Ciaconio," iii. col. 249, and Tomaso Inghirami, Orat. p. 82. P. Bembo, B. Castiglione, and Lod. Ariosto, in their Histories of Julius II. also praise his endeavours to restore the state of morals as well as his courage and love of justice.

of St. Peter in such a manner as to make it worthy the honour of being called the first Christian temple.

The monument intended to serve as a tomb for himself he entrusted to Michael Angelo, and he wished it to be stamped with the imposing character he himself desired to bear in history.[1]

He also commanded the powerful hands of Michael Angelo, accustomed to hew marble, to take the pencil and trace on the walls of the Sistine Chapel[2] the gigantic and immortal figures of the prophets and sibyls.

What was it that he now required of Raphael?

In the first place we must remember that Julius II. absolutely refused[3] to take possession of the apartments in the Vatican that had been inhabited by Alexander VI., and that when the master of the ceremonies spoke to him of having the mural portraits of that pope effaced, "Even if the portraits were destroyed," cried Julius, "the walls themselves would remind me of that simoniac, that Jew!"

The apartments in the upper story were then proposed to him, which already, under Nicholas V. and Sixtus IV., had been ornamented with paintings by Pietro della Francesca, Bramantino da Milano, Luca Signorelli, Bartolomeo della Gatta, and Pietro Perugino.

Raphael was commissioned to complete these decorations by painting the walls of the "Stanza della Signatura." The ceiling had been painted by Giovanni Antonio, surnamed Il Sodoma. The subjects of these ceilings, if we may judge from those that remain, were all drawn from mythology; a proof that, before the arrival of Raphael no idea had been formed of what subjects he would decide on. From this follows the probability that Julius had requested him to choose the subjects for the paintings.

In this splendid palace, the residence of the sovereign pontiff, in the midst of this brilliant, religious, learned, and warlike court, Raphael's

---

[1] Condivi relates, in his "Life of Michael Angelo," that, when Julius saw the design for his tomb he appeared satisfied with it, and asked Michael Angelo how much it would cost to carry it out?—A hundred thousand scudi," replied Michael Angelo. "A hundred thousand?" cried Julius. "No, but two hundred thousand!"

[2] It was Sixtus IV., the uncle of Julius II., who had built the Sistine chapel.

[3] As is related by Paris de Grassis. See "Notices et extraits des manuscrits de la Bibliothèque du roi," ii. p. 562, and "L'Histoire de la peinture en Italie," by Fiorillo," p. 97.

ideas expanded, and he soon found a subject which, by its sublimity, replied to the exigencies of the place and of its lord.

In the present day it has been contested that the original idea of these paintings, so learned even in the slightest details, belonged to Raphael; and it has, instead, been ascribed to the pope, or to some learned man at his court. But this deeply spiritual conception could not have come from Julius II., who all his life was governed by the most practical spirit.[1]

We willingly grant that, for certain personages, and certain details, as his letter to Ariosto indicates,[2] Raphael had recourse to learned men; but it is not the less true that the general invention belongs to him. At the commencement of his sojourn at Rome the literary men with whom he was intimate were not in the town: Castiglione went there a little later; Pietro Bembo only in April, 1510, and for a short time merely; Bernardino Divizio da Bibiena was at this time still at the court of Urbino.

Besides this, the subjects proposed by Raphael had been common in Italy from the fourteenth century. They were already mentioned by Boethius, Dante, and still more in the "Triumphs" of Petrarch. The germ of the "School of Athens" may be seen in the "Trionfo della Fama," and of the "Parnassus" in the "Trionfo d'Amore." In painting, Francesco Traini, a pupil of Orcagna's, had already executed, for the church of Santa Caterina at Pisa, a "Triumph of St. Thomas Aquinas," in which the figures of Plato, showing his "Timæus," and Aristotle his "Æsthetics," bear a certain resemblance to the figures in the "Dispute on the Holy Sacraments," as well as with those of the "School of Athens." Benozzo Gozzoli had painted a very similar subject, which is now in the Museum of Paris.[3] Raphael, in his travels, must certainly have seen this picture.

---

[1] When Michael Angelo had executed the model for the bronze statue of the pope at Bologna, Julius II. asked him, whether the right hand being raised signified blessing or cursing. On which the sculptor cleverly replied: "It orders the Bolognese to behave well."

Michael Angelo afterwards asked the pope whether he should place a book in the left hand.—"No, no!" Julius II. replied quickly, "give me a sword; for I am not learned."

[2] Jonathan Richardson: "Treatise on Painting," etc. p. 333. The chevalier Pozzo had this letter in his possession, but all trace of it is now lost.

[3] There is an engraving of this picture in the "Storia della Pittura Italiana," by Rosini, pl. xx. See the description of this picture in the Catalogue of the Louvre, No. 72, Italian Schools. "In the Cathedral, at Pisa," says Vasari, "behind the seat of

It came, then, quite naturally within the compass of his own knowledge to produce a composition which should represent the different religious and philosophic views of the time. It may readily be conceived that he would ask the advice of some of his friends; but most assuredly he did not, as certain writers have pretended, merely follow the directions of Inghirami of Sadoleto, nor of the young Beroaldo; the contrary is proved beyond dispute by his letter to Ariosto.

To characterize the Stanza della Signatura from the symbolical pictures it contains, we might name it the Hall of the Faculties, for, by Theology, Philosophy, Poetry, and Jurisprudence, Raphael has represented all the sciences which enable man to approach the divine truth.

And, if it be considered that these paintings were intended to decorate the place in which the head of the catholic church was to sign orders regulating the government of the Christian flock over the whole world, we must admire the wisdom of this choice.

The pope's satisfaction with the subjects increased when Raphael had executed the first fresco, "Theology." His expectation was far surpassed. He was so struck by the amplitude of Raphael's genius, that he immediately resolved to have the halls of the Vatican repainted by him. He gave orders for all the old frescoes in them, even those on the vaulted ceiling of the Stanza della Signatura, to be thrown down.

Nevertheless Raphael, approving the decoration of this vault, thought it well only to repaint the eight large panels, and to allow the small intermediate mythological subjects to remain, as well as the central picture of the pope's arms borne by genii.

He devoted the four large medallions on the ceiling to allegorical figures, serving as epigraphs to the great mural paintings of Theology, Philosophy, Poetry, and Jurisprudence. The oblong spaces in the angles of the vault, he employed in transition subjects; that is, bearing a double relation to the pictures on both sides below. All these pictures on the ceiling are executed on a gold ground, imitating mosaic.

We shall begin the description of the Stanza della Signatura by the

---

the archbishop, Gozzoli painted in distemper, on a small panel, a St. Thomas Aquinas, in the midst of a great number of doctors, who are discussing his works. Among these figures may be noticed Pope Sixtus IV. a number of Cardinals and the superiors of different religious orders. This picture is the best and most finished that Benozzo ever painted."—*Lacroix.*

THEOLOGY (LA DISPUTA)

figure of "Theology," which serves as an epigraph to the great picture on the same subject.

This figure, seated in the clouds, holds a book in her left hand, while with the right she points to the great picture which is below. Like Dante's Beatrice, she is crowned with laurel. She wears a red tunic and a green mantle; colours symbolical of the theological virtues, love and hope. Two small genii at her side hold tablets with the words: "Divinarum rerum Notitia."

The principal idea of the great composition of "Theology," frequently named also the "Dispute on the Holy Sacrament," symbolizes the relation of man to God through the redemption of the world and by the Eucharist.

In the upper part appear the three figures of the Holy Trinity, each surrounded by a glory. Above all is the Almighty Father, in the midst of the seraphim, cherubim, and a countless host of angels, who sing the "Holy, holy, holy, Lord God of hosts." Below the Father, amidst the saints of the celestial kingdom, the Saviour is enthroned; a little lower, the Holy Spirit is descending on men.

At the right of the Saviour, the Virgin is seated, bending towards him in adoration; and at her left is St. John the Baptist who is pointing towards him. On a large half circle of clouds, which extends to the extreme limits of the picture, are seated patriarchs, prophets, and martyrs, representing the communion of saints. Commencing at the extreme point to the right of Christ, we see the apostle St. Peter, holding the Holy Scriptures, and the two keys, as a sign of his being the guardian of the faith, and of his authority to bind and to unloose. At his side, in the expectation of mercy and pardon, is Adam, the father of the human race. Near Adam is St. John, the apostle loved by Christ, writing down his divine visions; afterwards, David, the head of the terrestrial family of our Lord, the sweet Psalmist who sang the praises of God; then St. Stephen, the first martyr; and lastly, a saint half concealed by the clouds.

On the other side, at the right of the spectator, is St. Paul, holding a sword, in remembrance of his martyrdom, and also as a symbol of the penetrating power of his doctrine. By his side is Abraham, with the knife to sacrifice Isaac, the first type of the sacrifice of Christ; then the apostle St. James, the third witness of the transfiguration of the Saviour, the religious type of hope, as St. Peter is of faith and St. John of love.

Moses follows, with the tables of the law. St. Lawrence corresponds to St. Stephen; and, lastly, we perceive a warlike figure, which is believed to be St. George, the patron saint of Liguria; in honour, no doubt, of Julius II., who was born in that country.

The Holy Spirit, under the form of a dove, surrounded by four cherubim, who hold the four books of the Gospel open, is descending upon the assembly of believers.

This sort of council, expressing theological life, is united in a half circle around the altar on which the Eucharist is exposed on a monstrance. Nearest to the altar, on both sides, come the four great fathers of the church, the columns of Roman Catholicism; to the left, St. Jerome, the type of contemplative life, absorbed in profound meditation on the Scriptures; near him are two books, one containing his "Letters," the other the Vulgate. Opposite is St. Ambrose, active especially in the militant church; he is raising his eyes and hands towards heaven, as if delighted with the angelic harmonies. St. Augustine, whom he converted to Christianity, is beside him, and is dictating his thoughts to a young man seated at his feet. His book on the "City of God," is lying by him. St. Gregory the Great, clothed in the tiara and pontifical mantle, is opposite St. Augustine. His book on Job, with the superscription, "Liber Moralium," is also on the ground beside him.

The name of the personage represented by the figure behind St. Jerome is unknown; it may perhaps be St. Bernard, the last of the fathers of the church. His hands are extended toward the monstrance. Opposite him, by the side of St. Ambrose, is a theologian wearing a long beard, who may possibly be Petrus Lombardus, named the Master of the Sentences, the founder of scholastic theology, and the first who wrote a discussion on the sacraments. A little further on is the Franciscan Scotus, and the Dominican Thomas Aquinas; afterwards, are standing a little behind St. Augustine, the Pope Anacletus, St. Bonaventura, reading in a book, and, on the lowest step, the Pope Innocent III. in profile, holding in his left hand a writing on the mass.

Amongst the figures in the background may be recognised Dante,[1]

---

[1] Benozzo Gozzoli, in the admirably painted choir of the church of the Franciscans, at Monte Falco, had already represented Dante, with the inscription, "Theologus Dantes, nullius docmatis expers." By the side of Dante the places of honour are shared by "Laureatus Petrarca, omnium virtutum monarca," and, "Pictorum eximius, Jottus (Giotto), fundamentum et lux."

the greatest Christian poet, and Fra Girolamo Savonarola, the austere preacher of Florence, put to death as a heretic at the instigation of Alexander VI., and who, under Julius II., was considered worthy of appearing in the Vatican amongst the most distinguished theologians of the church.

Quite in the foreground, a Christian philosopher clothed in antique garb, is speaking to a young Pagan, leaning on a balustrade, and is pointing out to him, as an example of obedience, the young man writing under the dictation of St. Augustine.

On the left side, Raphael has represented the clergy, the philosophers, the people, and even the schismatics, in the expression of their faith; the clergy are represented by two bishops; the philosophers by a man who, laying aside his personal opinions, symbolized by two books thrown on the ground, is turning towards the altar; the people by three young men, who bow before the Eucharist; and the schismatics, by priests and other persons discussing their opinions far from the altar. Heresy is still more decidedly characterized by the figure of a sectary, surrounded by auditors, interpreting a passage from the Scriptures. This group in the foreground corresponds to the group of the Christian philosopher and the young Pagan; for as the philosopher is exhorting the Pagan to submission, so here among the audience of the heresiarch there is a young man who, to recommend faith, is pointing towards the people engaged in adoration.

Lastly, at the extreme left of the picture is the portrait of the Dominican, Fra Angelico da Fiesole. A worthy homage rendered by Raphael to the holiest of painters.

The traditional title borne by this picture, the "Dispute on the Holy Sacrament," is quite a wrong one, in our opinion. The picture is rather an image of unity; in heaven by the union of the saints of the Old and New Testaments through Redemption; in the earth by the assembly of the theologians, all assisting at the consecration of the Eucharist.

The transition pictures painted on the ceiling, represent "Original Sin" by the side of "Jurisprudence;" and on the opposite side near the "Parnassus," "Apollo flaying Marsyas." The relation of this latter subject to Theology, may at first appear strange, but the meaning may be seen, on reading the first canto of the "Il Paradiso" of Dante, in which the poet prays Apollo, the god who despoiled Marsyas, to remove also his terrestrial covering and infuse the divine spirit into him, that he may thus be better able to recognise and describe the celestial scenes in Paradise.

The relation of the subject of "Apollo and Marsyas," with the picture of "Poetry" or the "Parnassus," is simpler and more evident; the victory of Apollo is that of true over false art, and threatens with divine chastisement those who are guilty enough not to employ the celestial gift for its proper use—the improvement of men and the glory of God.

The Marsyas of Raphael is taken from a fragment of an antique group; but instead of the Scythian, who, in the entire group is executing the judgment, are two shepherds covered with laurels; one holds a knife whilst the other crowns Apollo.

The allegorical figure of "Poetry" serves as an epigraph to the fresco of "Parnassus." This female figure is one of the most sublime creations of the master, and one of the most perfect works of art in all ages.

On a marble seat, placed in the clouds, is seated a woman in a garment strewn with stars. Her glance is inspired, her head crowned with laurels. With outspread wings, she seems to be ever rising, and to approach continually nearer to heaven. In one hand she holds her sacred tablets, in the other her golden lyre.

The eye is struck with this image, resplendent with youth and beauty, the everlasting flame of divine poetry.

Two little genii seated at her side, bear tablets with these words: "Numine afflatur."

In the large mural picture of Parnassus, Apollo, seated under laurels on the borders of the Hippocrenes is accompanying his songs on a chorded instrument. The Nine Muses, divided into two groups, surround him; graceful figures, but not sufficiently characteristic, the representation of the antique not being so familiar in the days of Raphael as in our times. Then come the great Greek and Roman poets, and also the Italian ones. Homer is singing his heroic songs, which a young man is writing down on a papyrus leaf. Virgil is conversing with Dante. Near the magnificent figure of Sappho of Mytelene are three lyrical poets, Alcæus, Anacreon, and Petrarch, conversing with Corinna of Thebes, whose beautiful hair flows down over her shoulders. Pindar, seated on the right in the foreground, is speaking to Horace. Not far from Sanazzaro, a lively discussion is being carried on between Ovid and three

---

[1] Contrary to the first sketch of Raphael's.

THE PARNASSUS.

poets, amongst whom may be recognised Boccaccio and Antonio Tebaldeo.

The conception of the subject is, as may be seen, as much Italian as antique, and the general arrangement presents a picture of a meeting of *beaux-esprits*, belonging to the highest class of Italian society of that time. Everywhere we see Italian manners, graces, and vivacity. Apollo even is accompanying himself on a violin, instead of on a harp, and reminds us of the improvisatore. It is probable that Raphael was induced to commit this anachronism by the Pope or some other influential person, who wished to perpetuate the features of some skilful virtuoso, perhaps Giacomo Sansecundo, whose musical talent Baldassare Castiglione, in his "Courtier's Book," praises with especial distinction.

Raphael employed the space on each side of the window, below the "Parnassus," for two small subjects in chiaroscuro, in which he rendered honours to the two great poets of antiquity. On one side Alexander is causing the poems of Homer to be placed in the tomb of Achilles,[1] on the other, Augustus is preventing Plautius Tucca and Varius, the friends of Virgil, from burning the Ænead, according to the wishes of its author.

The intermediary picture on the ceiling, symbolizes the contemplation of the stars, which suits as well to poetry as to philosophy. This figure serving as epigraph to the fresco of "Philosophy" is seated on a chair borne by two figures, resembling Diana of the Ephesians.[2] Her look is serene and meditative; on her knees are the books of Nature and Morals. The colours and ornaments of her drapery, ingeniously represent the four elements: the air, by a starry sky-blue, in the upper part of the garments; fire by a red flame-colour about the knees; lower down water, by the fishes which traverse a greenish sea-colour; and lastly, in the lower part the earth, by a brown tint strewn with plants.

At her side two children hold tablets with the inscription, "Causarum Cognitio."

The third great mural painting, so celebrated under the name of the "School of Athens," shows an assembly of the philosophers of antiquity

---

[1] This subject has no historical foundation; it owes its origin to the legend that Alexander envied the happiness of Achilles, in having been sung by Homer. Perhaps Raphael painted this subject at the instigation of Castiglione, who, in the first volume of his "Courtier" mentions this tradition as a proof of the sublimity of poetry.

[2] To indicate the study of the heavens.

in a magnificent hall. Arranged in groups of the different schools, they form a wonderfully clear picture of the historical development of Greek philosophy. And as it was especially from Athens that the sciences came, the designation of the School of Athens is well sustained.

It is now pretty generally believed that Raphael in the principal composition of the upper part, on the platform with the four steps, has assembled the masters of ancient philosophy, and in the lower part, in front, the masters of arithmetic, geometry and astronomy, those sciences having been recommended in Plato's "Republic," as preparatory to philosophy.

But, after a very careful examination, and considering that for the choice and arrangement of his subject, Raphael must have made use of some of the ten books—at that time very well known—of Diogenes Laertius, on the celebrated philosophers.[1] We believe that he intended to express, as we have said, the development of Greek philosophy. For we may see, by commencing at the left of the foreground, the most ancient of the philosophic schools, grouped around Pythagoras. Socrates, his pupils and adversaries, are in some sort the band of union with Plato and Aristotle, surrounded by their pupils, and occupying the centre of the picture, as supreme representatives of Greek philosophy in its double tendency.

Further on, to the right, are the Stoics, the Cynics, the Epicureans and some later philosophers ; and, lastly, in the foreground of the same side the masters of positive sciences, amongst whom is a mathematician, who may be either Euclid or Archimedes.

This chronology of the development of philosophy has not been proved until now. It will help us, for want of traditions, in endeavouring to discover, by bringing together incontestable portraits, the other individualities who figure in this magnificent assembly. We will endeavour then to explain the whole composition and to name all the personages, thanks to the assistance afforded us by the chronological order.

In the group to the left we recognize four founders of philosophic schools, as they are each placed in an isolated position in sign of independence.

---

[1] The first edition of this work, translated from Greek into Italian, appeared at Rome, the second at Venice, published by M. Jenson, 1475, fol. ; it bears this title, "Diogenis Laertii de vitis, dogmatibus et apophthegmatibus clarorum philosophorum."

The oldest is Pythagoras of Samos, who, five hundred and fifty years before our era, founded at Crotona in Italy a school of philosophy, the aim of which was intellectual, religious and moral culture. He also founded a school of mathematics, and, attributing to figures the principle of things, he grasped the science of arithmetic in its highest signification. Seated quite in the foreground, in the midst of his pupils, he is writing in a book, in which he seems to be inscribing his discoveries on the harmonious relations of music; for, before him a young man, probably his son Telanges, is holding a tablet, on which are noted the tones, octaves, fifths, fourths, with the words Diapason, Diapenta and Diatessaron.

Among the pupils grouped around him, the bald and bearded man is, it is believed, Archytas; he interpreted the doctrine of contrasts, which has caused the invention of the doctrine of *Categories* to be ascribed to him.

A little behind is Theano, the wife of Pythagoras; she is in profile, and is raising two fingers of her hand, apparently to signify the double consonants that Pythagoras discovered.

An Arab,[1] with a turban on, is leaning with curiosity over the books of Pythagoras; an ingenious myth of the initiation of the Arabs into Greek philosophy, or perhaps, of the improvements introduced by them into the science of numbers. On the other side of the picture the figure of Zoroaster indicates with equal subtlety, that the Greek philosophy had its origin in the east.[2]

At the extremity of the group to the right, in contrast with the ideal philosophy of the great man of Samos, the profound Heraclitus of Ephesus, who lived five hundred years B. C., represents the natural philosophy of the Ionic school; as the obscurity of his principles caused him to be surnamed Σκοτεινος (the obscure), he is clothed in dark grey. Seated near a pedestal, he is writing his speculative theories on the substance of things, and on the nature and life of man, theories which were little understood by his contemporaries, but which were at a later time grasped by more clear-sighted minds, such as Plato, Aristotle, and the stoics.

---

[1] It is believed to be Averroes, an Arab of the twelfth century, who transplanted the Greek philosophy into Arabian literature. Yet Averroes did not belong to the group of Pythagoras, but to the school of Aristotle, whose books he explained.

[2] This opinion was then generally adopted.

Between Heraclitus and Pythagoras, towards whom he is turning, the philosopher standing arguing on a book, is Anaxagoras, the friend of Pericles. From his education he belongs to the Ionic school; but, as he was the first to place the creative spirit of the world above matter, he forms the link between Heraclitus and Pythagoras, and the connecting passage between the school of Ethics (Εθιχος) and the school of Socrates. This is why he is placed immediately below the wise Athenian.

Behind him is standing a handsome young man, in whom Raphael has perpetuated the features of his Prince Francesco Maria della Rovere, Duke of Urbino, at that time at Rome. Vasari also notices that Raphael granted a similar distinction to the "prodigal son," Federico II. Duke of Mantua, only ten years of age, who was also at Rome at this time. We believe that we may recognize the young Federico in the child who is facing the spectator a little to the left behind the Arab.[1]

More to the left, on the same level, opposite the dark Heraclitus, Democritus of Abdera, the learned naturalist, so mistaken by his fellow citizens, the joyous traveller who saw only folly and not wickedness in the ill deeds of men, is leaning against a column and turning over the pages of a book. His studies related especially to five sciences, logic, physics, ethics, mathematics, and the arts of the Muses. He is crowned with ivy, to remind us, probably, that science did not prevent him from enjoying the pleasures of life; and that his practical principle was to seek for happiness in the tranquillity of the soul.

The young man who is placing his hands on the shoulders of Democritus is certainly one of his numerous disciples,—possibly Nausiphanes of Teios, subsequently the master of Epicurus.

The old man presenting a child to Democritus seems to be an allusion to the custom of the Athenians of asking the opinions of the philosophers on the dispositions of their children.

On the upper step we see, in the first place, some representatives of the Sophists, against whom Socrates struggled victoriously with his dialectic ethics. The man half-clothed hastening from the left with

---

[1] Vasari points out, as Federico de Gonzaga, the young man stooping down near the group of mathematicians. This is an evident error, for Federico, born in 1500, was still only a child at the time of the execution of the School of Athens. It was doubtless the sight of so many works of art at Rome which excited the enthusiasm of the young duke of Mantua, and induced him to set to work the celebrated Giulio Romano.

writings in his hand is Diagoras of Melos, the freedman, a disciple of Democritus. He is ranked among the Sophists, and his declared atheism forced him to leave Athens. The two other Sophists beside him are Gorgias of Leontini, a pupil of Empedocles, and Crites of Athens, who represented religion as derived from politics, and who was the constant adversary of Socrates.

But we now come to Socrates himself (born about 470 B.C.), one of the purest and most venerable men of antiquity. His clear common sense, irony, and luminous wisdom, rendered full justice to this crowd of unbelieving talkers. His precepts, directed towards practical and religious life, may be summed up in these words:—"Religion consists in honouring God by doing what is right. The supreme God is a reasonable being, the invisible author of all order, omnipotent, recompensing virtue and chastising vice. The soul resembles God, both by its reason and its invisible activity; it is on this account that it is immortal." Socrates preached these doctrines publicly, and introduced philosophy into private life; or, as Cicero says, "He caused it to descend from heaven into the abode of men." Thus we see him here teaching wisdom in the midst of a group of attentive auditors.

Opposite to him, in complete armour, is Alcibiades, whose life he saved. Like many other amiable and ductile natures, Alcibiades was not irreproachable in his morals; but his affection for Socrates proved that he was not destitute of noble sentiments.

Near him is one of the artisans with whom Socrates loved to converse, because their mind was not spoiled by false principles.

A little further back is the old Aristippus, brought up at Cyrene in sensual pleasures. The teaching of Socrates ennobled, however, this inclination for pleasure, and Aristippus became the founder of the school of Cyrene. According to him the destiny of man is to enjoy, preserving, however, an empire over himself and liberty of mind. His philosophy was the art of enjoying life.

By his side, and the nearest to Socrates, a young man, completely absorbed in his master's words, and leaning his elbow on the stylobate, is Xenophon of Athens. This great historian, the most intimate disciple of Socrates, has left us a faithful description of him in his writings.

To this group also belongs a man of low condition, Eschines, the poor sausage-seller. Always a fervent admirer of Socrates, he became subsequently one of the most celebrated orators of Greece. Extending his right arm towards the Sophists, he seems, by an imperative gesture, to warn them off, as if he had already guessed that the impious men would dare to accuse Socrates of impiety, and that their hatred would only be satisfied when the old man of seventy years of age, whom the Pythian oracle had named "the wisest of men," had drained the poisoned cup.

Further on, and more in the background, is Euclid of Megara, another of Socrates' admirers. He was the chief of the dialectic philosophy, based on the principal maxim of the Eclectic school, "All is but One;" and, inspired with the Socratic doctrine, he called that "One" not only the True, but also the Good.

We have now come to the most illustrious of the disciples of Socrates, Plato, who, with Aristotle, occupies the centre of the assembly. Their systems, which, in many important particulars, were opposed to each other, excited during the middle ages, and especially at the time of Raphael, the most eager conflicts between theologians and philosophers.

Plato (born 430 B.C.), descended from Solon, was one of the noblest and most gifted men that have ever lived. His genius and virtue render him worthy of standing by the side of his master, Socrates.

His travels, studies, and contemplations had raised his thoughts to heights undreamt of before. From this intellectual summit he collects into a whole the truths scattered throughout the various theories of his time. His profound intuition revealed to him that a superior God had formed objects from ideas; that the human soul, of celestial origin, had fallen through her own fault in terrestrial life, but that she would obtain redemption. It may be said that Plato thus obtained a glimpse of the doctrines of Christianity, and that he was its precursor.

Aristotle of Stagyra (born 384 B.C.), a disciple of Plato, and the tutor of Alexander the Great, was, on the contrary, the philosopher of reflective reasoning. In an exactly opposite manner to Plato he proceeded by analysis from the particular to the general; he rejected *à priori* ideas, and took as his aim, researches in nature—the study of what already exists, of what is called reality. His extraordinary perspicacity, and the extent of his knowledge, made him the head of the school of experimental philosophy.

In Raphael's fresco, the difference of the principles of these two men of genius is admirably expressed by their attitudes and gestures.

Plato, as the representative of speculative, contemplative, and theo-

THE SCHOOL OF ATHENS.

logical philosophy, holds his "Timæus" in his left hand, whilst he raises the other towards God, from whom everything is derived, and to whom everything returns.

Aristotle, representing the practical philosophy, holds his book of "Ethics," and advancing his right hand, seems to affirm that the object of the sciences is morality and the application of experience.

A numerous train of disciples of all ages surround them.

By the side of Plato is his sister's son, Speusippus of Athens, who remained faithful to the old Academy; also Menedemus of Eretria, the cynic; Xenocrates, the Chalcedonian; Phædon and Agathon, to whom Plato gave the most distinguished places in his "Symposium."[1]

By the side of Aristotle, and the nearest to him, is Theophrastus of Eresus, whom he named his heir and successor; Eudemus of Rhodes, Dikæarch of Messana, and Aristoxenus of Tarentum, the musician, are a little further back. The stoics Zeno[2] of Citium, in Cyprus; Cleanthus of Assus, and Chrysippus of Soli, are in the foreground. According to Diogenes Laertius, Chrysippus was the support of the Stoic school, founded by Zeno; his dialectics were celebrated, and his contemporaries said that, "if there were any book on dialectics amongst the gods, it could only be that of Chrysippus."

The two philosophers who walk behind the stoics are an allusion to the denomination of Peripatetics (*περι*, about, and *πατεῖν*, to walk), which was applied to the disciples of Aristotle, because their master walked with them in the Lyceum when instructing them.

On the middle step, Diogenes of Sinope, surnamed the Cynic, is lying negligently, holding a tablet in his hand, and seemingly engaged in profound meditation, without troubling himself about the illustrious men who surround him.

This singular man (born B.C. 414), a disciple of Antisthenes, founded

---

[1] The first of the younger figures has been frequently taken for Alexander the Great; but the real place for Alexander would be, as a disciple of Aristotle, on the opposite side. With greater probability the third figure has been recognized as the portrait of the celebrated Marsilio Ficino, translator of Plato, who died 1491 at Florence.

[2] In this proud old man, the portrait of Pietro Bembo, possibly on account of his long beard, has been recognized. This is an error; the celebrated friend of Raphael was then only forty years of age, and it was at a much later time that he allowed his beard to grow, as is seen by his letter addressed to Titian. Besides, Bembo was quite devoted to Platonism, and Raphael would not have placed him among the disciples of Aristotle.

the severe school of Virtue, which he interpreted to be an absolute renunciation of all the material things of life. He thus expressed the ground of his doctrine: "To need nothing, is the quality of the gods; to need but little, is to be like the gods." So by his side is merely his bowl, the only article he would allow himself to own, until the day when he recognized the superfluity even of this, on seeing a child drink out of his hand.

Contemporaneous with Cynicism and Stoicism, Epicureanism yet differed from them on many points. The founder of the Epicurean sect, Epicurus, (born B.C. 342 at Gargettus, near Athens), also took personal happiness as his aim; but he sought for it in the harmony of moral and sensual enjoyments. The Epicurean only practised virtue and wisdom with regard to their consequences and as a means of pleasure; he lived soberly and fraternally, and mastered joy as suffering.

The fresco shows Epicurus descending the steps of the platform; he is conversing with Aristippus,[1] surnamed Metrodidactus, a young man with curly hair, and wearing a rich costume, and points out to him the proud Stoic, disdaining all sensual enjoyments.

The Greek genius, in its searches for a solution of the universal enigma, has exhausted itself in its multiform endeavours. When the great men disappeared, there only remained small sects continually crossing and recrossing each other's path.

This confused transition is indicated by the young man leaning against the base of one of the columns. Standing on one leg, with the other crossed, he is writing on his knee, not what he has gathered from his own researches, but what he has heard here and there from others. He represents the Eclecticism which was about to commence.

But whilst Eclecticism is laying hold on all that to it appears true in the different systems, Scepticism arising at the same time declares that the falsity of all established truth may be proved; a tendency, the result of which would be the annihilation of all science and all philosophy.

Pyrrho of Elis (born B.C. 354) is the representative of this sceptical philosophy, to which his name has even been given (Pyrrhonism). We may venture to point out as Pyrrho, the philosopher standing inactive, who is leaning against the base of a column and looking sarcastically at the book in which the young Eclectician is writing.

---

[1] For this episode Raphael was inspired by a passage in Diogenes Laertius, Book ii. c. 8, No. 4.

The philosopher standing by his side, who, by a movement of hesitation, turns his head on one side and his body to the other, must be Arcesilaus of Pitane (born B.C. 318), the founder of the new academy, who in theory inclined towards Scepticism and in practice towards Stoicism. He in general only drew his inferences from problematical knowledge, and, as all reason is subject to contradiction, he considered himself obliged to abstain from any decided adhesion.

We may also admit that the philosopher advancing, wrapped in his mantle and a stick in his hand, is one of the later cynics, mocked by Lucian, who went about the country with a bag at their back. Lastly, the young man running away must indicate the close of the ancient Greek school.

It now remains to consider the group in the foreground of the right side.

Opposite to Pythagoras, representing speculative mathematics, we see practical mathematics. Leaving speculation more and more, the mind is carried on to the positive sciences. In the picture they commence by the study of geometry, which is taught by a master bending over the ground, and demonstrating with compasses the isogonal figure drawn on a tablet. Several pupils are grouped around him.

In this personage, Raphael has perpetuated the portrait of Bramante, his master in architecture. But it is difficult at the present time to decide whether he intended to represent Archimedes, the celebrated mechanician, by this figure, or else Euclid of Alexandria, the greatest mathematician of antiquity.[1]

The countenances of the young disciples express very clearly different

[1] An epigram of the hermit Paul Volgius, which was addressed to Georg Reisch, prior of the Carthusians, near Fribourg, and which was published by the latter in his work, then widely spread, "Margarita Philosophica" (Friburgi, 1503), designates Archimedes as the measurer of the earth, "Mensor et terræ Archimedes probatus." But the same book, in speaking of mathematics, considers Euclid as the prince of that science.

Luca Pacciolo del Borgo has also written an "Interpretazione di Euclide," and he gave lectures on this subject at Venice, at which Fra Giocondo, one of the architects of the works of St. Peter's attended. Euclid was held at this time in great esteem among the Italian artists.

Vasari has described perfectly the person in question, but without giving him any name. It was doubtless only under Paul III. that this figure was named Archimedes, on account of the small picture painted by Perino del Vaga on the socle, and which represents the "Death of Archimedes of Syracuse."

degrees of aptitude; the first, notwithstanding all his efforts is unable to seize the demonstration, whilst the young man leaning against him seems to have understood it already; a third kneeling at the side has understood the subject and is speaking of it to a companion behind who testifies his admiration.

Not far from this group, two venerable figures symbolize astronomy and geography. The man whose back is turned, covered with a royal mantle, with a crown on his head and a globe in his hand, is the geographer Ptolemy,[1] whose geography served as a guide for all travellers down to the sixteenth century. At this time he was confounded with the King of Egypt.[2]

The man with a beard, holding a celestial globe in his right hand, is the magician Zoroaster, who, according to tradition, was king of Bactria, in the time of Ninus. Petrarch also, in his "Trionfo della Fama," mentions Zoroaster as the founder of magic, a science closely allied to astrology.

At the extreme right of this group, Raphael has introduced himself with his master Perugino, as auditors.

To complete the analysis of this magnificent composition, we should also describe the architecture which surrounds it, and which imparts to the whole a solemnity of character perfectly in accordance with the rest. According to Vasari, Bramante must have made the design for this, and, as this superb hall is in the form of a Greek cross with a cupola, it is very likely that it gives an idea of the plan the learned architect intended to make use of for the church of St. Peter.

Among the statues which decorate the niches between the columns, we see opposite to us Apollo and Pallas: the god of poetic inspiration, on the side of the ancient idealistic philosophers, several of whom were poets; the goddess of wisdom and science, on the side of the philosophers of reason, experience, and practical life.

Below the statue of Apollo, two bas-reliefs, one over the other, relate to the sins of wantonness and anger which the god of the Arts knows how to appease. The upper bas-relief shows a sanguinary struggle; the other a Triton carrying off a nymph.

Opposite, under the statue of Minerva, a female figure with a wand

---

[1] See "Alexander von Humboldt," Cosmos ii. p. 224.

[2] The "Margarita Philosophica," Fribourg edit. 1503, contains a wood engraving representing this same philosopher, Ptolemy, crowned as a king.

in her hand in token of command and two attendant genii at her side, symbolize the victory of wisdom over brute instinct.

Between the fresco of Philosophy and that of Jurisprudence, the transition picture is a "Judgment of Solomon," a well chosen subject, as this celebrated Judgment, which might well be called a philosophical judgment, was not dictated by the written law, but by a knowledge of human nature.

The allegorical figure of Justice serves as an epigraph to the painting symbolizing "Jurisprudence." Her head is adorned by a diadem, and in her hands she holds the sword and balance, her usual attributes. Four little genii surround her, bearing this inscription: "Jus suum unicuique tribuens."

In the system of Aristotle, Morality is the basis of law.[1] The inscription is also in accordance with the definition given in the book of Ethics, which the philosopher of Stagira holds in his hands, in the fresco of the "School of Athens."

The wall below this figure of Justice, as well as that on which the Parnassus is painted, is pierced by a window in the centre. Raphael divided it into three compartments: an arch above the window, with the wider spaces on each side.

The arch presents the allegorical figures of Force, Prudence and Moderation, expressing with the Justice above, the four cardinal virtues, already celebrated both by Pindar and also by Plato, and without which any legislature is insufficient.

Prudence or Wisdom is in the centre. Seeing at once both the past and the future she has, like Janus, a double face, a profile of a young woman and of an old man. A genius is presenting her with the mirror of self-knowledge; another genius is waving a torch, the symbol of worldly knowledge, before the countenance of the old man. On her breast, as on that of Minerva, shines the Ægis with the head of Medusa.

"Force," clothed in armour, is holding an olive branch in token of peace; "Moderation" holds a bridle.

The paintings on either side of the window recall the guarantees of jurisdiction given by Justinian and Gregory IX., who collected and arranged, the former the ancient temporal laws, the latter the laws of the church.

---

[1] "Aristotle," ch. 5.

At the left the Emperor seated, crowned with laurels and clothed in a purple mantle, is giving the Pandects and the Codex to Tribonianus, who is kneeling before him. He is surrounded by jurisconsults, nearly all portraits, in the costume of their functions still used in the time of the artist. Two of them bear the Institutes decreed by Justinian.

On the right the Pope, seated in pontifical costume, is presenting to an advocate of the Consistory the "Decretals," collected under his order by the Dominican Pennaforte. But instead of painting the portrait of Gregory IX. of the house of Conti, Raphael introduced that of Julius II. The cardinals who hold up the pontiff's mantle are also portraits: Giovanni de Medici, afterwards Leo X.; Antonio del Monte, the uncle of Julius III.; and, further in the background, Alexander Farnese, who, in his turn, became Pope under the name of Paul III.

To this picture of "Jurisprudence" also belongs the little picture of "Original Sin," which we have already mentioned as serving as the transition between this and "Theology;" for original sin is also the cause of earthly laws.

Thus this sort of epic cycle is closed in. In it Raphael certainly succeeded wonderfully in showing with the greatest clearness, the tendencies of science and all the knowledge of the human mind.

Turning now to its artistic point of view, we notice immediately that the paintings of the ceiling, which were executed after the great fresco of "Theology," are very unequal in their execution. If some of them, for instance the allegorical figures of Poetry and Original Sin, show the noble and intelligent manner of Raphael, others, although very well composed, are cold and unsatisfactory in their execution, a proof that Raphael already employed his pupils or other artists for the least important parts of this Stanza. But in the principal pictures we should be unable to discover the slightest foreign co-operation.

As for the successive dates of these works, it is beyond a doubt that Raphael began the first Stanza in the Vatican by the great picture of Theology. This is proved by the faces which appear to be portraits—a peculiar characteristic of the Florentine school in the fifteenth century—by the frequent use of gold, and by the general style of the painting. For, notwithstanding the deep science with which he executed this fresco, we still feel a certain timidity in it. It was while executing it that Raphael discovered the secret of the marvellous facility of execution he afterwards displayed. This facility is already perceived in the lower part of the right side, where he had less need to have recourse to finishing touches on the distemper.

The arrangement of this composition, its wonderful richness, lofty significance, the nobleness and superb character of the figures, the fine arrangement of the groups, the lightness and harmony of the whole, make this "Dispute on the Holy Sacrament" a picture unequalled in modern art. If it be compared with ancient works, it may be perceived that it possesses perfection of drawing and beauty of form in an equal degree with them, but is far more attractive from the expression of lively faith which animates the Christian.

It also shows the progress made by the young master with respect to colouring: the head of St. Gregory, for example, is of a warm vigorous tone. The general harmony, so difficult to obtain in a fresco extending over a large surface, is also very satisfactory, especially when it is remembered that this was Raphael's first work of this nature.

The Parnassus, although it still resembles the style of the preceding picture, and is finished in every part with the same care, yet shows greater freedom. The style of the draperies, the distribution of light and shade, are an evident improvement. The drawing is everywhere more noble, although the outlines and movement of Apollo are not agreeable, and in general the character of that figure is not happy. The fine groups of the Muses, on the contrary, are very graceful and charming.

It was, however, in the School of Athens, that Raphael showed the full powers of his genius, and that he was completely master both of his style and of his execution.

In the part of this picture requiring great learning, it is possible, and indeed highly probable, that Raphael consulted the more erudite of his friends, and amongst others, the Count Castiglione, who had just come to settle at Rome.

However this may be, to Raphael alone belongs the great honour of having succeeded in representing in a single living and distinct image the development of Greek philosophy. It was Raphael who conceived the idea of grouping the personages according to the rank they occupy in history, and rendered the tendencies of these philosophers apparent—not merely by ingenious grouping, but also by their actions, their attitudes, and countenances.

This fresco, in which he rose to such dignity and to such a grand style, is justly considered as the most magnificent work the master ever produced. It does, indeed, unite the technical experience of drawing, colouring, and touch—the conquests of the more modern schools—to the severity bequeathed to them by the more ancient ones. The traditional symmetry of the painters of Siena and Florence, in the fourteenth century, which Perugino always observed, is also to be found in the "School of Athens;" but it is employed in a higher manner in the disposition of groups, so that the eye is not even arrested by these profound combinations, but may uninterruptedly enjoy the beauty of the lines.

Besides this, the figures are all individual, yet without being treated exactly as if they were portraits. Becoming more and more eager to attain a characteristic significance, Raphael sought rather the spirit of the features, if we may use such an expression, and avoided the two accidental forms of nature. He thus realized, by the union of character and beauty, what the old Italian masters had always sought for—he embodied an idea.

He has also succeeded admirably in the manner in which he treated the Grecian costume, although at that time many paintings and antique sculptures were not known. No one since that time has shown so much taste in this.

All these noble and fundamental qualities of the art of drawing Raphael has displayed in the "School of Athens;" he has also shown in it for the first time all the qualities peculiar to painting. The movement is free, the groups varied, the light and shade widely distributed; the perspective also is very skilful. These are, indeed, the means proper to painting, which place a barrier between it and sculpture, the natural principles of which are different. For this freedom of movement, picturesqueness of groups, and diversity in the size of the figures, all that forms the principal charm in painting cannot be applied to sculpture.

Raphael, however, understood well where this picturesque freedom was to stop. His sentiment of the beautiful—so fine and delicate—always prevented him from going to any of the extremes which characterized the latter half of the sixteenth century, and marked the decay of painting.

It is painful to say that it was Michael Angelo, that colossal genius, who first caused art to glide out of the noble route marked out by the ancient masters and the primitive schools of Italy.

Was it not this prodigious artist who delighted in producing violent and tortured attitudes, and a useless exaggeration of anatomical science? Even in his painting he has been the one who has the most abused the outline, thus sacrificing the immutable beauties of the plastic art.

The "School of Athens" is certainly one of the works of the sixteenth century which best unites all the qualities composing what is called the "elevated style," a qualification difficult to explain. It consists in a union of the severe and the true, in a general and particular knowledge of forms and characters, in the fulness of the lines and expression, and especially in the absence of all ephemeral puerility. Leonardo da Vinci, Fra Bartolomeo, and pre-eminently Raphael, are the representatives of the purest and noblest style of the great period of the art.

Many historians have sustained that it was the works of Michael Angelo which revealed this style to Raphael. Vasari, whose predilection for the Florentine master is well known, has exaggerated this supposition. Let us endeavour then to appreciate the influence, quite incontestable, of Michael Angelo on Raphael, and to judge of its results. Like all well-organized natures, Raphael in the first moment of enthusiasm, inspired by the work of a great master, could never resist the temptation of appropriating its most striking qualities. This was the case when he saw the pictures of Perugino, Leonardo da Vinci and Fra Bartolomeo. It was the same also with the works of Greek and Roman antiquity. It may be imagined, then, that his impressionable mind did not remain cold before the gigantic works of Michael Angelo. He sought to follow him, led by the power itself of the marvels, as much as by his own will. Some paintings executed after the first Stanza of the Vatican[1] testify to this irresistible attraction, for instance, the prophet Isaiah in the church of St. Augustine.

The influence is clearly seen here, but this prophet, in which it is most remarkable, is one of the weakest works of the painter.

The influence of Leonardo and Fra Bartolomeo had contributed much to the rapid and brilliant improvement of the young Raphael;

---

[1] It is certain that Raphael did not see the works of Michael Angelo at the Sistine before terminating his frescoes in the Stanza della Signatura. On Christmas day, 1512, the scaffolding of the first part of the paintings in the Sistine chapel were not yet removed, for we read in the "Diario" of Paris di Grassis, "1512, in vigiliâ N. C.: Pontifex voluit vesperis interesse in capellâ Sixtinâ. . . . Sed quia non erat ubi possemus ponere thalamum et solium ejus, dixit, ut illud facerem ego modo meo."

while, on the contrary, the influence of Michael Angelo arrested for a moment the onward flight of his genius. This phenomenon requires an explanation.

A great era in arts, as in literature, does not always follow the appearance of an extraordinary genius. It comes on gradually and its progress may be noted. It has its infancy, and with it the simplicity belonging to that age, then its youth, with the grace and sentiments natural to youth ; afterwards maturity with its increased power.

Raphael was the highest expression of the art of the sixteenth century, he attained its greatest perfection. He was a continuation of the chain of artists in his time, and was its last and brightest link.

Michael Angelo, on the contrary, never formed a part of this traditional chain : a unique, an incomparable genius, with a wonderful power of conception, never equalled either among the ancients or moderns, he possessed so many artistic qualities that it is hopeless to attempt an analysis of them. The only painter who might possibly have influenced him in his youth was Signorelli. Perhaps it would be more correct to say that Signorelli was the only contemporary artist whose works bore any resemblance to the noble conceptions of Michael Angelo. But, as we have already stated, this immense genius without any traditional fetters handed down from his predecessors, being only guided by his own inspirations, sometimes quitted the strict rules of art, and giving way to his impulse, created images, always astonishing in grandeur, beauty and power, but of exaggerated execution, notwithstanding his deep science, and was thus carried sometimes beyond the limits of nature. By studying him in an independent spirit, we may, doubtless, acquire both science and force ; but whoever seeks to imitate him, will infallibly fall into a hopeless exaggeration.

This was precisely the effect produced on Raphael. When the imitation is flagrant, the works are weak ; but, in those pictures in which, to the majestic and learned manner of the Florentine, Raphael united his own grace and ideality, and in which the fire of his own genius predominates, we must be struck with the fresh impulse and the grander tone imparted to them.

In our opinion, ancient art had far more influence on Raphael than the style of Michael Angelo. All his sympathies urged him in that direction, which was, besides, the general tendency of the period ; and the studies from the antique, which he was obliged to make for the

"School of Athens," contributed much to make him appreciate the beauties of Greek art.

In short, Raphael having received the most wonderful gifts from heaven, had also the rare talent of harmonizing in himself, yet without in the least injuring his own originality, nearly all the eminent qualities of the schools that preceded him, or of the contemporary artists.

We will now pass on to various occurrences happening during the early part of his sojourn at Rome.

It will be remembered that he formed a friendship with Francesco Francia at Bologna, in 1506. A few months after his arrival at Rome he wrote him the following letter:—[1]

" Dear Messer Francesco,

" I have just received your portrait, brought to me by Bazzotto, in excellent condition, and without any damage whatever. I thank you most heartily for it. It is most beautiful, and so full of life, that I sometimes deceive myself, and think you yourself are with me, and that I hear you speak. I entreat your indulgent excuse that I have so long delayed sending you my own, which from continuous and most important occupations, I have not as yet been able to finish with my own hands, as I promised you I would do. I might, indeed, have sent you one done by a pupil,[2] and retouched by myself, but this would have been most wrong; though, let who may paint it, the result will not equal the merit of your work. Excuse me, therefore, you, who know from frequent experience, what it is to live deprived of one's liberty, and at the command of patrons, who, when they need you not, lay you aside. Meantime, I send you by Bazzotto, who tells me he will return in a week, another drawing of the 'Presepio," very different, as you will see, from the one completed, and which you were pleased to commend so highly, as indeed you do with respect to all my works, covering me with blushes. I am ashamed of the trifle I send you, but you will value it more as a token of love and respect, than for any other reason. If, in return, you give me a drawing of your Judith[3] I shall place it among my dearest and most precious treasures.

---

[1] Published for the first time by Count Malvasia.

[2] This sentence shows that at this time Raphael had pupils or assistants; he had perhaps taken them with him from Florence. One of the first who worked under him was the Florentine Giovanni Francesco Penni, surnamed Il Fattore.

[3] This is probably the valuable drawing (preserved in the Albertine collection in

"Monsignor the Datary[1] is anxiously expecting his little Madonna, and Cardinal Riario[2] his large one, as you will hear from Bazzotto. I also shall view them with that satisfaction and enjoyment, which all your previous productions have given me—productions which no artist has surpassed in beauty, and in the expression of devotional feeling. Farewell, be of good courage, pursue the wise course you have hitherto adhered to, and be assured that I sympathise with you[3] as with myself. Continue to love me as I love you.

"Ever by serving you,

"RAPHAELLO."[4]

"Rome, 5th Sept. 1508."

Malvasia relates that, about 1511, Achilles Grassi (not yet a cardinal) sent an "Annunciation," by the hand of Raphael, to his brother Agamemnon, at Bologna. What became of this picture is not known; but the Gotha collection possesses a copy of it.

It was, most probably, after the arrival of this painting, that Francia

---

Vienna), in which Judith is advancing to place the head of Holophernes in a bag held by an attendant. It was published, wrongly, under the name of Giovanni Bellini, in the lithographed fac-simile. The Judith executed in fresco by Francia, in the Bentivoglio palace, was destroyed when that family was driven from Bologna by the Pope.

[1] Datario, Baldassare Turini da Pescia. He was one of Raphael's executors. Da Vinci painted two pictures for him in 1514, and Giulio Romano built his villa (Lante) on the Gianicolo.

[2] Rafael Riario, cardinal of San Giorgio, nephew or natural son of Sixtus IV. He lived in great style at Rome, and had the Cancelleria built by Bramante. He was very devoted to Julius II., and contributed to the election of Leo X. Although he had formerly taken part in the conspiracy of the Pazzi at Florence, and the murder of Giuliano de' Medici, he was appointed chamberlain by Leo X. But his resentment against the Medici afterwards revived, and he headed a fresh conspiracy against Leo X., which was discovered. However, thanks to the power of his party, he got off with banishment and a fine. See Carlo Fea, "Notizie intorno Raffaele Sanzio," &c., Rome, 1822, p. 83.

[3] Francia enjoyed the especial favour of the Bentivoglio family, the lords of Bologna, and he was much grieved at their expulsion by the Pope.

[4] Malvasia, in the "Felsina Pittrice," writes this signature: "Rafaello Sanzio." But it is a liberty that he takes, for Raphael always signs "Raphaello." The name of Sanzio added to the Christian name is also very suspicious, since no other signature bears this surname, and Raphael merely added to the Christian name, "Painter at Rome (pictor in Româ)." Besides this, the family name is written in every document "Santi" or "Sancti."

composed, in honour of Raphael, the sonnet that has been published by Malvasia; a touching testimony of friendship, and the high esteem of an older master of great celebrity.[1]

The following is Francia's sonnet:—

"All' excellente pittore Raphaello Sanzio
Zeusi del nostro secolo,
da me Francesco Raibolini, detto il Francia.

Non son Zeusi, ne Apelle, e non son tale;
Che di tanti tal nome a me convegna,
Ne mio talento, ni vertude è degna
Haver da un Raffael lode immortale.
Tu sol, cui fece il ciel dono fatale,
Che ogn' altro excede, e fora ogn' altro regna
L'excellente artificio a noi insegna
Con cui sei reso ad ogn' antico uguale
Fortunato Garxon, che nei primi anni
Tant oltrepassi, e che sara poi quando
In più provecta etade opre migliori?
Vinta sarà natura; et da tuoi inganni
Resa eloquente dira te lodando
Che tu solo il pictor sei de' pictori."

Amongst the easel pictures painted by Raphael during the three first years of his residence at Rome, we must mention the "Holy Family" for the church of Santa Maria del Popolo, erected by Pope Sixtus V. It was the Cardinal Riario who had ordered this picture; it is known by the name of the "Madonna di Loreto," because, at a later period it decorated the church at Loretto. It is now lost.[2]

Vasari, and also Sandrart, saw it exhibited on the grand feast days in Santa Maria at Rome, with a portrait of Julius II., also painted by Raphael about the same time, and presented by the Pope to this church, which he had taken under his especial protection.

This fine portrait, now in the Pitti Palace, shows Julius II. at an advanced age, but still full of vigour.

When Vasari says that this portrait is so true and life-like that one imagines one sees the Pope himself, and trembles, we must not conclude that Raphael has represented here, as in his frescoes, the imperious and

---

[1] It would seem to have been through false information that Vasari judged so ill of Francia.

[2] A picture was, however, discovered in 1857, which is supposed to be the original, and the Academy of St. Luke at Rome confirmed this judgment. This Madonna now belongs to Sir Walter Kennedy Lawrence, residing at Florence.

awe-inspiring sovereign; on the contrary, the expression is very mild, yet it shows all the individuality of an active and enterprising character.

The portrait of the young Marquis Federico of Mantua, with long hair covered by a red cap, and that of the Pope's favourite, the Parmesan, were painted at the same period. The former passed with the pictures in the Mantua gallery into the collection of Charles I., King of England. The other was given as a present by Ottaviano Sforza, Bishop of Lodi, to the Foscarini family at Venice, where the anonymous writer, edited by Morelli, saw it in 1530. We have no other information about the latter picture.

We think that the portrait of the "Young Man," which is in the Louvre,[1] must belong to the same period. It must be either of a young artist or of a friend of Raphael's. He is leaning on his elbow, and his blue eyes are full of tenderness and poetry.

To reply to the desires of his protectors, Raphael also painted several small Madonnas.

The beautiful round picture, known by the name of the "Madonna della Casa d'Alba,"[2] was obtained for the city of Nocera de Pagani, through the agency of Paolo Giovio, the bishop of that town.[3] Another Virgin, with the Infant Jesus, presenting a pink to St. John, was also at Rome, formerly in the Aldobrandini Gallery, the name of which it still bears.[4]

Raphael painted about 1511, a larger altar-piece for Sigismondo Conti di Fuligno,[5] private secretary to the Pope. This "Madonna di

---

[1] No. 386 of the Italian schools. This young man appears of about fifteen or sixteen years of age, according to the catalogue, in which M. Villot quotes Mariette's opinion in support of his own: "Some consider this painting," says Mariette in the description of the Crozet cabinet, "to be the portrait of the painter himself; but it is difficult to conceive that when still so young he could have painted a picture so unlike his first manner as this." M. Villot adds: "And indeed this painting, evidently in the painter's third manner, must have been executed between 1515 and 1520, and in consequence cannot represent himself." Thus Passavant and the catalogue of the Louvre differ materially as to the probable date of the picture. The approximate date of 1511, fixed by Passavant, would rank this picture in the second style of Raphael, and not the third. We believe him to be right. This portrait has too much simplicity, freshness, and poetry to belong to Raphael's third manner.—*Lacroix.*

[2] Engraved by Desnoyers.

[3] The Madonna della Casa d'Alba, bought by the Emperor Nicholas with a part of the Coesvelt collection at London, is now in the Hermitage at St. Petersburg.

[4] Now in the National Gallery. No. 744.

[5] He was descended from the noble family of Conti d'Anagni, one of whom became

THE MADONNA OF THE ALBA FAMILY

In the Hermitage, St. Petersburg

Fuligno," besides the splendid drawing and style displayed in it, is also admirable from its extreme freshness, and by the peculiar beauty of its colouring and the skilful use of chiaroscuro in it. It first adorned the Aracelli Church on the Capitol. The nun Anna Conti succeeded in getting it placed in the convent of St. Anne, founded at Fuligno by the Conti family. After having been in the Napoleon Museum it returned to Rome and was placed in the Vatican Gallery.

Raphael was also commissioned about this time by John Gorizius of Luxembourg, to paint the "Prophet Isaiah" in fresco, on a pillar of the church of St. Augustine. This Gorizius, also called Janus Corycius, was a great patron of the arts and sciences, and at his house all the artists and scientific men were frequently assembled. He it was who ordered the beautiful group in marble of the Virgin with St. Anne, by Andrew Sansovino, which was placed in 1512 against a pillar in the church of St. Augustine.

It was on the upper part of this pillar that Raphael painted the Prophet of which we have already spoken as betraying an imitation of Michael Angelo.

Vasari relates that Raphael had at first painted another Isaiah, but, that having seen the works of Michael Angelo in the Sistine Chapel, he had it destroyed in order to replace it by a new figure in his rival's style, "Much more perfect than the former one," adds Vasari. We doubt this, however, as the praises he lavishes on this second fresco, can only be attributed to his enthusiasm for everything that resembles the style of his master the Florentine.

It has been much discussed, in what years Raphael painted the "Prophet Isaiah." And yet the Greek inscription on the group of Andrea Sansovino, of 1512, indicates that Gorizius caused the painting

---

Pope Innocent III. Since the time of Innocent III. the rich Conti family resided at Rome, and were always firm protectors of art. It became extinct in 1808. Sigismondo Conti, whom Giovanni Santi (in his dedication to the Duke of Urbino) mentions as a distinguished writer, has left a history of his times, from the year 1475, in nine books, which Giustiniano Pagliarini intended to publish at Rome. See Pungileoni, p. 111. Sigismondo Conti was *cameriere segreto* to Pope Julius II., which is equivalent to private secretary. According to P. Casimiro ("Memorie d'Aracelli," Roma. 1736, p. 242), he also bore the title of secretary, which was also *abbreviatore del sacro Palazzo apostolico;* now called *viso di Curia.* He died February 23rd, 1512. See C. Fea, "Nuova Descr. de' mon. ant." Rom. 1819, p. 72.

[1] Desnoyers has also made a good engraving of it.

and the sculpture to be executed at the same time. Besides this the arms of Julius II. painted in fresco, which were formerly above a fire-place in one of the apartments of Pope Innocent VIII. in the Vatican, were supported by two children's figures, precisely similar to those which surround Raphael's "Prophet," Julius II. having died February 21, 1513, it follows that the execution of the painting, as well as of the blazon, cannot be fixed later than the end of 1512.

We must now examine another statement concerning Raphael. Condivi says that when Michael Angelo had completed one half of the ceiling of the Sistine, Bramante, at the instigation of Raphael, endeavoured to persuade the Pope to have the remaining half finished by Raphael. Michael Angelo was very uneasy at this step, and the question was only decided in his favour by his vigorous representations to the Pope.

Vasari also mentions the same fact, omitting, however, the instigation of Raphael, and he throws all the blame on the jealousy of Bramante.

But a passage from a letter of Michael Angelo,[1] seems to prove that he himself had suggested these versions to the two Italian biographers; this letter ends thus:—"The jealousy of Bramante and Raphael da Urbino was the cause of all the misunderstandings between the Pope and myself. This jealousy, and the intention they had to ruin me, prevented the mausoleum of Julius II. from being finished during his life. It must be confessed that Raphael had good reasons for this; for whatever he knew of art he had learned from me."[2]

The tone of this letter shows the great irritability of Michael Angelo, who from his youth had always a feeling of animosity towards his brother artists, who had not entirely yielded to him.

It is sufficient to remember his bitter sarcasms in the gardens of the

---

[1] Published by Sebastiano Ciampi: "Lettera di Michelangiolo Buonarroti, per giustificarsi contro le calunnie degli emuli e de' nemici suoi, sul proposito del sepolcro di passa Giulio II. trovata da S. Ciampi." Firenze, 1834, p. 7.

[2] Condivi writes almost the same: "Michael Angelo was never jealous of the works of others, even in his own art, more from natural kindness than from his opinion of himself. He was more given to praising everyone universally, even Raffaello da Urbino, with whom he had had some dispute in painting, as I have written; however, I have heard him say that Raffaello had not received his art from nature, but by long study." As for the particular qualities of the two masters, Vasari, elsewhere so partial, says with greater justice: "The world received the gift of this artist from the hand of Nature. When vanquished by Art in the person of Michael Angelo, she deigned to be subjugated in that of Raphael, not by art only but by goodness also."

THE MADONNA DI FOLIGNO.

In the Vatican.

Medici palace, when one of his fellow disciples, unable to bear it any longer, gave him a blow that broke his nose; his intrigue against Baccio d'Agnolo, which prevented the completion of the cupola of the cathedral; his hard judgment on the painting of Perugino, whom he called an ignorant man in matters of art; his bitterness against Francia, when, on seeing for the first time that painter's handsome son, he remarked—"Thy father knows better how to make living figures than painted ones," arising from an old grudge that when Francia was looking at the statue of Julius II., he praised the metal without praising the sculpture; his violent quarrel with Leonardo da Vinci, under Leo X. at Rome, which resulted in Da Vinci's leaving the town; and, lastly, his ill-temper with all other artists, which prevented the accomplishment of the Pope's project, of terminating the façade of San Lorenzo at Florence.

These facts, and many others that might be mentioned, prove not only that Michael Angelo was always excessively irritable and unsociable, but that he placed himself far above all other artists, and usually treated them with disdain.

His presumptuous words then about Raphael lose all value. It is impossible to believe that Raphael, with his undoubted modesty and simple admiration for Michael Angelo, should have really been inspired by the jealousy and ill-intentions thus imputed to him. It is easy to contrast the characters of the two great men, by opposing to the last sentence of Michael Angelo's letter the following passage from Condivi himself:—"Raphael frequently observed that he considered himself happy to have been born in the time of Michael Angelo, as that great artist had revealed to him a side of art which was never seen in the old masters."

But to return to the works of Raphael. To this same year, 1512, also belong some magnificent portraits; that of a woman, thought to be Raphael's mistress, in the Tribune at Florence, and the portrait of Bindo Altoviti, erroneously called by the name of the painter himself, in the Pinacothek at Munich.[1]

---

[1] In the Munich gallery are two portraits, said to be of Raphael, painted by himself. "Both are half-length figures; in one he is dressed in violet velvet, on a dark background; in the other he is in black, the background being a garden scene. A note added to the description of the latter in the catalogue, confesses frankly that Raphael, having necessarily to paint himself in a glass, could scarcely have coloured the right hand with such perfection, and that his portrait may be taken for that of the

In the greater part of the portraits which he executed at this time, Raphael employed a vigour of tone which his other pictures were far from equalling. The two latter portraits, indeed, possess such vigorous colouring, that they might even compete with Giorgione's works. On this account the portrait dated 1512 has been frequently attributed to him, the fact being altogether overlooked that the Venetian master had died in the preceding year. The drawing and general spirit of this picture are, besides, quite Raphaelesque.

This perfection of colouring, however, makes it probable that Raphael had seen some Venetian pictures, either by Giorgione himself, or by one of his pupils. It may be noticed also, that Sebastiano del Piombo, one of the best painters of the Venetian school, had arrived in Rome in 1511, where he had been summoned by the famous banker, Agostino Chigi, who was a friend of Raphael.

There have been many controversies as to who are the two persons represented in these portraits.

The beautiful woman, of southern amplitude and ardent glance, received, in the middle of last century, the name of the Fornarina, the supposed mistress of Raphael.[1] This title is, however, an error, as will be seen when we speak of the authentic portrait of Raphael's mistress.

Who, then, is the person represented?

In the inventory of the objects of art in the Florence gallery, in 1589, this portrait is inscribed without any name being attached. The woman was, then, even at that time unknown.

Can it be the portrait of Beatrice Ferrarese, mentioned by Vasari?

It is useless to devote a single instant to the supposition often brought forward, of its being a princess of the house of Este, since the work of Litta, so exact in its information about every member of the celebrated families of Italy, does not mention any princess of that name of the house of Este. The Beatrice of Ferrara mentioned by Vasari,

---

Duke of Urbino." (Viardot, "Musées d'Allemagne," p. 115.) As for the other portrait, he hesitates, notwithstanding the assertion of the catalogue, to find any resemblance in it to the other portraits of Raphael, for this portrait, in which we seek vainly for "his calm features, his large black eyes, and the genius visible in the whole countenance," recalls in its attitude, and even in the features the celebrated portrait of the "Suonatore di Violino," which is at Rome in the Sciarra gallery; but, adds M. Viardot, "we find in this neither the wonderful execution nor the striking effect of the other." —*Lacroix.*

[1] Engraved as such by Raphael Morghen.

was probably a lady of high distinction and cultivated mind. She may possibly have possessed the talent of improvisation, as the crown of enamelled gold on her head seems to imply. The attitude, the choice of the costume, the penetrating glance of her beautiful eyes, confirm our conjecture. Besides which, in a letter addressed to Cardinal Bembo, Oct. 27th, 1523,[1] Gratiosa Pia of Ferrara "commends to him herself and her *Beatrice*." Everything, then, would lead us to suppose that the portrait in the Tribune represents this Beatrice of Ferrara in connection with Bembo, the friend of Raphael.

Hypotheses, nearly all confused, have been formed since the time of Bottari, respecting the portrait of the "Young Man," of the Altoviti house at Florence.

Bottari had a perfect mania for discovering everywhere portraits of Raphael. Resting on a passage of double meaning of Vasari's,[2] he was the first to assert that the portrait in question, although for more than two centuries it had been handed down in the Altoviti family as that of their ancestor Bindo, in reality represented Raphael himself.

Certainly, it is surprising on what slight grounds certain writers advance the most arbitrary facts. Here is a man with fair hair and blue eyes; Raphael, in every authentic portrait, has dark hair and eyes. This, however, does not prevent Bottari from boldly making his assertion. The portrait, besides, in its execution, differs much from the style of Raphael in 1505 and 1506, yet is quite in harmony with his manner in 1512, a date which agrees exactly with the age of Bindo Altoviti, then entering his twenty-second year, since he was born Sept. 26th, 1490. Besides, even admitting what is not the case, that the eyes and hair have been repainted, the countenance has nothing of the ardent and meditative expression, which is so attractive in the portrait of Raphael, painted by himself at Urbino, in 1506.

Notwithstanding so many contradictions, Bottari's opinion has found many warm partisans; and Raphael Morghen, in his engraving, has also given the name of the painter to the portrait of Altoviti.

Bindo Altoviti was celebrated at Rome for his beauty. Being also

[1] See the correspondence of Pietro Bembo, among the "Lettere da diverse principesse et altre signore," Lib. ii. p. 29, 6.

[2] "Ed a Bindo Altoviti fece il ritratto suo, quando era giovane, che è tenuto stupendissimo."

an amateur in art, he commissioned Raphael to paint him a "Holy Family," with St. John the Baptist, the patron saint of Florence.

The inexhaustible genius of Raphael succeeded in imparting a peculiar charm to this subject, which has been so often repeated, by borrowing a little scene from domestic life. The Virgin, standing, is taking the Child from the hands of St. Elizabeth; he is trying to spring towards his mother, but at that moment a young woman behind Elizabeth touches him, and he is looking round and smiling at her.

On account of a window in the background being covered with a cloth, this picture bears the name of the "Madonna dell' Impannata." It is now in the Pitti palace. Its authenticity has frequently been doubted; but the beauty of the composition, and a drawing by the hand of Raphael in the royal collection in England, prove that the design is by the master, if not the execution, in which much stiffness and inequality may be noticed. It was doubtless painted by one of his pupils. It was some years later than the portrait of Bindo.

Amongst the Madonnas executed about 1512, is that of the Orleans gallery, which has passed into the gallery of the Duke of Bridgwater. The head of the Virgin, and the exquisite drawing of the Child from the shoulders to the feet, are especially admirable; it is a masterpiece of life and grace.

More simple, but not less attractive, is a "Madonna" formerly at the Tempi house, and now in the Pinacothek of Munich. The Virgin has a touching expression of maternal happiness.

The poet, Samuel Rogers,[1] in London, possessed a small "Madonna," in which the infant Jesus, standing on his mother's lap, and leaning against her, is looking smilingly out of the picture. This painting, like that in the Bridgwater gallery, came from the Orleans gallery. It is a good deal injured, unfortunately.

The Holy Family which Raphael painted for Lionello Pio da Carpi, is, on the contrary, in excellent preservation. It is in the Museum of Naples, with the original cartoon. It was formerly in the Farnese Gallery. The Virgin, and St. Elizabeth, with their children, are seated near a ruin. The little St. John is expressing his tender adoration for Jesus, who, taking his hand from that of St. Elizabeth, is blessing him.

---

[1] Samuel Rogers died in 1856, and his collection was sold in London. Raphael's Madonna formed a part of the Manchester Exhibition (No. 140).—*Lacroix.*

St. Joseph is walking under the arcade of a building. Marco of Ravenna has preserved for us in an engraving the first thought for this picture; instead of a ruin was a landscape with a palm tree.

At each fresh "Madonna" of Raphael's we are always struck with the variety he imparts to a subject the form of which is almost imposed, and of the noble style which he never for a moment leaves, even while taking his accessories from simple domestic life. The Virgins of Raphael do not always bear the stamp of religious mysticism which characterizes those of his predecessors, and of several of his contemporaries, and yet they remain as the types of the "Madonna."

Raphael devoted himself to the worship of the beautiful and of the true, and this explains his power. His love for all the beauties of nature must remove him from the mysticism of past forms and of inflexible traditions. In the "Madonna del Pesce" and the "Madonna di San Sisto," and in a few others, of which we shall soon speak, Christian poetry has found its highest expression; for it is poetry which touches all nations the most deeply, and beauty alone can give an idea of divinity.

About the year 1513, Raphael received various orders from the rich merchant, Agostino Chigi, the protégé of the Popes Julius II. and Leo X.[1] Chigi owed this favour of the Popes as much to his probity and the uprightness of his character, as to the services he had rendered to the State. Yet his name, then so well known, and held in such high estimation, would long since have been forgotten, if his love for art had not united his memory to the fame of the great artists whose works he had ordered.[2]

Baldassare Peruzzi built for him, in the ancient gardens of Geta, one of the finest dwellings in Rome, now known by the name of La Farnesina, and he also painted the ceiling of the large hall in it. Sebastiano del Piombo, Raphael, Antonio Razzi, and Giulio Romano, decorated the interior of the palace.

Chigi, a generous and gallant man, led a princely life. The feasts

---

[1] Chigi was likewise a patron of letters; he had founded a printing-press, the sole aim of which was to spread, at his own expense, the Greek classics, such as Pindar Theocritus, &c.

[2] Julius II. thought so highly of Chigi, that he authorized him to assume the name of Rovere, and the arms of that illustrious family. See Carlo Fea: Notizie, &c. p. 88. There we find the document relating to this authorization of Julius II., September 9th, 1509.

he gave in his sumptuous dwelling recall, by their luxury, the feasts of Rome in the olden days. He assembled in his house all the nobility, the literary men, and artists of Rome. Women held a high place there; and Paulo Giovio relates that Chigi was a passionate admirer of the courtesan Imperia, famous for her beauty and gallantries.

The first document which bears on the relation of Raphael to this Mæcenas is a contract of the 10th November, 1510, between Chigi and the sculptor Cesarino, of Urbino, a friend of Raphael's. According to this contract, Cesare di Francesco, called Cesarino, was to execute two round goblets in bronze, at the price of twenty-five ducats of gold, for which "Raphael of Urbino, the son of Giovanni Santi," had made the designs.

One of these drawings, preserved in the Dresden collection, represents Neptune, passing joyously through the waves, surrounded by tritons, nymphs, and loves. The other sketch, on a similar subject, is in the collection at Oxford.

The commands of Chigi to Raphael for the decoration of chapels in the churches of Santa Maria della Pace and Santa Maria del Popolo were of far higher importance. The two churches, built by Sixtus IV., were especially under the protection of his nephew, Pope Julius II. Santa Maria della Pace, built in remembrance of the efforts of Sixtus IV. to bring back peace to Christianity, had been entrusted, in 1482, to the care of the Lateran chapter. Santa Maria del Popolo, restored according to the plans of Baccio Pintelli, was decorated by the superb mausoleums of the Cardinal Ascanio Maria Sforza, and of the Cardinal Girolamo Basso, named di Recanati, the works of Andrea Sansovino.

Agostino commissioned Raphael to build, at the side of the latter church, a chapel which was to contain his mausoleum. Raphael made the plans for it, but neither he nor Chigi lived long enough to see it completed. We shall return to this at the proper place; but we shall at once describe the frescoes of Santa Maria della Pace, in order not to interrupt afterwards the description of the second Stanza of the Vatican, commenced at the same period.

On the wall above the arch of the chapel are four Prophets, with four angels, and below them four sibyls receiving the revelation; to the left the Sibyl of Cumæ; then the Persic sibyl, opposite the Phrygian, and, lastly, the Tiburtine. Celestial genii hold strips of parchment, or tablets, with Greek inscriptions on the divine decisions. At the key-stone of the arch, an angel bears a lighted torch, a symbol of the light which these predestined women were to hand down to men.

Indeed, all that is known of the sibyls is extremely problematical; and even the church has not adopted all the fictions invented of them in the early times of Christianity. Nevertheless, these women, agitated by divine fury, "furore divinationis convulsæ," as Cicero says, have been frequently represented, since the fourteenth century, both in sculpture and painting, in the churches of the West.

Whether myths or realities, the sibyls, on account of the romantic mystery of their history, and the diversity of their countries, have always been one of the happiest subjects for art.

In originality and grandeur, nothing can surpass the sibyls of Michael Angelo. In beauty of outline and form, in charm of expression and grace, nothing can equal the sibyls of Raphael. The former strike the mind from their majesty; the latter by their gentleness and nobility at once elevate and touch the soul.

The four Prophets are weaker in composition, but especially in execution. The young Daniel is seated on the left, holding a tablet and looking at King David, who is seated near him in sacerdotal costume. On the tablet is written, "I am alive again, and am ever near thee." On the other side, near the Prophet Hosea, Jonah is seated, showing the words, "God will raise him up after two days, on the third day;" an allusion to the resurrection of Christ, and at the same time to the deliverance of Jonah.

This fresco of the Prophets is so inferior to the Sibyls that Raphael can certainly have only made the cartoons, and must have entrusted the execution to one of his pupils. Vasari speaks of the co-operation of Timoteo Viti in the execution of the Sibyls; but we may see at the first glance, that this co-operation could only have applied to the painting of the "Prophets."

Cinelli, in his "Bellezze di Firenze" (edition of 1677, p. 277), mentions, in connection with this fresco, the following anecdote:

"Raphael of Urbino had painted for Agostino Chigi, at Santa Maria della Pace, some Prophets and Sibyls, on which he had received an advance of 500 scudi. One day he demanded of Agostino's cashier (Giulio Borghesi) the remainder of the sum at which he estimated his work. The cashier being astonished at this demand, and thinking that the sum already paid was sufficient, did not reply. 'Cause the work to be estimated by a judge of painting,' replied Raphael, 'and you will see how moderate my demand is.'

"Giulio Borghesi thought of Michael Angelo for this valuation, and begged him to go to the church and estimate the figures of Raphael. Possibly he imagined that self-love, rivalry and jealousy would lead the Florentine to lower the price of the pictures.

"Michael Angelo went, accompanied by the cashier, to Santa Maria della Pace, and as he was contemplating the fresco without uttering a word, Borghesi questioned him. 'That head,' replied Michael Angelo, pointing to one of the Sibyls, 'that head is worth a hundred scudi!' 'And the others?' asked the cashier. 'The others are not worth less.'"

Some who witnessed this scene related it to Chigi. He heard every particular, and ordering in addition to the five hundred scudi for five heads, a hundred scudi to be paid for each of the others, he said to his cashier, "Go and give that to Raphael in payment for his heads, and behave very politely to him, so that he may be satisfied; for if he insists on my also paying for the drapery, we should probably be ruined."

After the works in the church of Santa Maria della Pace, Raphael had already undertaken the paintings in the second stanza of the Vatican, generally named from the subject of the principal fresco, the Stanza di Eliodoro. To make room for the works of Raphael the Pope had the old frescoes of Bramantino of Milan and of Pietro della Francesca thrown down; but, as they contained portraits of many celebrated men, Raphael's pupils first made copies of them, which were afterwards given by Giulio Romano to Paolo Giovio, Bishop of Nocera de' Pagani.[1]

The new paintings for this second room were to represent the promises of God to the patriarchs, relative to the coming of the Messiah, and the traditional facts, showing how the divine wrath fell on the enemies of the Church.

For the first subjects, Raphael chose the ceiling, preserving, however, as in the Stanza della Signatura, the old arrangement of the ornamental part. Here the ceiling is divided into four parts, by wide bands, covered with mythological subjects, combats, triumphs, and sacrifices, which meet in the centre, decorated with the arms of the Popes.

---

[1] Vasari, in the "Life of Pietro della Francesca." These copies must now be in England, they formed a part of the collection of the late W. Roscoe, Esq., author of the "Life of Leo X."

Wishing to give these paintings on the ceilings an appearance of lightness, Raphael has represented them as painted on loose sheets attached to the ceiling.

The first of these subjects has been very variously interpreted. Vasari, and Platner after him, see in it the promise of a great posterity which God gave Abraham; Montagnani, the order given to Noah to leave the ark; Bellori, the thanksgiving of Noah after leaving the ark. But the three children besides the father and mother, seem to us to refute all these suppositions.

In our opinion, the subject of this picture relates to the words in the Scriptures preceding the order to build the ark: "Noah found grace in the eyes of the Lord. . . . And Noah begat three sons, Shem, Ham and Japhet." And we are confirmed in our opinion by this subject comprehending also the idea of the blessing of God on all future humanity. The Almighty, accompanied by two angels, is appearing to Noah. The patriarch holding one of his children in his arms, is standing before the door of the house.

This work is one of the finest by this master, and is full of majesty.

The second subject is the sacrifice of Isaac. An angel is arresting the patriarch's arm, another is bringing him a ram for the burnt-offering.

The third subject is "Jacob's Dream." A weak composition which Raphael afterwards painted again for the Loggie, with his usual qualities.

The fourth subject, "Moses prostrate before the burning bush," is full of power and energy. Dazzled by the celestial effulgence, Moses is veiling his face, whilst an angel is revealing the Almighty to him by parting the flames.

The paintings on the roof have lost much of their colours from the defects in the plaster, which has likewise proved fatal to two of the frescoes in the Stanza della Signatura. Fortunately Raphael perceived it, and was able to avoid this inconvenience in the great mural paintings.

The first of these mural paintings represents Heliodorus driven out of the temple in Jerusalem; where, by the orders of King Seleucus, he was taking the money destined for widows and orphans.

The scene passes in the temple itself. Surprise and fear agitate the assembly of the people and priests; for three celestial messengers, one of whom, in golden armour, is mounted on a magnificent horse, have rushed through the air with the violence of a thunderbolt, and have just struck the spoliator, in the very scene of his crime. Heliodorus, overthrown by them, has let his treasure fall; his two terrified acolytes are endeavouring to save themselves by flight. This magnificent group shows the highest degree of grandeur and correctness in movement and expression; it occupies the right of the foreground, leaving the whole space empty from them to the priests in prayer; thus indicating the promptitude of the flight of Heliodorus and his people, as well as the rapidity of celestial vengeance.

Yet the spectator cannot fail to be surprised to see, on the left side, Pope Julius II., borne by four attendants.

Raphael was obliged to introduce this anachronism on account of the Pope's desire that this fresco should likewise contain an allusion to the expulsion of his enemies from Rome.

In the first sketch, this foreign incident is not to be seen; it is wrong then to reproach Raphael for it; for all resistance on his part would have been utterly useless before the inflexible will of Julius II.

However, this little incident contains one point of interest to us: the foremost bearer of the pontifical chair is the celebrated engraver of Raphael's drawings, Mark Antonio Raimondi; and the personage standing beside him is the secretary of the "Memoriale," Giovanni Pietro de' Foliari, of Cremona.

In respect to colouring, this fresco is of great interest. Its date justifies our foregoing observations on the two portraits which, by their warmth and strength of colour, recall the principles of the Venetian colourists. We feel at once that Raphael wished to treat this fresco on the same system, and give it all the force of oil-painting. In other respects, too, we notice the introduction of a new element. The details are more sacrificed than in the works of the first room; the execution is wider and grander and there are greater masses in the ordering. All the resources of expression abound in it in an inimitable manner, without, however, diverging from the true principles of beauty, so that the dramatic sentiment attains its greatest height, without passing its just limits.

If the idea of the Heliodorus was to show the protection granted by God against his enemies, the idea of the Miracle of Bolsena, the second fresco in this room, was to show the divine assistance against unbelievers.

According to the tradition, in 1263, under the pontificate of Urban IV., a priest, who doubted the reality of transubstantiation, saw the blood

HELIODORUS DRIVEN FROM THE TEMPLE

flow from the host which he had just consecrated, when celebrating the mass in the church of St. Christina, at Bolsena. This miracle gave rise to the feast of Corpus Christi, which was not, however, regularly introduced into the church until fifty years later.

The wall, on which this tradition was to be represented, was pierced in the middle by a window. Raphael utilized this window very ingeniously, by placing the altar with the priests and assistants, as well as the Pope Urban[1] in prayer, on the horizontal line above the window. On the two spaces on each side the window the steps are drawn leading to the altar, and at the bottom are the Pope's suite and other spectators.

What strikes us the most in this painting is the expression of repentant humility in the officiating priest, the demonstrations of surprise from the assistants, the wrathful glances of one of the cardinals standing behind the Pope towards the incredulous priest, and the marvellous characteristic simplicity of the five Swiss soldiers, kneeling in the right of the foreground. Their calm features and simple countenances form a happy and picturesque contrast to the vivacity of the Italian crowd, in great agitation at the sight of the miracle, and also to the grave dignity of the priests of the papal court. Amongst the cardinals may be noticed Cardinal Raffaele Riario, famous for his hatred to the Medici family, and his conspiracies against them.[2]

At this period of Raphael's career, the colouring is improved in each fresh work. In this, the local tone, the half tints, and variety of the colours are admirably true and very vigorous. Raphael has brought out resources unknown in fresco painting until that time. Thus the celebrated frescoes by Titian in the Scuola di San Antonio, at Padua, are inferior to those of Raphael, not only in drawing and style, but also in colouring.

This fine composition was nearly finished when the death of Julius II. occurred February 22, 1513. We must in consequence stop our account of Raphael's works during this reign; but it seems advisable not to interrupt the description of the paintings in the second stanza of the Vatican, the

---

[1] This is also a portrait of Julius II.

[2] Carlo Fea (Notizie, &c., Roma, 1822, p. 83) has published interesting documents relative to the conspiracy against Leo X.; at first the indictment of the conspirators, at the Consistory of June 22, 1517; then a recognisance of 50,000 ducats, from Agostino Chigi, engaging to pay that sum to the Pope on the cardinal's account. We have already spoken of Riario, p. 106.

more so, as the honour belongs to Julius, although his successor may have chosen the other subjects.

The death of Julius II. scarcely interrupted the labours of Raphael at all, for Giovanni di Medici, raised to the pontificate under the name of Leo X., also loved art passionately, and the great painter found another powerful protector in him. The composition of the frescoes yet to be executed, however, in the Stanza di Eliodoro had to be modified in order that the allusions to the life of the Pope who had just died, might be transformed into allusions to the living Pope.

The third fresco is executed on a wall, having a window in the middle, like that on which the "Mass of Bolsena" is painted. This fresco represents in three scenes the "Deliverance of St. Peter from Prison."

Above the window St. Peter is seen through an iron grating, chained to the two soldiers. All three are in deep sleep. An angel resplendent in light has appeared to save the prisoner. To the right of the window, the angel is leading St. Peter through the sleeping soldiers who guard the approach to the prison. To the left the soldiers are seen awaking, and in great consternation at this unexpected flight.

The two former subjects are lighted up by the luminous figure of the angel; the latter by a torch borne by the soldiers, and the feeble light of the moon. These different lights give a peculiar aspect to the picture, at once striking and original. It was one of the first examples in Italy of this sort of effect, and it excited universal admiration.

The soldiers wear the steel cuirasses and arms of the sixteenth century, contrary to historical truth, from which Raphael did not usually deviate. This anachronism would confirm the opinion of Bellari, that the "Deliverance of St. Peter" is an allusion to the almost miraculous escape of Leo X., after he had been taken prisoner by the French at the battle of Ravenna, where he was present as papal legate. The first anniversary of this escape happened to fall on the very day of his elevation to the pontificate, and it is very probable that he intended to perpetuate this remembrance in the fresco of St. Peter.

The fourth mural painting of this room shows Attila arrested in his march on Rome, by the apparition of St. Peter and St. Paul. Pope Leo I. coming to meet him decided him to leave Italy.

According to history the Emperor Valentinian III. sent out the Bishop Leo, to negotiate a peace with the king of the Huns, advancing on Rome in 452. Leo met Attila on the banks of the River Oglio, near the fortress of Governolo, offered him presents, informing him of the special protection St. Peter had always granted to Rome, and reminded him that Alaric, having ill-treated that city, had been punished by a premature death. According to the tradition a gigantic man appeared at this moment, by the side of the Pope, threatening Attila with his sword. This vision appeased the conqueror, who retired from Italy with his rich booty.

In the fresco, Attila is on horseback in the centre of the group. The sight of the patron saints of Rome seems to inspire him with fear. A frightful hurricane is raging at the same time, and the savage hordes of the Huns are filled with terror; the horses are neighing in fear, and amidst all this confusion the trumpets sound the retreat.

An earlier sketch, now in the Louvre, contained, in the foreground to the left, groups of horsemen and pedestrians, seized with a secret terror yet without seeing the apparition. St. Leo was more in the background.

This drawing, highly finished, was submitted by Raphael to the approbation of the Pope. But Leo X., who had just succeeded, 1513, by the assistance of the Swiss, in driving the French under Louis XII., out of Italy, thought it as well that the fresco should contain some allusion to this long desired event.[1] Raphael, then, had to replace St. Leo and his train, by Leo X. with his court. A few very animated groups of soldiers had to be sacrificed; but on the whole the composition gained by the alteration, from the contrast of the calm gentleness of the pontiff with the ferocity of the barbarians.

In execution this fresco may be considered as one of the most perfect by this master. We have already drawn attention to the variety of the groups, the clearness of the ordering, the truth and movement of the figures. We must also admire the fulness and facility of the execution, the correctness of the drawing, the beauty of the colouring, especially in the group of the Pope and his train; the brilliancy of the two figures in

---

[1] A Latin poem of Gyraldi's, brought to light by W. Roscoe, Esq., celebrates the same event taken in the same form from the tradition, the expulsion of the Huns by St. Leo. The masquerade at Florence, which in the year 1514 represented the triumph of Camillus over the Gauls, was also an allusion to the same incident. It was at this time a very common practice in Italy to symbolize contemporary events under the forms of antiquity.

the apparition, and the picturesque effect of the masses which surround Attila.

In the lower part of the walls eleven caryatides, painted to resemble white marble, support the moulding painted below the frescoes; small pictures of bronze colour fill up the intervals. The subjects and the signification of these caryatides are so many allegories of the prosperity of the state under Leo X.

If we now compare the two series of works which decorate these two Stanze of the Vatican, we shall notice that the works in the first room are especially remarkable for the grandeur of their subjects, the depth of thought displayed in them, the pureness of the drawing, and the severe beauty of the execution, whilst those in the second Stanza show greater experience in technical points. The execution is bolder, the colouring superior, the general disposition grander. The subjects are also more dramatic. Life and the violent feelings of the soul prevail in it, and carry away the spectator irresistibly.

The Stanza della Signatura does not show the same richness of painting as the Stanza of Heliodorus; but the subjects which are of a more elevated character, and treated with such magnificent simplicity, may perhaps give more entire satisfaction to the soul.

Chapter IV.

RAPHAEL UNDER LEO X.

(1513—1520.)

UNDER Julius II. Raphael had served a prince at once severe, courageous, persevering, and ambitious of illustrating his reign through the productions of art. The period was propitious for great enterprises, and by his ambitious ideas and the austerity of his character, Julius II. gave a fresh impulse to all that was going forward. The vast field for exertion which he opened to artists excited a fruitful emulation, and art was bringing forth marvels of all kinds at the time when the young painter of Urbino was executing his masterpieces.

Leo X., no less a friend of art than his predecessor, was, however, of a very different character. His high birth, brilliant education, his delicate taste—a family inheritance—his affable manners, and great prodigality, all contributed to gain the affection of all that approached him. His liberality to authors, poets, and artists, who flocked to Rome from all the states in Italy, has for ever rendered his name famous.

His predecessor, however, far surpassed him in energy and in the depth of his combinations. Julius II. pursued firmly and unhesitatingly his great aim of the consolidation of the papal power, and the deliverance of Italy from the foreign yoke, whilst, on the contrary, the politics of Leo X. were narrower, as he sought principally the advancement of his own family. Julius II., by the wise administration of his resources, was able to ensure the continuation of his gigantic labours in art; whilst Leo X., by his exaggerated magnificence and unbounded generosity, so squandered his enormous income, that he often found himself in urgent need of money.

Posterity sees Leo X. in such glowing colours, because, far more than his predecessor, he patronised authors and poets, who in their turn extolled the name of Medici as a protector of arts and letters far more highly than that of Rovere.

On examining, however, the literary and artistic works during the reign of Leo X., we see a prevailing tendency to imitate too closely the antique style, so useful as a study; but at the period of which we speak it became a passion, and carried its votaries far beyond the natural limits: they no longer sought merely to imitate the perfect forms and the sentiment of the beautiful with the ancients, but even carried their enthusiasm so far as to admire their failings.

In painting, we find already amongst the artists who commenced their labours at the time when art had already reached its highest limits, a certain relaxing and an increasing propensity to a sort of sensualism. This propensity, at first scarcely sensible, soon degenerated into a vicious licence, and the rapid decay of art ensued.

Raphael, more than any other artist, resisted this general fascination. He felt, indeed, a profound sympathy for the works of the Greeks and Romans of ancient times, but his noble nature always preserved him from the corrupting influences then beginning to be felt. His mythological subjects even, so marvellously endued with ancient taste, are always chaste and pure. He never deviated from the true path of art.

At the accession of Leo X. Raphael had already passed five years at Rome. His position as an artist procured him the acquaintance of the most distinguished personages at the court, besides those whom he had formerly known at Urbino and Florence. All those who at first were merely admirers of his genius, through his extreme kindness and amiability, had become his firm friends.

The Count Baldassare Castiglione[1] occupies one of the first places amongst the friends of Raphael. He had come to Rome on a mission from Francesco Maria, Duke of Urbino, to Leo X., newly elected Pope. How great must his emotion have been on seeing these magnificent works of Raphael! He was delighted to see him again. He also met

---

[1] He was born at Casatico, near Mantua. We have already spoken of him several times.

at Rome Jacopo Sadoleto, Pietro Bembo, Federico Fregoso, Filippo Beroaldo the younger, Antonio Tebaldeo, Andrea Navagero, Agostino Beazzano, all old friends of his. His amiable qualities, learning, and interest in art and science, made him the foremost in this remarkable circle.[1]

Raphael painted two portraits of Castiglione; one only in bust, the other half-length. The latter is in the Louvre. It corresponds perfectly to the idea we form of this cultivated gentleman from reading his "Cortegiano."

Pietro Bembo, another intimate friend of Raphael's, is already known to us. He had only paid short visits to Rome in 1510 and 1511; but in 1512, having accompanied Giulio de' Medici to that city, he remained there for seven consecutive years. Leo X., before becoming Pope, had chosen him as his private secretary, with a salary of three thousand scudi per annum. Bettinelli says that Bembo brought back the times of Cicero and Virgil, and that his style recalled that of Petrarch and Boccaccio. At Rome Bembo formed an intimacy with a certain Morosina, much praised for her beauty. By her he had two sons and a daughter. In 1519, he returned to Padua, his onerous duties having injured his health, already very delicate. At a subsequent period, when Paul III. was raised to the pontificate, he returned to Rome, where

---

[1] The following verses prove that he was much admired as a poet in the antique style. They are by Marcantonio Flaminio ("Carmina, L. i. De laudibus Mantuæ"):

> "Felix Mantua, centiesque felix
> Tantis Mantua dotibus beata;
> Sed felix magis, et magis beata,
> Quod his temporibus, rudique sæclo
> Magnum Castaliona protulisti."

Another poem of Flaminio's praises Castiglione both as a warrior and a poet:

> "Si truculenta ferox irrumpis in agmina, Marte,
> Diceris invicto Castilione satus;
> At molli cithara si condis amabile carmen,
> Castalia natus diceris esse Dea."

The Count of Castiglione was ambassador from the pontifical Court, to Charles V. in 1525, and he died in Spain, Feb. 2nd, 1529. His body was conveyed to Mantua. His tomb, in the church of the "Madonna della Grazie," five miles from Mantua, was executed from the designs of Giulio Romano. Bembo wrote the funeral inscription. There is an engraving of this tomb in the "Monumenti di pittura, scultura, trascelti in Mantova, o nel suo territorio."—*Mantova*, 1827, pl. xx.

he spent the rest of his days in intimate relation with his old friends the Cardinals Contarini, Sadoleto, Cortese, and Reginald Pole.[1] He died in 1547, more than seventy years of age.

Sadoleto received the same distinction as Bembo; he also was named private secretary by Leo X., while the latter was still a cardinal. A great theologian, a distinguished poet, a learned archeologist, and an intimate friend of Erasmus of Rotterdam,[2] he was the only one of the Roman prelates who in matters relating to the reformation remained moderate.

Andrea Navagero and Agostino Beazzano, both distinguished authors, were also intimate with Raphael, Castiglione, and Bembo. A letter from Bembo to Cardinal Bibiena, of April 3rd, 1516, gives an interesting testimony to these relations—"To-morrow, after twenty-seven years, I shall once more visit Tivoli, in company with Navagero, Beazzano, the Signor Baldassare, Castiglione, and Raphael. We intend to see everything, the antique and the modern. We are going for the pleasure of the Signor Andrea, who will return to Venice after Easter."

Raphael painted the portraits of these two distinguished writers, on one panel, for Bembo. This is proved by a letter of Bembo's, and by the copy of the portraits, which is preserved in the Doria palace at Rome; but they have been wrongly called by the names of Bartolus and Baldus. Navagero, with black hair and beard, has a very grave expression; Beazzano looks more agreeable.

This latter assisted Bembo in various business either connected with matters of the state or of science. He was employed in many important missions by Leo X. After the death of this Pope he left the court, and lived[3] at Treviso during the last eighteen years of his life.

Navagero, who was of a noble family, was born in the same year as Raphael. An active member of the Venetian academy, he continued, at the request of the Senate the "History of Venice," left incomplete by Sabellicus; but he afterwards burned his manuscript, with several others

---

[1] Cardinal Pole was an Englishman who enjoyed great consideration at the Papal Court and in the literary world.

[2] Erasmus was at Rome at the time of the election of the successor of Julius II. The evening before the day on which Giovanni di Medici arrived, Erasmus being in the company of several gentlemen, he said, greatly to their surprise, that none of the cardinals then at Rome would be elected pope. See the "History of Leo X." by Paolo Giovio.

[3] According to the testimony of Ariosto.

of his works. Having been sent as ambassador to the court of Francis I. at Blois, he died there in 1528. His friend and fellow-citizen Beazzaro wrote a poem on his death, which is praised by Bembo.[1]

Raphael also counted among his friends two of the greatest poets of the time, Jacopo Sanazzaro and Antonio Tebaldeo, members of the Neapolitan Academy.

Sanazzaro, born in 1458, was obliged, after the disasters that had befallen his country, to take refuge at Rome under Leo X., and he there wrote his celebrated poem, "De partu Virginis."

Tebaldeo likewise came to Rome at the beginning of Leo's pontificate. He had composed a poem in honour of the Pope, who received him with distinction, and presented him with five hundred ducats.

Bottari was the first to recognise that Raphael had introduced the portraits of these two poets into his "Parnassus." We may add with certainty that Raphael also painted the portrait of Tebaldeo in oil. Bembo mentions it with high praise in a letter of April 19th, 1516, to Cardinal Bibiena. But it is not known what became of this portrait, and none of those, said to be it, represent the right person.

Raphael also kept up a friendship and correspondence with Ariosto, according to Richardson. We have already spoken of the letter, which, according to the same writer, was in the possession of the Chevalier del Pozzo, and in which the painter asked the poet's advice as to the personages to be introduced in the "Dispute on the Sacrament." Ariosto, however, did not remain long at Rome. He had known Giovanni de' Medici before his elevation to the pontificate, and hoped to find a protector in him. And, indeed, the Pope received him with much cordiality, did not suffer him to remain kneeling before him, and promised him his favour. But, alas! the great poet obtained nothing, unless, indeed, it were permission to publish his poem of "Orlando Furioso." Deceived in his expectations, he quitted Rome, determined never to return.

Amongst the men of high rank who protected Raphael were the Cardinals Riario and Giulio de' Medici, afterwards Clement VII. We have already alluded to the former; Giulio de' Medici, natural son of Giuliano, was legitimatized by his uncle, Leo X., who first nominated him Archbishop of Florence, then cardinal, and afterwards chancellor. He was of a serious disposition, much attached to his family, and especially

---

[1] See the letter addressed to Beazzaro, June 29, 1529, in Bembo's correspondence.

to the Pope, to whom he rendered signal services. It was for him that Raphael painted his last work, the "Transfiguration." He also made for him a design for a villa (now called the villa Madonna) on Monte Mario.

The President of the Chancery, Baldassare Turini da Pescia, and Gio. Battista Branconio dall' Aquila, were also amongst the number of Raphael's friends. He nominated them afterwards his executors. For Branconio dall' Aquila, he painted the superb picture of the "Visitation" in the Madrid Museum, and drew the plan for the façade of a palace situated formerly opposite the church of St. Peter's. This palace of Branconio has frequently been erroneously indicated as having been the residence of the artist himself.

After Raphael's death, his pupil Giulio Romano built for President Turini the beautiful villa (villa Lante) on Monte Janiculus, where the proprietor caused, amongst other portraits, those of Raphael and his mistress to be painted in one of his apartments.

Raphael had also very intimate relations with Bernardo Divizio da Bibiena, whom we have already met at the court of Urbino, and who was named by Leo X. Cardinal of Santa Maria in Portico.

We shall see presently[1] that the cardinal wished to attach Raphael more closely to himself in bonds of relationship, by giving him the hand of one of his nieces.

Raphael has painted a magnificent portrait of Bibiena,[2] in which the statesman and man of the world are powerfully depicted.

He also painted immediately after the elevation of Leo X. the portrait of a distinguished individual, the librarian Tommaso Phædra Inghirami, of a noble family at Volterra.

Having lost his father in the civil disturbances of his country, Tommaso, when only two years of age, had been taken to Florence, where the Medici took him under their special protection. When he had attained his thirteenth year, he was sent to Rome, and his precocious talents soon brought him into notice.

---

[1] In a letter from Raphael to his uncle Ciarla. See p. 141.

[2] It was taken to Spain by Count Castiglione. It now adorns the Museum of Madrid.*

---

* It is no doubt the picture marked No. 905 of the Catalogue: "Portrait of a Cardinal—unknown. . . . It is thought that it may represent Giulio de' Medici. . . ." M. Viardot also considered it to be a portrait of Giulio de' Medici.

His name of Phædra was given him in consequence of a singular proof of talent and presence of mind. One day he, with several of his friends, was acting in the palace of the Cardinal di San Giorgio, the tragedy of "Hippolytus," by Seneca, in which he took the part of Phædra, when some disturbance took place in the machinery, and the play was interrupted. Inghirami then advanced towards the auditory, and amused them by an improvisation of Latin verse. Immense applause followed, and the spectators shouted, "Viva, Phædra!" This name clung to him, and he afterwards added it to his own.

Inghirami was sent by Alexander VI. on an embassy to Maximilian, who was a patron of the arts and sciences, and who conferred on him the title of Count Palatine, with permission to add the Imperial eagle to his arms. In 1510 he was appointed Bishop of Ragusa by Julius II., and at the conclave in which Giovanni de' Medici was elected Pope, he filled the office of secretary. It was in the costume of this office, which was entirely of red, that Raphael painted him. This portrait is in the Pitti palace. He is represented as being very stout, and with a cast in his eye. He holds a pen, and is raising his eyes, as if listening to a discussion, in order to take it down afterwards. The truth of the expression is surprising; the head, modelled with the greatest care, is in full light. This effect reminds us of Holbein's portraits. It is possible that Raphael may have seen some paintings by this master; for Erasmus, who was then at Rome, possessed some pictures by his friend Hans Holbein.

At this time Raphael had attained a high position. His fortune had increased with his renown. He wished to have a house for himself, and made plans for it, after having chosen a site on the Via di Borgo Nuova, in the vicinity of the Vatican. His intercourse with Bramante had developed his talent in architecture, in which he always took a deep interest. The plan for his own house was very elegant and tasteful. Bramante conducted the works, and for some salient parts, such as the columns and the bossage, he employed bricks and mortar, shaped in wooden moulds, a new process, which had great success at the time.

The ground floor of the façade was of rustic architecture, with five arched doors, four of which were for the offices, and the one in the centre for the entrance to the house. The upper story was of Doric order, with coupled columns, and five windows surmounted by triangular pediments. The entablature which surmounted the whole was of a severe style, imitated from the antique.

This beautiful building no longer exists. The angle of the right of the basement which now forms a part of the Accoramboni palace, is the only part that remains. We owe our acquaintance with its façade to the engraving published by Antonio Lafrerio in 1549, under the title "Raph. Urbinas ex lapide coctili Romæ extractum." The only copy of this engraving known is in the library of Prince Corsini at Rome. It has been copied by Pontani in his work on the architecture of Raphael.

The friendship between Raphael and Bramante never failed.[1] The painter and the architect mutually assisted each other with their advice. When Bramante, at the desire of Cardinal Grimani, caused wax models to be executed for the group of the Laocoon, to be afterwards copied in bronze, he showed them to Raphael, that he might decide which was the finest. Vasari names amongst the candidates, Zacchèri Zachi, of Volterra, the Spaniard Alonzo Berruguete, the old Giovanni of Bologna, and Jacopo Sansovino. Raphael much preferred the model of Sansovino, which was accordingly cast in bronze.

This group, yielded by the cardinal to the Government of Venice, adorned the hall of the Council of Ten. In 1534 it was taken to France by the Cardinal Guise of Lorraine; and now, if we are not mistaken, it is in the gardens of the Tuileries.

We shall speak later of the numerous pupils and artists who ranged themselves round the master of Urbino. Here we will only remind our readers that the influence of Raphael was so great, that all those who approached him laid aside their own artistic individuality, and sought to adopt his mind and manners.

This fact was so general that Raphael said smilingly one day to Cesare da Sesto, one of the most distinguished pupils of Da Vinci, and whom he was very fond of, "How does it happen, dear Cesare, that we live in such good friendship, but that in the art of painting we show no deference to each other?"[2] At a later period Cesare was likewise subjugated, and endeavoured to unite the particular styles of the two great masters.

Yet Raphael could not succeed in attracting to Rome, two of his dearest friends and early companions, Domenico di Paris Alfani, of Perugia, and Ridolfo del Ghirlandajo, of Florence, with whom he much

---

[1] In his "Tempio della pittura" (p. 14), Lomazzo relates that Bramante wrote a Treatise on the proportions of men and horses, which he afterwards presented to his relative Raphael da Urbino.

[2] Lomazzo, "Tempio della pittura," p. 107.

wished to renew his intimacy. One was detained at home by domestic cares, and nothing could prevail on the other to pass the limit from whence, as the Florentines say, he would be able to see the dome of the cathedral.

To make up for this deprivation, however, Raphael had the pleasure of meeting his friend Fra Bartolomeo again. The frate had yielded to his desire to behold the works with which Michael Angelo and Raphael had so much adorned the eternal city. He himself undertook some works in that town, but the climate not proving favourable to him, he was obliged to leave, and he entrusted to Raphael the completion of a St. Peter and St. Paul, which had been ordered by Fra Mariano Fetti, for the church of San Silvestro on the Monte Cavallo. These two pictures are now in the Quirinal. Raphael's hand may be especially noticed in the St. Peter, by a certain energy and resolution, which are never found in the other works of Fra Bartolomeo.

Two cardinals with whom Raphael was very intimate visited him at the very moment when he was busy with these pictures. They had arranged to get him into a discussion on art, and not knowing exactly how to set about it, they remarked that the heads of the apostles were too red. Raphael had guessed their intention, and, to save the honour of his friend, he replied, smiling, "You need not be surprised, I have given them that colour after deliberate reflection; for it may well be supposed that the apostles St. Peter and St. Paul must blush as deeply in heaven as in these pictures, on seeing the church governed by such men as you." [1]

At this time Leonardo da Vinci also visited Rome, attracted, like Bartolomeo, by the works of Michael Angelo and Raphael. According to a notice written with his own hand,[2] he left Milan September 24, 1513, followed by his pupils Giovanni Boltraffio,[3] Francesco Melzi, Salai, Lorenzo and Fanfoja.

The journey commenced under happy auspices, for Leonardo met

---

[1] This anecdote is related by Count Castiglione, in the first chapter of his "Cortegiano," p. 213. It is not indeed stated that the pictures had been commenced by Fra Bartolomeo; but, as Raphael has only this once painted the isolated figures of these two Apostles, and as the colouring of Fra Bartolomeo rather inclined to the red, there is every probability that this refers to the pictures of the Florentine master.

[2] Codex B. of the Ambrosian library, now in the library of the Fine Arts in Paris. It is not known exactly whether it was in 1513 or in 1514 that Leonardo da Vinci came to Rome.

[3] Passavant, Waagen (in his Catalogue of the Berlin Museum), and the greater part of the Germans write Boltraffio, following Vasari. The Catalogue of the Louvre writes Beltraffio.—*Lacroix.*

Giuliano de' Medici, who showed him particular attention, and who, charmed to obtain so delightful a companion, invited him to travel with him. It is said that to beguile the long journey, and amuse the prince, the artist, ingenious in everything, modelled a quantity of small fantastic figures in wax, so light that when laid on the hand they flew away.

At Rome, he was received with great favour by the Pope, who ordered paintings of him. It was at this period and when at Rome that he executed a "Holy Family," said to be that now at St. Petersburg.[1]

Raphael must certainly have been filled with admiration for him, and with his natural amiability would have shown the greatest respect to the master, who was growing old, though still a "Prometheus," as Lomazzo called him.

It was not the same with Buonarroti,[2] who had violent quarrels with Leonardo, and involved him in serious embarrassment. Da Vinci in consequence quitted Rome, the following year; and in January, 1516, he even left Florence when the influence of Michael Angelo had caused him to be excluded from the competition for the plan of the façade of the basilica of San Lorenzo.

It was about this time that the relations of Raphael with Albrecht Dürer commenced. Their genius was much alike in character; in both was there the same richness and even depth of imagination. Both were equally dramatic in their arrangement, both likewise excelled in other branches of art.

Their physical nature was also in harmony. Dürer was remarkably handsome, and his beauty was set off by qualities which endeared him to others—goodness and devotion.

His activity was ceaseless. If he had been initiated in ancient art, if, instead of being born in the Gothic Nuremberg, he had first seen the day in Rome or Florence, this master, admirable as he was, would have attained the height of a Leonardo da Vinci or a Raphael.

Albrecht Dürer, when he went to Bologna, had taken with him some of his engravings, Raphael had probably seen them in the house of Francia, and they doubtless made him anxious to enter into communications with the Nuremberg master. However this may be, it is certain that Albrecht Dürer sent some drawings to Raphael, among which was

---

[1] M. Viardot in his "Musées de Russie," (p. 469), contests this Holy Family with great energy, calling it "une page défectueuse . . . où tout est laid, dis-gracieux grimaçant," etc.—*Lacroix.*

[2] See Vasari.

his own portrait, painted in water-colours, on such fine linen that the painting might be seen on both sides. The lights had not been laid on with white, but had been managed on the linen itself, which Raphael admired very much.

Giulio Romano afterwards possessed this portrait, as a bequest from his master, and held it in high honour;[1] Sandrart saw it in the collection of works of art at Mantua. It is not known whether it passed with the other pictures in this gallery into that of Charles I. of England, but at present all trace has been lost of it.

Raphael in return, sent several drawings to Dürer. One of these drawings (in the Albertine collection at Vienna),[2] is a fine study in red crayon of two naked men, one of which served for the captain standing by the side of the Pope in the "Victory of Ostia." Dürer wrote on it the following note: "1515. Raphael da Urbino, who is so highly esteemed by the Pope, has drawn this study from the nude, and has sent it to Albrecht Dürer at Nürnberg, in order to show him his manner of drawing."

The two great masters always remained in friendly relations, as Vasari relates in his "Life of Marcantonio." This may also be seen from Dürer's journal, where he makes the remark, in 1520, that he had given to Tommaso of Bologna[3] a complete copy of his engraved works, in order that another painter might take it to Rome, and that Raphael might send back in exchange, engravings from his own works.[4]

According to Dolce, Raphael had already many works by German artists in his studio, and praised them highly.[5]

---

[1] See Vasari.

[2] Richardson, in his "Travels," p. 13, mentions another: "A sketch of Raphael's, with a drawing by Albert Dürer on the reverse, in the Crozat collection."

[3] Dürer names him Thomas Polonius, and adds, "Polonius has taken my portrait, and wishes to take it to Rome." See "Reliquien von Albrecht Dürer," p. 98. As a portrait of Dürer was engraved by Andrew Stock, in 1629, from a drawing by Tommaso Vincidoro of Bologna, it appears probable that this Polonius was no other than Vincidoro.

[4] The entry in Dürer's journal records that it was not until the Monday after Michaelmas in 1520, that he sent his engraved works to Rome; he could not therefore possibly have meant that Raphael himself was to send back engravings—"Ding," as he calls them, in exchange, Raphael having died in the preceding April. In a previous passage in the journal, also, Dürer states that "Raphael von Urbino's things were all scattered after his death." It was probably some of these scattered "things"—drawings and such like, that he sought to possess.—*Trans.*

[5] "Dialogo della pittura," by Ludovico Dolce, surnamed Aretino, because Pietro Aretino had supplied the materials for these dialogues.

As we are speaking of engravings from Raphael's drawings, we ought to mention here that Marcantonio Raimondi came from the school of Francia to Rome, about 1510. After his first engraving of a "Lucretia," from one of Raphael's drawings, the latter was so much pleased with it, that he immediately set about fresh drawings, intended to be multiplied by engraving and spread over the world like those of Albert Dürer.

According to Vasari, the plates that Raimondi undertook for Raphael, after this "Lucretia," were the "Judgment of Paris," "Neptune subduing the Sea" (which plate is also named the "Quos ego,") the "Massacre of the Innocents," &c.

The study for the figure of a man in this last work, is also on the same sheet as a study of the figure of a woman for the "Judgment of Solomon," in the Stanza della Signatura. The "Massacre of the Innocents" must have been engraved then about 1510, in the same year as Raimondi engraved, from the cartoon of Michael Angelo, the "Climbers," a plate which clearly shows the hand of a master. For this reason we believe that the arrival of Marcantonio at Rome must have been in 1510, and that he immediately commenced his numerous studies from Raphael's drawings.

The plates that Raphael received from Raimondi he gave to a certain Baviera, a servant of his mistress. This Baviera printed them, superintended the sale and had a share in the profits, which were very considerable. Seeing this success, several artists began to engrave the works of Raphael, amongst others Marco da Ravenna and Agostino Veneziano. In this way nearly all the works of the great master have been preserved to posterity.

Hugo da Carpi has also immortalized several of Raphael's drawings by wood engravings from several blocks of wood, a method of printing already known in Germany, and which is called engraving in chiaroscuro.[1]

It is whilst speaking of these engravings that Vasari first mentions

---

[1] The most ancient engravings from two blocks with a date, are two wood engravings by Lucas Cranach, "Venus and Cupid," and a "St. Christopher;" they are dated 1506. Jost de Nocker, (born at Antwerp,) in a letter from Augsburg which he addressed to the emperor Maximilian, says that he is the inventor of engraving in chiaroscuro from three blocks; and indeed we possess engravings of this kind from his hand, according to Hans Burgkmair, with the date of 1510. Hugo da Carpi was not then, as Vasari asserts, the inventor of this style of engraving, since his works are dated 1518, and consequently are much later than those of the German masters.

Raphael's mistress. Many investigations have been made on the subject but without any satisfactory result. The interest of the subject, however, justifies us in giving all the information we have been able to collect.

During the early part of his residence at Rome, in the flower of youth, and full of the brightest hopes, when he was occupied with the frescoes for the first Stanza of the Vatican, Raphael fell in love, and even endeavoured to express his passion in three sonnets. The rough copies of these poems are written on several of the studies for the "Disputa," preserved in the collections of Vienna, London, Oxford, and Montpellier.

These sonnets do not possess a high poetic value. However, a certain grace may be perceived in them, especially in the following, the original of which is in the British Museum :

"Un pensier dolce e rimembrare e godo [1]
Di quello asalto, ma più gravo el danno
Del partir, ch' io restai como quei c' anno
In mar perso la stella, s' el ver odo.
O lingua di parlar disogli el nodo
A dir di questo inusitato inganno
Ch' amor mi fece per mio grave afanno
Ma lui più ne ringratio, e lei ne lodo.
L' ora sesta era, che l' ocaso un sole
Aveva fatto, e l' altro surce in locho
Ati più da far fati, che parole.
Ma io restai pur vinto al mio gran focho
Che mi tormenta, che dove l' on sole
Diserar di parlar, più riman fiocho."

But who could this young girl have been whom Raphael loved? All that we can say with any certainty is that she was named Margarita, for she is mentioned by this name, in a note written in the sixteenth century on the margin of an edition of Vasari of 1568, which belongs to the barrister Giuseppe Vannutelli at Rome. This note is written by the side of the passage in which Riviera, who served Raphael's mistress, is spoken of: "Ritratto di Margarita donna di Raffaello;" and by the side of these words, "che pareva viva," the name Margarita is repeated.[2]

---

[1] The last word of this line no longer exists in the original ; it seems tolerably well replaced by "godo." In a rough copy of the same sonnet (in the Albertine Collection) there is "in modo," but afterwards the second line takes a different turn.

[2] See Visconti, "Istoria del trovamento delle spoglie mortali di Raffaello Sanzio da Urbino" Roma, 1833, p. 85.

She has also been given the name of the Fornarina, and according to Missirini[1] she was the daughter of a soda manufacturer, who lived near Santa Cecilia, on the other side of the Tiber. A small house, No. 20, in the street of Santa Dorotea, the windows of which, decorated with a pretty framework of earthenware, is pointed out as the house where she was born.

The beautiful young girl was very frequently in a little garden adjoining the house, where, the wall not being very high, it was easy to see her from outside. So the young men, especially artists—always passionate admirers of beauty—did not fail to come and look at her, by climbing up above the wall.

Raphael is said to have seen her for the first time as she was bathing her pretty feet in a little fountain in the garden. Struck by her perfect beauty, he fell deeply in love with her, and after having made acquaintance with her, and discovered that her mind was as beautiful as her body, he became so much attached as to be unable to live without her.

This story is certainly very attractive, and it is supported by a small picture, attributed to Sebastiano del Piombo, in which Raphael is seated near the fountain in the garden, with his lady-love.[2] But recent investigations have proved that this story is a pure invention, and even that the name of the Fornarina was only invented about the middle of the eighteenth century.[3] We must, then, content ourselves with the very

---

[1] M. Missirini to R. Arregoni, "in Longhena," p. 657.

[2] This little picture, belonging to Lord Northwick, was engraved in aqua-tinta by Reynolds, as a work of Sebastiano del Piombo's. But it was made up in the last century. The lower part of the drapery and the feet are imitated from the allegorical figure of "Poetry" by Raphael.

[3] Missirini asserts that he received his account from the conscientious writer, the late Abbé Francesco Girolamo Cancellieri, who had found it in a manuscript in the library of Cardinal Antonelli. But the Chevalier V. Carnuccini declares that Cancellieri merely wished to prove that Raphael's death was not caused by a woman. Pungileoni also says that Cancellieri, with whom he was intimate, never told him that he had made any discoveries as to Raphael's mistress.

The name of Fornarina, the origin of which is unknown, seems to have been mentioned for the first time in the "Real Galleria di Firenze" (vol. i. p. 6,) of T. Puccini. Bottari and the later writer G. della Valle, do not speak of Raphael's mistress by this name.

M. de Rumohr ("Italienischen Forschungen," vol. iii. p. 113,) takes up the tradition, long since abandoned as untenable, that Raphael had had a *liaison* at Urbino with the daughter of a potter, and he quotes in support of this, "a plate on which was painted

simple statement of Vasari—that Raphael loved a young girl, who lived with him, and to whom he was devotedly attached to the last moment of his life.

According to the same writer,[1] we might believe that Raphael painted several portraits of his mistress. Two are known which have good pretensions to represent her.

The first is of a young girl, only half-clothed, seated in a myrtle and laurel wood. A striped yellow stuff surrounds her head as a turban, and imparts something distinguished and charming to features which otherwise have little expression. With her right hand she holds a light gauze against her breast. Her right arm, encircled with a golden bracelet, rests on her knees, which are covered by red drapery. On the bracelet Raphael has inscribed his name with the greatest care.

The original, of which many old copies are to be found at Rome, is noticed since the year 1642, as being among the pictures in the Barberini palace at Rome, and cannot be the one that Vasari mentions as having belonged in his time to a merchant named Matteo Botti, a friend of Raphael's; for, until the year 1677, this latter picture is mentioned in the Belezze di Firenze as still belonging to the descendants of Botti.

But since 1824 there has been the portrait of a woman in the Pitti palace, at Florence, whose name is not inscribed in the catalogue of the Tribune, and which came from the collection of the Grand Duke of Tuscany. This must be the portrait of Raphael's mistress mentioned by Vasari.

---

a fair young man, embracing a young girl in a pottery workshop." Dr. G. K. Nagler (" Raphael als Mensch ") even supposes that this potter's daughter went to Rome and was no other than the pretended Fornarina ! Without taking much trouble to confute these stories, we need scarcely remark that at this period there was no manufactory of Majolica at Urbino. There was one at Fermignano, three miles off ; another at Urbania, formerly Castel Durante, at a distance of sixteen miles, and the most ancient of all at Gubbio, on the other slope of the mountain.

[1] " Raphael painted the portrait of Beatrice of Ferrara, with those of other ladies ; that of his own innamorata is more particularly to be specified ; but he also executed others." In another place Vasari says : " Marco Antonio subsequently executed a number of engravings, which were afterwards given by Raphael to il Baviera, his disciple, who was the guardian of a certain lady, to whom Raphael was attached till the day of his death, and of whom he painted a most beautiful portrait, which might be supposed alive. This is now at Florence, in the possession of the good and worthy Botti, a Florentine merchant of that city, who is the friend and favourer of all distinguished men, but more especially of painters ; by him the work is treasured as if it were a relic, for the love which he bears to the art, but more especially to Raphael.

This portrait in the Pitti Palace bears a strong resemblance to the Madonna di San Sisto (Dresden Museum), with this difference, however, that the features of the Virgin are ennobled. The woman in the portrait is a handsome Roman, but of quite individual character. Her form is powerful, her costume sumptuous, her beautiful black eyes flash, her mouth is refined and full of grace.

If this portrait, as may well be believed, represents the same person as that of the Barberini house, we are compelled to admit that the countenance, always intelligent, of this young girl, had become wonderfully animated in the time between the execution of the two portraits. However, if this really be the portrait of Raphael's mistress, it would be indeed astonishing if constant intercourse with the author of so many masterpieces, and one of the most perfect human organizations that nature ever produced, should have failed to influence the facile character of a young girl.

This second portrait, to judge by the manner in which it is painted, must belong to the last years of Raphael's life, as it is not completely terminated.

Two sentences of Vasari's and these two portraits, are all the authentic information we have as to the mistress of Raphael.

But we have a valuable document by the hand of the master himself, containing details of the highest interest as to his own position and prospects. This is a letter which he wrote from Rome to his uncle Simone Ciarla, at Urbino. The most important information, however, contained in this letter relates to the instructions given to Raphael by Leo X., when superintending the works in the church of St. Peter's. We shall return to that at a later time.

The following is the letter—

"To my uncle, dear to me as a father, Simone di Battista di Ciarla da Urbino, at Urbino.

"I have received your dear letter, and am happy to see by it that you are not angry with me, though indeed you would be wrong, if you consider how difficult it is to write without a serious motive. To-day, as there is something of importance to say, I reply to you at once.

"In the first place, as to taking a wife, I will say in regard to her whom you destined for me, that I am very glad, and thank God for not having taken either her or another. And in this I have been wiser than you who wished to give her to me. I am convinced that you see yourself that I should not have got on as I have done. I have already property at Rome to the amount of 3,000 ducats of gold (£862 10*s.*), and an income of 50 ducats (£14 7*s.* 6*d.*). Then his Holiness, our Lord, has proposed to me some works in the church of St. Peter, with a salary of 300 ducats of gold (£86 5*s.*), which will not fail me as long as I live. This is not all. Besides this, they will pay me for my work whatever may seem right to me. The paintings also in another hall that I have undertaken will produce 1,200 ducats of gold (£345). Thus, then, dear uncle, I am doing honour to you as well as to my other relations and to my native town. I bear you continually in my heart, and, when I hear you mentioned, it seems as if I heard my father named. Do not complain of me, then, if I do not write oftener, since it should be rather I to complain of you, who have a pen in your hand all day, and yet allow six months to pass between one letter and another. Notwithstanding all, however, I am not angry with you, as you are unjustly with me.

"I had left off speaking of my marriage, but return to it, to tell you that the Cardinal of Santa Maria in Portico wishes to give me one of his relations,[1] and that with the consent of my uncle the priest (D. Bartolomeo Santi) and your consent, I have placed myself at the disposition of his lordship. I cannot withdraw my word; we are nearer than ever to the conclusion, and I will inform you immediately of everything. Do not be vexed if this affair end well; but if it should not, I will do what you wish. And know that if Francesco Buffa finds good matches, I can do so too; for I might have a beautiful young lady at Rome, and, by what I hear, both herself and her relations of good reputation, with a dowry of 3,000 scudi of gold; and be sure that 100 crowns at Rome are worth more than 200 at Urbino.

"As to my sojourn in Rome, I cannot from love for the works of St. Peter's, remain long elsewhere, for I have at present the place of Bramante. And what city in the world is worthier than Rome, and what enterprise greater than St. Peter's, the first temple in the world? It is the greatest building ever seen, and will cost more than a million of gold (£287,500). The Pope has granted 60,000 ducats (£17,250) a year

---

[1] Her name was Maria; she was the daughter of Antonio Divizio da Bibiena, the nephew of the cardinal. In January, 1515, the cardinal married another of his nieces, named Chiaretta Marietta, or Marianna, the daughter of his brother Pietro, to Bernardino Peroli da Urbino, the treasurer-general of the Pope's army, and gave her a dowry of 5,000 gold scudi. See "Pungileoni," pp. 160, 166, and 241.

for the works, and he thinks of nothing else. He has given me as a colleague a very learned frate, of at least eighty years of age, and who has not long to live. His Holiness gave me this man of great reputation and great learning for a colleague, that I might profit by him, and if he has a noble secret in architecture, that I might learn it also, and thus attain perfection in the art. He is named Fra Giocondo. The Pope sends for us every day, and speaks to us for some time about the works. I pray you to go to the duke and duchess and tell them all this; for I know that it gives them pleasure to hear that one of their subjects is doing them honour, and commend me to their highnesses, as I also commend myself to you. Salute all my friends and relations in my name, and especially Ridolfo, who bears such great and kind affection to me.

"This July 1st, 1514.

"Your RAFAEL, painter at Rome."

It would seem from this letter that Raphael had consented rather through condescension than inclination to the marriage proposed for him with the niece of Cardinal Bibiena.[1] We know, however,[2] that two years later, 1516, he was still very intimate with Cardinal Bibiena, and that the project for the alliance still subsisted. This is proved besides by the inscription in memory of Maria da Bibiena, in Raphael's sepulchral chapel in the Pantheon, and from which it appears that Maria died before Raphael. It has been supposed that Maria, being very delicate, it was necessary to delay the marriage, and that her death alone put an end to these projects and hopes. Notwithstanding this, many have imagined that Raphael himself was reluctant to realize his union with Maria da Bibiena. Some writers have attributed to him, without any proof, a decided aversion to this marriage. Others have repeated the assertion of Vasari that he always endeavoured to defer this alliance, because he hoped to obtain a cardinal's hat, as a compensation for the money that the Pope owed him; but this is entirely imaginary, for all the works were paid for punctually[3] at the time fixed. There could not, moreover, be

---

[1] Angelo Maria Bandini: "Memorie per la vita del card. Divizj," Livorno, 1758, p. 25. "The cardinal was extremely anxious to give him a wife, and at length Raphael resolved to be guided by Bibiena, and accepted a niece of the cardinal's as his bride."

[2] From Bembo's letters to Cardinal Bibiena. See "Delle Lettere di M. Pietro Bembo," Venezia, 1560, pp. 14-22.

[3] On Aug. 1, 1514, Raphael received the last 100 scudi still owing of the 1,200 gold

any question of this kind in 1514; and it would have been an unheard of thing that artistic merits should lead to such eminent dignities in the church. Except Vasari no cotemporary author has mentioned this supposition.

During the execution of the second Stanza in the Vatican, Raphael painted several pictures of large dimensions, especially the magnificent altar-piece for the church of San Domenico Maggiore at Naples. This is the "Madonna del Pesce," thus called in Spain, where it was afterwards carried. It is now in the Museum of Madrid.

The Virgin is seated on a throne with the child. The young Tobit, led by an angel, has come to implore a cure for his father's blindness. The infant Saviour is looking at him, and laying his hand on an open book, which St. Jerome is holding open before him.

The union of these personages is explained by the place the picture was intended to adorn. Diseases of the eyes being very common at Naples, a special chapel had been erected for those who were thus afflicted. Raphael's Madonna was intended for this chapel.

It is one of the finest works of the master, for in it we see the grand and powerful style of his manhood combined with the qualities of ardent faith which distinguish his earlier manner. The head of St. Jerome is noble and full of character; the angel appears living, and is of celestial beauty; the child is radiant with divine beauty, and even Raphael never surpassed the ideal loveliness of the Virgin. We may with perfect justice apply to this Madonna of Madrid the enthusiastic eulogy Vasari bestows on Raphael's Virgins in general: "Raphael has shown all the beauty which can be imagined in the expression of a Virgin; in the eyes there is modesty, on the brow there shines honour, the nose is of a very graceful character, the mouth betokens sweetness and excellence." The colouring also is vigorous, clear, and perfectly harmonious, and the tones are disposed with the greatest intelligence.

About the same time, Raphael undertook the celebrated fresco of "Galatea," in a hall of the Chigi palace, built by Baldassare Peruzzi. This architect had, in the first place, himself adorned the ceiling of the painted hall with pictures relating to the "History of Medusa," and

---

scudi for the "Stanza di Eliodoro." On the 1st April, 1519, the administration of the works of St. Peter's paid him the sum of 1,500 ducats, for his salary during five years. See Fea, "Notizie," etc. p. 9.

other mythological subjects. Sebastiano of Venice, afterwards surnamed del Piombo, had also painted subjects of the same nature in the lunettes of the arches round the hall. One only of these lunettes has not been painted, but in the place of a fresco there is a colossal head drawn in charcoal by Michael Angelo.

One day when Michael Angelo came to the Chigi palace to meet Sebastiano, who was not there, he left this magnificent head behind him as a visiting card. It has been asserted that he traced this head after a visit paid to Raphael, in order to induce him to adopt a grander style. However ridiculous this story may appear, we may as well answer it.

Sebastiano completed his lunettes in 1512, before Raphael had commenced the painting underneath, and it is scarcely probable that he would have left one of the lunettes empty, with its rough plaster work, in order that Michael Angelo, several years later, might give a lesson to Raphael. Besides this, after the scaffolding had been removed, even Michael Angelo's arm would have been unable to reach to the height of that head. We have only made these remarks in order to show, what very slight foundation some of these apocryphal stories possess. The "Galatea" is dated 1514. The subject is taken from the narrative of Philostratus about the Cyclops. The ancient poet shows us Galatea sailing in a conch shell drawn by dolphins, and accompanied by several nymphs. A red drapery floats in the wind over the head of the beautiful nereid, and protects her from the sun.

The painter followed the poet. In the fresco, Galatea is gently sailing on the waves. Love guides the shell, which is drawn by dolphins and surrounded by tritons and marine centaurs, who bear the nymphs. Little cupids in the air are shooting arrows at them. All these figures form a contrast with the beautiful Galatea, whose languid eyes are raised to heaven, the centre of all noble aspirations.

Galatea is an image of beauty of soul united to that of the body. It is, indeed, a sort of glorified nature; or rather a goddess clad in human form.

Raphael's genius defies all comparison; and has attained in this masterpiece a height which approaches very nearly to perfection.

"Galatea" met with a wonderful success from the very first. The following letter of Raphael's, replying to Count Castiglione, will enable us to judge of this:—

"Signor Count,

"I have made, in different styles, several drawings from the suggestions of your lordship. Every one is pleased with them, if every one does not flatter me. But, in my own judgment I could not be satisfied, for I fear not to satisfy you. I send you these drawings that your lordship may choose, if one be found worthy of you. Our Lord (the Pope), by giving me an honour has imposed a great burden on my shoulders. This is the care of the works for St. Peter's. I hope not to fail in it, the more so as my model pleases his Holiness and many other distinguished persons. But my thoughts rise higher. I want to find the beautiful forms of ancient buildings. I do not know whether it will be a flight of Icarus. Vitruvius gives me some light, yet not sufficient.

"As for 'the Galatea' I should think myself a great master if it possessed one half the merits of which you write, but I read in your words, the love you bear to myself. To paint a figure truly beautiful, I should see many beautiful forms, with the further provision that you should yourself be present to choose the most beautiful. But good judges and beautiful women being rare, I avail myself of certain ideas which come into my mind. If this idea has any excellence in art I know not, although I labour heartily to acquire it.

"I commend myself to your lordship,

"From Rome,

"RAFAEL."

One sentence of this letter appears remarkable to several theorists. It is the one in which Raphael says that, for want of a sufficiently perfect model, he made use of a certain idea or ideal. These writers have fancied they discovered in this expression, the germ of the arbitrary ideal tendency, which so soon induced a decay in art.

Raphael's thought is however clear enough, and he expresses it quite distinctly. It was not that he did not wish to draw from a living model; on the contrary he sought one, but finding nothing which came up to his refined taste, and the perfection of form which the study of the ancients had revealed to him, he was obliged to replace it from his own resources, and with a kind of second sight belonging to a really gifted artist. Neither the art nor the ideal of Raphael has anything conventional about it. Nature was its basis; and it is the perfection of nature which forms the ideal. Happy are those to whom Heaven has granted the power of feeling and expressing this ideal! for neither study nor reflection can bestow it. The drawings that Raphael sent to Castiglione were sketches for a medallion that the count,[1] according to the custom of the time, wished to wear in his cap, and the subject of which was to be the emblem of his principles.

A copy of this medal, in the Mazzuchelliani museum, shows on one side the portrait of Castiglione, and on the other, Phœbus descending from his car, with two allegorical figures of the hours holding his fiery horses. The inscription it bears is, "Tenebrarum et Lucis."

There has been much discussion as to the meaning of this subject. It symbolizes doubtless the idea of the propagation of light, to which the count devoted his active life.

Marcantonio Raimondi has also engraved from Raphael a similar work, "Aurora in her car, coming out of the waves." Two allegorical figures lead the horses.

It would appear then, that two of Raphael's compositions for the medal have been preserved. We have seen by the letters to Castiglione and to Ciarla, that Raphael had been nominated architect of St. Peter's. Bramante when dying[2] had recommended him as being the most suitable for the superintendence of the works. The Pope however wished to ascertain for himself Raphael's capacity in architecture; he asked him for some particulars as to the plan he would follow, and a general estimate of expenses. Raphael had a wooden model of his plan executed, which obtained universal admiration, and he was then named superintendent of the works of St. Peter's. His nomination,[3] dated August 1st, 1514, in the following terms:

---

[1] See Antonio Beffa Negrini, "Elogj de personaggi della Famiglia Castigliona," Mantova, 1606, p. 428.

[2] He died March 11, 1514. Baldassare Turini wrote to Lorenzo de' Medici, "Da Roma, hora 4 noctis, 12 marzo, 1514. . . . M. Bramante mori hier mattina, et Fra Mariano nostro ha havuto il loco suo." This was referring to his "Uffizio del Piombo." See Gaye "Carteggio," vol. ii. p. 135.

[3] It is printed in the "Petri Bembi epistolarum, Leonis decimi Pont. Max. nomine, scriptarum libri xvi." Lugduni, 1538. It is the third letter in the ninth book.

Although the nomination is dated Aug. 1st, it would appear from the books of the administration, that Raphael had already entered on his functions on the 1st April, 1514: "Maestro Raffaello d'Urbino deve havere ducati 1500, per sua provisione d'anni cinque cominciati a di 1 aprile, 1514, e finito a di 1 aprile, 1519, a ducati 300 l'anno,

"To Raphael of Urbino.

"Besides the art of painting, in which you are universally known to excel, you were, by the architect Bramante, equally esteemed for your knowledge in that profession; so that when dying, he justly considered that to you might be confided the construction of that temple, which by him was begun in Rome to the prince of the apostles; and you have learnedly confirmed that opinion by the plan for that temple requested of you. We, who have no greater desire than that the temple should be built with the greatest possible magnificence and despatch, do appoint you superintendent of that work, with the salary of three hundred golden crowns per annum (£150) out of the money laid aside for the said construction. And we order that you be paid punctually every month, or on your demand, the proportion due. We exhort you to undertake the charge of this work in such a manner, that in executing it you have due regard to your own reputation and good name, for which things the foundation must be laid in youth. Let your efforts correspond to our hope in you, to our paternal benevolence towards you, and, lastly, to the dignity and fame of that temple, even the greatest in the whole world, and most holy; and to our devotion for the prince of the apostles!

"Rome, August 1st, the second year of our Pontificate."

The artists united with Raphael and receiving the same salary, were Giuliano da San Gallo and Fra Giocondo da Verona. They had been already employed under Bramante in the works at St. Peter's.[1] They were of an advanced age, and San Gallo so ill, that he soon retired to Florence. Giocondo probably died in 1518. For, after that date neither he nor San Gallo are mentioned in the account books of the administration.

Raphael remained then the only architect of St. Peter's.

It is much to be regretted that the model executed by him, is no

---

come appare nel conto di M. Simone Ricasoli=D. 1500.—A di 10 maggio 1520, duc. 300 per sua provisione di un anno finito primo aprile, 1520. Pagati da M. Simone Ricasole=Sc. 300. C. Fea, "Notizie," etc. p. 9, first published this document with other extracts from the archives of the administrations of the buildings ordered by Pope Alexander VII. MS. II. II. 22 in the Chigi library.

[1] Carlo Fea, "Notizie," etc. p. 12; and Luigi Pungileoni, "Elogio storico di Raff. Santi," p. 165.

longer in existence; we only possess the plan published by Serlio.[1] This plan forms a Latin cross, with a large cupola in the middle of the transepts. Its length is divided into three aisles, with five chapels on each side. The square pillars have a niche on each surface. The choir and transepts have each a hemicycle, composed of two pillars in niches on the four sides and twelve columns always grouped in fours. The façade, with three large principal entrances, has no towers. The vestibule, raised on steps, rests on thirty-six columns, arranged in twelve groups, in lines three deep, and so disposed that the groups at the end and the two in the middle are more closely drawn together than the others.

This architectural work is grandly and simply combined. Although the dome is at some distance behind the façade, as in the present church of St. Peter's, the vestibule is not so high, and the general effect would have suffered less. On the whole, it may well be believed, to judge from this sketch and the architecture of Michael Angelo in general, that Raphael's plan realized would have been much richer, and at the same time of greater repose as a whole than the St. Peter's of Michael Angelo.

When Raphael set to work with his two colleagues, they perceived that the four columns which were to support the cupola had too weak a foundation, and that Bramante, constantly urged forward by the impatience of Julius II. had made too much haste. They strengthened the pillars very considerably, under the directions of Giocondo, by digging at suitable distances deep square holes which were filled with heavy stone work. Afterwards from one foundation to another they threw arches, and thus obtained a wider and more substantial basis.

It does not appear that any thing else was done under Raphael, because in the first place subterranean works require much time, and in the second, the money destined for St. Peter's was otherwise employed. Raphael was unable even to terminate with Doric columns the central enclosure, which was to serve for the celebration of the Papal high mass. This enclosure, commenced by Bramante, was finished by Raphael's successor, Baldassare Peruzzi; certainly a curious work, but which was afterwards destroyed.

Raphael was more fortunate in the execution of another edifice,

---

[1] Sebastiano Serlio, "Regole generali d'Architettura," Venezia, 1545, pl. xxxvii. Phil. Bonanni also gives an engraving of it in his work, "Templi Vaticani Historia," Romæ, 1696.

undertaken under Bramante, the court with three stories known as that of San Damaso in the Vatican. He drew a fresh plan for this, richer and more beautiful than the first, and caused a model in wood to be executed of it. This work when finished fulfilled the highest expectations; and even now this court, open on one side, is considered to be one of the finest things of that sort ever built. Without entering into details, we shall merely mention that the staircases, of such easy ascent leading to the Loggie, were built from the plans of Raphael.

Raphael's letter to Count Castiglione shows that he was already endeavouring to fill his place of chief architect with conscientious care. Two documents which relate to these functions are records both of his zeal for science and, also, of his amiable character.

The first of these documents is a translation from "Vitruvius," made for him by the learned Marco Fabio Calvo of Ravenna, and which he used in his architectural studies. This is proved by several notes in his hand, on the margin of the valuable manuscript in the Munich Library.[1] This translation is written very clearly on two hundred and seventy-three sheets. The last page states that Marco Fabio Calvo of Ravenna had made this translation from Latin to Italian, according to the desire, and even in the house, of Raphael.[2] We cannot tell what journeys this manuscript may have taken, it is probable however that Giulio Romano possessed it after the death of Raphael; its last journey was from the Bavarian Library to the Royal Library of Munich.

This translation is also remarkable from being the oldest edition of Vitruvius in Italian; for the first printed edition bears the date 1521.

Already, from 1510 to 1515, Calvo, at the demand of Giulio de' Medici (afterwards Clement VII.), had translated the works of Hippo-

---

[1] The few notes by the hand of Raphael are not very important. They are usually merely a rapid summary of the text.

For example, page 58, where the temple of Diana is mentioned, "I travi del tempio de Diana efesia e la imagine de essa dea e di cedro."

Page 59, "Come Cesare vide la prova del arice che non abrusia."

Page 60, "La ragia delo arice e bona al mal del tisicho."

Page 61, "Li abeti sono migliore per edifici quelli che sono volti a mezzo di che quelli del setentrone."

[2] The following note is written on the margin at the end of the tenth book, page 273, by the same hand as the manuscript: Fine del libro di Vitruvio, architecto tradotto di latino in lingua et sermone proprio et volgare, da Marco Fabio Calvo Ravenate in Roma, in casa di Raphaello di Giovanni di Sancte da Urbino, et a sua istantia."

crates. His work appeared in 1525, accompanied by an address expressing the gratitude of the physicians of Rome to the Pope. Calvo died in 1527.

This learned man, who lived in poverty, found a warm reception in the house of Raphael. A letter of Caelio Calcagnini's, the first secretary of the Pope, to the celebrated mathematician Jacob Ziegler,[1] gives the following interesting particulars of these details:—

"Fabius of Ravenna is an old man of stoical probity, and of whom it would be difficult to say whether his learning or affability is the greater. Through him Hippocrates speaks Latin, and has laid aside his ancient defective expressions (an allusion to the translations of the middle ages). This most holy man has this peculiar and very uncommon quality of despising money so much, as to refuse it when offered to him, unless forced to accept it by the most urgent necessity. However, he receives from the Pope an annual pension, which he divides amongst his friends and relations. He himself lives on herbs and lettuces, like the Pythagoricians, and dwells in a hole which might justly be named the tub of Diogenes. He would far rather die than not pursue his studies; and die is really the word, for the old man of eighty years old is suffering from a serious and even dangerous illness. He is cared for as a child by the very rich Raphael da Urbino, who is so much esteemed by the Pope; he is a young man of the greatest kindness and of an admirable mind. He is distinguished by the highest qualities. Thus he is, perhaps, the first of all the painters, as well in theory as in practice; moreover he is an architect of such rare talent, that he invents and executes things which men of the greatest genius deemed impossible. I make an exception only in Vitruvius, whose principles he does not teach, but whom he defends or attacks with the surest proofs, and with so much grace, that not even the slightest envy mingles in his criticism. At present he is occupied with a wonderful work, which will be scarcely credited by posterity (I do not allude to the basilica of the Vatican, where he directs the works); it is the town of Rome which he is restoring in almost its ancient grandeur; for, by removing the highest accumulations of earth, digging down to the lowest foundations, and restoring everything according to the descriptions of ancient authors,

[1] See "Cael. Calcagnini protonotarii apotolici opera aliquot," (Basileæ, 1554, p. 100). Or, "Caelii Calcagnini Epist. crit. et fam." (Amberg, 1618, lib. vii. ep. 27, p. 255).

he has so carried the Pope Leo and the Romans along with him, as to induce every one to look on him as a god sent from heaven to restore to the ancient city her ancient majesty. With all this he is so far from being proud, that he comes as a friend to every one, and does not shun the words and remarks of any one; he likes to hear his views discussed in order to obtain instruction and to instruct others, which he regards as the object of life. He respects and honours Fabius as a master and a father; speaking to him of everything and following his counsels. . . ."

This letter was written towards the close of Raphael's life, since Calcagnini—who had resided in Hungary and been present at the election of the Emperor Charles V. at Frankfort-on-the-Maine—only returned to Rome in 1519.[1] We shall return to this later.

The other document we alluded to is a brief given by Leo X., at the entreaty of Raphael. He always showed the anxiety of a true artist as to the preservations of ancient inscriptions. The learned world will always owe him a debt of gratitude on this account.

"To Raphael of Urbino,

"It is of the greatest importance for the works of the Roman temple of the Prince of the Apostles, that the stones and marbles, of which a large number are required, should be obtained easily from places near us. And since we know that the Roman ruins yield them abundantly, and that both those who build in Rome and in its environs, and those who are engaged in making excavations, find marbles of all kinds abundantly and in all directions among the ancient ruins, I grant to you, being architect in chief of St. Peter's, the general inspection of all excavations and discoveries of stones and of marbles which shall be henceforward made in Rome, and within a circumference of ten miles, in order that you may purchase what may be necessary for the construction of the new temple.

"To this end I command every one, of whatever condition or rank he may be, noble or not, titled or of low estate, to make you, as superintendent of this matter, acquainted with every stone or marble which shall be discovered within the extent of country designated by me, who desire that every one failing to do so shall be judged by you, and fined from 100 to 300 gold crowns." And further on:—"As moreover it has been

[1] G. Tiraboschi, "Storia della letteratura ital." vi. p. 67.

reported to me that workers in marble carelessly use and cut antique marbles, without regard to the inscriptions which are engraven thereon, and which contain certain monuments important to be preserved for the study of the Latin language and learning, I prohibit all who belong to this profession from sawing or cutting any written stone, without your order or permission; and I desire that if they do not obey they shall be subjected to the same penalty.

"Rome, this 27th August, in the third year of our Pontificate."

The object of this brief was, as may be seen, to give Raphael the means of procuring stone and marble at a low price for the building of St. Peter's, and also to prevent the destruction of curious monuments. Some writers have interpreted this document as being the nomination of Raphael to the post of director of antiquities, a title conferred on Winkelmann two centuries and a half later. Such an office was not then necessary; for the collection of antiques in the Pope's palace, was still extremely small, although there were, even at this time, several masterpieces [1] amongst them: the group of the "Laocoon," discovered in 1506, and in honour of which Sadoleto wrote a poem of some celebrity; [2] the "Apollo Belvedere," which had been acquired by Julius II. before becoming Pope; the "Torso," that Michael Angelo preferred to any other work of antiquity; the "Ariadne" that was sung by Count Castiglione; [3] the "Antinous;" the groups of the "Tiber" and the "Nile;" the "Salustia Barbia Orbiana," wife of Alexander Severus, as Venus; and others. In certain cases, however, Raphael did perform the office of director, for instance when Gabriel de' Rossi bequeathed a statue for the capitol.[4]

---

[1] Carlo Fea, "Notizie," etc. p. 50.

[2] "Sadolet," Oper. iii. p. 245, Verona, 1738. Francesco da San Gallo gives the following account of the discovery of the Laocoon in the Baths of Titus: "It was a few years ago, the first time that I was in Rome, that it was told the Pope that certain very beautiful statues had been found in a vineyard near Santa Maria Maggiore. The Pope commanded an equerry to go and tell Giuliano da San Gallo to go at once to see them. He went immediately; and as Michael Angelo Buonarotti still lived in the house in which my father had placed him, and had confided to him the tomb of the Pope, he wished him also to go with him, and thus we started, I accompanying my father. I uncovered before the statues, and my father said at once, 'This is the Laocoon that Pliny speaks of.' They enlarged the hole in order to draw them out, and we quickly returned here to dinner." See Carlo Fea, "Notizie," etc. p. 21.

[3] Fabroni, "Vita Leonis X." p. 306.

[4] D. Salv. Leoni found the following note in book xxxvi. p. 45, of the secret archives

In order to give a complete sketch of the architectural works of Raphael in Rome, we shall mention here the buildings in Rome for which he made the plans, although several of these works belong properly to the later years of his life.

The chapel for Agostino Chigi at Santa Maria del Popolo, was one of the first buildings erected from his plans.

It is on the left side of the church, and forms an octagon with unequal sides, the narrowest of which are decorated with pilasters and niches. A small cupola, resting on the pilasters receives light from the eight windows of the lantern. It appears that according to Raphael's plan, this cupola was to contain in mosaic the history of Adam from his creation to his fall; then the prophecy of the coming of Christ, represented by four statues of prophets, in marble, which he wished to carve himself; and lastly, underneath, the accomplishment of this prophecy, in three great mural pictures.

But these projects were not all destined to be realised: Raphael only executed the image of the Creator on a golden background, with the allegorical figures of the sun, the moon, and the planets, according to Dante's description.[1] Of the statues he only completed the "Jonah," and did not touch the "Elijah," which had been roughly prepared by the sculptor Lorenzetto.

For both Raphael and Agostino Chigi died in April, 1520.

Subsequently the works in this chapel were resumed. Sebastiano del Piombo painted the "Birth of the Virgin," in oil, on the centre wall, and Francesco Salviati, though not until 1554, the history of the Creation and of the first sin, in fresco on the cupola. At a still later period Bernini erected the tomb of Chigi, and added two more prophets to the "Jonah" and "Elijah."

---

of the Capitol: "1518, 15 Julii, Raphael de Urbino, volens quamdam statuam ab hæredibus quondam Gabrielis de Rubeis, conservatores asseruerunt, velle eam transportare ad Capitolium juxtà formam testamenti supradicti. Pacificus Nardus de Pacificis Not." See Pungileoni, "Elogio Storico di Timoteo Viti." Urbino, 1835, p. 103.

[1] According to Dante, an angel is placed in every star. In canto ii. of "Paradise," he says:

> "The virtue and motion of the sacred orbs,
> As mallet by the workman's hand, must needs
> By blessed movers be inspired."

Then, in his Convito, "Le movitori del cielo della luna siano dell' ordine degli Angeli, e quelli di Mercurio siano gli Archangeli, e quelli di Venere siano li Troni."

The question has frequently been raised whether Raphael did not merely have these two statues executed according to his own ideas, by the Florentine Lorenzetto, or if he really applied his own hand to the work.

Good reasons tend to confirm the latter supposition; in the first place the great perfection of the "Jonah," which does not merely deserve to be admired for its general form, and for the beauty of its lines, but also, for the great finish in the details. At any rate it is superior to anything that Lorenzetto ever produced. On the other hand, the statue of Elijah is very weak in character, and has not even the appearance of a finished sculpture, although, however, it still bears some traces of its Raphaelesque origin. It proves that after Raphael's death Lorenzetto was no longer capable by himself to attain the same perfection as the master had reached in an art with which he was not familiar. The inferiority of Lorenzetto's talent is betrayed still more in the "Madonna del Sasso," which he executed for the tomb of Raphael in the Pantheon.

These considerations, without seeking for others, appear to us to remove all doubt and to confirm the fact that Raphael himself completed the statue of Jonah.

Another proof that Raphael sometimes worked in sculpture is that in a letter to Andrea Piperario, his intendant at Rome,[1] Count Castiglione says: "I wish to know if Giulio Romano has still the 'Young Boy' in marble, by the hand of Raphael, and the lowest price at which he would allow me to have it." We have no more certain and exact information as to the sculpture; Cavaceppi however possessed and sold to M. de Breteuil a group in marble, of a child mortally wounded, borne by a dolphin through the waves.[2]

The natural attitude of the child, the style of the head and hair, the form of the dolphin's head, which reminds us strongly of the dolphins in the picture of the "Galatea," all lead us to believe that this child is the one spoken of by Castiglione. Possibly it was the count himself who

---

[1] Of May 8th, 1523. See "Lettere Pitt." v. p. 245, No. 5.

[2] In his work entitled, "Raccolta d'antiche statue," Cavaceppi mentions this little group as being a work of Lorenzetto, under the directions of Raphael. This group afterwards passed into the collection of the earl of Bristol, bishop of Derry, who carried it to Ireland; it is now in the collection of works of art at Down Hill. The "Penny Magazine" of July 17th, 1844, published a wood engraving of it. There is also a copy of it among the plaster works of Mengs."

had recommended to Raphael this subject, taken from the book of Ælian,[1] where we read that dolphins are very devoted to men, and that one of them bore a dead child to the shore.

It is to Raphael also that is owing the beautiful fountain called delle Tartarughe. There is nothing to show whether he made a design for it, or ever so small a model, nor even that he executed it entirely. No contemporary speaks of it. But a glance is sufficient to recognize on this monument the most decided stamp of the genius and grace of the master of Urbino.

Four young men, entirely naked, are leaning against the base of a large basin. They are seated, and place their feet against fantastic dolphins, whose mouths throw out streams of water into large shells also forming basins. They each hold up a tortoise, as if to make him drink, towards the upper basin, which throws the water into the air, and out by four masks into the lower basins.

Nothing can be more charming than these youthful figures of the most elegant forms, whose sculpturing is perfectly scientific and graceful. The heads possess that distinction inseparable from the works of Raphael, and we confidently repeat what we said before, that he alone would be able to produce such a work.

It would appear that Raphael also made the design for a medal with the effigy of Lorenzo de' Medici, Duke of Urbino, during the residence of that prince in Rome, in the year 1517.[2]

After these digressions we must return to the architectural works of Raphael at Rome.

According to Vasari, he designed for Agostino Chigi the plan of the stables by the side of the small palace, built in 1509 and 1510, by Baldassare Peruzzi, and now named the Farnesina, near the Tiber. It would indeed be worthy of Raphael; but the severity of its architecture would seem rather to indicate the style of Baldassare Peruzzi.

Several fine houses in the Borgo San Pietro, which Vasari mentions as having been built from designs by Raphael, have been destroyed for the colonnades of the piazza San Pietro. Vasari describes as especially remarkable the palace of Giovanni Battista Branconio dall' Aquila, the façade of which was richly decorated with bas-reliefs in stucco by

---

[1] On the Nature of animals.

[2] See Gaye, "Carteggio," ii. p. 143.

Giovanni da Udine. An engraving has been made of this façade, and the house is always described wrongly as having been the residence of Raphael himself.

A house named de' Berti, which may still be seen in the Via del Borgo Nuovo, has completely the character of the Raphaelesque architecture. It was built in 1515 for the Pope's surgeon, Jacopo da Brescia, and not for Jacopo Sadoleto, as has been erroneously stated, notwithstanding a decisive inscription which it formerly bore.

It is solidly built of hewn stones and of bricks, and has on the façade five windows with pediments alternately triangular and circular, according to Raphael's habitual custom. The bossage and the cornices also show the master's usual style.

For the Cavaliere Coltrolini Raphael made the design of a palace, which was erected near the church S. Andrea della Valle, and subsequently bore successively the names of Caffarelli, Stoppani, and Acquaviva. It now belongs to the Cardinal Vidoni.

The lower story is of very powerful rustic architecture. The one above, which had originally seven windows, is decorated with coupled pillars of Ionic order, surmounted by a rich cornice of corresponding style. This latter palace, of the most perfect proportions, was much enlarged by the architect Niccolò Sansimoni, who added a third story quite out of harmony with the original parts. Nevertheless the eye is still delighted by the lines of the original plan.

The seal that Raphael impressed on his works is ineffaceable, notwithstanding all the mutilations they have undergone during more than three centuries.

A short time before his death he commenced building a villa for Cardinal Giulio de' Medici (afterwards Clement VII.) on Monte Mario. Giulio Romana continued it, but with many changes of his own introduction. The three arcades or porticoes, still admired so much by visitors at this villa (now named the Madama villa), show the grandeur of the primitive plan.

According to Vasari, Raphael must also have competed for the church that Leo X. charged Ludovico Capponi, the Florentine consul at Rome, to have built in the Via Giulia, near the Tiber, in honour of St. John the Baptist. But the plan of Jacopo Sansovino was chosen.

These brief sketches of the architectural works of Raphael at Rome must suffice for the present. When we find him at a later period in competition with Buonarotti at Florence for the façade of the church of San Lorenzo, we shall mention the buildings erected there from his designs. Here we will merely add a few reflections as to his particular qualities in architecture.

What distinguishes the style of Raphael from that of Bramante, whose pupil he may be considered to be, is that in minor details, such as the frameworks of the windows, the entablatures and cornices, he gives a greater projection and greater amplitude in the profiles. He did not follow scrupulously the examples of Roman architecture, but what he sought most zealously was picturesque arrangement and richness of form. He frequently employed coupled columns, nearly always surmounted his windows by pediments alternately triangular and circular, and decorated them at the base with projecting balustrades.

Notwithstanding, however, this inclination for picturesque effect, he yet possessed in the highest degree a just sentiment for grand architectural masses, and he was always guided by his instinct for beautiful forms and fine proportions. His plinths and cornices are never broken in their lines, and have an agreeable appearance. In short, the buildings erected by Raphael may be considered as among the most perfect of the sixteenth century. Peruzzi is the only one who can dispute the first rank with him, because that with an equal sentiment for fine proportions and equal skill in employing new forms, he knew, also, how to keep his inventions within the strict bounds of rational architecture, whilst Raphael sometimes passed them.

But in comparison with Michael Angelo, the relation is quite reversed. Raphael never made use of anything arbitrary either in the forms or ornaments; and in general in every part of the art he differs from Michael Angelo by possessing greater harmony and purity of style.

To return to his works in painting, we will mention the oil pictures, which he executed at the commencement of the pontificate of Leo X. before passing to the great frescoes with which he decorated the Vatican.

In October, 1513,[1] a noble Bolognese lady, Elena Duglioni, named del' Oglio, and subsequently canonized, had felt herself inspired to build a chapel to St. Cecilia in the church of San Giovanni in Monte, near Bologna. With this design, she applied to the Florentine Antonio

[1] P. Meloni, "Alti e memorie di Santi Bolognesi," vol. iii. p. 333. "Pungileoni," p. 144.

Pucci, her relation and guardian. Pucci undertook, at her cost, the care of the erection of the chapel, and his uncle, Lorenzo Pucci, just made Cardinal of Santi Quattro, begged Raphael to paint the altar-piece for it.

A sudden inspiration called forth this picture, and it was in one of his most inspired moments that the master composed this exquisite painting. Everything in it speaks of faith and zeal. All the noble countenances bear the divine stamp, and yet, whatever may be the exultation of their souls, their attitudes are full of the calmest majesty.

St. Paul, leaning on a naked sword, represents knowledge and wisdom, whilst on the other side St. John shows the full blessing of divine love. Mary Magdalen, holding a vase of perfumes, is opposite to St. Paul, as if to indicate that, if the repentance of the apostle, and his unwearied activity in the church, obtained forgiveness for him for his former sins, she also had been forgiven much, because she had loved much. And as St. Paul, converted through a vision, is by the side of the loving St. John, so St. Augustine, also converted to the faith of Christ, is by the side of the Magdalen.

Surrounded by these great and touching figures, St. Cecilia is standing, radiant with ecstasy, listening to the divine harmonies sung by the angels in heaven. The earthly organ falls from her hands, she trembles with holy enthusiasm, and her soul seems longing to fly away to the heavenly country.

The beauty of the style, and the depth of expression are not the only things that render this a masterpiece ; but the combination of these with harmony, richness, and powerful colouring. The colouring responds to the poetry of the subject ; it carries us into an ethereal and mysterious atmosphere. No colourist has ever equalled this splendour, which we may almost call divine. Titian's "Assumption" excites feelings of joyfulness, Correggio's "St. Jerome" a gentle emotion, but Raphael's "St. Cecilia" brings us nearer to heaven.

Although this picture was ordered in 1513, and had doubtless been sketched in the first fire of its conception, it does not appear that it was completed at once; for it was only placed in the chapel in 1517. Raphael had sent it to his friend Francia, with the request to "make any correction he pleased, if he noticed any defect," or to repair any accident the painting might have suffered in the transport, and to get it framed.

What must Francia's emotion have been when he received this picture from his illustrious friend. All Bologna was equally filled with enthusiasm at the sight of this divine work,[1] and its praises were sung in countless Latin and Italian poems.[2]

It was also for an inhabitant of Bologna, the Count Vincenzo Ercolani, that Raphael executed the small picture of "Ezekiel's Vision." Vasari observes, very judiciously, that this representation of Jehovah, surrounded by the attributes of the four Evangelists, is not much in accordance with the Gospels, and that Raphael has rather given him the appearance of a Jupiter in the powerful style of Michael Angelo. In our opinion, however, for this subject from Ezekiel, Jehovah should rather correspond with what we learn of him in the prophets.

The original picture, which decorates the Pitti palace, at Florence, was already inscribed in the catalogue of the works of art in the Tribune, in 1589. Several ancient copies of it still exist.

Vasari mentions with praise a "Birth of Christ" (Mary and Joseph adoring the infant Saviour), that Raphael sent to the Count Canossa, at Verona, about this period. He praises particularly the rising sun in the landscape background. The count thought so highly of this picture, that he never would give it up, although princes offered him high sums for it. With much difficulty Zucchero succeeded in obtaining leave to make a copy of it for the Duke of Urbino. Both the original and the copy are now lost, and Vasari's description of it is the only one that has come down to us.

Greater works were awaiting Raphael in the Vatican. He had to decorate the third hall of the Pope, named the Stanza di Torre Borgia,

---

[1] It has been asserted that at sight of this picture, Francia, jealous of Raphael's superiority, felt such excessive grief that he died from the effects of it. We do not believe this story. Malvasia, in the good intention to contradict is, however, mistaken, when he mentions as being by Francesco Francia an altar piece, bearing the date 1526, several years after the arrival of the St. Cecilia. This picture, which represents the Virgin with saints, and which was transferred from the Felicini Chapel in the Church of the Franciscans to the Pinacothek of Bologna (No. 84), is by the son of Francesco, Giacomo Francia. It is signed thus, "J. J. FRANCIA, AVRIF. BONON. FE MDXXVI." According to the Bolognese Chronicles and the "Memorie" of Francesco Raibolini of Calvi, Bologna, 1812, p. 41, Francesco Francia died January 6th, 1517, at the age of sixty-seven; he was then director of the mint in that town.

[2] Vasari has preserved the two following lines:—

"Pingant sola alii referantque coloribus ora;
Cæciliæ os Raphael atque animum explicuit."

the vestibule of the Palafrenieri, and the Loggie of the second story. His pupils were to assist in the work, to satisfy the impatience of Leo X. He gave up to them, therefore, the painting of the Loggie and the Palafrenieri, after having merely sketched the compositions. But for the Pope's own apartment he made special cartoons, which he executed in part himself.

Perugino had already ornamented the ceiling with groups of Christ and the apostles, saints, angels, and allegorical figures. Although these subjects bore no connection to those that Raphael intended to paint, he would not allow them to be sacrificed, as had been done to so many other pictures in the adjoining apartments.

In the second hall the "Atila," a subject drawn from the life of Leo I., was an allusion to the dispersion of the enemies of Italy by Leo X. In the third Stanza he had to represent the glory of the papacy, the extraordinary events which distinguished the reigns and persons of two other Popes of the name of Leo.

Of these fresh paintings, the first in chronological order shows Leo III. refuting, by an oath on the Holy Gospels, the accusations brought against him by the nephew of the late Pope Adrian I.

The scene takes place in the church of St. Peter at Rome, where the Emperor Charlemagne had assembled the chiefs of temporal as well as of spiritual authority. But, at the moment in which he interrogates the august assembly on the accusations brought against Leo, a voice was heard stating that the right belonged to no one of judging the supreme sovereign. On which Charlemagne stopped the enquiry, and was satisfied with the oath of purification.

Below the painting are inscribed these words: "To God and not to man belongs the judging of Bishops." This fresco symbolizes, then, the supremacy of the pontifical authority over temporal power, since the church has only to render an account to God.

The second mural painting represents the "Coronation of Charlemagne, by Leo III." and signifies that temporal power flows from spiritual power. It recalls at the same time the alliance of Leo X. and Francis I. at Bologna in the winter of 1515-1516, since the two principal figures are portraits of these two sovereigns. The page holding the crown of Lombardy behind the kneeling emperor is the young Ippolito de Medici, a child of extreme beauty and intelligence. Leo X. felt such affection for him as to give him apartments in the Vatican near himself.[1] This fresco also contains many other portraits, especially among the bishops. Vasari mentions, among others, Gianozzo Pandolfini of Florence, who was indebted to Raphael, whose friend he was, for the plan of his palace in that city.

The two frescoes relating to Leo III., through the nature of the subject, only possess a secondary interest. This sort of solemn ceremonial leaves no scope for the artist to develope the action, the different expression, and contrast the effects;[2] the interest is broken up in every figure and every detail.

Anastasius the librarian, in the "Life of Leo IV." relates that the Saracens, after having conquered Theodosius, admiral of the Emperor Michael's fleet, pillaged Tarentum and the coast of Dalmatia, undertook an expedition against the States of the Pope, and attempted to land in the port of Ostia. But the Romans, assisted by the Neapolitans and Gaetans, fought a naval battle against them, and, by the help of God, who sent a violent tempest, they obtained a complete victory.

The picture shows the confusion of the combat in the port, some of the enemy's vessels being driven by the tempest, others stranded on the shore, where the conflict still rages. The Pope (it is still the portrait of Leo X.), accompanied by the cardinals Giulio de' Medici and Bernardo Divizio da Bibiena, is seated on the shore, with clasped hands, and eyes raised to heaven. Prisoners in chains are lying at their feet.

Raphael has represented in a striking manner all the aspects of a naval battle; here in the foreground, the fury, the vengeance and fierce joy of the conquerors; there, on the other side, the humiliation, the agony, the despair of the prisoners. And these dramatic agitations form an excellent contrast to the holy calm of the praying Pontiff.

The most remarkable picture, however, in this room, is the "Conflagration of the Borgo Vecchio at Rome," entirely by the hand of Raphael.

In 847, according to the same Anastasius, a fire broke out in the suburb inhabited by the Saxons and Lombards, which extended from the Vatican to the mausoleum of Adrian. A frightful hurricane spread the fire so much, that its progress could not be arrested. The danger was

---

[1] Ippolito was the natural son of Giuliano de' Medici and Pacifica Brandani, a noble lady of Urbino.

[2] This is what Emeric David called "tableaux d'apparat." See his definition in an article published under this title by the "Revue Universelle des Arts," vol. iii. p. 289. —*Lacroix.*

becoming imminent for the church of St. Peter's, when Pope Leo IV., imploring earnestly divine assistance, suddenly saw the flames on the buildings assume the form of a cross, and the fire was at once arrested.

It was this moment that Raphael chose to represent.

In the background is perceived the old basilica of St. Peter's, and in a loggia, since destroyed, the Pope is in prayer, with his suite, surrounded by a multitude praying and lamenting. In the foreground women and children are running about in despair. The fire is still blazing in the buildings on the foreground, both to right and left. Here all the horrors of such a disaster are depicted, as well as the sublime self-devotion it arouses.

Several of the figures in the "Conflagration of the Borgo Vecchio" are considered as perfect and inimitable, amongst others the two beautiful and powerful women who are bringing water in vases, and whose forms are so admirably delineated under their garments agitated by the wind; the group of the mother who forgets her own danger, while the father is endeavouring to save their child; the figure of the naked man who is sliding down from the top of a wall; the group of the strong man carrying his old father on his shoulders, his most precious possession, followed by his young son and an old woman laden with various household utensils.

These incidents gave an opportunity for Raphael to display his profound knowledge of the human body, by painting nude figures of both sexes and of different ages: in the figure of the father manly strength; in the old man, the weakness of extreme age; in the children the grace of youth.

It has been frequently observed that Raphael wished thus to enter the lists with Michael Angelo, but that the latter is superior in energy of drawing, in his anatomical science, and in his outlines, which are so just and true, that in every muscle life seems in complete activity.

We agree cordially in this judgment, but declare nevertheless, that Raphael possesses a larger share of one particular quality which is very precious; he is more varied than Michael Angelo in the character of his forms, and is simpler and truer in the drawing.

This quality of Raphael's would be sought for vainly in the works of his rival, who disdained delicate forms and aspired only to a single ideal, very grand, doubtless, but which he wrongly considered to be the only one worthy of art.

The pictures in this third Stanza have unfortunately suffered still more than the preceding ones; so much so, in fact, that to be able to appreciate rightly their truth and character, we are obliged to have recourse to the studies which still exist.

As this deterioration set in very quickly, especially in the "Victory of Ostia," Sebastiano del Piombo touched up the frescoes in several places. One day when he was showing this part of the Vatican to Titan, the latter, annoyed by these restorations, asked:

"Who is the arrogant and ignorant man who has dared thus to daub over these heads?" At this apostrophe, says Dolce, with a pun,[1] Sebastiano became literally *del piombo* (of lead).

We pass by in silence the pictures on the socles and several figures of protectors of the church, which Giulio Romano originally executed in camaieu from his own designs, and the small pictures in the embrasures of the windows, with Biblical subjects. We will merely notice here that Raphael and the artists who worked with him frequently introduced contemporaneous facts into their works, and thus excited a greater amount of public sympathy.

Giovanni Barile, the skilful sculptor who decorated so richly the doors and window shutters of the Pope's state rooms[2] with works in mosaic of all colours, made use of them still more freely. On the door which separates the Stanza del Borgo Vecchio from the Stanza della Signatura, he represented a comedy which amused the whole town, and of which the hero was the very bad improvisatore Baraballo of Gaeta. This abbot, to whom the Pope delighted in paying sarcastic praises, considered himself a greater poet than Petrarch, and at the instigation of Cardinal Bibiena, he seriously accepted the proposition to be crowned at the capitol. The supposed solemnity was fixed for the festival of St. Cosmo and St. Damianus, the patron saints of the house of Medici, a day on which the Pope was in the habit of dining in public. The abbot Baraballo, clothed in a Roman toga, was gloriously seated on a rich chair, placed on the back of an elephant which the King of Portugal had given to the Pope in 1514. The procession, accompanied by trumpets and cymbals, set out thus from the Vatican, and began its march towards the capitol. But when it had gone as far as the bridge of St. Angelo,

---

[1] "Dialogo della Pittura," di M. Lodovico Dolce, intitolato Aretino (Venezia, 1557), p. 11.

[2] Extract from the account books of the church of St. Peter, MS. in the Chigi Library, H. ii. 48: "Giovanni Barile deve havere ducati 420 d'oro per provisione d'anni sette, cominciati a di 1 di Novembre, 1514, e fimiti per tutto Ottobre, 1521."

the elephant, impatient at being the object of the yells of the crowd, shook his sides maliciously, and the poor abbot slipped off his seat; the general hilarity soon made him understand that there was to be no crowning at the capitol for him.[1] Raphael himself, as an inscription published by Cancellieri informs us, has left a memento of this elephant.[2]

The Pope's menagerie was also very useful to Giovanni da Udine, for the decoration of the hall of the Palafrenieri, where he painted all sorts of foreign animals, in the frieze below the saints and apostles, executed in enamel in the niches, from designs by Raphael.

The greater part of these paintings were destroyed when Paul IV. divided the hall into four little rooms; under Gregory XIII. it was wished to bring it back to its original form, and Taddeo Zucchero endeavoured to restore the figures of the apostles, but he was obliged to repaint them altogether, and it is only with great difficulty that anything of the principal figures can be recognised. A St. John the Baptist as a child, in chiaroscuro, with two parrots near him, is the only one that can give us any idea of what the others were. Happily an engraving of Marcantonio has preserved the apostles. Imitations may also be found painted in fresco, on the pillars of the church of St. Vincent and St. Anastasio, named *alle Tre Fontane*, but they are very unreliable.

The Loggie leading to the apartments of the Pope were painted still more richly than the latter apartment. These Loggie consist of thirteen arcades arched in cupolas. Each of the arcades contains four principal pictures. Out of the whole fifty-two, forty-eight of the subjects are taken from the Old Testament, from the creation down to the building of Solomon's Temple, and four from the life of Christ. This series of pictures is usually called "Raphael's Bible."

For these subjects he made sketches washed and relieved with white, some of which have come down to us; but he left the execution entirely to his pupils, principally to Giulio Romano, who drew all the cartoons and directed the whole work. The bas-reliefs in stucco and groteschi, were entrusted to Giovanni da Udine, whose knowledge of botany and zoology rendered him well suited for this sort of decoration.

Raphael felt such a strong attraction for this artist's talent, that he

---

[1] Montagnani, in his work of the "Stanze of Raphael" (p. 75), gives an engraving of Barballo seated triumphantly on the elephant.

[2] Francesco Cancellieri, "Storia de solenni possessi de Sommi Pontefici," p. 62.

took a great delight in looking through Giovanni's sketch book. Frequently also they took artistic excursions together.

It was in one of these excursions to the Baths of Titus, which had recently been discovered, that both were struck by the freshness of the stucco and coloured ornaments, which are still so much admired. Giovanni took the designs, studied the material composition, and succeeded by a mixture of travertine, chalk, and marble, in composing similar works of equal beauty. Raphael encouraged this discovery of his pupil as far as possible, and utilized it for the decoration of the Loggie. Thus these celebrated pictures were produced, as astonishing as poetical inventions as in their execution.

In them, not only has Raphael's genius expressed in shining characters the majestic simplicity of the Bible, but his rich and charming fancy gave to the decorations, however unconnected they may appear at first, the most ingenious harmony with the principal subjects; a quality which would be sought in vain in the ancient decorative system, the want of unity in which was so justly blamed by Vitruvius. According to the taste of the period, Raphael united in it both the elements of antiquity and of Christianity, as Dante had done in his "Divina Comedia," and the pupils of Giotto, in 1410, in the paintings in the great hall at Padua.

These decorations of the Loggie, besides forming an elegant framework for the subjects taken from the Bible, also serve, so to speak, to complete the universal history. Nature, mythology, science, and art, are symbolized in them in a variety of motives, which are connected with each other. Frequently also the ornaments nearest to the principal subjects bear a direct relation to them.

Angels in adoration decorate the first and last cupola, which contain the "Creation" and the "Incarnation." The *grotteschi* of Adam and Eve and of the First Sin represent loves fighting with harpies, lions, and tigers, which is intended to symbolize the struggle of divine love with the savage passions of fallen nature. Distant architecture surrounds the scene of the "Building of Noah's Ark." At the "Destruction of Sodom and Gomorrha," there is a combat of fantastic monsters. By the side of the "Moses saved from the Water," and of the "Deliverance from Egypt," are children dancing joyfully, and garlands of flowers. Around the "Conquest of Palestine," is a combat of genii with wild beasts. Around the "History of Solomon," symbols of peace, &c.

Others of the scenes relate to contemporaneous events, which no longer possess the same interest, and an analysis of which would take too long.

Raphael, to respond to the sumptuous tastes of Leo X., brought into use all the resources of art. He entrusted to Gian Barile the carving for the doors; for the flooring, he made use of slabs of coloured and glazed earthenware from the Florentine manufactory *della Robbia*, which imitated in their brilliant tints a carpet, with the Pope's arms.

All these works executed under the influence of Raphael, excited an inexpressible ardour amongst the artists and inhabitants of the town. Everyone felt that from these works in the Vatican there would result lasting glory for the country, for religion, and for art.

Three centuries have confirmed this presentiment, and as long as a love for the beautiful and the true shall coexist among men, no one will visit the Pontifical dwelling without feelings of enthusiasm and respect in presence of the works we have just described.

Raphael intended likewise to decorate the other Loggie of the same story with a series of subjects taken from the New Testament, and embracing the history of the apostles, and of the principal saints of the church. His premature death prevented the execution of these plans.

The second suite of "the Loggie" was painted under Gregory XIII. by the ornament maker, Marco da Faenza, whom Vasari praises in so exaggerated a manner.[1] His paintings show the rapid decline of good taste after the disappearance of Raphael.

If in "the Loggie" we are struck by the fertile talent and wonderful imagination of the master, we see his genius on a vaster scale in the tapestries of the Sistine. The Pope, Sixtus IV., who erected this chapel, had caused various subjects from the Old and New Testaments to be painted in it by the best artists of the time; and under Julius II. the incomparable paintings of the roof had been executed by Michael Angelo.

It may easily be imagined how Raphael would be spurred to fresh exertions, when he was commissioned to paint the cartoons for these pieces of tapestry, which were to decorate the same chapel and undergo a constant comparison with those of Michael Angelo. The lower part of the walls had in the first place been covered with paintings imitating tapestry, the effect of which was pretty successful. This inspired Raphael with the idea of causing his compositions to be copied in fabrics of wool or of silk and gold, which might be hung up before the wainscoting on high festivals, according to the customs of the Byzantines and Romans.

---

[1] In the "Life of Primaticcio."

The ten pieces of tapestry, made in Flanders[1] with unexampled magnificence and perfection, arrived at Rome in 1519, only a few months before the death of Raphael, and were hung up in St. Peter's on the feast of St. Stephen in the same year. The master had thus the happiness of seeing his work crowned with complete success; for the enthusiasm of the Romans was indescribable. Vasari speaking of these tapestries says, "that they seem rather to have been performed by miracle than by the aid of man."

The choice of the subjects was all indicated. To "the History of Moses," painted under Sixtus IV., Michael Angelo had added "the History of the Creation," and the "Prophecy of a Saviour" (the Prophets and Sibyls). Raphael continued the series[2] by taking his subjects from the Acts of the Apostles, and adding a "Coronation of the Virgin" for the altar.

The interior space in the chapel, as far as the iron-gate, is divided by ten pilasters into as many panels of different sizes. The tapestries were to correspond to the size of these panels; four on each side, and two at the end near the altar, where Michael Angelo subsequently painted the "Last Judgment."

To the left of the throne, were placed four scenes from the life of St. Peter, and the "Stoning of St. Stephen;" to the right as pendants, five subjects from the life of St. Paul.

The pilasters are covered with arabesques—masterpieces of their kind: "the Theological Virtues," "the Fates," "the Divisions of the Day," &c.

Seven of the original cartoons for these tapestries have come down to us, and are now in England;[3] they are "the Miraculous Draught

---

[1] That is to say at Arras, famous for its manufacturing of tapestries of high warp in the middle ages. See the work of M. de Laborde, "Les Ducs de Bourgogne. Etudes sur les Lettres, les Arts, et l'Industrie pendant le XVe siècle;" 2nd partie, vol. i. and ii.—*Lacroix.*

[2] Michael Angelo closed it by representing subsequently the "Last Judgment," a symbol of the end of the history of the world.

[3] Formerly at Hampton Court, now in the South Kensington Museum. It is said that five cartoons, which had already disappeared in the time of Rubens, are still in existence in a church in France. "These cartoons," says M. Viardot (Musées d'Angleterre), "are not, like ordinary cartoons, drawings in chalk on white or grey paper. To serve as models for tapestries, and not merely as a preparation for pictures, they had to be coloured. Thus they are really pictures in distemper." M. Waagen, in his works on the arts in England, gives full details of these cartoons. See vol. i. p

of Fishes," "Christ's Charge to St. Peter," "the Healing of the Lame Man," "The Death of Ananias," "Elymas struck with blindness," "Paul and Barnabas at Lystra," and "St. Paul preaching at Athens." In our catalogue of Raphael's works we shall give further details on these cartoons. Here we will merely examine the subjects drawn from the life of the Apostles.

"The Miraculous Draught of Fishes." St. Peter seeing his frail bark overladen with fish and in danger of sinking, throws himself at the feet of Christ, exclaiming, "Depart from me for I am a sinful man, O Lord." But Christ says to him, "Fear not, from henceforth thou shalt catch men."

This grand scene in which Christ chooses this poor and ignorant fisherman to be the first of the apostles, is rendered with sublime poetry. Peter, whilst his companions in the second boat are still busied in drawing in their nets, has just been penetrated by the divine power. His humble attitude contrasts with the calm and majestic demeanour of the Saviour. The beautiful outlines of the landscape and of the lake make a magnificent surrounding to this group.

The charge to St. Peter, "Feed my Sheep." These words, which Christ after his resurrection addressed to St. Peter, after the twice repeated question, "Simon, son of Jonas, lovest thou me?" form the subject of the second picture. St. Peter is kneeling before Christ who is showing him a flock of sheep. His countenance expresses the liveliest faith and emotion. The other disciples are standing a little apart, as if to indicate that though their master was still on the earth, his reign had already begun in the heavens. "The Healing of the Lame Man." The apostles St. Peter and St. John going into the Temple, found a beggar lying in the porch, lame from his birth, who asked alms of them. "Silver and gold have I none," answered St. Peter, "but such as I have give I thee; in the name of Jesus Christ of Nazareth, rise up and walk." The lame man immediately stood up and walked. The scene is represented in the midst of a vestibule with twisted Corinthian columns, taken from those which adorn St. Peter's church at the altar in the chapel of the Holy Sacrament, and which according to the tradition were brought from the temple in Jerusalem. The noble figures of St. Peter, St. John,

---

360. Quatre de Quincy does not hesitate to give them as Raphael's masterpiece. "In these cartoons he indeed rises above himself. The collection of these memorable works ought to be here pronounced what in truth it is, the climax, not only of the productions of Raffaello, but of all those of modern genius in painting."—*Lacroix*.

FEED MY SHEEP.

and the men, women and children united at the entrance of the temple, contrast with the ugliness of the lame man, and of another beggar, also lame, who is dragging himself towards the disciples of Christ.[1] These men are a fine example of the power of style in the arts; it would be difficult to imagine human beings, more entirely the opposite of beautiful than these two beggars, and yet their ugliness is neither horrible nor common-place. These figures successfully demonstrate an immutable principle, namely that when ugliness is necessary in a work of art, it is only acceptable in the most elevated style. And, if it fulfils this condition, it comes more within the bounds of art than mere vulgar, accidental beauty without style.

"The Death of Ananias." "Ananias, why hath Satan filled thine heart to lie to the Holy Ghost and to keep back part of the price of the land?" Scarcely had St. Peter pronounced these words, than Ananias fell down dead. The persons nearest to him are struck with terror. On one side of the platform on which the apostles are standing St. John is distributing alms; on the other, some of the faithful are bringing offerings. In this group may be distinguished Sapphira, the wife of Ananias; she is quietly counting the money, without any presentiment of the punishment that awaits her crime.

"The Martyrdom of St. Stephen." The false witnesses, fanatical partisans of the Pharisees, have dragged the young deacon out of the town and are stoning him. He, kneeling, raises his arms and his eyes to heaven, where Christ appears to him in glory. At this vision he cries out, "Lord, lay not this sin to their charge!" Saul at whose feet the clothes of the false witnesses are lying, seems to be applauding the martyrdom of the saint. Notwithstanding the energy with which the rage of the executioners is expressed, it is the noble and inspired figure of the young martyr that attracts the first glance.

"The Conversion of St. Paul." Saul the unwearied enemy of the Christians, had gone to Damascus to persecute them. But "suddenly there shined round about him a light from heaven; and he fell to the earth and heard a voice saying unto him, 'Saul, Saul, why persecutest thou me?' And he said, 'Who art thou, Lord?' And the Lord said, 'I am Jesus, whom thou persecutest.'" As in the biblical narrative, the pic-

---

[1] These figures have frequently been imitated by painters, even by Rubens in his magnificent picture of St. Martin giving his mantle to a poor boy (in her Majesty's collection at Windsor).—*Lacroix.*

ture shows Saul prostrate before the celestial vision, whilst his frightened companions are dispersing in disorder.

Raphael has rendered this scene with wonderful clearness, not disturbing the general unity through the confusion. The eye is at once attracted to the miraculous revelation which was to transform Saul the persecutor into the apostle St. Paul.

"Elymas struck with Blindness." Paul and Barnabas, who had met with a favourable reception from the proconsul Sergius Paulus, had to undergo the violent hostility of a magician named Elymas. But St. Paul full of the Holy Ghost, looking steadfastly at Elymas said, "O full of all subtilty and all mischief, thou child of the devil, thou enemy of all righteousness, wilt thou not cease to pervert the right ways of the Lord? And now, behold, the hand of the Lord is upon thee, and thou shalt be blind, not seeing the sun for a season. And in the same moment there fell upon him a mist and a darkness; and he went about seeking some one to lead him by the hand."

In this composition, Elymas, in total darkness, tottering, with his head thrown back is groping around him for some support. Sergius Paulus, astonished, seems to ask those near him, "What have you to oppose to the proofs of Paul?" Here again Raphael has depicted with admirable clearness this dramatic scene; the profound faith of St. Paul, the humiliation and pain of Elymas, and the noble satisfaction of Sergius Paulus. The whole effect, notwithstanding the picturesqueness of the details preserves that noble simplicity, so necessary for biblical subjects.

"Paul and Barnabas at Lystra." St. Paul having healed a lame man at Lystra, the people took the disciples of Christ for the gods Jupiter and Mercury, and entreated the priests to offer sacrifices to them. "Then Paul and Barnabas rent their clothes, and ran in among the people, crying out, and saying, Sirs, why do ye these things?"

Raphael has chosen the moment when the sacrifice was being prepared. But the protestations of the apostles stop this idolatrous ceremony and cause a new emotion to circulate amongst the crowd. A young man, interpreting their thought, seizes, by a rapid movement, the arm of the priest, which is already raised. An old man is curiously lifting the garments which cover the legs of the restored cripple, as if to seek some traces of the miracle, whilst the man himself, no longer in need of his crutches is casting a grateful look on the apostles.

The Greek architecture of the background by its richness, purity and elegance is a fresh proof of Raphael's profound knowledge of that art.

It has frequently been remarked that the group containing the sacrifice was taken from an antique bas-relief.[1] But who could dare to blame the master for this! He was certainly fortunate in being able from an authentic monument, to give this part of his subject the seal of historical fidelity.

"St. Paul preaching at Athens." Amongst a numerous audience, St. Paul, standing on the steps is announcing his divine message. His look and gestures are inspired, his whole bearing is imposing. The personages listening to him are very well characterised. We may study all the different impressions produced on the crowd. In the foreground Dionysius, the Areopagite, accompanied by his wife Damaris, is coming up the steps and testifying his enthusiasm. On the other side is a well-fed Epicurean, who seems very attentive but still feels doubts; near him is a proud stoic. The sophists who are seated are already discussing the words of St. Paul amongst themselves. This masterly work is the image of the first gigantic struggles of the Christian church, not yet with ignorance and barbarism, but with the whole pagan philosophy and the worship of false gods.

This picture, like the preceding ones, is distinguished for the grandeur of its ordering, the life and movement which animate it, the character and precision of the types and the beauty of the architecture.

"St. Paul in Prison." The apostle having preached at Philippi, was arrested and thrown into a dungeon with Silas. But at midnight when they were praying and singing praises to God, an earthquake shook the prison, the doors opened and the apostles were at liberty.

To indicate this earthquake, Raphael has placed under the ground of the building the allegorical figure of a gigantic man who shakes the foundations of the building by his wide shoulders.

This tapestry is the narrowest of the whole, its proportions being made to correspond with those of the panel nearest the tribune of the choir.

The whole of these superb works show that Raphael thoroughly understood the Christian epic. In representing all these historical characters he kept closely to the type authorized by tradition. But his

---

[1] Reproduced, pl. x., in the work of Pietro Santi Bartoli, entitled "Amiranda Romanorum," &c., 1793; it is most probably this bas-relief that is now in the collection in the Mantua Library. Another ancient bas-relief, almost similar, is the one preserved in the collection Degli Uffizi at Florence, but in this there is only one child playing on the flute near the altar. In general Raphael only made a very free use of the antique models.

figures are far from possessing the stiffness of the later academic schools. Although guided by nature, Raphael never fell into that brutal naturalism, so much admired by vulgar minds.

A pure and true expression, a harmony between the spirit and the time to which his subjects belong, the moral and physical reality of his personages, a clearness of ordering, in which everything concurs to the general idea; these are the qualities which when united constitute the great historical picture. The works of Raphael will be immortal examples of this. They all tend towards a direction which ennobles man. Nothing is ever to be found in them which can disturb the serenity and dignity of history.

There are no superfluous accessories, no strange liberties, nothing at all arbitrary. The delicacy of his genius always dictated a respect for historic facts, which should serve as a lesson to succeeding ages; when representing them his soul only added to them the grandeur, truth, and beauty, which are the essence of true art.

Besides the history of the apostles, Raphael also made another cartoon for a tapestry destined for the altar of the chapel. This tapestry represents the coronation of the Virgin. The Madonna is seated on a throne with Jesus, who is placing a crown on her head. The Father and Holy Spirit are hovering above their heads in a glory. Two angels are drawing aside a curtain, on each side. In the lower part to the left St. John the Baptist is pointing to the Saviour; to the left is St. Jerome in prayer. Near the steps of the throne two little angels are singing.

Here Raphael returned to the symmetric and calm style required by allegorical subjects.

The coronation of the Virgin is at the same time an image of the Holy Trinity; it symbolizes also the divine reason for the agitations, struggles and martyrdoms related in the Acts of the Apostles; and lastly, it is a summary containing the highest expression of Christian faith, and as such, should terminate the series of sacred history.

Whilst Raphael was thus occupied with his sublime creations, Leo X., who was at Florence during the winter of 1515 and 1516, summoned him to that town. Having resolved to add a façade to the church of San Lorenzo, which his ancestor had caused to be erected by Brunelleschi, the Pope wished to consult all the great architects in Italy.

He did not merely summon Raphael: Baccio d'Agnolo, Giuliano da San Gallo, Andrea and Jacopo Sansovino, and Michael Angelo were also invited to send in their designs. His intention was that all these artists should consult together to arrive at a decisive plan. But Michael Angelo would not allow the admission of other artists. Through him the work was allowed to languish for some time, and at last he alone was charged with the work.

The Pope required that instead of Carrara marble, that of Tuscany should be employed, to which place it was necessary first to make a road. In the meantime years passed on, and the funds destined for the completion of the church were partly dissipated, partly devoured by political necessities; and thus it happened that San Lorenzo still wants a façade.

We have no certain information as to Raphael's design. It is probable, however, that a slight drawing, formerly in the Crozat collection, and now in the Albertine collection at Vienna, was the first sketch. The three principal entrances are at the end of a vestibule formed by three large arcades. At the sides are two towers, which are surmounted by high spires, flanked with four little pyramids. These three-storied towers are decorated with coupled columns. The pediment in the centre, pierced by a large round window, is sustained on each side by counterforts in the shape of a prostrate S (ᔕ), the form usually adopted in the churches of the fifteenth century in Tuscany.

This design, very rich and picturesque in its effect, shows several of the peculiar characteristics of Raphael, and there is not the slightest doubt that it is by him.

During this visit to Florence, Raphael also made two designs for private houses, which were built at a later time; they may be considered as amongst the most beautiful in Florence.

The first, built for Giannotto Pandolfini, Bishop of Troy, is in the Strada di San Gallo, and now belongs to the Countess Nencini.

The principal façade, about seventy feet wide, has four windows in a line, surmounted by pediments alternately circular and triangular, accompanied by small Tuscan columns on the ground floor, and Ionic ones on the first floor. The balustrades of the upper windows stand out strongly and rest on the string-course equally projecting of the lower story.

The façade looking into the gardens has more simple frame works for the windows, and in the lower part a beautiful "loggia" of about thirty-six feet wide, with three arcades, supported by graceful columns the chapiters of which are decorated with dolphins and foliage.

A cornice of Ionic order surrounds the house.

Raphael had commissioned Giovanni Francesco da San Gallo with the execution of his plan; but Francesco having died in 1530, his brother Bastiano Aristotile superintended the works.

The second house is the Palazzo degl'Uguccioni family, on the Piazza di Gran-Duca. Besides his design, Raphael had a model made of his plan.

The façade of about fifty-feet wide is of rustic architecture in the ground floor. It has three doors. On the first-story coupled Ionic columns rest on pedestals. This story has three windows with circular pediments, and a balcony with double balustrades, which extends along the whole width of the house. The windows of the second story have triangular pediments with Corinthian coupled columns. The cornice, which was to be Corinthian, is yet wanting, and the house is still covered by a very projecting temporary roof. Possibly the expenses of the building exceeded the means of the proprietor, a case which frequently happened in Italy, especially in the sixteenth century.

On his return to Rome, Raphael, overwhelmed with orders of all kinds, was compelled to refuse many; for instance, he was unable to satisfy the Cardinal Gregorio Cortese, of Modena, who demanded a picture for the refectory of the convent of Saint Polidoro, in that town. This excess of work prevented the execution of many pictures promised or even commenced. Thus the picture for the church of the convent of Monte Luce, near Perugia, was never terminated; it had been commenced in 1505, and in 1516 a fresh agreement had been signed that it should be delivered August 15, 1517.

In the same way the picture for the church of San Spirito, commenced at Florence for the Dei family, remained in the state in which he had left it, as well as the fresco of San Severo at Perugia, the completion of which was vainly longed for.

But to his friends, and especially to his pupils, Raphael constantly gave proof of the most eager devotion. He recommended his pupils, he employed them in great works, he made sketches for them, and assisted them by every possible means.

Thus he sent drawings to his fellow citizen Antonio Battiferri, chief apostolical notary, who had them painted in fresco, on the façade of his house at Borgo San Pietro, by Vincenzo da San Geminiano.

In allusion to the name Battiferri (beater of iron), he had chosen the fable of Vulcan forging the arrows of Cupid, and that of the Cyclops forging the bolts of Jupiter. One of these compositions has come down to us through the fine engraving of Agostino Veneziano; it represents Venus in Vulcan's forge, distributing bows and arrows to little loves.

It would appear that this Battiferri was in friendly relations with Raphael, since their united arbitration was demanded in order to settle a dispute that had arisen at Urbino between the archdeacon, Vincenzo Brancarini, and D. Girolamo Vagnini, Raphael's cousin, on the subject of an ecclesiastical benefice.

The relations of Raphael with Baldassare Turini, the president of the Chancery, are also proved by a curious document of 1518. A political agitator, after having roused the people of Urbino in favour of their legitimate duke, Francesco Maria, had been taken prisoner by the usurper, Lorenzo de' Medici. Raphael did not fear to intercede for him with the chancellor Turini.

He was still more intimate, as we have already seen, with Bernardo Divizio da Bibiena. This cardinal possessing no house in Rome, inhabited in his quality of private secretary of the Pope, some rooms in the third story of the Vatican, which communicated with the upper Loggie. He claimed Raphael's assistance and talent for the decoration of a bath room, and the subjects chosen for it were allusions to the action of love in nature. A strange subject for a cardinal to choose, but quite in harmony with the manners of the time, at the court of Leo X.

Raphael had already made some sketches for these compositions, when the cardinal quitted Rome. He went to Pietro Bembo for news of him, who at the very moment was writing to their mutual friend. This interesting letter has come down to us. It runs as follows:—

"I hear that you took cold at Rubiera and have a fever, which has made me uneasy on your account . . . Raphael has just painted our friend Tebaldeo with so much truth that Tebaldeo does not more resemble himself than this painting resembles him. For myself I have never seen a more striking resemblance. You may judge of this by what Monsignor Antonio (Tebaldeo) says of it, and the value he attaches to it; he is, indeed, quite in the right. The portraits of Monsignor Baldassare Castiglione, and that of the duke of honoured memory, seem to be as regards likeness merely sketches made by a scholar, by the side of Tebaldeo's portrait. I am jealous of it, and think of having my portrait also taken by the hand of Raphael . . . . I had written as far as this in my letter, when Raphael himself came in. He seems to have guessed that I was writing about him. He begs me to add this: that you will let him know the other subjects you desire to have in your little bath room; send him a description of them, for the subjects already decided on will be commenced this week . . . In good truth I am not joking, but Monsignor Baldassare has also just arrived . . . He wishes me to tell you that he has decided to remain this summer in Rome, in order not to changé his good customs, and also because Monsignor Tebaldeo wishes it much. On this I kiss your lordship's hands and commend myself to your goodness . . . . etc.

"April 19th, 1516, at Rome. "PIETRO BEMBO."

Another letter of Bembo's to the same, mentions that Raphael had been unable to place in the bath room a statue of Venus, belonging to the cardinal, the niche intended to receive it being too small. Bembo entreats his friend to allow him to have this Venus, and concludes his letter thus :—" If my demand seem to you too bold, Raphael, *whom you love so much* will make my excuses, for it was he who encouraged me to make this demand. I think then that you will not be able to refuse *your* Raphael . . . . etc."

We are happy, after all the difficulties we have encountered in our researches, to be able to produce some authentic documents, especially when they do honour to the person of Raphael no less than his talent.

The bath room of which we have been speaking was, in conformity with the instructions of the cardinal and the sketches of Raphael and Giulio Romano, decorated in the following manner.

The vaulted ceiling, divided in the antique style into several compartments bordered with gold, contains subjects relating to the combat of Nature with Beauty and Love, and the omnipotence of Love.

Thus we see savage beasts devouring peaceful ones ; two women in chariots, guiding fiery horses and bulls ; and four Loves in different attitudes. On the upper part of the walls, near the windows and three niches, are seven allusions to the victory of Beauty and Love ; whilst Saturn in the heavens drives his father from the throne, the goddess of Love and Beauty appears on the earth ; this Venus, emerging from the foam of the sea, is radiant with life and beauty ; then she crosses the sea with Love, borne by marine monsters ; in the next picture, wounded by Cupid's dart she complains to the god himself, who stands near her ; in the last she is taking out a thorn which has pierced her.

According to the fable, it was the drop of blood that flowed from this slight wound, that falling on a white rose imparted to it its colour.

These four episodes from the history of Venus all bear the stamp of Raphael's genius. In it he has displayed the most graceful movements and lovely forms, with an ever new charm. Nature interpreted thus in all its beauty and variety produces a magical effect without any search for a deeper significance.

The three other pictures in the bath room are of a very different character. Two of them, designed by Giulio Romano, are voluptuous in style; they represent "Syrinx surprised when bathing by Pan," and "Venus and Adonis." The third, of less merit in its composition, is a "Pallas struggling with Vulcan." "The Victorious Loves," engraved by Maestri, decorate the socle below.

It appears strange at the present day, notwithstanding the modest beauty of Raphael's compositions, that a prelate should have decorated his private dwelling, in the very palace of the Pope, with such subjects; the more so as the subjects sketched by Giulio Romano, are decidedly of a voluptuous tendency. But it must be remembered that at this time the court of Rome had a singular predilection for everything antique and classical, an instance of which has been left by Cardinal Bibiena, in his comedy of "Calandra." The paintings in the bath room had a great success, as is proved by their having been engraved, and also by the repetitions made of them in the ancient vestibule of the Villa Pallatina. The coats of arms and some other subjects still to be seen on the ceiling, seem to indicate that Giulio Romano must have painted these repetitions for a Duke Mattei. The loggia in which they are is supported by three Ionic columns. It looked out formerly on a garden; but, having been surrounded by new buildings, it is now in the centre of a large hall.

Here again we see, amongst other subjects, in the small compartments of the white ceiling, the contest of Love in Nature, symbolized by cupids fighting with wild beasts and marine monsters. On the five panels of the walls are the same subjects from the history of Venus, but in figures the size of life.

We must not forget the paintings in another villa, said to be that of Raphael himself, which was situated in the park of the great Borghese villa, and which was destroyed during the commotions of 1848. The ceiling of the hall had been decorated in the time of Raphael. Three small frescoes, of historical and mythological subjects were surrounded by four female portraits, which have been falsely termed the "Mistresses of Raphael." It is now proved that this villa never belonged to Raphael. It belonged possibly to some rich merchant, a friend of the arts, as there is a figure of Mercury amongst the ornaments of the ceiling.

The proprietor had fortunately caused the three principal frescoes to be removed in 1845. These are the "Marriage of Roxana," from a composition of Raphael's; the "Passions," allegorical figures, who, during the sleep of Cupid, are shooting at a target, from a design by Michael Angelo; and "Vertumnus and Pomona," which appears to be by Perino del Vaga, as well as the other ornaments of that room.

Here we have only to examine Raphael's Roxana. Seated on a couch of antique form, she bends her beautiful head towards Alexander, as a flower before the rays of the sun. The hero feels himself vanquished, and urged by a little cupid, he offers her a crown. Ephestion, with a torch in his hand, is standing near the god Hymen. Little Loves are carrying away the veil and sandals of Roxana; others are playing gaily with Alexander's arms; one of them has slipped into his cuirass, and is trying to lift it, crawling on his hands and feet. Greater beauty could not be imagined. It would have been very interesting to compare this painting with that of the ancient painter, Ætion, of which Lucian has left a complete description; for it was from this very description that Raphael made his drawing.

We must now mention a fresco executed from a composition of Raphael's, by one of his best pupils, in the little hunting box, called the Magliana, situated near the Tiber, about five miles from Rome. It was built by Innocent VIII., enlarged by Julius II., and frequently visited by Leo X., who was extremely fond of the chase. The Cardinal of Pavia, in order to please Julius II., had had a chapel erected in it, which was decorated by one of Perugino's pupils. These paintings were probably either deteriorated, or the assassination of the cardinal had prevented their completion, for it was here that Leo X. caused a fresco to be executed from a composition of Raphael, on the "Martyrdom of St. Cecilia," wrongly named the "Martyrdom of St. Felicia," so well known through the engraving of Marcantonio.

For a long time past only half of this picture was to be seen, the wall having been pierced to make a gallery; what remained of the picture has lately been removed from the wall, and sold by auction. Raphael thus gave his pupils work as frequently as he could. It was an immense advantage for them, doubtless, to have such a master, constantly to feel the inspiration of his genius, to receive the counsels of a man who had attained to the climax of his art, to profit by his experience, and to be in some degree animated by his noble and generous heart; all

—both master and pupils—being at that age when hope is ardent and conviction complete.

But Raphael would not allow these young artists, the greater part of whom were masters themselves, to sacrifice their career to him; he encouraged them to give free course to their talents, and to execute their own compositions, as was done by Giovanni da Udine, in the paintings for the lower loggie, and Perino del Vaga in concert with Da Udine, for the large hall of the same story.[1]

Vasari also relates that Raphael, who had such taste for elegance, and who kept a princely house, was always followed by the train of his numerous disciples when he went to the court, a striking contrast to the customs of Michael Angelo, who usually went alone.[2]

Amongst the pictures that Raphael sent out of Rome between the years 1516 and 1518, is that of "Christ bearing the Cross," painted for the church of the monks of Monte Oliveto, Santa Maria della Spasimo, at Palermo. Jesus, borne down under the weight of the cross, is saying to the women who follow him, "Daughters of Jerusalem, weep not for me, but weep for yourselves and for your children," &c.

This picture, which is in the finest manner of the master, is well known through the brilliant engraving of Toschi. In life and movement, dramatic unity, power of drawing, and sentiment of the beautiful, it is perhaps more perfect than any other of Raphael's works. The irresistible charm of Raphael's ordinary paintings, arises from the depth of the characters and expressions; but here the exterior is more masculine and full of energy. The artist is seen in all the strength of mature age. The sight of this masterpiece always awakens the thought, that art could not rise to a grander style.

The "Bearing of the Cross," which is frequently called "Lo Spasimo," had an almost miraculous escape. The ship which was carrying it to

---

[1] They decorated the ceiling with symbolical figures of the sun, the moon and the planets, surrounded by the signs of the Zodiac and the hours. These paintings are so much in Raphael's style that they have been frequently attributed to him. But a conscientious examination reveals the want of spirit and fancy always to be found in the great master; the general arrangement too has not that sentiment of the beautiful to be found in all the works directly emanating from him.

[2] The anecdote related by Lomazzo is not the less improbable: "One day Raphael, accompanied by his pupils, met Michael Angelo, who said to him, 'Where are you going, surrounded thus like a general?' 'And you, alone, like the hangman!' replied Raphael." M. Horace Vernet has painted a well known picture on this subject, which was exhibited in 1833, under the title of "Raphael au Vatican."—*Lacroix.*

Palermo was wrecked, and all on board, both crew and cargo, perished. The case containing the picture alone floated towards the port of Genoa, and was picked up before the water penetrated into it. There was great joy in the whole town, and the news of the event immediately spread over the whole of Italy. But when the monks of Palermo claimed their masterpiece, the inhabitants of Genoa were not willing to restore it; and it was only given up on the Pope's intervention.

During the Spanish dominion it was bought for the chapel of Philip IV.; under the French empire, it figured in the Napoleon Museum; it is now in the Museum of Madrid.

Raphael painted another altar-piece, a "Visitation," for the church of San Silvestro dell' Aquila, in the Abruzzi. Mary, with a degree of maidenly embarrassment, is greeting her cousin Elizabeth, who advances to meet her. The latter, filled with holy joy, is so marvellously life-like, that we seem to hear the words, "Blessed art thou among women!"

The background is a landscape, traversed by the Jordan, in which may be seen small figures of Christ being baptized by John the Baptist. This anachronism is an allusion to the donor, Giovanni Battista Branconio, who had ordered the picture.

For his young patron, who was afterwards Duke of Mantua, Raphael composed a Holy Family, expressive of the joys of domestic life. Giulio Romano was charged with its execution, and accomplished it with extraordinary care.

When, after the dispersion of the gallery of the unfortunate Charles I. of England, Philip IV. received this Madonna, which he had caused to be bought for him in London, he was so much enchanted that he exclaimed, "That is my pearl!" And this name has ever since remained.[1]

In Spain there are likewise two other Holy Families, belonging to

---

[1] Emeric David, who was able to study this picture at Paris in the studio of the painter and restorer Bonnemaison, does not appear to believe that Giulio Romano had assisted in it. "A chef-d'œuvre of taste," he says, after having lovingly described this "Holy Family." (See "Notices Historiques sur les Chefs-d'œuvre de la Peinture Moderne," p. 48). "This picture possesses every perfection proper to the subject, and the most severe critic would have difficulty in discovering any negligence. The composition, drawing, expression and colouring, are almost perfect." M. Viardot, in his "Musées d'Espagne," does not say that Giulio Romano assisted in the slightest degree in this picture: "Although the background is rather dark, there is a prevailing tint rather violet than brick colour, but, at all events, perfectly graceful; and the whole composition, even to the slightest details of the ground and drapery, is completed with the same finish that is admired in the works of Leonardo."—*Lacroix.*

the school of Raphael, and for which the master appears only to have made the sketches. One of these is the "Holy Family under the Oak-tree;" the other the "Virgin with the Rose or with the Legend."

We now come to a picture entirely by the hand of Raphael, and one of his most celebrated ones, too, the "Madonna della Sedia." Vasari does not describe it. It is mentioned in the catalogue of the Tribune in 1589. It is now to be seen in the gallery of the Pitti Palace.

What strikes us the most in this Madonna is that it presents rather an image of maternal and filial love, than an image of the mother of the Redeemer. Created by Raphael in one of his poetical inspirations, it is of magical and fascinating beauty. Perhaps no picture has ever been rendered so popular by copies and imitations of every sort.

Although the attraction of the Virgin is derived rather from her incomparable beauty than from a Christian significance, the head of the infant Jesus with its gentle simplicity, and the young St. John in adoration, give to the picture, if not the religious character of the primitive masters, at all events a character completely removed from the familiar style.

The "Madonna della Tenda," thus named because of a curtain which decorates the background, bears some resemblance to the Madonna of the Pitti palace; it was formerly in the palace of Madrid. King Louis of Bavaria bought it of Sir Thomas Baring, and it is now in the Pinacothek of Munich.[1] Several ancient copies are known of it.

The Madonna named "of the Candelabra" is much finer than that of Munich. Its name arises from the two angels who hold candelabra. These angels are not by Raphael, but were added subsequently. The Virgin's head is totally different from that of the Madonna della Sedia.

---

[1] This Madonna has been frequently contested. M. Viardot, in his "Musées d'Allemagne" (1855, p. 114), says, "The one of Raphael's pictures which the Bavarians seem most proud of possessing, is a small Holy Family, or rather a Madonna, reminding us in its arrangement of the marvellous "Madonna della Sedia" in the Pitti Palace. It was bought, it is said, for the sum of 64,000 florins. Mary seated and seen in profile presses the Infant Saviour to her breast, whilst he is worshipped by the young St. John rather further back. This resemblance to the "Madonna della Sedia" is less an advantage, in my opinion, than a formidable danger. For those who have seen the incomparable masterpiece at Florence, and who have shed tears of enthusiasm before it, the Munich Virgin is like a distant portrait of a lost friend; a sight of it only inspires us with regret. If Andrea del Sarto—whose wonderful copy of the portrait of Leo X., sent by the Medici to Naples, so long passed for an original—had sometimes imitated the painter of Urbino I should say that this Madonna was by Andrea del Sarto rather than by the divine founder of the Roman school. Drawing, colouring—all, except the style, remind us of him rather than of Raphael.—*Lacroix.*

Her countenance is full of majestic calm and a divine modesty; her eyes are humbly cast down. We feel the influence of her faith that her smiling child is the Son of God and the Saviour of the world.

This magnificent picture, of circular form, passed from the Borghese gallery to that of Lucien Bonaparte, then into that of the Duke of Lucca. It is now in the possession of Mr. Munro, in London.

We cannot fail to be surprised when we come to enumerate the easel pictures executed at this period by Raphael, who was overwhelmed with labours of far higher importance. His productiveness was as inexhaustible as his imagination. It is said that one of his pupils asked him one day how he had succeeded in producing so quickly such a large number of works; he replied, "From my earliest childhood I have made it a principle never to neglect anything." And, indeed, his long studies, his sustained attention, his constant observations, his care of details, had rendered him so completely master of his execution, that his hand followed the rapidity of his thought.

Amongst the masterpieces that he produced at this time, we must mention first the painting that Lorenzo de' Medici commissioned him to execute for Francis I.[1]

A political motive was the origin of this order.[2] Lorenzo de' Medici, who had usurped the duchy of Urbino, hoped to obtain the protection of

---

[1] See Gaye, Carteggio, ii. p. 146-8, and our Catalogue-article on the "St. Michael," where all the letters concerning these pictures are given.

[2] M. Villot, in his excellent catalogue of the pictures in the Louvre, has done justice to all the accounts given by historians of the two pictures. "Historians say that Francis I., in his admiration for the picture of St. Michael which Raphael had sent him, recompensed the great artist with such munificence that he, in his turn, wished to recognise the liberality of the monarch by painting him a Holy Family, which he entreated him to accept as a present. Francis I. replied to Raphael that men celebrated in art, sharing the immortality of great kings, might treat with them." He accepted the picture, doubled the price he had given for the "St. Michael," and invited the artist to come to his court; but Leo X. would not permit his departure from Rome. Father Dan, after stating that Francis I. paid 24,000 livres for the Holy Family, adds that in his time a famous painter, "la considérant exactement, offrit d'en faire 20,000 écus, s'il estoit à vendre," and says that it was a present from Pope Clement VII. to the king. Unhappily facts come in to contradict the anecdotes of historians and the accounts of Father Dan, who should have remembered that Leo X. died in 1521, and that Clement VII. was not Pope in 1518." It might be admitted, however, without being at variance with facts and dates, that Francis I. had requested Lorenzo de' Medici to order the two pictures in his own name, but on account of the king of France. It would not be impossible that that prince had written to the painter sending him a present, if not the price stipulated between Lorenzo de' Medici and him.—*Lacroix.*

THE MADONNA WITH THE CANDELABRA.

In the Munro Collection.

the King of France by sending him two of Raphael's works. The first picture is a St. Michael, in allusion to the order of knighthood bearing the name of the archangel; the second, a Holy Family, which, from its dimensions and the number of the figures, surpasses all that Raphael had executed before.

The St. Michael represents the irresistible power of the divine will, or the triumph of good over evil. The archangel is descending on Satan with the rapidity of lightning, and overthrowing him with a touch of his foot. His youth, beauty, and heroism bear a supernatural character. The spectator's glance scarcely rests on the prostrate demon, whose fantastic ugliness Raphael has partially concealed by a skilful foreshortening.

The large "Holy Family" (thus named because it is the largest work of this subject painted by the master) expresses the happiness, love, and adoration of the Holy Family. The nobility and richness of the ordering, the purity of the style, are still further increased by the presence of two angels who take part in the joys of the domestic hearth.

The Virgin is holding out her arms to the Infant Saviour, still in his cradle; St. Elizabeth, kneeling, is teaching the young St. John to worship the Saviour, and St. Joseph appears absorbed in contemplation.

But how is it that this idea so simple in itself, is yet capable of arousing such elevated thoughts, and of causing all the highest faculties God has given us to vibrate? The reason is to be found in the sacred mission and the grandeur of art. It is because Raphael, divinely endowed, has imparted to his works the inspiration with which he was himself animated. In his mind was grandeur and harmony, and the sentiment of his works is of all that is purest in nature.

In the execution of these pictures, Raphael employed the assistance of Giulio Romano,[1] but he completed them both himself, and traced his

---

[1] All connoisseurs in art have, indeed, declared that the "St. Michael," to which they attach comparatively little value, was not painted by Raphael; they scarcely even recognise his hand in any part of this large painting, which appears to have been executed in his studio from his drawings. As for the "Holy Family," which went to France with the "St. Michael," it is, on the contrary, looked upon as one of the best works of the master. The picture was formerly closed by two wings which were probably destroyed at the time of the revolution, when the picture was transferred to canvas. The following note is to be found in the inventory of Bailli, guardian of the king's pictures in 1710:—"Painted on wood and with a gilded border, with two wings lined with green velvet, painted over with ornaments relieved with gold."

Mr. Waagen (Kunstwerke in Paris, 1839, p. 439) says:—"The share that Giulio

name on them with the date 1518. In the month of June of that year, and as if to prevent all fear of accidents,[1] they were sent by land (by Florence and Lyons) to King Francis at Fontainebleau, where Lorenzo de' Medici was at the time.[2]

It may be imagined what were the joy and admiration of Francis I. at beholding these masterpieces. However great the fame of Raphael was and the opinion that had been formed in France of his talent, all the king's expectations were surpassed. He therefore used every means to attract the great Italian artist to his court. But Leo X. could not consent to this desire of the King of France, and besides, nothing could have persuaded Raphael to quit Rome and Italy.[3]

Being unable to accomplish his design of bringing Raphael to Paris, Francis I. seems at all events to have claimed his talent in some great works, and to have recompensed him royally; for Félibien,[4] speaking of the small Holy Family in which the Infant Jesus, standing up in his cradle, is embracing the young St. John, relates that Raphael painted it for Adrian Gouffier, Cardinal de Boissy, who had rendered him services

---

Romano had in these two pictures is unmistakeable. . . ." And, indeed, Vasari, in his life of Giulio Romano, says, "Lavorò sopra un bellissimo quadro d'una Santa Elisabetta che tu fatto da Raffaello e mandato al Re Francesco di Francia." This St. Elizabeth, as Bottari has already remarked, could be no other picture than the "Holy Family" of 1518.—*Lacroix*.

[1] The shipwreck of Raphael's "Spasimo" (see p. 182) was probably not forgotten, for it had been at first proposed to transport the pictures by sea to Provence, says the correspondence of Gorio Gheri; but he writes, May 17th, 1518: "As for the paintings, I hear that our lord (the Pope?) wishes them to go by land. Let his Holiness's pleasure be performed. Do not forget to remind Raphael that he must arrange them and take every precaution that they be not injured on the way, especially if it should rain." —*Lacroix*.

[2] The presence of Lorenzo de' Medici at Fontainebleau is proved by the correspondence of Gorio Gheri, of Florence, with Baldassare Turini at Rome, and with Lorenzo himself. See Gaye, "Carteggio," vol. ii., n. xc. and xci.

[3] See "Extraits des différents ouvrages publiés sur la vie des peintres," by M. P. D. L. F. (Papillon de la Ferté), Paris, 1776, vol. i. p. 38.

[4] Felibien asserts that this small Holy Family is not by the hand of Raphael, but that he merely retouched and completed it. Mariette ("Recueil d'estampes de Crozat, vol. i. pl. 9,) believes that he recognises the execution of Garofalo in this picture. According to a tradition related by Felibien, Giulio Romano painted it from an original which Mazarin commissioned the Chevalier del Pozzo to buy at Rome. "It may be seen," says M. Villot ("Catalogue des Table des Ecoles Italiennes," p. 217), "that these critics all agree in attributing this composition to Raphael, though they are not unanimous as to the name of the artist who executed it.—*Lacroix*.

at the court of France.[1] This small Holy Family had a wing on which the allegorical figure of Plenty was painted in chiaroscuro, which is now exhibited in the Louvre, but separated from the principal picture.[2]

Amongst the orders given to Raphael by Francis I., we believe we may include the cartoons for the tapestries with subjects drawn from the life of Christ, which he wished to present to the Pope in gratitude for the canonisation of San Francesco di Paula.[3]

But of all these undertakings Raphael had only completed, when death came to interrupt his labours, the one composition of the "Massacre of the Innocents." The cartoons for the other subjects were subsequently executed by his pupils.

It is supposed that the St. Margaret[4] had been painted for Francis I. in allusion to the name of his sister, Marguerite de Valois. The saint with the calm and moral force given by faith, is victoriously treading down the dragon. This picture is much deteriorated, and has been almost entirely repainted. But everything in it gives us to suppose that in its primitive state it was worthy of being placed amongst the other works of Raphael of the same period.

In his life of Giulio Romano, Vasari says that another picture sent to Francis I., the portrait of Joanna of Aragon, of which, however, Raphael had only painted the head, all the rest having been executed from his designs by Giulio Romano. According to Father Dan and Lépicié, this

---

[1] He was sent there in 1519, as papal legate.

[2] Félibien says that this picture was covered by a wing of painted wood, and adorned in a manner as agreeable as it was learned. M. Villot, who had not recognised this wing in the picture of "Plenty" (see the editions of his catalogue anterior to 1855) was, no doubt, led astray by the rather vague information afforded by Félibien: "The fate of this wing," he observed, "is not known. It has entirely disappeared, and for a long time has been separated from the picture." After having described this same wing under the No. 387, as being a "model for a fountain," he adds, "This picture is attributed in the inventory of Bailly (1709-10), to Giulio Romano. It has likewise been attributed to Giovanni Nanni da Udine, who frequently painted the arabesques and ornaments in Raphael's pictures; also to Francesco Penni, called *Il Fatore*."—*Lacroix*.

[3] Francis I. had ardently desired this canonisation which took place May 1st, 1519. See P. Isidoro Toscana, "Vita di San Francesco di Paula" (Roma, 1731), and the 'Magazin Encyclopédique," in the third year of the Republic (1795), vol. iii. p. 379.

[4] M. Villot quotes Vasari, who pretends that this picture, probably painted for the king or for his sister Marguerite, was entirely painted by Giulio Romano from Raphael's drawing. This picture was first restored ten years after its arrival in France; it has undergone many restorations since, and is now so entirely repainted that the tip of the saint's toe is the only part in the light.—*Lacroix*.

picture was a present from Ippolito de' Medici; this is an error, however, since that prince was only nine years of age at the death of Raphael.[1] We imagine that this was rather a present from Lorenzo de' Medici who knew the passion of the King for beautiful women.

Joanna of Aragon, the wife of Ascanio Colonna, Prince of Tagliacozzo, was at this time the most accomplished beauty at Rome. More than three hundred poets sang of her brilliant beauty and of her virtues. Amongst them was Augustinus Niphus, in his book on "Beauty and Love."[2] As an introduction, he added to this book an extremely enthusiastic letter of Cardinal Pompejus Colonna, the chancellor of the Pope: "I have read your book on 'Love and Beauty' with the greatest care," says the cardinal, "and I am much delighted with it. Nothing could be found more agreeable to me, nothing more useful to posterity or more glorious to you. You explain divine and mortal beauty with reasons which are quite decisive, and you illustrate all this by the celebrated and almost divine Joanna of Aragon, in order that there may not remain the slightest doubt as to what beauty must take the first place amongst gods and men. Such models, however, are most rare in humanity, for nature is not lavish of her choicest gifts. But in our times, nature, the generous creator, wishing to show the world something marvellous, perfect, and resembling the immortals, has created Johanna Aragonia Colonna; and has conducted her through all the degrees of perfection, from the cradle until this day, when she is in all the flower of life. . . . Nature has likewise endowed her with extraordinary virtues, adding chaste dignity to a body of divine form, so that it would be difficult to find any fault in her unless it be her mortal nature. Her brow and her mouth have so much serenity, her eyes dart such dazzling rays, her whole body is so perfect, that the most insensible are compelled to love her, and are so drawn into the contemplation of perfect beauty. Of great piety, and possessed of eloquence beyond her sex, she is a model of virtue. One might call her a luminary fallen from the heavens to bring light amongst us. . . . . ."

It is beyond doubt that the portrait in the Louvre is indeed the one spoken of by Vasari; the hand of Giulio Romano may be recognised in

---

[1] M. Villot points out the same error, but he supposes that the picture was given by Giuliano de' Medici (Clement VII.) and not by Lorenzo.—*Lacroix*.

[2] The work of Agostino Nilo, Professor at the University of Pisa, who wrote under the name of Niphus, is entitled "De Amore et Pulchro;" it was printed at Leyden in 1549, with the book "De Remedio Amoris," of Platina.—*Lacroix*.

SAINT MARGARET.

In the Louvre.

all the accessories, which are skilfully and powerfully treated. Yet we must confess that the head, which alone is attributed to Raphael, surprises us by showing a certain dryness of execution, a certain stiffness and even littleness in the drawing, very little in accordance with the noble and spiritual manner of the master.[1] However this may be, the picture in the Louvre is undoubtedly the best of all the repetitions known of it.

These works for France did not prevent Raphael from producing others at the same time for the Medici Family.

Already, about the year 1514, he had painted the portrait of the Pope's younger brother, Giuliano de' Medici, who had just abdicated the government of Florence. Four years later he also took the portrait of Lorenzo de' Medici, the son of Pietro Francesco, Duke of Nemours, who had succeeded to his uncle Giuliano as gonfalonier of Florence, in 1516.

According to Vasari these portraits which were of very fine colouring, were, in his time, in the possession of Ottaviano de' Medici at Florence. It is not known what has become of them. Copies of them alone have been preserved : that of Giuliano, by Alessandro Allori, is in the Florence gallery ; that of Lorenzo, in the Fabre Museum, at Montpellier.

But we still possess the chef d'œuvre which places Raphael in the first rank of portrait-painters. The portrait of Leo X. surrounded by his nearest relations, Giuliano de Medici whom he named cardinal of Santa Maria in Domenica, and who was subsequently Pope Clement VII. and Lodovico de Rossi, also a nephew of Leo X., brought up under the same roof as he, and who remained his inseparable companion in all the vicissitudes of his life.

Filled with gratitude to his powerful protector, Raphael has almost surpassed himself in this work, which in every respect occupies a unique place in art. The countenances are living, the light plays through it, everything seems in motion. Grandeur, truth, style, colouring, execution, all are carried to the highest possible perfection in it.

We do not attach much credence to certain anecdotes told of Raphael, but we will give, merely as a proof of the resemblance of these portraits to their originals the anecdote related by Federico Zucchero.[2] Baldassare Turini the president of the chancery, was so deceived by the

[1] M. Waagen also criticises and contests a little the Joanna of Aragon in the Louvre.—*Lacroix.*

[2] "L'Idea d' scultori, pittori," etc., lib. ii. cap. 6.

painting, that he knelt before it, presenting a pen and ink to the image of the Pope that he might sign some bills.

The well-known portrait of the young violinist,[1] although less imbued with reality is by the same pencil. It adorns the Sciarra palace at Rome. The date it bears is 1518. We have been unable to determine exactly whom it is intended to represent. It is possibly Andrea Marone, of Brescia, who accompanied himself with the violin in his improvisations, and who met with great success under Leo X. He was a great favourite of the Pope, and gained the prize for improvisation at a feast of St. Cosmo, which Leo X. held annually in honour of his ancestors. The laurel leaves which the young musician holds in the same hand as the bow, would seem to be an allusion to this fact.

Vasari informs us that Raphael painted many other portraits; some of these have disappeared; others do not show the master's touch in every part. We will mention however the noble portrait of Cardinal Borgia, in the Borghese palace, and that of the Archdeacon Carondelet, in the collection of the Duke of Grafton in London.

About the same period, the Benedictines of St. Sixtus at Placentia asked Raphael for a picture in which might be introduced the Madonna with the Child, St. Sixtus and St. Barbara. It was the last Virgin created by the genius of Raphael; and as if he had foreseen that this Madonna would be his last work, he made it an apotheosis.

In the midst of an immense and profound glory filled with cherubim heads, the Virgin is standing holding in her arms the Infant Jesus. Her feet scarcely touch the cloud which bears her; she stands out from the mystery of the heavens and appears in her sweet and majestic glory. Beneath her St. Sixtus on the left and St. Barbara on the right, are kneeling in adoration. Two little angels of celestial beauty, leaning on a cornice at the bottom complete the composition.

In Raphael's idea, the faithful are supposed to be in prayer before his work; St. Sixtus is pointing to them with a gesture, and is praying the Virgin for them; St. Barbara is also praying for them with an admirable expression of charity.

Let us endeavour as far as possible to appreciate this sublime

---

[1] "Cantatore alla viola," an improvisatore accompanying himself on the violin. Castiglione, in the first volume of his "Corteggio," quotes the style of the "cantare alla viola," as the most suitable to represent musical talent.

picture, although words are very powerless to describe so much beauty, magnificence, elevation, and faith.

The features of the Virgin whose triumphant majesty is unequalled, wear an expression of nobleness, innocence, sweetness, and modesty; her son whose attitude is simple and child-like, bears in his whole countenance a divine character, and his penetrating glance goes straight to the heart. It is no longer the graceful smiling child of the other Madonnas, but the Son of God, the Saviour of the world, who at the last day will become the sovereign judge.

Wonderful power of art! in that little head, so calm, so sweet and yet so severe, reside both the flame of the purest poetry and all the depth of Christian faith.

The "Madonna di San Sisto" is indeed an apparition, clothed in the forms of nature, but animated, and to some extent rendered divine, by the genius of the most ideal artist that God has ever created. This Madonna is certainly the work which contributed most to procure Raphael the surname of "the divine." Even in its technical part it does not resemble any of the other works of Raphael; although its execution is of extreme simplicity, it has none of that art which is only formed for delighting the eye. All in it is seen by the light of enthusiasm; and but for the little angels at the bottom, painted as an after-thought on the clouds, we should scarcely see a trace of human hands in the picture.

This is why this picture cannot be worthily represented by copyists, either painters or engravers. The outline flies when we seek to seize it; and even supposing that were rendered correctly, some parts, we may safely affirm that what Raphael has imparted of his own soul, so to speak, in the countenances of the Virgin and the Infant Jesus, can never be rendered by another hand.

It was before this "Madonna di San Sisto" that Correggio exclaimed, "I also am a painter." Although we can well understand the emulation that would be aroused in the breast of a gifted artist, by the sight of such a picture, yet we confess that this exclamation, which has become celebrated, loses much of its value when we think of what different directions the painter of Parma and the painter of Urbino follow in art. In Raphael's Virgin there is a total absence of all pretensions to colouring, brilliancy, and powerful tones. Correggio, then, could see nothing in this picture of what rendered himself famous. On the contrary, this great colourist must have been struck by the fact that the sublime conceptions of Raphael, assisted by the simplest technical means, the severity of his thought and the noble drawing, made the resources of colouring almost undesirable. There was no reason, then, for Correggio's exclamation.

We certainly should not receive too implicitly all the anecdotes concerning great artists and great men in general; but in comparing two of these anecdotes, that which depicts the humility and even the despair of Francia, that despair, which it is said, prevented him from touching a pencil again, and was the real cause of his death, at the sight of Raphael's "St. Cecilia," is more touching than the proud language of Correggio.

The town of Placentia allowed the "Madonna di San Sisto" to be carried away from it by the Elector of Saxony, who bought it at eleven thousand sequins, without counting some presents. On its arrival in Dresden, the picture obtained a rare honour; the Elector wishing to place it in the large reception-room in the palace, it was perceived that the place occupied by the throne was precisely that best lighted and most favourable to the picture. The Elector immediately ordered the displacement of his throne, and even assisted himself in the operation.

The "St. John the Baptist in the Desert," painted on canvas for Cardinal Colonna, is of about the same date. Seated near a spring of water, he is pointing to the luminous rays emitted by a reed cross. A panther's skin hangs around one of his arms and his loins.

This picture, in science and taste in the drawing, does not quite come up to the superb and masterly drawing Raphael had at first made for it. It resembles rather an academic study than a religious or historical scene. We must conclude that a pupil assisted in its execution.

But, on account of the taste then professed for the nude, the St. John the Baptist obtained excessive admiration and was frequently copied. It was presented, in the first place, by the cardinal to the physician Jacopo da Carpi, who had treated him during a severe illness; it afterwards passed into the possession of Francesco Benintendi at Florence, and since the year 1589 it has been in the Tribune.

Now, however, Raphael wished to undertake the paintings in the Loggie of the Chigi Palace, in which he had already represented Galatea. Induced by the success which the Commentary on the Fables of Apuleius, published by Beroaldo the elder, was then obtaining, he chose as a fresh subject the fable of Cupid and Psyche.

For the fourteen medallions of the vestibule he sketched, in allusion to the omnipotence of love, little victorious Loves, playing with the attributes of the gods; for the pendants, the "Jealousy of Venus," the "Trials and Victory of Psyche;" for the roof, the "Reception of Psyche in Olympus," and her "Marriage with Cupid;" two large compositions which, like those in the hall of Heliodorus, are painted to look like tapestries fastened to the ceiling.

He was extremely anxious to avoid the disagreeable effect of a number of figures foreshortened from top to bottom; a fault very usual with later painters, and which shows always a want of taste and good decorative qualities in mural paintings of an elevated style.

But, overwhelmed with commissions at this time, he was only able to execute the cartoons for the greater part, and merely painted with his own hand, as a model for the rest, one of the three Graces (the one seen from behind), to whom Cupid is showing Psyche.

Unfortunately, the master's model did not inspire the disciples with the sentiment of beauty and life which animates this female figure, treated in a style of sufficient amplitude, but with very delicate outlines and fresh colouring.

The frescoes were painted heavily; the drawing is wanting in delicacy; the half-tints are of a brick-red colour. The high qualities peculiar to Raphael's style have alone given to this picture the charm it still possesses, notwithstanding its successive deteriorations.

Much criticism was aroused by these paintings in the Chigi palace, and by many other oil paintings which had come from Raphael's studio, but which had been almost entirely executed by his pupils; and the opinion soon spread that the talent of the great master of the Roman school was on the decline.

This decision of the public was sensibly felt by Raphael, who resolved to refute it by some brilliant work which should only be touched by himself. He accepted, then, with joy an order from Cardinal Giuliano de' Medici for a "Transfiguration," for a church in the diocese of Narbonne. The cardinal had likewise ordered at the same time a picture representing the "Raising of Lazarus,"[1] from Sebastiano del Piombo, whom Michael Angelo wished to oppose to Raphael.[2] Michael Angelo even

[1] This picture is now in the National Gallery. Mr. Wornum in his Catalogue of the National Gallery says:—"This picture remained in the cathedral of Narbonne until it was purchased by the Duke of Orleans early in the eighteenth century. It was brought to England in 1792, with the rest of the Orleans gallery, and came into the possession of Mr. Angerstein, with whose pictures it was purchased for the nation in 1824."

[2] The high opinion Sebastiano himself entertained of this painting may be seen from the following passage in one of his letters to Michael Angelo, of December 29th, 1519:—"E credo la mia tavola sia meglio disegnata che i panni drazi che son venuti da Fiandra." He was alluding to the tapestries by Raphael. The original letter was

made several drawings for this Lazarus,[1] thinking that, with the beautiful colouring of his friend the Venetian, the result would be overpowering for the painter of the "Transfiguration." Raphael was informed of this, and replied gaily, "Michael Angelo pays me a great honour, since it is in reality himself he offers as my rival and not Sebastiano."

The "Transfiguration" being the last picture painted by Raphael, we shall examine it last. In the meantime we have to speak of another work, which occupied much of the time of the last years of his life.

Our readers will not have forgotten the letter from Caelio Calcagnini to Jacob Ziegler, in which the writer relates that Raphael, passionately fond of everything beautiful or great, especially in ancient art, sought to discover the plans of ancient Rome from what remained of the buildings, and from the description of Latin authors. The same Calcagnini has left the following epigram on this attempt of Raphael's, which interested in the highest degree all the learned men in the town:—

"RAPHAELIO URBINATIO INDUSTRIA.

Tot proceres Romam tam longa exstruxerat ætas,
Totque hostes, et tot sæcula diruerant,
Nunc Romam in Româ quærit reperitque Raphael.
Quærere, magni hominis; sed reperire, Dei est."

Amongst those who especially assisted Raphael in his researches were the Count Castiglione and the antiquarian Andrea Fulvio. The latter had also made use of Raphael in his archæological enterprises; for, in a preface[2] addressed to the Pope, he says that he had been occupied in preserving from destruction the remains of ancient Rome, adding that, from his indications, Raphael da Urbino, a few days before his death,

---

in the possession of Sir Thomas Lawrence, and is printed in "Alcune Memorie de Michel Angelo," da MSS. F. de Romanio (Roma, 1823).

[1] "Sir Thomas Lawrence was in possession of some drawings of parts of this composition, ascribed to Michael Angelo, including two sketches of the figure of Lazarus, now in the British Museum; they were some time in the collection of the late King of Holland at the Hague."—*Wornum, Catalogue of National Gallery.*

[2] At the head of the folio work entitled "Antiquitates Urbis per Andream Fulvium Antiquarium R. nuperrimè editæ." The privilege granted by Clement VII. is dated, "die 15 Februarii, 1527." The following is the text of the passage alluded to:—"Ruinas Urbis . . . ab interitu vindicare ac litterarum monumentis resarcire operam dedi, quæ jacerent in tenebris nisi litterarum lumen accederet: priscaque loca per regiones explorans observavi, quas Raphael Urbinas (quem honoris causâ nomino) paucis antè diebus quam e vita decederit (me indicante) penicillo finxerat; tametsi nullum ingenium ad attollendam urbem satis est, nec ejus faciem qualis antè fuerit exprimendam."

had reproduced with his pencil several ancient monuments. Unhappily, he does not add the plan made and the edifices drawn by Raphael.

But there likewise exists a much more remarkable document on this subject, it is that which Raphael himself addressed to Pope Leo X. It informs us that he had been commissioned by the Pontiff to draw out a plan of the city of Rome, to make out a drawing of the buildings, with the assistance of the discoveries being made, and that Raphael worked eagerly at it.

After bitter lamentations over the fate of Rome, he gives a sketch of the architectural characters of the various periods: first of antiquity; then of the earlier style of the middle ages, of the round arcades, a style which he calls Gothic, according to the custom of old Italian authors; then the pointed style, which he calls the German style; and lastly, the style contemporaneous with himself.

He relates afterwards, in a very circumstantial manner, how, by the assistance of a compass and an instrument for measuring, and provided with a polarized needle and a rule in optics, he had taken his plans, elevations, and the sections of buildings. He concludes by entreating that the destruction of ancient monuments may be stopped.

Two manuscript copies of this letter have been preserved: one is in the Munich library; the other, about one year earlier, belongs to the Marquis Scipione Maffei, and was first published by the brothers Volpi amongst the works of Castiglione (edition of Padua, 1733), as being by the count himself. But towards the close of the eighteenth century, Francesconi [1] endeavoured to prove that this letter could only be by Raphael,—an opinion which has since been fully confirmed. We will confine ourselves to stating three of the most decisive proofs.

In the first place, the author of this manuscript says that he had been eleven years in Rome, which is perfectly applicable to Raphael in 1519. but not to Count Castiglione, who never remained there for long together, but always paid it merely a short visit.

Secondly, the author shows that he was possessed of an amount of geometrical knowledge which would be scarcely probable for a courtier.

And thirdly, he says that he had undertaken this work at the Pope's order, which certainly can only refer to an architect or artist in the

[1] "Congettura che una lettera creduta di Baldassare Castiglione sia di Raffaello d'Urbino," dall' Abate Daniele Francesconi, Firenze, 1799.

service of Leo X., but in no case to a diplomatist in the service of the Duke of Mantua.

However, we willingly accede to the general opinion, that Castiglione assisted in this letter through his talent as a writer. We even believe that the learned and amiable statesman must have assisted his friend the artist in the work itself; for, in one passage of the letter, the writer speaks in the plural, "and *we* have adopted this method (of measuring), as may be seen in the course of *our* writing." Everywhere else the author employs the first person, singular.

The count probably intended to write a description of ancient Rome, with the assistance of Raphael, and this letter to the Pope would have served as an introduction.

The second manuscript, that of the Munich Library, improved in many parts, is also less adulatory ; it names Publius Victor, whose directions Raphael had especially followed, and who is not spoken of in the first copy. But the conclusion is wanting.[1]

Raphael did not restrict his researches to Rome and its environs ; his ardent zeal, his passion for antique art, led him to send artists into all the countries of Italy, and even into Greece,[2] in order to collect a series of studies from the old monuments, and thus to increase his knowledge. An engraving of the basement of the Column of Theodosius at Constantinople, engraved by an artist of the period, has a note inscribed on it to the effect that the original drawing had been sent to Raphael da Urbino. The beautiful bas-relief with the Loves, formerly at San Vitale at Ravenna, and which was engraved by Marco Ravegiano in 1519,[3] was likewise the work of his school.

As studies from the antique by the master himself, we may notice, amongst all those attributed to him, the beautiful drawing of a Roman emperor in armour, in the collection of the Duke of Devonshire, and the torso of a Venus at Oxford.

It is also believed that drawings from several ancient sculptures, engraved by Marc Antonio and his pupils—amongst others a statue of Ariadne, and the bas-relief of the two Fauns carrying a child in a basket —are by Raphael.[4]

The universal genius of the great painter of Urbino, which extended

---

[1] See Passavant's "Life of Raphael," (French edition).

[2] This is asserted by Vasari.

[3] Bartsch, vol. xv. p. 57, No. 4, and vol. xiv. No. 242.

[4] *Ib.* vol. xiv. Nos. 199 and 230.

over all the categories of human intelligence, also led him towards historical studies. History interested him so much that he even thought of producing something himself in that science, for which his position offered him exceptional advantages. He left a writing on art, with historical notes, which was extremely useful to Vasari in his biographies of artists. It is a great misfortune that this writing is lost, and that there is even no hope of finding it again; for we possess no other information which could guide our researches, and all those that have been made hitherto have remained fruitless.

Raphael, as we have seen, had at this period cultivated every branch of art, with the enthusiasm of genius and the perseverance of a great character. His name was surrounded with glory. Sovereigns honoured him; the greatest men had eagerly desired his friendship; around him a whole generation of eminent artists were grouped, who lived by his breath, and who revered him as a father. With what indescribable feelings do we remember the young orphan of Urbino, leaving the happy scenes where his childhood had been passed, supported alone by that mysterious force given by genius and virtue! We have followed him step by step in his vast and brilliant career; but, alas! death was soon to put an end to his existence, and we have now to examine his last works, which his hand had not even time to finish!

He had received the important command for the paintings in the large hall leading to the Pope's apartments in the Vatican. It was intended to symbolize in it the dominion of the Church by the most memorable events in the life of Constantine. Thinking to obtain more power and tone with oil painting, he determined to make a trial of it upon the wall. He had a wall prepared with this intention, after having made some sketches and completed the cartoon of the "Battle of Constantine."

We will now return to the altar-piece already alluded to, the "Transfiguration of Christ," the last work of the master.

Raphael divided his subject into two distinct parts. In the upper part, Christ has just risen into the air above Mount Tabor, and has appeared to his apostles, in the midst of a dazzling and supernatural light, of which he himself is the centre. His eyes and arms are raised to heaven. At his side, likewise self-supported in air, are figures of Moses and Elijah. On the mountain itself the apostles Peter, James and John are lying prostrate on the ground, their eyes being unable to bear the brilliancy of the supernatural light; and it is at this moment that the mysterious voice is heard saying: "This is my beloved Son; hear him."

But when our eyes descend from this height to the lower part of the picture, we are struck by the most striking contrast between the celestial apparition, which is so full of majesty, and the human and demoniac nature in its most disturbed state; for the principal subject of this part of the composition is a father, who has just brought his son, possessed by a devil, and is vainly seeking help from the apostles. The physical and moral suffering, the misery and weakness of human nature on the earth, are heartrending sights; but this feeling, which the master wished to arouse as a contrast between things celestial and terrestrial, finds its consolation and true Christian interpretation in the different gestures of the apostles, directed towards the Christ, the Saviour of men. These gestures, so animated by faith, unite the two scenes in the composition, and form them into one of the greatest richness and divinely combined depth.

It would seem superfluous to speak of the sublime qualities of this work, now so universally known, and which many writers call the masterpiece of masterpieces. We agree perfectly in all the praises that have been lavished on its perfection, and we might have terminated here our own remarks on it, had the "Transfiguration" only shown the same tendencies as the other works of the master. But this is not the case; this last work of an incomparable genius reveals an entirely new aspiration, worthy of being studied. This examination will, perhaps, interfere with our historical narration; on this account, therefore, with all the care required by so noble a subject, we will return to it in our separate and more detailed judgment on Raphael's art.[1]

However, before leaving this wonderful picture, we must remark a strange and almost miraculous coincidence. The last picture that Raphael painted of the history of Christ was the "Transfiguration," as the last picture of the Madonna, which terminated his many representations of the Virgin, is the "Madonna di San Sisto," in which the Virgin seems transfigured by the celestial light which surrounds her. It may be said, too, that these two masterpieces are those that have excited the most constant admiration and the greatest veneration during three centuries throughout all Christendom.

Raphael had not yet completed the picture of the "Transfiguration," when he suddenly felt his last hour approaching, at the moment of his greatest activity, and when still scarcely beyond the flower of youth. A

[1] See the last chapter of the "History of Raphael."

violent fever had seized him during his researches amongst the ruins of Rome, and his delicate organization, over-excited by the incessant efforts of his genius, gave way at the first attack of the malady.

Notwithstanding the suddenness of the attack, he was able to arrange his earthly affairs. Margherita, the young girl whom he had always loved, was left richly provided for. His relations at Urbino received a thousand ducats in gold; but the fortune of his father Giovanni passed to the brotherhood of Santa Maria della Misericordia. To the cardinal Bibiena, who had no house in Rome, and of whose annoying financial position he was aware, as well as of the difficulty of his relations with the Pope, he bequeathed, with a noble delicacy, his beautiful house near the Vatican. To his pupils Giulio Pippi, called Romano, and Giovanni Francesco Penni, he left all that he possessed in objects of art. He commissioned them at the same time to terminate, by agreement with the persons who had ordered them, all the works in course of execution.

He had already, some time before, chosen his tomb in the Pantheon, and he had caused one of the chapels to be restored for this purpose. According to his directions a vault was made under the niche, and the altar placed in front. It was an architectural arrangement which he had been the first to introduce in the Pantheon, as is seen by a drawing of the interior of that edifice, by San Gallo;[1] for in this drawing we may still see the pedestals of the figures of the gods, formerly placed in the niches. Raphael ordered besides, that the altar should be decorated by a marble statue of the Virgin, the execution of which he entrusted to Lorenzetto. He devoted the sum of a thousand gold crowns to the purchase of a house, the rent of which would go to the service of the chapel and the payment of the chaplain, charged to say every year some masses for his soul.

As his testamentary executors, he named (but not in writing as would appear) the president of the chancery, Baldassare Turini of Pescia, and the Pope's chamberlain Gio. Battista Branconio dall' Aquila, both of them amongst his oldest friends.

After having thus arranged his worldly affairs, he received the sacraments of the church, and commended his soul to the mercy of God.

The general uneasiness was great at the dangerous turn Raphael's illness had taken. Not only were his pupils and near friends troubled at the misfortune which threatened them, but the whole population of Rome

[1] This drawing is preserved in the Barberini Library.

feared losing the young master who had done so much to render the capital of the Christian world famous.

No one had yet seemed to have conceived the possibility of that career whose end appeared so distant, being thus suddenly cut short.

The Pope, who felt a true friendship for Raphael, and who in him always found fresh inspiration for his grand projects, shared painfully in the universal anxiety. He sent frequently to him during the fortnight that his illness lasted, and did every thing in his power to re-assure and encourage him.

Great was his fright when the apartment he occupied and which had been built by Raphael fell down! He was obliged to move from it as fast as possible, and his fear redoubled when he learned, almost immediately, that the great master had breathed his last.

Raphael died at thirty-eight years of age, on the anniversary of his birth, April 6th, 1520, which fell on Good Friday.

The grief caused by his death was inexpressible. His body lay in state in his house on a catafalque, surrounded by lighted tapers, in order that all who had known him might once more look on his loved features, and give the last pledges of affection. Behind the catafalque stood the unfinished picture of the "Transfiguration." This, the last work produced by his genius, expresses better than any human words the greatness of the loss which art and Italy had experienced.

An immense crowd accompanied his remains to the Pantheon. Every one was in mourning. The body was placed under the sepulchral vault behind the altar, near the place on which is the inscription to the memory of Maria da Bibiena, his betrothed bride.

On one side of the tomb was engraved the Latin inscription that Pietro Bembo had written for Raphael:

D. O. M.
RAPHAELI . SANCTIO . IOANN . F . URBINATI
PICTORI . EMINENTISS . VETERVMQ . AEMVLO
CVIVS . SPIRANTES . PROPE . IMAGINES . SI
CONTEMPLERE NATURAE . ATQVE . ARTIS . FOEDVS
FACILE . INSPEXERIS
IVLII II . ET LEONIS . X . PONT . MAXX . PICTVRAE
ET . ARCHITECT . OPERIBVS . GLORIAM . AVXIT
VIX . ANNOS . XXXVIII . INTEGER . INTEGROS
QUO . DIE . NATVS . EST . EO . ESSE . DESIIT
VIII . ID . APRILIS . MDXX.
ILLE HIC EST RAPHAEL TIMVIT QVO SOSPITE VINCI
RERVM MAGNA PARENS ET MORIENTE MORI.

FROM the letter that a noble Venetian, Marcantonio Michiel de Ser Vettor, addressed, a few days after the death of Raphael, to Antonio di Marsilio at Venice, we extract an account of the last moments of the great artist and the mourning that followed his death:

"On Good Friday night, at three o'clock on Saturday morning, died the noble and excellent painter Raphael da Urbino. His death caused universal sorrow, especially amongst learned men, for whom more especially, although also for painters and architects, he had drawn in a book —as Ptolemy drew the configuration of the world—the ancient buildings of Rome, with their proportions, forms, and ornaments; and so faithfully, that he who has seen these drawings might almost assert that he had seen ancient Rome. He had already completed the first zone. He did not merely represent the plan and place of the constructions, which he had traced with great pains and great skill, from their ruins, but also the façades with all their decorations; and, when there remained no ruins to guide him, he made his drawings from the descriptions of Vitruvius, according to the rules of architecture and the descriptions of ancient authors.

"But death interrupted this noble and glorious enterprise; it carried off the young man at the age of thirty-four (it should be thirty-seven), on the anniversary of his birth. The Pope himself felt intense grief; he had sent at least six times during the fifteen days that the illness lasted, to ask for fresh news. You may judge, then, of what others did. And as on precisely the same day the Pope's palace was menaced with destruction, so much so that his Holiness was compelled to seek refuge in the apartments of Monsignore Cibo, there are many people who say that it was not the weight of the Loggie placed above which caused the accident, but that it was a miracle to announce the death of him who had worked so long at the adornment of the palace.

"And in truth an incomparable master no longer exists! Lamentations for his death should not be merely expressed in light and fugitive words, but by serious and immortal poetry. And poets, if I am not mistaken, are preparing in great numbers for the work.

"It is said that he leaves a fortune of sixteen thousand ducats, of which five thousand is in silver specie, the greater part of which is to be distributed to his friends and servants. To the Cardinal of Santa Maria, in Portico, he has bequeathed his house, which belonged formerly to Bramante, and which he bought for three thousand ducats.[1]

"He has been interred in the Rotunda, where he was borne with great honours. His soul has doubtless gone to contemplate the edifices in heaven, which are not subject to destruction. His name and memory will long live in his works and in the remembrance of all honest men.

"Far less important in my opinion, although it may appear otherwise to the multitude, is the loss the world has just sustained in the death of the Signor Agostino Chigi, which happened last night. I shall not speak much of him here, as it is not yet known to whom he has left his property. I learn merely he has left to the world eight hundred thousand ducats, in ready money, letters of exchange, loans, properties, sums placed at interest in banking houses, plate, and jewels.

"It is said that Michael Angelo is ill at Florence. Tell our Catena[2] of this, that he may be upon his guard, since great painters are threatened.

"God be with youth.

"Rome, April 11, 1520."

A great deal of poetry which has not come down to us shows sufficiently the deep regret caused by the death of Raphael. We shall now terminate our recital by the few words so full of sadness that the Count Castiglione addressed to his mother, Maria Aloisa Gonzaga da Castiglione.

"I am in good health, but it seems as if I were not in Rome, since my poor Raphael is here no longer. May his blessed soul be with God!"

---

[1] According to Vasari, Bramante built this house for Raphael, and, as we have endeavoured to prove, from Raphael's own plans. Although the Cardinal da Bibiena had inherited Raphael's house, he never lived in it; for he died shortly after, on the 9th November, 1520, whilst still residing at the Vatican.

[2] An excellent portrait painter, whose works were frequently confounded with those of Giorgione.

RAPHAEL'S PAINTINGS

CHRONOLOGICALLY ARRANGED.

Paintings executed under Perugino's superintendence.

1.

THE INFANT JESUS WITH ST. JOHN THE BAPTIST.

St. John, holding a cross, embraces the Holy Child, who is seated on a golden step. The figures, almost nude, are rather smaller than life. This is a copy in distemper of a larger picture by Perugino, and is in the sacristy of S. Piedro Maggiore at Perugia.

2.

THE RESURRECTION OF CHRIST.

On wood; height 90¼ inches, width 66¼ inches.[1]

Christ, supported on a cloud, blesses the world as he leaves his tomb; two guards, thought by some to resemble Perugino and Raphael, sleep near, whilst two more are running away in the distance.

This work has often been attributed to Perugino, but it is now certain that it is from Raphael's own hand. Two studies for it are in the Oxford collection, and the painting itself, originally intended for the Franciscan church at Perugia, was carried away by the French, and sent to the Vatican after the treaty of 1815. It has been several times engraved.

3.

THE ARCHANGELS MICHAEL AND RAPHAEL.

Two pictures; figures half life-size.

The Archangel Michael is on foot, holding a shield before him, and reminds us of Donatello's "Saint George" at Florence.

---

[1] The sizes are given in English inches, and the terms *right* and *left* always refer to the position the spectator is supposed to occupy opposite the picture.

The Archangel Raphael is leading the young Tobit, who holds a small box in the left hand, and looks lovingly at his celestial guide.

These two paintings were formerly placed on either side of Perugino's "Birth of Christ," and adorned the splendid altar of the Carthusian church at Pavia. We have no formal proof that they are by Raphael; but many of the best judges, Von Rumohr, for instance, attribute them to him; and a study of one of the angels, now at Oxford, which is undoubtedly by Raphael, confirms their opinion. These altar pieces changed hands more than once, and are now in the Louvre. The figures have been rendered familiar by numerous copies, and the entire works have been engraved. It would be useless to enumerate all the works at which Raphael is said to have assisted when under Perugino. Much information may be found in the French edition of Passavant's "Life of Raphael," vol. i., Appendix V., and vol. ii., pp. 5 and 6.

Paintings by Raphael in Perugino's style. 1500-1504.

4.

Church Banner in S. Trinita at Citta di Castello.

Two canvases in distemper.

(1.) The Holy Trinity: God the Father, seated on clouds in a halo of glory, holds the crucifix in both hands; the Holy Spirit hovers above. Saints Sebastian and Roch kneel in prayer on either side. Figures half life-size.

(2.) The Creation of Man (on the reverse of the banner). On the left, Adam lies asleep; on the right, the Creator approaches him in the form of an old man. Two adoring angels are seen above.

Each picture is about 64 inches by $38\frac{1}{2}$ inches.

5.

The Coronation of Saint Nicolas of Torentino.

According to Vasari and others, this was one of Raphael's earliest works. It was the altar piece of St. Agostino at Città di Castello. "The Virgin and St. Augustine, partly hidden in a cloud, are crowning the saint . . . who treads the Devil under foot; on either side stands an angel with a roll of parchment . . . and above we see a half-length figure of God the Father beneath a halo of cherubim's heads . . . The group is arranged in a kind of temple." (From Lanzi's *Storia pittorica dell' Italia.*) This altar piece was damaged by an earthquake, and sold in 1789 to Pius VI., who cut it into several pieces, which were lost after the taking of Rome by the French.

6.

Christ on the Cross, and Four Saints.

On wood; height $87\frac{1}{2}$ inches, width $67\frac{1}{4}$ inches.

Christ is nailed to a very high cross. In the air, on either side, a little angel with a vase is collecting the blood which flows from the Saviour's wounds. The Virgin stands at the foot of the cross in an agony of grief, and near her kneels

CHRIST ON THE CROSS.

In the possession of Earl Dudley.

St. Jerome, striking his breast with a stone. On the other side, St. John, with Mary Magdalene, in an attitude of devotion. In the sky we see both the sun and the moon. At the foot of the cross, in golden letters, is written: "Raphael. Urbinas. P."

This picture was painted for the Gavri or Gavari family, about 1500, and remained in the Dominican church at Citta di Castello for three centuries, when a Frenchman bought if for 4,000 scudi, and a bad copy, now in the place of the original. Prince Canino bought the original for 10,000 Roman scudi of Cardinal Fesch, and in 1847 it passed into the hands of Lord Ward.

7.

THE MADONNA OF THE SOLLY COLLECTION.

On wood; height 24¼ inches, width 16 inches.

The Virgin, seen in profile, is reading; the Holy Child, with one foot in her left hand, is playing with a goldfinch. The influence of Perugino is very clearly seen in this painting, and we believe its date to be about 1500. It is now in the Berlin Museum (No. 141).

8.

MARY MAGDALENE AND ST. CATHERINE.

The two saints are represented on foot on two panels, which were formerly the shutters of a small Madonna by Perugino. Although much spoiled, we still recognise Raphael's style in the Magdalene's head. In 1845 they belonged to the famous painter Camuccini of Rome.

9.

THE MADONNA OF COUNTESS ANNA ALFANI AT PERUGIA.

On wood; height 19¾ inches, width 13 inches.

The Virgin in profile, is seated on a bench holding the Infant Jesus with both hands. The Holy Child is standing, clinging with the right hand to the thin veil which covers his mother's breast, and looking towards the spectator with a sweet expression. Above, on either side, we see a cherub's head. This picture is executed with the finish peculiar to Raphael, but his master's influence is very evident. It belongs to the Countess Alfani, and is in excellent preservation.

10.

THE VIRGIN WITH ST. JEROME AND ST. FRANCIS.

On wood; height 14 inches, width 11¾ inches.

The Virgin, in profile, holds the Infant Jesus on a cushion on her knees and looks lovingly at him, whilst he, clasping his mother's hand in his left, raises the right in benediction. St. Jerome in a cardinal's hat, kneels on the left, and St. Francis in ecstasy, on the right. In the distance we see a town at the foot of high mountains.

The execution of this painting, which is well preserved, is very delicate and the colouring powerful. Its date appears to be about 1503, and after changing hands several times, it was obtained by the Berlin Museum in 1820.

11.

THE CORONATION OF THE VIRGIN.

Cabinet picture painted on wood for the Franciscan church at Perugia, and afterwards transferred to canvas.

Height, $117\frac{1}{4}$ inches, width $66\frac{1}{4}$ inches.

This picture is divided into two parts; in the upper the Virgin, with clasped hands and downcast eyes, waits to receive the crown from the hands of her divine Son. Four small angels playing the harp, the violin, and the tambourine, surround this group. Above we see eight winged cherubim's heads, and below two angels looking on the scene.

The lower part of the picture represents the empty tomb of the Virgin, in which flowers are springing up. The Apostles stand round it. Saint Thomas between Saint Peter and Saint Paul, is looking at the girdle the Virgin has left behind her, and the figure on the left is probably Saint John.

This picture still betrays Perugino's style, but the genius of Raphael himself is also very apparent; his figures are now more life-like than those of his master.

We have already said that this altar-piece was painted for Maddelena degli Oddi in 1503; it was one of the ornaments of the Franciscan church at Perugia until 1792, when it was sent to Paris for the museum of the Republic, and the wood being moth-eaten, it was transferred to a single canvas, suffering considerably in the operation; the principal parts are, however, in a fair state of preservation. By the treaty of 1815, this picture was restored to Italy, and is now in the Vatican. Numerous studies for it are treasured up in different collections, and it has been engraved and copied several times.

Predella of the Painting.

On wood, height 15 inches, width $66\frac{1}{4}$ inches.

Three separate compartments containing the Annunciation, the Adoration of the Magi, and the Presentation in the Temple, divided from each other by grotesque designs in red on a black ground; they are now in the Vatican.

(*a.*) The "Annunciation." The angel is approaching the Virgin, who is seated in a colonnade; a landscape forms the background, in which we see God the Father and the Holy Spirit.

The original drawing for this painting belonged to the Lawrence collection, it passed into the possession of the late King of Holland, and from thence to the Louvre. The outlines, drawn with the pen, are pricked for tracing.

(*b.*) "The Adoration of the Magi." The Virgin, the Infant Jesus and Saint Joseph are seated near a ruined house, and the three Kings occupy the centre of the painting, their suite being on the left.

(*c.*) "The Presentation in the Temple." The Virgin, with Saint Joseph, presents the Infant Jesus to the High Priest. Three women stand in the portico on the left and four men on the right.

The original cartoon, pricked for tracing, was in the possession of the late Mr. Chambers Hall, of London, and Maria Ricci, of Rieti, has copies on canvas of all three paintings.

12.

THE MADONNA OF COUNT STAFFA.

On wood; 6¾ inches square.

The Virgin holding the Infant Jesus on her arm and a book in her hand, which the child also grasps; a background of meadows and mountains.

The painting itself is round, but the four black angles of the square panel are ornamented with red arabesque figures grotesquely interwoven; Raphael soon perceived how inappropriate such ornaments are to sacred subjects, and we do not meet with them again in his works.

This painting has never been restored; it has lately become slightly cracked, but it has never been removed from its original frame. It is an heirloom in the Staffa family. A fine pen sketch for this Madonna is in the Royal collection at Madrid, and it has been copied many times.

13.

THE VISION OF A KNIGHT.

On wood; 7¼ inches square.

A young knight in armour resting on his shield at the foot of a small laurel, which forms the centre of the foreground. He is asleep and dreaming. A woman clad in purple and violet, is at his right hand, offering him a book and a sword as though to prepare him at the same time for study and conflict. In the background rises a castle on a rock. At the young man's left hand stands another woman in bright array offering him flowers as types of the pleasures of the world. A fine town near a river, with mountains in the distance, complete the scene.

This picture, bearing Raphael's signature, is in excellent preservation. It has changed hands many times, and is now in the National Gallery of London, having been bought in 1847 for £1,050 sterling. The original design for it hangs beside it.

14.

PORTRAIT OF A YOUNG MAN.

In the Kensington Museum. On wood; about 17 inches square.

Bust portrait of a youth of fifteen with flowing locks, in a close-fitting vest, fastened at the collar with round gold buckles, bearing the inscription: "Raffaello —Urbinas, Fec." A landscape with a stag in the background. This picture is unfortunately much deteriorated.

15.

THE MARRIAGE OF THE VIRGIN. (1504.)

Arched picture. Figures rather less than half life size. (On wood.)

In this picture, commonly called the "Sposalizio," the Virgin is on the left and St. Joseph on the right giving her the wedding ring; the High Priest being in the centre holding their hands. The Virgin is attended by five women and St. Joseph by five young men who were once Mary's suitors. The despair of the lovers is shadowed forth by the reeds they hold; they will never flower; and the handsomest youth is breaking his across his knees. In the background we see a temple, and on the moulding of the central arch is written: "Raphael Urbinas MDIIII.;" the first known signature with a date on Raphael's works.

We know that this picture was painted for the Church of the Franciscans at Citta di Castello, and remained there for three centuries, when it was seized by Count Giuseppe Lechi, at the head of a French brigade; and after changing hands several times it was finally acquired by the Brera of Milan, with a few unimportant works, for about 53,000 francs.

According to Pungileoni this picture is but a copy, with some slight alterations, of Perugino's celebrated painting in the Museum at Caen. Raphael's "Marriage of the Virgin" is in a good state of preservation, but unfortunately the colours for the draperies were ill chosen, and they have in some parts become black. This work was engraved by Longhi at Milan, in 1812, and has been copied several times.

16.
SAINT SEBASTIAN.

On wood; height 17 inches, width 12¾ inches.

A half-length figure of the Saint, seen full-face, with the instrument of his martyrdom in his hand. The landscape in the background is exquisitely finished, and the execution as a whole resembles that of the "Sposalizio;" it probably belongs to the same period of the artist's life. It is well preserved, but the sky and the head of the Saint have been slightly retouched.

It was bought by G. Longhi, the engraver, for 3,000 Milanese lire, and is now in the possession of the Count of Lecchi at Bergamo.

17.
CHRIST ON THE MOUNT OF OLIVES.

Painted for Duke Guidubaldo of Urbino. On wood; height 24 inches, width 27½ inches.

The Saviour, with clasped hands, and eyes raised to heaven in imploring anguish, kneels upon a hillock, against which lean the sleeping Apostles. An angel is descending on the left, bearing the cup of bitterness, and at a little distance, on the right, Judas approaches with six armed men. In the background we have verdure-covered hills and a town in the distance.

This picture has passed through a great many hands; in 1820 it was stolen from its owner, Prince Gabrielli, and sold to a merchant named Gigli, for 40 scudi. The loss was accidentally discovered by the blowing aside of the silken curtain put up to protect it, and the prince, hearing that it had been unsuccessfully offered for sale at various German courts, called in the aid of the law, and recovered his treasure, giving the merchant 10 scudi as compensation. It now belongs to Mr. Maitland of Stanstead, Sussex.

THE VISION OF A KNIGHT

18.

SAINT GEORGE WITH THE SWORD.

On wood; height 11⅓ inches, width 10 inches.

The mail-clad knight on a white horse, is about to give the dragon his death-stroke. A barren rock-strewn landscape, with a woman running away, completes the picture.

Raphael is said to have painted two groups of St. George and the Dragon; the one now under consideration is that alluded to by Lomazzo as forming part of the Fontainebleau collection.

19.

SAINT MICHAEL.

On wood; height 12¼ inches, width 10 inches.

The Archangel Michael, in golden armour and full of youthful vigour, stands on the largest of the monsters around him, and is about to drive home the death-stroke with his sword. A red cross stands out on his white shield. In the back-ground, on the left, penitent sinners in leaden mantles pass slowly by the Town of Dis, which is in flames; on the right are the hypocrites and thieves tormented by serpents.—See Dante's "Divina Comedia," Cantos 8, 23 and 24 of the Inferno.

The colouring of this delicate little picture is powerful and brilliant; it was painted on the back of a chess-board. It is now in the Louvre in excellent preservation.

20.

THREE SMALL ROUND PICTURES.

In the Berlin Museum. On wood; about 6½ inches in diameter.

A Pietà on a black ground; Christ with arms extended is seated on a sarcophagus, with the half-length figures of the patron saints of Perugia, Lodovicus and Herculanus.

These little pictures evidently formed part of a predella, but to what altar-piece they belonged is unknown. They were bought by Von Rumohr, and given by him to the Prince Royal of Prussia.[1] In the "Researches in Italy" (vol. iii. p. 41) it is suggested that they formed part of the "Coronation of the Virgin," and that the painter Wicar possessed a fourth, representing St. Catherine, which belonged to the same work.

Raphael's Paintings executed at Florence. 1504-1510.

21.

MADONNA OF THE GRAND DUKE OF TUSCANY.

The Virgin, in profile, is standing holding the Infant Jesus on her left arm and gazing upon him with downcast eyes. The child looks towards the spectator, and rests his right hand upon his mother's breast.

---

[1] In the Catalogue they are said to have been bought by the Museum of Von Rumohr.

The figure of the Madonna, in a flowing blue mantle, stands out distinctly against the background, which is of a powerful tone.

Although this charming picture is full of Raphael's own genius, we still detect the style of Perugino. At the end of last century it was in the possession of a poor widow, who, ignorant of its value, sold it to a bookseller for twelve scudi. It was obtained by Puccini, director of the Florence Gallery, for the Grand Duke of Tuscany, Ferdinand III., who took it with him wherever he went. It has lately been placed in the Florence Gallery.

It was engraved in 1823 by Raphael Morghen, and has been reproduced in many different ways.

22.

Madonna of the Duke of Terranuova.

On wood; round, 35 inches in diameter; now at Berlin.

The Virgin is seated with Jesus lying on her knees. St. John, on the left, looks lovingly at the Saviour, and offers him a scroll, on which is written, "Ecce agnus Dei." On the right another child, with a halo round his head, leans against the Virgin; he is probably one of the future apostles. On the breast of the mother's robe is the letter M, which might lead to doubts about the authorship of the painting, if we did not know that it was a common custom to embroider the initial of the proper name on the borders of the garments of men and women.

This picture remained in the Terranuova family until 1854, when it was bought by the King of Prussia for about 30,000 thalers.

23.

Lord Cowper's Madonna.

On wood; height 25½ inches, width 18 inches.

The Virgin, in profile, seated near a wall, leans slightly forward, and supports the Holy Child with the left hand. Jesus rests one foot on his mother's out-spread palm, and clings to her with both hands. Violet drapery, covered with a transparent veil, falls over Mary's head, and for background we have a landscape with a church.

This work was evidently produced about 1505. The execution is light and easy, but the hands, especially those of the Virgin, are almost fastidiously elegant, and we fancy that the picture is not entirely from Raphael's own hand.

It was, we believe, preserved at Urbino until bought by Lord Cowper, English ambassador at Florence, for his beautiful collection at Panshanger, near Hertford.

24.

Portrait of a Young Man of the Riccio Family.

On wood; height 20¾ inches, width 16 inches.

Bust portrait of a youth about twenty years old, with straight heavy locks falling from beneath a little black cap, and Raphael's signature on the fastenings of his vest. In the background we see coloured marble columns, and a meadow with a wood, in which a stag is grazing, watched by a lynx.

This picture is well preserved; it belonged to the Riccio family for a long time, and after constantly changing hands it was bought by Louis of Bavaria for the Pinacothek of Munich.

25.

ALTAR-PIECE FOR THE MONASTERY OF ST. ANTHONY OF PADUA AT PERUGIA.

Raphael painted a picture for this convent with a *lunette* and a *predella*, containing five subjects, which he began as early as 1504, before his journey to Urbino, but did not finish until his return to Perugia.

The Central Picture.

On wood; almost square. Figures two-thirds the size of life.

The child Jesus on the right knee of the enthroned Virgin, raises his right hand in benediction over St. John, who approaches him in adoration. On the left stand St. Catherine and St. Peter, and on the right St. Dorothea and St. Paul; the women holding palms as symbols of their martyrdom. The colouring of this painting is powerful, and the execution betrays the influence of the Florentine school, although the Virgin and child retain the tenderness of expression peculiar to Raphael's earlier works.

The Lunette.

A half-length figure of the Eternal Father with the terrestrial globe in the left hand, an angel on either side, and two cherubim's heads in the sky above.

In 1678 the nuns sold these two paintings to Count Bigazzini at Rome for about 2,000 scudi, receiving into the bargain a copy of each for their high-altar. They were transferred to the Colonna Gallery, and at the end of last century became the property of the King of Naples. They are well preserved, although the central picture is cracked right across.

Paintings of the Predella.

In 1663 five subjects were sold to Christina of Sweden by the nuns, for 601 Roman scudi; later they passed into the possession of the Duke of Orleans, and in 1798 they were sold in London, and distributed among various English amateurs.

(*a.*) "Christ in the Garden of Gethsemane." Height 9½ inches, width 10½ inches.

The Saviour kneels in prayer, whilst an angel approaches him with the cup of suffering, and the apostles sleep near. This picture is feeble, and we fancy it must have been executed after a drawing by Raphael by one of his fellow-students. It is now in the possession of Lady Burdett Coutts.

(*b.*) "Christ bearing the Cross." Height 9½ inches, width 24½ inches.

Two horsemen open the procession, followed by Christ, bending beneath his burden, and accompanied by the executioner and two soldiers. Simon of Cyrene tries to relieve the Saviour of the weight of the cross; on the right the Virgin is fainting away, and is ministered to by St. John and three women. This is the best of the Predella paintings; it is well preserved, and is now at Leigh Court, near Bristol.

(*c.*) "Virgin supporting a dead Christ." Height 9½ inches, width 10½ inches.

The Saviour lies on the Virgin's knees; St. John supports his head and shoulders, and Mary Magdalene kisses his feet; on either side stand Joseph of Arimathæa and Nicodemus. This is a very fine painting; the drawing is pure and full of feeling, and the general style reminds us of Perugino. It is now at Barrow Hill, near Ashborne, Derbyshire.

(*d.*) and (*e.*) "Saint Francis and Saint Anthony of Padua. Height 9½ inches, width 5½ inches.

The former, turning to the right, holds a red book and a cross; the latter, turning to the left, a green book and a lily. It is doubtful whether these paintings are by Raphael himself, but they were at least produced under his superintendence. They are now in Dulwich College.[1]

26.

THE MADONNA OF THE ANSIDEI FAMILY (1505).

On wood; full-length figures, rather less than life size.

The Virgin on a high throne, with Jesus on her right knee and an open book on the left, from which both mother and child are reading. On the left stands John the Baptist pointing to the Saviour with the right hand, and holding a cross in the left; on the right we see Bishop Nicolas of Bari reading; his crosier in his hand.

This altar-piece was originally painted for the chapel of St. Nicolas of Bari in S. Fiorenzo, at Perugia, but it was sold to Lord Spencer in 1764, and by him presented to his brother, the Duke of Marlborough, in whose palace at Blenheim it still remains.

This picture formerly had a *predella* with three small subjects from the life of St. John, but the only one in anything like good preservation is that now at Bowood, the seat of the Marquis of Lansdowne. It represents the preaching of St. John.[2]

27.

"PAX VOBIS."

Profile figure on wood; height, about 16 inches.

The risen Christ, with red drapery round the body and on the right shoulder, and the crown of thorns upon his head, raises one hand in benediction, and with the other points to the wound in his side. The knowledge of anatomy shown in this picture, and the general beauty of the execution, &c., authorise us in supposing it to have been produced in 1505. It is in perfect preservation, and passed from the Mosca family to Count P. Tosi, of Brescia.

28.

A CHILD'S HEAD, PAINTED IN FRESCO ON A BRICK.

This head (which may be either that of a boy or a girl) is nearly full-faced. The hair, parted down the middle, falls in heavy masses on the shoulders, and the features have the peculiar expression, bordering on affectation, which we

---

[1] In the Catalogue they are attributed to Perugino, not to Raphael.

[2] The Cartoon of the Preaching of St. John the Baptist is in the Stirling Collection.

sometimes meet with in Raphael's earlier works. This head was probably a study for the large fresco of S. Severo; and in any case it belongs to the same period. By some chance it fell into the hands of a broker of Perugia, who, ignorant of its value, sold it for 5 paoli (about 2*s.*); and, later, Louis, of Bavaria, bought it of Count G. Cesarei for 1,000 scudi, and placed it in the Pinacothek at Munich.

29.

THE FRESCO OF SAN SEVERO (1505).

Raphael executed this mural painting in an ancient side chapel of the church of the Camoldoli convent at Perugia, on his return from his first journey to Florence. He was called to Rome when he had finished the upper part only, but the monks clung to the hope that he would return, and it was not until they heard of his death in 1521 that they commissioned Perugino to complete his pupil's work.

The subject chosen by Raphael is the celestial reunion of sainted Camoldoli monks around the Holy Trinity. In the centre we see God the Father and the Holy Spirit, with Christ below them, raising His hands in benediction; four adoring angels are in attendance, and on either side, rather lower down, are three Camoldoli monks seated on clouds.

Unfortunately this picture has suffered very much, but in our own day its decay has been to a great extent arrested by G. Carattoli, and, as it was nearly hidden by new structures, the monks have raised a scaffolding before it, to facilitate its examination. Of Perugino's six saints in the lower part we need not now speak.

30.

THE VIRGIN WITH THE GOLDFINCH.

On wood; height 39½ inches, width 31 inches. Figures full length, half life size.

The Virgin is seated holding a book, and looking with loving eyes at St. John, who is offering a goldfinch to the infant Saviour. The latter, leaning against His mother's knees, is about to caress the bird. A landscape with trees and a bridge forms the setting of the group. Vasari tells us that this Madonna, painted for Lorenzo Mazi, of Florence, was broken in 1547, in the fall of the house in which it was kept, and that the pieces were very cleverly joined together. It has been again restored since its admission to the Florence Gallery, but, although its first value is of course lessened, it still glows with the divine genius of Raphael.[1]

It was engraved in 1814 by Raphael Morghen, and has been also reproduced many times by less famous artists.

31.

THE MADONNA IN THE MEADOW. (1505-6.)

On wood; height 46 inches, width 13¼ inches.

This picture takes its name from the flower-strewn meadow in the foreground.

---

[1] A replica of this work is in the Raphael Gallery at South Kensington.

The Virgin is seated with the infant Jesus before her. On the left, St. John on his knees, offers a cross to the Holy Child, and the latter, grasping it in his right hand, gazes at the donor with a grave but sweet expression.

This was one of two Madonnas painted by Raphael for Taddeo Taddei; in 1688 it was still in his family, but now, after many changes of residence, it is in the Belvidera of Vienna.

32.

MADONNA OF THE TEMPI FAMILY.

On wood; height 30 inches, width 20¼ inches.

Mary, on foot, is about to embrace Jesus, who leans against her. There are some faults in the drawing of the Madonna's hands, but the picture is so full of pure and tender beauty that we scarcely notice them.

It is said that this painting was left unnoticed and covered with dust in the Tempi mansion for a long time, but a year after its discovery it was bought by Louis of Bavaria, for 16,000 scudi for the Pinacothek at Munich. Engraved by B. Desnoyers.

33.

THE HOLY FAMILY UNDER THE PALM TREE.

Painted on wood, and transferred to canvas. Round; 42¾ inches diameter.

The Virgin, seated near a palm, holds Jesus on her knees, covered with her veil. St. Joseph, kneeling before them, offers flowers to the Holy Child, who receives them with a look of ineffable sweetness. We presume that this precious Madonna is the second executed for Taddeo Taddei. It was bought by the Duke of Bridgwater for £12,000 sterling, and is now in the possession of Lord Ellesmere in London.

34.

PORTRAITS OF ANGELO DONI AND MADDALENA STROZZI, HIS WIFE.

Angelo Doni, aged about thirty, is seated near a balustrade on which he rests his left arm. He wears a black surtout, a red waistcoat, and a black cap; his figure stands out against a background of sky and landscape; the colouring is warm but the drawing is not quite correct, and we miss the purity characteristic of Raphael's later works.

The portrait of Maddalena Doni, *née* Strozzi, is nearly full faced. She wears red and blue, a gold collar and chain, with a pear-shaped pearl pendant. Although this picture shares, to some extent, the faults of that above described, there is an extraordinary charm about it, and it was evidently painted with real pleasure.

For a long time the authenticity of these portraits was doubted, and after it was found out by Metzger, the great picture restorer, and confirmed by Falere, Leopold II. bought them for 5,000 scudi in 1826, and entrusted them to Domenico del Podesta to be cleaned. The latter having wetted them too much with spirits of turpentine, was terrified at seeing picture and varnish dissolving together. He hurried to Metzger, who saved them by ordering them to be dried in the open air, and greater care taken in future. They are now in the Pitti Gallery.

35.

PORTRAIT OF A WOMAN.

In the Tribune at Florence. On wood; height 30 inches, width 18¼ inches

The youthful Florentine turns slightly to the right; the details of her dress are exquisitely painted, but unfortunately the picture is very much worn, and it is only in parts, in the hands especially, that we can still recognise the great master's touch.

36.

THE ADORATION OF THE SHEPHERDS.

This picture is lost and we know nothing of its fate, nor have we any authentic copy or engraving to guide us in describing it. For the various conjectures on the subject we refer our readers to the French edition of Passavant's "Life of Raphael," pp. 41 and 42 (vol. ii).

37.

SAINT GEORGE WITH THE LANCE.

On wood; height 11¾ inches, width 8¼ inches.

The knight, on a white horse, is springing from the right to the left and plunging his lance into the heart of an enormous dragon, who emits poisonous vapours in his death agony. On the left, behind the monster, we see the cavern, and on the right the princess kneeling in prayer. On the harness of the horse is Raphael's signature, and on St. George's garter the word "Honi" which is explained by the well attested fact that Raphael painted the picture for the Duke of Urbino, as a present for Henry VII. of England, when the Duke was made a member of the order of the Garter, or St. George.

The fate of this picture is doubtful; it was engraved by Vorsterman in 1627, and was then in the possession of the Duke of Pembroke; later it belonged to Charles I., and was sold for £150 sterling; according to Florent le Comte it is now in the Hermitage Palace at St. Petersburg.

38.

A HOLY FAMILY, WITH ST. JOSEPH WITHOUT A BEARD.

On wood; height 27 inches, width 21¼ inches.

The Virgin, turning to the left, is seated in a room with Jesus on her knee. St. Joseph stands near, resting both hands upon a staff; the head of the latter, a portrait probably, is not pleasing. On the right we see a landscape through an arched window.

There is little doubt that this picture was painted in 1506, for the Duke of Urbino; it is now in the Hermitage Palace at St. Petersburg.

39.

THE SMALL MADONNA OF THE ORLEANS GALLERY.

On wood; height 11¼ inches, width 8½ inches. Profile figures.

The Virgin is seated on a chair, holding Jesus with the left hand, and looking lovingly at him. The child is trying to climb up to his mother and clings to her dress, gazing out of the picture with a grave expression. The background represents the wall of a room with a greyish red curtain and a little shelf with vases on it. These accessories were evidently added later, and they are so entirely in Teniers' style that we can hardly help thinking that he is their real author.

After changing hands no less than seven or eight times this picture was bought by M. Delessert for 24,000 francs.

40.

Portrait of Guidubaldo, Duke of Urbino.

This likeness was probably taken in 1506; it is unfortunately lost, but it is alluded to in a letter from Pietro Bembo (dated from Rome, April 19, 1516), and also in Baldi's *Della Vita e de Fatti di Guidobaldo.* A portrait in the Lichtenstein Gallery is said to be that by Raphael of the Duke, but in reality it neither represents Guidubaldo, nor is it from the great master's hand.

A descriptive list of the portraits of other members of the Urbino family attributed to Raphael, is given in the French edition of Passavant, vol. ii. pp. 45-49; but we refrain from enumerating them here, as our business now is with Raphael's authentic paintings alone.

41.

Portrait of Raphael by himself.

At the age of twenty-three: bust without hands. On wood; height 19¼ inches, width 13½ inches.

The artist has represented himself three quarters faced, turning to the right. He wears a black cap, and his luxuriant chesnut hair falls in curls upon his bare neck, which is of a beautiful shape. He looks at the spectator with the gentle melancholy of a young and noble nature, and the expression of his mouth is most fascinating. The face is pale, the eyes are brown, the nose is thin and slightly bent, the chin round and rather long. The background is of a greyish green tint.

It is probable that Raphael painted this portrait in his native town as a keepsake for his parents in 1506. In any case it remained at Urbino until transferred to the Academy of St. Luke at Rome. It passed later into the collection of portraits of painters by themselves in the Florence Gallery. It has unfortunately suffered both from decay and restoration, but not to the extent represented by Von Rumohr. It has been engraved many times, by F. Muller and F. Forster amongst others.

42.

The Three Graces.

On wood; 7½ inches square.

The figures are grouped in the antique style; that in the centre with her back to the spectator, rests one hand on the shoulder of the female on the left, and turns her head towards a golden apple in her right hand. The other two look out of the picture, each holding a golden apple in one hand and resting the other on the shoulder of the central figure. Coral chains adorn the hair of the Graces on either side, and the third wears a coral necklace. In the distance we have a landscape with hills.

The nude portions of these figures are grandly drawn in the master's second manner; we believe the date of the picture to be 1506, and that it was painted by Raphael for one of his friends at Urbino, after a drawing that he made of the antique group in the *Libreria* of the Cathedral of Sienna. The picture itself is now in the possession of Lord Dudley; it was engraved by F. Forster in 1841.

43.
Portraits of Two Monks.

Busts without hands, rather larger than life; painted in distemper on wood.

The heads of the monks are in profile, with the eyes raised, and we believe they were meant to hang on either side of a crucifix, so as to look up at Christ. They were painted in the Monastery of Vallombrosa, in distemper, probably because suitable oil could not be obtained.

The chief of the order, Don Blasio, is a pious old man of ordinary character, treated in Raphael's usual manner, with brown-grey shadows, reddish half-tints and white lights. The background is of a vigorous tone.

Don Baldassare, turning to the left, is in the prime of life; he is rather thin, his complexion is dark, and the earnest thoughtful expression of his face is that of a man of high intelligence. The name of the person represented is inscribed on each portrait.

These likenesses are full of truth and power, and we already recognise in them the hand of the great author of the celebrated fresco of the "Dispute of the Holy Sacrament." They passed from Vallombrosa to the Florence Gallery, where, according to Bottari, they were erroneously attributed to Perugino.

44.
Portrait of a Young Woman. (About 1507.)

On wood. In the Pitti Palace. Profile figure, seated.

A woman, still young, not strictly beautiful, but with something very attractive in her face. Her long dark brown hair is loosely confined in a net, she rests her right arm on a table, and holds a pair of gloves in her hand. The execution of this charming portrait is extremely delicate, the shape of the head and hands is perfect, the colouring of the flesh, fresh and clear, and the drawing of the whole far less laboured than in the portraits of the two Doni.

This picture is well preserved, and has been lately added to the Pitti collection.

45.
The Holy Family of the Canigiani Family.

On wood; height 51¼ inches, width 42 inches.

The Virgin is seated in a meadow; with her right hand she holds Jesus on her knees, and in the left a small book. St. Elizabeth kneeling, with St. John before her, offering the Holy Child a scroll with the words, "Ecce Agnus Dei," and St. Joseph, standing leaning on a staff, are grouped in such a manner as to form a pyramid. In the distance we see a landscape with a town, and in the clouds there were formerly three small profile angels, which gave ease to the whole, but they were so much damaged in the cleaning of the picture, by Colin, a Frenchman, that it was thought best to efface them entirely.

The style of this painting is very similar to that of the "Entombment," and it must have been executed about the same time, 1506; indeed, this date is said to have been marked on the Virgin's robe. It was given to Anna Maria, daughter of Cosmo III., on her marriage with Johann Wilhelm, Elector of the Palatinate, and is now in the Pinacothek of Munich. It has been engraved some dozen times, by René Boyvin, G. Bonasone, and others less celebrated, and the copies of it are nearly as numerous. See Passavant's "Life of Raphael," French edition, vol. ii. pp. 53, 54.

46.

THE HOLY FAMILY WITH JESUS SEATED ON A LAMB. (At Madrid.)

On wood; height 16 inches, width 9½ inches (Spanish measure).

The Virgin, half kneeling, holds Jesus on a lamb, whilst St. Joseph looks on leaning on his staff. In the beautiful landscape in the distance, the "Flight into Egypt" is represented in miniature.

This precious picture was probably executed about 1506 or 1507; it is remarkable for the delicacy of the drawing and the agreeable colouring. For a long time it was, so to speak, buried in the Oratorio of the Escurial at Madrid, and looked upon as a picture of little value; until one day the Infant, Don Sebastian, a great lover of art, saw it for the first time, was struck by its beauty, and examining it closely, found to his astonishment that it bore Raphael's signature. It was then removed to the Museum of Madrid, and has been reproduced by Raphael Morghen and others.

47.

SAINT CATHERINE OF ALEXANDRIA.

On wood; height 28¾ inches, width 22½ inches. Nearly life-size.

The saint's figure is represented down to the knees: she is turning to the left, resting her right hand on her breast, and her left arm on the wheel, the instrument of her martyrdom. She raises her head with an expression of devout enthusiasm, towards a bright beam gleaming from the sky, and her face, though animated, is divinely peaceful. In the distance we have a river bordered by trees and houses.

The execution of this painting is light and spirited, and the colours are so thinly spread that we can distinguish the pen strokes on the panel, prepared with chalk. Except for a few retouches on the forehead and at the roots of the hair, this beautiful picture is in perfect preservation. It is now in the National Gallery, and was engraved by A. B. Desnoyers in 1824, and by Leroux in 1845.

48.

THE ENTOMBMENT, 1507.

On wood, about 6½ inches square.

Two young men are carrying the dead Christ to the tomb in a sheet. The elder of the two, with a short beard, is about to mount the steps leading to the sepulchre, walking backwards; the younger, seen in profile, supports the legs of the Saviour. Mary Magdalene, anxious to take one last look at the divine man, has seized his left hand; Joseph of Arimathæa is behind her, with St. John leaning over his shoulder. On the right, rather further back, the Virgin is fainting in the arms of three women. In the distance we see Mount Calvary with the three crosses. The figures are rather smaller than life size, and on the step on the left is inscribed: "Raphael Urbinas pinxit. MDVII."

Raphael painted this picture by order of Atalanta Baglioni, for the church of St. Francesco de' Conventuali at Perugia. He made the cartoon at Florence, and then, having seen Michael Angelo's design for the "Bathers of the Battle of the Pisans," and made friends with Fra Bartolomeo, he returned to Perugia, and executed his work with such consummate skill, that it will be an object of study and admiration to artists for all time.

We will not pause to enumerate the eulogisms of the admirers, or to examine the criticisms of the great writers who have studied this work;[1] but merely state in what it appears to us to differ from its predecessors.

We are, then, chiefly struck by the severe and profound study manifested, by the power of expression and beauty of form which proved Raphael's superiority over contemporary artists, and raised him to the unrivalled position which he still occupies. There is, it is true, something hard and dry about the outlines, and the colours of the draperies are perhaps too much glazed, but these slight imperfections are lost in the vivid truth of action and expression.

This altar-piece remained for a century in its original position; but in 1607 the monks sold it to Pope Paul V., who had it removed to the Borghese Palace, Rome. It was replaced by an excellent copy by the Cavaliere di Arpino; but the Perugians were very indignant with the monks for selling a picture given to their church, and made many fruitless endeavours to interest the Pope in their favour.

We cannot enumerate the many copies and engravings of this famous picture; but full details will be found in Passavant's "Life of Raphael," French edition, vol. ii. pp. 60, 61.

The Lunette of the Picture.

As usual in altar-pieces, Raphael added a small arched picture above the principal group; it is a half-length figure of God the Father, and is now surrounded by eleven small angels, supposed to have been added by Stefano Amadei of Perugia, who flourished about 1630. It was not sold with the large picture,

[1] See Passavant's "Life of Raphael," vol. ii. pp. 57, 58, and 59.

but forms the lunette of a "Nativity" by Orazio Alfani, in the same church of St. Francesco, at Perugia.

The Predella of the Picture.

The predella is composed of three compartments, each containing a profile figure of a theological virtue, in a medallion, with a companion angel in a niche. They are painted in grisaille on a grey ground. The predella was carried away by the French in 1798, restored to Italy after the treaty of 1815, and placed in the Vatican. A copy of it occupies its former place on the altar of the church of St. Francesco. We will briefly describe the three figures: "Faith" holds the chalice, with the host, in the right hand; on either side stands an angel clothed, and holding a tablet. "Charity" is seated with two children on her knees, and two leaning against her; one holds a pan of burning incense, and the other is scattering pieces of money; they symbolize the warmth and abundance of Christian charity. "Hope" is a profile figure, turning to the right, with clasped hands, and eyes raised to heaven. The angels on either side have their hands crossed.

The entire predella was engraved by Desnoyers (1811) and others, and the three figures have been reproduced separately several times.

49.

THE MADONNA WITH THE PINK.

A small picture; figure to the knees.

The Virgin is giving a pink to the Holy Child, who, seated in her lap, receives the flower with a gesture of delight. A room with an open window, through which we can see a distant landscape, forms the background.

There are many ancient copies of this charming picture, but we have never yet been able to discover the original; it is said to be in the possession of Count Francesco Spada at Lucca, but we think this a mistake. There are several good copies at Rome, and one fine imitation on canvas by Sassoferato at Basle. The engravings after these pictures are equally numerous; a list of them is given in Passavant's "Life of Raphael," vol. ii. p. 63.

50.

THE VIRGIN WITH JESUS ASLEEP.

Full length figures; two thirds the size of life.

The Virgin, turning to the left, is bending over the sleeping Jesus; and, raising the veil which covers him, gazes lovingly at him. St. John, kneeling near her, is looking towards the spectator and pointing to his divine companion with an expression of childlike joy. In the distance we see a landscape with a town on the left, a monastery on the right, and figures in the fields.[1]

This is the subject of a series of paintings all after one original by Raphael,

[1] Raphael painted a small picture like this, but with St. John in prayer, called the "Virgin with the Diadem." It is now in the Louvre.

which unfortunately cannot be found. The cartoon for it is, however, preserved in the Academy of Florence; and it is evident that these copies are not after it, for they all have a landscape exactly alike in Raphael's style, which is wanting in the former. For a detailed list of engravings and copies after this painting, see Passavant's "Life of Raphael," French edition, vol. ii. pp. 64, 65.

51.

THE MADONNA DELLA CASA NICCOLINI, 1508.

From the Niccolini Gallery at Florence. Figure to the knees; life size.

The Virgin, seen nearly in profile, is seated with Jesus on a white cushion on her knees. She gazes at him with the sweet purity of expression peculiar to Raphael's Madonnas, whilst the Child seizes his mother's dress, and looks round at the spectator with a smile. There is some little affectation about the figure of Jesus, but the drawing is perfect and, with the exception of one hand, the whole picture is in excellent preservation. It was bought by Earl Cowper of the Niccolini family when he was ambassador to the court of Tuscany, and it is now in his collection at Panshanger, near Hertford. It was engraved by Doo in 1835, under the title of the "Messiah," and has been reproduced in various forms by other less famous artists.

52.

MADONNA DI CASA COLONNA.

On wood; height 31½ inches, width 26⅛ inches. Figure to the knees.

The Virgin, her eyes fixed on Jesus, supports him with her right hand, and the Child, in trying to climb up to her, rests his left hand on his mother's right arm and clings with the other to her dress. The Virgin holds a small book in her left hand, and a landscape forms the background.

This is an unfinished picture; the hair and veil are scarcely coloured, and much of the shading and glazing is left out; from which we conclude that the gold ornaments were added by another hand, as they are generally not put in until the last. Imperfect as it is, however, this sketch is very valuable, as it shows how fully the great master's thought was embodied in the first touches of his brush.

This Madonna was bought by Bunsen, when Prussian Ambassador at Rome, for the Berlin Museum; it has been engraved and copied several times.

53.

LA BELLE JARDINIÈRE. (Arched picture.)

On wood; height 46½ inches, width 37½ inches. Figures full length.

This picture is so named because the Virgin is seated on a stone in a meadow full of plants and flowers. She looks down upon her Divine Son, who leans against her, with an expression of indescribable beauty, whilst he returns his mother's gaze with eyes full of love. St. John, kneeling on the right and resting on his cross, contemplates his companion with tender admiration. In the distance we see a hilly landscape with a river and a town.

Although the hands and feet are not quite finished in this picture, it is one of the most beautiful works ever produced by Raphael; the heads especially are full of soul and expression.

According to Lepicié and Mariette, this is the picture painted by Raphael for a gentleman of Sienna, which he left unfinished when called to Rome, requesting his friend Ridolfo Ghirlandajo to complete the Virgin's blue mantle. This assertion is borne out by the fact that the mantle is not in Raphael's style, but resembles that in the "Coronation of the Virgin," known to be by Ghirlandajo.

Francis I. bought "*La Belle Jardinière*" of the Siennese gentleman, and it is now in the Louvre. The original cartoon is at Holkham, the seat of the Earl of Leicester. The painting has been engraved by A. B. Desnoyers and many others, and a long list of ancient copies is given in Passavant's "Life of Raphael," vol ii. pp. 69 and 70 (French edition).

54.

The Madonna del Baldacchino.

On wood; height 128¼ inches, width 76¾ inches.

The Madonna, seated on a high throne, with Jesus on her knees, encircles him with one arm, and holds his arm against her breast with the right hand. On the left are St. Augustine and St. James; on the right St. Peter and a canonised Camoldoli monk (St. Bruno?). Two small angels, holding parchment scrolls, are singing in front of the throne, and above, two more raise the canopy.

Raphael painted this altar-piece for the chapel of the Dei family in the church of the Santo Spirito at Florence; but he had proceeded no further than the sketch when he was summoned to Rome, and he never found time to finish his work. After the great master's death, Baldasarre Turini bought this painting for the church of Pescia, and in 1697 it was obtained at a very high price of the Bonvicini family, to whom it belonged by right of patronage, by Prince Ferdinand, son of the Grand Duke Cosmo III.; but it was necessary to remove it in the night, lest its loss should cause a riot among the people. It was replaced by a copy by Carlo Sacconi.

This painting, which was restored with great care by Gio. Agostino Cassana, or Niccolo Cassana, is now in the Pitti Gallery. Like many other great works, it was taken to France by Napoleon, and returned to Italy after the treaty of 1815. It has been engraved by Morghen and others.

55.

The Madonna with the Infant Christ and the Young St. John.

Merely a sketch for a small picture. On wood; height 10½ inches, width 8½ inches.

The Holy Child is seated on a hillock, and the Virgin, kneeling before him, holds him with both hands. St. John, kneeling on the left, close to Jesus, is reading attentively from a parchment scroll, and for background we have a landscape with ruins surrounded by trees, and a mountain on the right.

This picture was probably left unfinished at the same time as the "Virgin with the Canopy." It was given to the Empress Elizabeth by Pope Clement XI. of the Albani family, and is now in the Esterhazy collection at Vienna. On a slip of paper, stuck at the back of the panel, the following words, in German, are inscribed in Elizabeth's own hand-writing—"This picture of the Virgin by Raffael of Urbino, together with the case set in precious stones, was given to me as a present by Pope Albany.—ELIZABETH R."

Paintings executed at Rome, under Pope Julius II. 1508-1511.

56.

THE STANZA DELLA SIGNATURA, IN THE VATICAN.

From 1508 to 1511.

The Stanze were three rooms decorated with Frescoes by Raphael under Julius II. and Leo X., for each of which he received 1200 gold ducats. Beginning with the Stanza "Della Signatura," we will give a brief summary of the subjects represented.

57.

THE FRESCO OF THEOLOGY.

Height 192 inches, width 320½ inches (arch-top picture).

This painting, also called the "Dispute on the Holy Sacrament," is divided into two parts; in the upper the Holy Trinity is surrounded by the heavenly host, the Saviour being placed between the Virgin and St. John the Baptist; with six saints, chosen from the Old and New Testament, on either side.

In the centre of the lower part the Eucharist is displayed upon an altar, round which are grouped forty-three figures: popes, bishops, theologians, &c., some of which, those of Dante, Savonarola, and Fra Angelico da Fiesole, for instance, are portraits.

This magnificent fresco surpasses anything of the kind before produced; we are struck alike by the grandeur and variety of the subjects treated, and the harmony of the whole. The execution is admirable, the great master had now acquired facility in the use of the materials at his command, and we see no more finishing touches added on the dry fresco. That this perfection was not obtained without much trouble, is proved by the great numbers of studies and sketches made for this composition, of which a list is given in the French edition of Passavant's "Life of Raphael," vol. ii. pp. 75 and 76.

The fresco itself has unfortunately suffered a great deal, the colours are faded, and it is cracked in three places, one crack cutting Christ's figure in two, another passing across John the Baptist, St. Thomas Aquinas and the writer below, and the third spoiling the figure of Dante. Measures have recently been taken to prevent any further deterioration.

It has been engraved by G. Mocetto, Keller, Volpato, and many others.

58.

THE PARNASSUS.

Height 192 inches, width 256¼ inches.

Apollo with a violin is seated beneath some laurel bushes near the fountain of the Hippocrenes, surrounded by the Muses. On the right stand four epic poets, amongst whom we recognise Homer, Virgil, and Dante, the fourth being unknown. In the group below, on the left, there is but one portrait, that of Petrarch; the others are supposed to represent Alcæus, Anacreon, Corinna and Sappho. Opposite to them, on the other side of the picture, are eight poets, Pindar, Horace, and others, four being evidently Italians, but their names are doubtful.

This fresco is executed in much the same style as that of the "Disputa;" it is not quite so carefully finished, but this is atoned for by a better distribution of light, and a grander treatment of the draperies. It is not characterized by the same richness of invention as the former, but this is accounted for by the subject. It is full of serenity and calm; a faithful representation of the tranquil lives of Italian poets in Raphael's time. The "Parnassus" seems to have been almost entirely executed by the great master himself; it has suffered slightly from decay. There is a fine engraving by Marc Antonio of a sketch of the whole composition in Bartsch's work, vol. xiv. No. 247, and the separate figures have been reproduced in various ways many times.[1]

59.

THE SCHOOL OF ATHENS.

Height 192 inches, width 320½ inches.

Plato and Aristotle occupy the centre of this composition with Zeno, chief of the Stoics, and other disciples; Diogenes is lying on the steps, and Aristippus is passing near him talking to Epicurus: sixteen figures in all. In the lower part of the picture, on the left, we see Pythagoras with Archytas and other pupils; Anaxagoras standing, Heraclitus alone, and Democritus, surrounded by young men leaning against the base of a pillar; altogether thirteen figures, amongst which are portraits of Francesco Maria della Rovere, Duke of Urbino, and of the young Prince Federico, of Mantua. On the steps in the corner on the left, Socrates is conversing with Alcibiades and others, and near this group are three sophists, eleven figures in all. Amongst the six figures on the right are two sceptic philosophers, Pyrrho and Arcesilaus, and in the group of nine figures below we recognise Euclid or Archimedes teaching mathematics to four young men. Ptolemy and Zoroaster, representing geography and astronomy, are talking together near Raphael and Perugino.

We know that Raphael consulted a scholar on the choice and arrangement of

---

[1] For sketches and studies see Passavant's "Life of Raphael," French ed. vol. ii. pp. 78 and 79.

the figures in this fresco, and in our description of them, we have been guided by the great authority on ancient philosophers; the book of Diogenes Laertius, which was much thought of in the sixteenth century. We find that the book and picture agree entirely, and that in this, as in almost every composition, Raphael has followed a chronological order in the arrangement of his groups.

After the death of Raphael the true sense of the "School of Athens" was entirely lost sight of: Vasari saw in it the union of theology and philosophy by means of astronomy, and he took the figure of Pythagoras for that of the Evangelist St. Matthew, and other less well known critics have hazarded equally distorted explanations. The honour of giving a true interpretation of the painting belongs to Bellori, see his "Descrizione delle immagini dipinte da Rafaello nelle camere del Vaticano" (Roma, 1695); but his want of classical knowledge led him into absurd mistakes, and it was Adolphus Trendelenburg who worked out the idea suggested by Bellori, and reduced his crude expressions into a reasonable statement. (Raphael's "School of Athens," a lecture delivered at Berlin in 1843.)

The "School of Athens" is considered superior both to the "Disputa" and the Parnassus, but it has unfortunately suffered more than any of the paintings in this room; this deterioration is partly owing to the neglect with which these great works was treated until 1702, but still more to the injurious custom of making tracings on the frescoes, which, damaging the even surface of the painting, spoilt the precision and purity of the outlines. Carlo Maratti, aided by his pupils Bartolomeo Urbani, Pietro de Pietri, and Andrea Procacini restored all the "Stanze" very carefully in 1702, and all tracing was strictly forbidden, but it was too late to remedy the mischief.

Several engravings of single studies for this work are given in Ottley's "Italian School of Design" and a sketch of "Philosophy," for the bas-relief beneath the statue of Minerva, was engraved by Marc Antonio (Bartsch XIV. No. 381) and copied by Agostino Veneziano and others. The whole fresco has been engraved more than sixteen times, but the great masters contented themselves with reproducing parts of it; by Marc Antonio we have "The figure of Apollo in the niche" (Bartsch XIV. Nos. 334 and 335); by Agostino Veneziano, the group of "Pythagoras," and that of "Alcibiades" leaning against an altar.[1]

60.

The Three Allegorical Figures.

In an arch, above the window; height 87½ inches, width 256¼ inches.

Prudence, with a Janus head, is seated in the centre, one genius offers her a mirror and another holds a torch before her. On the left, near a young oak, sits Fortitude or Force, with two small spirits; and on the other side Moderation holds a bridle towards which a genius, seated near her, is pointing.

If possible, there is more power in this painting than in the "School of

---

[1] For further details see Passavant's "Life of Raphael," vol. ii. pp. 85, 86, (French ed.)

Athens;" it is in perfect preservation, and has been engraved by Raphael Morghen, and others.

61.

The Emperor Justinian giving the Pandects.

A narrow painting, on the left, near the window.

The Emperor, in a purple mantle, is seated, presenting the law-books to Tribonianus, kneeling before him. Behind his throne stand six jurists, two of whom, Theophilus and Dorotheus, hold books containing the new "Institutiones" and "Constitutiones," given by the same Emperor. An architectural niche forms the background of this group. Owing to a flaw in the plaster of the wall, the colours of the fresco have become very pale.

62.

Gregory IX. giving the Decretals.

A narrow painting, on the right, near the window.

Pope Gregory (with the features of Julius II.) is seated in a niche, blessing the Decretals, as he hands them to a kneeling jurist of the Consistory. On the left stand three prelates: Giovanni de' Medeci, afterwards Leo X.; Alessandro Farnese, afterwards Paul III.; and Antonio del Monte. On the left are three other figures. This painting has also lost much of its colour; it has been engraved with the other pictures and ornaments of this room by Franc. Aquila.

63.

Allegorical Figure of Theology.

Round painting on the ceiling, on a gold ground, mosaic style.

This figure is seated on clouds, with a book in the left hand, typical of the tenets of the church, and the right hand pointing to the upper part of the chief picture. Two small attendant spirits hold tablets, with the respective inscriptions, "Divinar. Rer." and "Scientia." Beautiful as it is, we do not think this figure is from Raphael's own hand; we miss the combined severity and grandeur of the great master's style. It has been engraved by B. Audran, Raphael Morghen, and others.

64.

Allegorical Figure of Poetry.

Round painting on the ceiling, on a gold ground, mosaic style.

A female figure, with outspread wings and crossed legs, is seated on a block of marble covered with theatrical masks, emblematical of dramatic poetry. In the right hand she holds a book, and in the left a lyre. In the clouds rest two little spirits with tablets, on which are written: "Numine afflatur."

This figure, which is of supernatural beauty, is entirely from Raphael's own hand, and in his best manner. It has been engraved by Marc Antonio, B. Audran, Raphael Morghen, and many others.

65.

ALLEGORICAL FIGURE OF PHILOSOPHY.

Round painting on the ceiling, on a gold ground, mosaic style.

This figure, turning a little to the left, is also seated on marble, which is ornamented with small figures of Diana of Ephesus; symbolical representations of the four elements are woven into her dress, and on her knees are books bearing the titles, "Naturalis et Moralis." Two spirits stand near holding tablets with the inscriptions, "Causarum—cognitio."

Although this fine work has suffered much from restorations, we still recognise Raphael's hand in every part. It has been engraved by B. Audran, Raphael Morghen, and several others.

66.

ALLEGORICAL FIGURE OF JURISPRUDENCE.

Round painting on the ceiling, on a gold ground, mosaic style.

This figure, crowned with a diadem, holds a sword in the right hand and the scales in the left. A spirit on either side holds a tablet with the inscription, "Jus suum unicuique tribuens." This is the feeblest of the four figures; it is evidently by one of Raphael's pupils. It has been engraved by Morghen and others.

67.

ORIGINAL SIN.

A small painting on the ceiling, on a gold ground.

Adam, seated on the left under a fig tree, turns towards Eve, who offers him the forbidden fruit with one hand and with the other takes hold of a branch of the tree, on which we see the serpent with a woman's head.

This beautiful composition is executed in the most spirited style; it has been engraved by Virgilius Solis, Fr. Muller, and others.

68.

APOLLO FLAYING MARSYAS.

A small picture on the ceiling, on a gold ground.

Apollo seated, with his lyre in the left hand, is ordering a shepherd to flay Marsyas, who is bound to a tree; a second shepherd is crowning the god with laurel.

This fresco was executed by one of Raphael's feeblest pupils, and has only been engraved two or three times.

69.

ASTRONOMY; OR THE CONTEMPLATION OF THE HEAVENLY BODIES.

A small picture on the ceiling, on a gold ground.

A female figure, leaning against a transparent celestial globe, gazes admiringly at the planets, amongst which we can distinguish the earth. Two child spirits, holding books, stand beside her on clouds.

70.

THE JUDGMENT OF SOLOMON.

A small picture on the ceiling, on a gold ground.

Solomon, seated on his throne on the right, has just pronounced judgment; a young man on the left is about to cut the child in two; the false mother is on her knees in the foreground, whilst the true is hurrying to stay the execution of the sentence.

71.

ALEXANDER THE GREAT PLACING THE POEMS OF HOMER IN THE TOMB OF ACHILLES.

One of the paintings in grisaille, under the Parnassus, on the left.

The young conqueror, standing on the right, is ordering a bearded man to place a volume in a sarcophagus, the cover of which is raised by a youth who is nearly nude. Six warriors stand behind Alexander, and on the left are six other men, three of whom are looking into the tomb with evident curiosity. Engraved by Marc Antonio and others.

72.

THE EMPEROR AUGUSTUS FORBIDDING THE BURNING OF VIRGIL'S ÆNEAD.

Painted in grisaille, under the Parnassus, on the right.

In compliance with the last wish of Virgil, his friends Tucca and Varius are about to throw his unfinished poem of the Ænead into the flames, and the Emperor, crowned with laurel, advances to prevent them. On the right we see eight figures.

73.

THE SMALL PICTURES IN THE EMBRASURES OF THE WINDOWS.

These ornamental paintings in grisaille, relieved with gold, are executed after drawings by Raphael; they represent candelabra or grotesques, with a small picture in the middle, and a larger one at the top. They have suffered so much, that it is in most cases impossible to compare the engravings after them with the originals. The supposed subjects are enumerated in Passavant's "Life of Raphael," vol. ii. p. 92 (French edition).

74.

THE PAINTINGS ON THE SOCLE OF THE "STANZA DELLA SIGNATURA."

We know that Raphael placed sculptured wood panels, the work of Fra Giovanni of Verona, all round this room; but they were removed by Paul III. and replaced by paintings by Pierino del Vaga, which in their turn were restored by Carlo Maratti and his pupils. We will briefly name their subjects, as they have reference to the larger works by Raphael himself:—

Under the fresco of Theology:

(*a.*) "The Knowledge of Divine things;" allegorical female figure.

(*b.*) "The Sibyl of Tibur showing the Emperor Augustus the vision of the Holy Virgin."

(*c.*) "Saint Augustine watching a child on the beach attempting to drain the sea with a spoon."

(*d.*) "A Heathen Sacrifice."

Under the "School of Athens:"

(*e.*) "Speculative Philosophy;" allegorical female figure.

(*f.*) "Oriental Scholars and Magicians arguing on the terrestial globe."

(*g.*) "The Siege of Syracuse."

(*h.*) "The Death of Archimedes."

Under "Jurisprudence:"

(*i.*) "Moses giving the Tables of the Law to the People of Israel."

(*k.*) "Solon addressing the people of Athens."

75.

Portrait of Pope Julius II.

On wood; height 39½ inches, width 25½ inches. Figure to the knees.

The Pope is seated in an arm chair, holding a handkerchief in the left hand, on which he wears three rings. On his head is a red velvet cap, his white beard falls upon his breast, and he looks thoughtfully on the ground. The background is green.

We believe that Raphael painted this portrait for the Pope himself, by whom it was given to the church of Santa Maria del Popolo at Rome; at all events it was there in the time of Vasari and also of Sandrart, and was exhibited on high fête days with the Madonna of Loretto, also by Raphael. We do not know how it became the property of the Medici family.

Although this portrait suffered from too much cleaning in its brief visit to France before the treaty of 1815, it is still a magnificent work. It has not been engraved by any of the great masters, but the copies are numerous, and we have one in our own National Gallery (height 42 inches, width 32 inches).

76.

Portrait of the Marchese Federico of Mantua.

On wood; height 16½ inches, width 9 inches.

In the catalogue of the works of art belonging to Charles I. drawn up by Van der Doort,[1] this portrait is described in the following terms: "Bought by the king. A young man's head, without a beard, in a red cap, whereon a medal and some part of his white shirt, without a ruff, in his long hair; being the Marquis of Mantua, who was by the Emperor Charles V. made the first Duke of Mantua. The picture being only a head, so big as the life. Upon a board in a black frame, painted upon the right light."

This portrait is said to have belonged to Cardinal Richelieu, but however that may be, it was in the possession of Mr. Ed. Gray, of London, in 1831, and is now

[1] "A Catalogue and Description of King Charles I. Capital Collection of Pictures, etc. from an original MS. in the Ashmolean Museum at Oxford. London, 1757."

in the collection of Mr. Lucy, of Charlcote Park near Warwick. It represents a very handsome youth in the costume of his time (beginning of the sixteenth century).

77.

Portrait of Raphael himself.

To the knees, three-quarter-face.

Raphael is seated, resting his right arm on a table and holding his fur-trimmed doublet with the left. His plentiful brown hair, parted down the middle, falls upon his neck and shoulders; he wears a cap a little on one side and pushed back from his forehead. For background we have the wall of a room with a window looking out upon a landscape, with buildings, one of which resembles the tomb of Cecilia Metella, near Rome.

In this portrait, Raphael appears to be about twenty-five years old; he has a long, finely shaped nose, a mouth full of character, and a well-developed chin; a high forehead with delicately arched eyebrows. He looks out of the picture with a sweet but penetrating gaze, and in the beautiful contour of the left cheek, we note that refined delicacy often characteristic of a vigorous and enthusiastic nature.

We believe this to be the likeness which Raphael promised to Francesco Francia, in a letter to him, dated the 5th of September, 1508; but where it is now, or if it be still in existence, is uncertain. We have an engraving by Paul Pontius said to be after the original; and copies and engravings of them are extremely numerous; for full particulars on the subject we refer our readers to Passavant's "Life of Raphael," vol. ii. pp. 97, 98 (French edition).

78.

The Mistress of Raphael, or La Fornarina.

Figure to the knees, turning to the left.

A beautiful half-nude girl, in the bloom of youth, is seated, surrounded by flowers. She wears a yellow drapery about her head, and her hair is bound with a circlet of gold with leaves and flowers garnished with precious stones. With one hand she holds the light drapery upon her breast, whilst the other falls carelessly on the red garment over her knees. On the bracelet on her left arm is inscribed: "Raphael Urbinas." There is something both artless and sensual in the expression of this woman's face, and the features are somewhat wanting in animation and refinement, but the execution and colouring are alike very fine.

From the style of this work we believe it to have been produced about 1509; there are a great many copies of it, but the painting in the Barberini Gallery is certainly the original; for a long time it was neglected and allowed to remain covered with dust, but in 1820 Palmaroli cleaned it with great success. It has been engraved by Domenico Cunego and others. A list of the copies is given in the life of Raphael referred to above, p. 99, together with the engravings after them.

PORTRAIT OF A YOUNG MAN.

In the Louvre.

79.

BUST PORTRAIT OF A YOUNG MAN.

In the Louvre. Height 23½ inches, width 17 inches.

This portrait represents a handsome youth of fifteen, with light hair falling from beneath a cap. He is seated with his elbow on the table, resting his head on his hand, and looking at the spectator. His dress, of a sober green, stands out clearly against a background of the same colour, but lighter. The execution of this picture is easy, but the drawing not quite correct; by some it has been supposed to be Raphael's own likeness; but we do not share this opinion, as it is in his third manner, and he is not likely to have departed so entirely from his master's style at the early age of fifteen.

Engraved by H. Edelinck, F. Forster, and others.

80.

THE MADONNA DI LORETO.

Figure to the knees. Life size.

The Virgin, standing behind the couch of the infant Jesus, lifts the veil which covers him, and raises her right arm in the air. The child, resting on a cushion, stretches his arms towards his mother. St. Joseph leans on a staff behind the Virgin, and a curtain forms the background.

This picture was formerly in the church of S. Maria del Popolo, at Rome, with the portrait of Julius II.; it was there as late as 1675, as it was seen by Sandrart. We have no positive information as to its subsequent fate, but it is generally believed that Girolamo Lottorio, of Rome, gave it to the shrine of Loreto in 1717; hence its present title. The copies are very numerous, and the discovery of the original has been more than once positively announced, but, as we think, without any sufficient evidence of a trustworthy kind. For a long list of copies and supposed originals, see Passavant's "Life of Raphael," vol. ii. pp. 101-105.

81.

MADONNA DELLA CASA D'ALBA.

Round picture on wood; 9½ inches in diameter.

The Virgin is seated on the ground in a landscape, holding Jesus with the left hand, and an open book in the right. The Holy Child embraces his mother with the left arm, and grasps a small cross, offered to him by St. John, in the right hand. The landscape in the background resembles the banks of the Tiber.

This valuable picture is extremely well preserved; for some unknown reason, the landscape was at one time completely painted over, but the colours of the new coating were so thick that they were removed without spoiling the painting. Judging from the style of this work, we believe it to have been executed soon after Raphael's arrival at Rome. It was formerly in a church at Nocera de' Pagani in the Neapolitan States, and was bought by the Marchese del Carpio, Viceroy of Naples, for about 1000 scudi. We meet with it later in the gallery of the Duke of Alba at Madrid, and according to an old tradition the Duchess of Alba left it and a copy to her doctor, as a reward for curing her of a dangerous disease. Her death almost immediately after making her will, in 1801, led to suspicions of poison; the doctor was arrested, and not set at liberty until his cause was espoused by the Principe de la Paz. In his gratitude he presented one of the pictures to his benefactor, and sold the other, the original, to Burcke, Danish ambassador at Madrid. After passing from hand to hand, it was finally bought for the Emperor of Russia for £14,000 sterling, and is now in the Hermitage Palace at St. Petersburg, having fortunately escaped injury in the last great fire.

It has been engraved by A. Boucher-Desnoyers, and others, and the ancient copies of it are very numerous.

82.

Madonna of the Aldobrandini Family.

On wood; height 14½ inches, width 11¾ inches. Figures to the knees.

The Virgin, wearing blue-green drapery, relieved with gold, is seated on a bench with Jesus on her knees; with one arm she spreads her mantle round the Holy Child, and with the other embraces St. John, who stands on the right. Jesus leans against his mother's breast, and offers the future prophet a pink; the latter stretches out one hand to receive it, and rests the other, in which he holds a cross, upon the bench. For background we have a landscape with factories.

The clear and brilliant tone of the flesh tints in this picture contrast well with the quiet colouring of the drapery and landscape; and the ornaments, relieved with gold, show it to have been produced soon after Raphael's arrival in Rome.

This Madonna at first formed part of the Aldobrandini collection, but, according to Buchanan, it was bought by Lord Garvagh, of London, for £15,000 sterling, of Mr. Day.[1] It has been several times engraved, and copies of it are distributed all over Europe.

83.

The Virgin with the Diadem.

Also known as the "Vierge au Linge," the "Vierge au Voile," the "Slumber of Jesus," and the "Silence of the Holy Virgin."

On wood; height 26½ inches, width 19¼ inches.

The Virgin, wearing a blue diadem, is stooping over Jesus asleep upon the ground; and raising the veil which covers him to show him to St. John, who is kneeling near.

In the distance we see a town, and recognise the ruins in the Sachetti vineyard, which still exist in Rome, near the basilica of St. Peter's.

Tradition says that this painting, cut in half, was once used to cover some casks in a cave at Pescia, but that an amateur bought the two pieces, and had them so skilfully put together that it is almost impossible to see the joins; how-

---

[1] This painting was purchased for the National Gallery in 1865, for the sum of £9,000.

ever this may be, we know that it was once in the celebrated collection of M. de Chateauneuf, at Paris, and that it is now in the Louvre.

It has unfortunately been both too much cleaned and injudiciously retouched. We have engravings after it by Boucher-Desnoyers, François de Poilly, and many others, and antique copies of it are very numerous.

84.

MADONNA DI FULIGNO.

On wood, transferred to canvas; height $113\frac{3}{4}$ inches, width $74\frac{3}{4}$ inches.

The Virgin, seated on clouds in a golden glory, is surrounded by a number of half-length angels, faintly indicated against the azure blue sky; with one hand she embraces the Holy Child, standing beside her, and with the other holds some drapery round him. Both look down on the kneeling votary, Sigismondi Conti, who is presented to the holy mother by St. Jerome. St. John the Baptist, standing on the left, points to the Saviour, and St. Francis kneels more in front, in ecstasy; a little naked angel, with a tablet, completes the group. A burning globe, with a rainbow above it, is falling from the sky. According to tradition this globe is a bomb, and bears reference to the danger incurred by Sigismondi at the siege of Fuligno, his native town, and the rainbow may be considered symbolical of the reconciliation of the donor with God. A hilly landscape, with a town, forms the background.

We believe this picture to have been painted about 1511, for Sigismondi Conti,[1] and to have been intended for a votive offering.

According to Vasari, it first adorned the high altar of the church of Ara Cœli on the Capitol, at Rome; but it was at Fuligno from 1565 until it was carried away by the French. It was in a very bad condition on its arrival in Paris, and was transferred to canvas by M. Haquin, and restored by Herr Roser, of Heidelberg. On the removal of the wood from the panel, the whole drawing was distinctly seen traced with the brush, in brown colour, and it was noticed that St. Jerome's right hand was drawn in two different styles, and that one only was executed by the painter. After the treaty of 1815, this painting was restored to Italy, and is now in the Vatican. The entire work has been engraved by Boucher-Desnoyers, and several others, and part of it by Marc Antonio, &c.

85.

THE PROPHET ISAIAH (1512 at the latest).

In fresco; height 102 inches, width, 64.

The prophet is seated, turning his head to the left, and holding a strip of parchment towards the spectator, on which the second verse of the 26th of Isaiah is written in Hebrew: "Open ye the gates, that the righteous nation which keepeth the truth may enter in." Two children, placed on the architrave a little above, hold a cartouche with the following dedication in Greek: "To Saint Anne, mother of the Virgin; to the holy Virgin, mother of God; to Jesus the Saviour; Johann Corizius."

[1] S. Conti was private secretary to the Pope: he died in 1512.

Raphael painted this fresco on a pillar, supporting a marble group of the Virgin, Jesus, and St. Anne, by order and at the expense of a German gentleman, Johann Gorizius by name, who is sometimes called Janus Corycius Lucumburgensis.

Vasari relates that Raphael had just finished this fresco, when Bramante showed him Michael Angelo's paintings in the Sistine Chapel, and that he was so disgusted with his own work after seeing them, that he had it destroyed, and produced another prophet in grander style. This story is doubtful at the best, although we know that the artist of Urbino was at one time much influenced by Buonarotti. Another equally improbable anecdote is told by Richardson. He informs us that the person who ordered this painting thought the price too high when it was finished, and consulted Michael Angelo on the matter. The latter having seen the fresco, replied: "The knee alone is worth the price demanded."

This painting has suffered greatly; an over zealous sacristan washed it, and spoilt it so much that Paul IV. (1555) had it restored, unfortunately making matters worse. It has been engraved by Henry Goltzius, N. Visscher, Nic. Chapron, and many others.

86.

Two Children, with the Armorial Bearings of Julius II.

Above the chimney-piece of the room named after Innocent VIII. in the Vatican, the coat-of-arms of Julius II. was painted, upheld by two children, attributed to Raphael. Pungileoni discovered that they were exact copies of those in the fresco of Isaiah; and when the Vatican was enlarged about twenty years ago the whole painting was cut out and exchanged for some engravings by Marc Antonio. One of the children belonging to this fresco is said to be in England, and the other is in the Academy of Saint Luke, at Rome.

87.

Portrait of a Woman (1512).

In the Tribune at Florence; height 26 inches, width 22 inches.

This bust portrait represents a young and beautiful lady, seen nearly full face, and turning to the left. On her head she wears a circlet of gold, enamelled with green leaves, and with one hand she holds back the fur-trimmed mantle which covers her dark blue velvet bodice. All the ornaments, and even the lights of the hair in this picture are relieved with gold, as in Mantegna's and Holbein's portraits, and the colouring is so warm and powerful that we are forcibly reminded of Giorgione, to whom, as well as to Sebastiano del Piombo, this work has been attributed. It is, however, incontestably from Raphael's own hand.

Unfortunately, although much has been written on the subject, and many conjectures have been hazarded, we do not know the name of the lovely woman represented; we ourselves are somewhat disposed to think that she is the poetess and improvisatrice, Beatrice Ferrarese, who was famous at the time this likeness was painted; but we have nothing to warrant our idea but her peculiar attitude, her rapt and inspired expression, and the crown of golden leaves upon her head.

This portrait has been engraved by Raphael Morghen, and others less celebrated.

88.

Portrait of Bindo Altoviti.

On wood; height 23½ inches; width 17½ inches.

A handsome youth, with blue eyes and long fair hair, wearing a black cap and looking over his right shoulder.

This portrait remained in the Altoviti family until 1808, when it was bought by Prince Louis of Bavaria for about 3,500 zecchini. For a long time, however, it was hidden by John Metzger, the agent employed, lest it should excite the cupidity of the French government. It is now in the Pinacothek of Munich, in a state of excellent preservation.[1]

Although Vasari and others have hazarded a different opinion, there is no doubt that this is the portrait of Bindo Altoviti, who was born on the 26th of September, 1490, and was consequently in his twenty-second year when it was painted. It has been engraved by Raphael Morghen, and many others.

89.

Madonna of the Bridgewater Gallery.

Painted on wood and afterwards transferred to canvas; height 34 inches, width 23½ inches. Figures to the knees.

The Virgin, turning to the left, with the infant Jesus lying across her knees, and supported by her right arm. The child, who is full of vivacity, grasps his mother's veil in his right hand, and looks up into her face. The drawing and modelling of this painting are excellent, and it would be impossible to conceive a more beautiful line than that of the figure of the child from the shoulder to the sole of the foot. In parts the coating of colour is so thin that the lines of the drawing can be seen through. This beautiful picture passed from the Seignelay collection to that of the Duke of Orleans, and was transferred to canvas by Haquin. The Duke of Bridgewater bought it in London for £3,000 sterling, and it now belongs to Lord Ellesmere. It has been engraved by Nic. de Larmessin, Boulanger, and many others.

90.

Madonna with Jesus standing.

Painted on wood and afterwards transferred to canvas; height 32 inches, width 25½ inches. Figure to the knees.

The Virgin is seated on a bench, on which Jesus is standing; she presses her son lovingly to her breast, and holds his foot in her left hand. Her eyes are

[1] Erroneously called Raphael's own portrait in the Catalogue.

downcast; she is wrapt in happy meditation. The child twines his arms round his mother's neck, and looks out of the picture with a smile.

This painting has unfortunately suffered greatly; it is so worn in parts that the sketch alone remains.

It has been engraved no less than thirteen times.

91.

The Holy Family of Naples.

On wood; height 23 inches, width 19 inches.

The Virgin, seen almost in profile, is seated on the ground, looking at Jesus, who is on her knees. St. Elizabeth, on the right, takes one of the child's hands, as if to persuade him to bless St. John, who kneels before him in adoration. We recognize St. Joseph in the buildings in the background.

The whole, or at least the principal parts, of this painting are from Raphael's own hand, in his most superior style. It is in excellent preservation, and was originally painted for Lionello da Carpi, Signore da Meldola; later it passed into the Farnese Gallery at Parma, and was inherited by Ferdinand I., King of the two Sicilies. In 1805, when Naples was invaded by the French armies, the queen took this painting, with other valuable objects, to Palermo, and from thence to Vienna, and it did not return to Naples until after her death.

The sketch of this group has been engraved by Marc Antonio, but the composition itself has not been reproduced by any of the great masters of chiaroscuro, although the antique copies are extremely numerous.

92.

The Virgin with the Fish.

Painted on wood and afterwards transferred to canvas; height 77½ inches, width 63½ inches.

The Virgin is seated on a throne with Jesus on her knees. The holy child bends lovingly towards the young Tobit, who, holding a fish in his hand, is presented to the Son of God by the angel Raphael. On the right, near the throne, stands St. Jerome, with his lion at his feet, reading from a large book, on the leaves of which Jesus has placed his hand. A curtain forms the background, and we see a small piece of the sky on the right.

It is said that the Viceroy of Naples, Duke of Medina, took this picture and others away from the Dominican convent at Naples without the consent of the authorities, and that when the prior complained to Rome of the outrage, the Duke revenged himself by ordering him to quit the kingdom of Naples in a few hours, and had him escorted to the frontier by fifty horsemen. The Viceroy took the "Virgin with the Fish" to Spain about 1644, and in 1656 it became the property of Philip IV. and was placed in the Escurial, where it received the name of "La Virgen del Pez." When the French were compelled to evacuate the

Peninsula in 1813, they carried away this coveted picture. It arrived in Paris in a very bad condition, and Bonnemaison was carefully transferring it from its worm-eaten panel to canvas, when the treaty of 1815 was concluded. The Duke of Wellington, however, urged him to finish his task, and it was not until 1822 that it was restored to Spain. Although it suffered in some parts in the transference to canvas, it is still the finest work in the Italian Gallery of the Madrid Museum; and if possible, it surpasses even the "Madonna di San Sisto" in the expression of the figures. The whole composition has been engraved by Boucher Desnoyers, and others, and the Virgin and Child alone by H. S. Beham, &c.

93.

The Stanza di Eliodoro, in the Vatican (1512-1514).

This room was formerly decorated with paintings by Pietro della Francesca and Bramantino, but they were removed by order of the Pope to make room for Raphael's. Before they were destroyed, however, the great master had copies of them made by his pupil Giulio Romano, which were in the possession of the late Mr. Roscoe, of Liverpool, in 1831.

In the room which he undertook to decorate, Raphael left untouched the small antique subjects in grisaille, relieved with gold, which formed the framework of the ceiling paintings. He only executed the four large subjects, and to make them look lighter he imitated stretched canvas. He received 1,200 gold ducats for his work.

94.

God appearing to Noah.

Painting on the ceiling.

God the Father is descending from Heaven, accompanied by two small angels, and is about to address Noah, who kneels before him in profound adoration. One of the patriarch's young sons is near him, the other two are with their mother, who is looking out from the door of her house, with her youngest child in her arms. This painting probably bears reference to the warning before the Deluge, but it has been otherwise interpreted. Vasari thinks it represents the Covenant with Abraham, and Montagnani Noah adoring the Almighty on leaving the ark.

This fresco has become very pale in consequence of the bad material on which it is executed, and we notice a similar alteration in the other ceiling paintings.

95.

The Sacrifice of Isaac.

Fresco on the ceiling.

Abraham is holding Isaac in a kneeling posture on a stone altar, and is about to complete the sacrifice, when an angel arrests his arm. Another angel is descending from Heaven, head downwards, with the ram which is to replace the victim. Raphael has painted several angels flying with the head downwards in an ungraceful position, in the "Virgin with the Canopy," for instance; and this is the more surprising, as his figures are generally remarkable for simplicity and beauty of attitude.

96.

JACOB'S DREAM.

Fresco on the ceiling.

The patriarch is lying asleep on some flat stones. In the clouds we see a ladder on which five angels are ascending and descending, and above Jehovah in glory with outstretched arms. This is the feeblest of the four frescoes on the ceiling; Raphael has treated the same subject in a very superior manner in the Loggie.

97.

MOSES PROSTRATE BEFORE THE BURNING BUSH.

Fresco on the ceiling.

Moses, as a shepherd, is kneeling before the burning bush, with his face hidden in his hands, and the Lord is issuing from the flames attended by angels and seraphims.

In this splendid composition the grandeur of Michael Angelo is combined with the grace of Raphael. It is much to be regretted that the colours have faded as in the other ceiling frescoes. It has been engraved, with some alterations, by G. Audran and others.

98.

HELIODORUS DRIVEN OUT OF THE TEMPLE.

Mural painting.

Heliodorus, who intended stealing some of the treasures of the Temple of Jerusalem, is turned out by two avenging angels, sent by God (2 Maccabees iii. 23-28). In the interior of the temple we see the High Priest Onias praying with the people before the tabernacle and the seven-branched candlestick; and in the foreground their prayer is answered. Heliodorus is already overthrown, and the soldiers are fleeing, pursued by a celestial horseman, accompanied by two angels with whips. The left side is occupied by the assembled people, amongst whom we notice several women manifesting great enthusiasm at the Divine interposition.

In the foreground Julius II. is looking on from his chair of state, carried by four men. One of the bearers in front is the celebrated Marc Antonio Raimondi, and another, standing rather further back, is thought to be Giulio Romano; the young man near Raimondi, holding a cap and sheet of parchment with the inscription: "Jo. Petro de Folicarius Cremonens," was secretary of briefs to Pope Julius.

We refer our readers to the explanation of this painting given in our "Life of Raphael," and will only add that it is executed in the new style, now called the picturesque, alluded to by Vasari, which consists in sacrificing strictness of drawing to the general effect produced by large masses of light and shade.

It is much to be regretted that the plaster on which this fresco is painted, seems likely to fall in several places. Measures should be at once taken to arrest the evil.

We have engravings after this painting by And. Meldolla, Mochetti, and many others.

99.

THE MIRACLE OF BOLSENA.

Mural painting.

This painting covers the wall, with the window looking out upon the court of the Vatican. Beneath this window Raphael has represented a priest saying mass at an altar in the presence of Urban IV., with the features of Julius II.; it was at this service that the miracle of the bleeding of the Host was performed, which led to the institution of the feast of Corpus Christi. On the left are the astonished people, and on the right the bearers of the Pope's chair.

The "Miracle of Bolsena" has been engraved by Raphael Morghen, and several others.

100.

THE DISCOMFITURE OF THE HORDES OF ATTILA.

Mural painting.

Attila, King of the Huns, was marching towards Rome at the head of his wild warriors, when Saints Peter and Paul, patrons of the Holy City, suddenly appeared to him in the clouds, waving their flaming swords. This vision so terrified Attila that he was compelled to submit to the terms of Leo I. and leave Italy.

Attila is represented in the middle of the picture on a black horse with white spots, two soldiers before him are pointing out the Pope coming to meet him. On the right are two barbarian chiefs mounted on spirited horses, and in the background a crowd of soldiers are issuing from a defile in the mountains. On the left Leo I. (with the features of Leo X.) approaches with calm dignity, mounted on a sober steed, led by an esquire. All the figures of the Papal retinue appear to be portraits.

101.

THE DELIVERANCE OF ST. PETER.

This fresco, which covers the right wall, is divided into three compartments: in the central one we look through the bars of the prison at St. Peter, lying asleep between two guards, who are slumbering at their post, whilst an angel of dazzling brightness approaches to deliver the apostle. In the right compartment St. Peter is seen leaving the prison with the angel, and passing between two soldiers asleep on the steps; and in the left the keepers are awaking in dismay at the disappearance of their charge. The two first subjects are illumined by the light from the angel only, and the third by the glimmer of a torch held by one of the soldiers, and by the moon in a cloudy sky.

In this beautiful painting we have fresh proofs of Raphael's minute and careful study of nature, and of his exalted appreciation of the true, the beautiful, and the picturesque in everything which came under his notice.

102.

Paintings of the Socles and Allegorical Figures in the Stanza d'Eliodoro.

The lower part of these mural paintings is occupied by eleven allegorical figures and four caryatid statues; between the latter are marble slabs with small paintings below them, bearing reference, together with the allegorical figures, to the industries, &c. of the States of the Church. Both caryatides and paintings have suffered greatly; they were partially retouched in 1702 and 1703 by Carlo Maratti and his pupils, but we still recognize Raphael's own style.

The eleven allegorical figures represent Religion, Law, Peace, Protection, Nobility, Commerce, the Navy, Navigation, Plenty, Husbandry, Agriculture, and the Cultivation of the Vine. They are all standing female figures with small capitals on their heads, which apparently support the cornice beneath the large paintings. The greater number of them have been engraved by Gerard Audran and others.

The subjects of the small paintings are, "The Harvest;" "Rome protecting the Arts and Sciences," and "Minerva banishing Discord;" "Agriculture;" "The Vintage;" "The Thrashing of Corn;" "Abundance, produced by Commerce and Good Laws;" "Husbandry;" "Rome and the Tiber;" "The Navy;" two Warriors; and a Matron, with a young girl kneeling before her.

103.

The Embrasures of the Windows in the Stanza d'Eliodoro.

The grotesques in grisaille, relieved with gold, and the small accompanying pictures in these embrasures are terribly spoilt, and have been entirely repainted; indeed, in one we recognize the man of the Apocalypse with the brazen feet, after Albert Durer's wood engraving. We believe the subjects to have been the following:—"Joseph before Pharaoh;" "The Red Sea;" "Moses receiving the Tables of the Law;" "The Annunciation;" "The Pope celebrating Mass;" and "The Emperor Constantine giving the town of Rome to Pope Sylvester." Pietro Santo Bartoli has published etchings of them all.

Paintings of Raphael executed at Rome under Leo X.

1513—1520.

104.

Portrait of Phædra Inghirami.

On wood; height 35½ inches, width 23½ inches. Profile figure.

This person is represented turning to the left, and looking up; one eye squints very much. He has a pen in his hand, and paper and ink before him, ready to exercise his functions as secretary to the conclave of cardinals which elected Leo X. pope. He wears a red garment, and a cap of the same colour.

Near him, on the left, is an open book on a small desk, and a green drapery forms the background.

This interesting portrait was for a time in the Napoleon Museum, but was restored to the Pitti Gallery, where it now is, in 1815.

105.

THE PROPHETS AND THE SIBYLS.

Frescoes in the church of Santa Maria della Pace, at Rome.

Agostino Chigi, a wealthy merchant of Siena, had the first chapel on the right in S. Maria della Pace decorated at his own expense, and commissioned Raphael to paint four prophets and four sibyls on the wall above the arcade leading to the altar.

The four prophets, which are above the sibyls, were executed by Timoteo della Vite, in 1514, after drawings by Raphael, and are far feebler than the female figures. On the left are the young Daniel seated and King David standing, and on the right Jonas on foot looking up to heaven and Hosea sitting down and pointing to the inscription on his tablet. Behind each group is an angel in repose, and above another, smaller, flying.

The fresco beneath the prophets, on the arcade which forms the entrance to the chapel, contains four sibyls and seven angels. On the left the Cumæan sibyl is seated, holding up a scroll in her right hand, which is half opened by an angel flying above her, and reveals the inscription in Greek—"The resurrection of the dead." Near her sits the Persica, writing on a tablet held by an angel, "He will have the lot of death." A little angel holding a torch is kneeling on the key-stone, and another, seated near, points to the tablet in his hand, with the inscription—"The heavens surround the sphere of the earth." The two other sibyls on the right look down; the young and beautiful Phrygia is standing, leaning against the curve of the arcade, and the old Tiburtina is seated at the edge of the picture. A little angel between the two last-named figures holds a tablet, with the inscription—"I will open and arise," and above him floats another with an open scroll, on which is written—"Another generation already" ("Jam nova progenies," from Virgil's "Eclogue IV." line 7). As in the fresco of the prophets, the background represents architecture of a dull colour, against which the figures stand out clearly.

The magnificent figures of the sibyls are executed in a masterly manner; and there is no doubt that they are entirely from Raphael's own hand. In some respects they resemble the three virtues of the "Stanza della Segnatura," but they are executed with even greater ease, and the colouring is warmer.

These frescoes were finished about 1519; they had suffered considerably soon after Raphael's death, and were restored by order of Pope Alexander VII. under the superintendence of the Cavaliere Fontana (1656-61), and in our own day they have been carefully gone over by Palmaroli. They have been engraved several times, but by none of the great masters. A list of drawings for the prophets and sibyls is given in Passavant's "Life of Raphael," vol. ii. p. 142, (French edition).

106.
Galatea.

Fresco painting in the Farnesina. Galatea is borne over the waves in her shell, drawn by two dolphins, and guided by a cupid. Tritons and sea-nymphs play around; behind the goddess a youth, mounted on a sea-horse, is blowing in a Venus shell, and above her three amorini are discharging their arrows, whilst a fourth, half hidden in the clouds, is preparing his darts.

This fresco, which is still in excellent preservation, was painted by Raphael, in 1514, in one of the rooms of the Farnesina Palace, which then belonged to Agostino Chigi. It is supposed to be an allegorical representation of the superiority of spiritual over material joys, and is more remarkable for its life and action than for beauty of drawing or grandeur of style. It has been engraved by Marc Antonio, Marco Dente or Marco of Ravenna, Henry Goltzius, and several others.

107.
Portrait of Giuliano de' Medici.

Raphael painted two portraits of this Giuliano, but both are lost; a copy of one is in the Florence Gallery; it represents a young man with the characteristic features of the Medici family, wearing a black cap, a scarlet vest, a black doublet, and a sort of grey greatcoat trimmed with brown fur. A copy of the other, merely a head, was formerly in the Cammucini collection at Rome; but it, too, is now lost.

108.
Portrait of Bernardo Dovizio da Bibiena, Cardinal of Santa Maria in Portico.

On wood; height 33¾ inches; width 26 inches. Spanish measure.

This portrait is in the Madrid Museum, and was for a long time thought to represent Cardinal Granvelle, although that great statesman was only seventeen years old when Raphael died. It is the likeness of a middle-aged person, seen nearly full-face, and turning slightly to the left. The face is thin, the nose somewhat bent, and the eyes bright, with long lashes, altogether quite the Italian type of countenance. The cardinal wears a red hat and a red collar; he rests his left arm, in a white sleeve, on a stone balustrade, and lets the right hand fall.

The presence of this portrait of an Italian cardinal in the Madrid Museum is accounted for by the fact that it was bequeathed by the owner to Castiglione, Spanish ambassador at the court of Clement VII., and by him carried to Spain. It is one of the finest likenesses painted by Raphael, and has been well engraved by Ludwig Grüner, but under the erroneous title of "Giulio de' Medici."

109.

SAINT CECILIA.

Painted on wood and afterwards transferred to canvas; height 92 inches, width 57½ inches.

The saint, in the centre of the picture, is listening to the celestial singing of six angels, with her eyes raised to heaven in ecstasy. Her little organ is slipping from her hands, and half-broken instruments of terrestrial music are lying at her feet. On her right hand is St. Paul, leaning on his sword, and behind him St. John the Evangelist; on the other side St. Mary Magdalene, with St. Augustine, father of the church.

This painting, one of the finest compositions ever produced by Raphael, is also a masterpiece of colouring. The contrasts are admirable, but the half tints are so judiciously managed that there are no abrupt transitions, and the whole forms one beautiful scale of colour, of which the eye is never weary.

This beautiful work was painted about 1517, for the chapel of St. Cecilia in the church of S. Giovanni in Monte, near Bologna. It was carried to Paris in 1798, transferred to canvas by Haquin in 1803, and returned to Bologna after the peace of 1815. It is now in the Pinacoteca of that town. The sketch for it was engraved by Marc Antonio, and the composition itself by Robert Strange, and many others.

110.

THE VISION OF EZEKIEL.

On wood; height 19¾ inches, width 14½ inches.

Jehovah is seated in a glory, composed of a multitude of cherubim's heads, which are scarcely visible in the exceeding brightness round about his person. Near him are grouped the four symbolic animals which represent the Evangelists, and two small angels with outstretched arms. The glory is surrounded by grey clouds, which seem to be rolling back to reveal the celestial vision.

This little painting is but a sketch, with some small errors of drawing; but for all that it is a grand work. The symbolic animals are, so to speak, transfigured; they are full of nobility and divine power. Jehovah himself is not represented in the traditional style; he bears some resemblance to Jupiter, with the upper part of the figure nude, and the lower limbs draped in purple.

The "Vision of Ezekiel" was painted for Count Vincenzo Ercolani of Bologna; for a time it adorned the Napoleon Museum at Paris, but is now in the Pitti Gallery at Florence. It was mentioned in the Inventory of the Tribune as early as 1589. It has been engraved by Longhi, Calamatta, and others, and antique copies of it are very numerous.

111.

THE BIRTH OF CHRIST.

This painting is unfortunately lost, and we have no authentic copy or engraving of it to guide us in our researches. Our best plan, therefore, will be to quote the passage in which Vasari refers to it: "Raphael sent a large picture of equal beauty with the 'Vision of Ezekiel,' representing the Nativity, to the Count Canossa at Verona. The effect of the aurora, and the figure of St. Anne are especially admired." In his life of Taddeo Zucchero, the same writer says: "When the Duke of Urbino, at that time general of the Venetians, went to inspect the fortifications of Verona, he took Taddeo with him, that he might make a copy of Raphael's painting preserved in the palace of the Canossa family." Another copy is alluded to by C. Ridolfi, in his "Life of Paolo Veronese," but, alas! all efforts to discover their fate have hitherto been fruitless.

112.

Portrait of Count Baldassare Castiglione.

On wood; height 21¼ inches, width 25½ inches.

The count is represented nearly full face, turning slightly to the left. His well-opened blue eyes look out of the picture with a benevolent expression; his fine and well-developed forehead bears the impress of a cultivated mind; and his bushy eyebrows and beard give manliness to his face, which is redeemed from sternness by the sweetness of his mouth. He wears a black hat with a very broad brim, a white shirt, a black vest, and a sort of light brown doublet with wide sleeves.

This faithful and life-like portrait of the accomplished author of the "Cortegiano," who was also a warrior and diplomatist, is executed in a masterly style. It has passed through many collections, and is now in the Louvre. Various copies exist of another portrait of the count by Raphael, but we have no positive information on the subject of the original.

113.

The Stanza of the Incendio del Borgo, or Di Torre Borgia.

The frescoes on the ceiling of this room are by Perugino, and the walls are decorated with four paintings by Raphael, of which the "Incendio del Borgo" is not only the most remarkable, but also the best preserved; probably the others were in part executed by his pupils, under his superintendence. The figures of the princely patrons of the church on the socles, were originally painted by Giulio Romano, but they were so entirely altered by Carlo Maratti, when he was entrusted with their restoration, that they may now be considered his work.

114.

The Oath of Leo III.

Leo III., with the features of Leo X., is standing before the altar with his hands on the gospels, defending himself before Charlemagne against the accusations of the nephew of the deceased Pope Adrian I. The deacons beside him hold back his mantle, and a young priest stands behind him with the triple crown. On the left, in front of a group of bishops, stands the King of the Franks in the costume of a Roman senator, with his hand raised, appealing to the synod he has convoked for judgment on the conduct of the Pope. According to Anastasius, the librarian, a voice replied that no one had a right to judge the supreme sovereign (" prima sedes a nemine judicatur"). Behind the bishops is a vast crowd; and on the steps of the altar are guards and mace-bearers, in the Italian costume of the sixteenth century. It is not easy to judge this picture, as it has suffered much from decay, and is badly lighted. The arrangement is, however, worthy of Raphael, and we believe the actual execution to have been entrusted to one of his pupils.

115.

The Coronation of Charlemagne.

Leo III., with the features of Leo X., is seated in the foreground, and is about to place the crown on the head of the kneeling emperor, who is represented as Francis I., in allusion to the treaty of Bologna, concluded between the latter and Leo X. in 1515. The young Ippolito of Medici, in the costume of a page, holds the crown of the Most Christian King. Cardinals with their train-bearers (caudatari), are seated on either side of this imposing group. In the background we see a young warrior wearing a helmet encircled with a crown, supposed by Montagnani to be Pepin, who was anointed and consecrated by Leo III. at the same time as his father. Opposite the throne, near the altar, is a raised gallery for the musicians, before which officers are passing, bearing the offerings of the new Roman emperor. In the background we have some fine Doric architecture, Raphael's design for the church of St. Peter.

Although this painting has lost much of its clearness of tone in the various restorations it has undergone, we still recognize Raphael's own hand in the masterly treatment of the heads, especially those of the bishops. We have but few engravings of this great work.

116.

The Incendio del Borgo; or, the Conflagration of the Borgo Vecchio.

The district of St. Peter, called the Borgo Nuovo, is in flames; the conflagration has made such progress that all efforts to arrest it are useless; the fire is even threatening the church. In the extremity of the danger Leo IV. appears in the portico of the Vatican (now destroyed), and, making the sign of the cross, addresses an earnest prayer to Heaven for deliverance, whilst the assembled crowds fall on their knees to receive the benediction of the Holy Father. This solemn scene, with a view of the old façade of St. Peter, forms the background of the painting. In the foreground, on the left, a small house is burning; and on the wall a young woman, forgetful of her own peril, is trying to save her child, holding it out to a man who is struggling to reach it. Near this group a young man, who has escaped from his bed without any clothing, is sliding along the wall, measuring its height from the ground with his eye. More in front, a strong muscular man, accompanied by his young son, is hurrying over the rubbish with his old father in his arms. The centre of the foreground is filled with women and children. Nothing could surpass the figure of the young girl with both arms raised in supplication, nor could anything be more touching than the group of the mother making her child join his little hands in prayer as if feeling, more confidence in his innocent petition than in her own. Further back, on the left, a mother, overwhelmed with terror, kneels with her child clasped close to her, whilst another, hesitating and trembling, is urging her children on in the direction of the flying fugitives. On the right, men and women are trying to put out the flames, amongst whom we must notice the woman giving a young man two jars of water, whose blue robes, roughly disordered by the wind, reveal the beautiful outlines of her figure, and the girl coming down a staircase with a vase full of water on her head, whose grace is even more remarkable.

In this fresco Raphael has shown himself an accomplished master; the dramatic interest of the subject, the beauty of the design, and the majestic style of the execution combine to place it in the highest rank; but at the same time we cannot help regretting, with Vasari, that in the "Incendio del Borgo" the great artist has endeavoured to imitate Michael Angelo in his treatment of the nude, instead of remaining true to his own ideal, the exquisite beauty and truth of which is seen in his studies for this very fresco.

117.

The Victory over the Saracens.

Leo IV., with the features of Leo X., is seated on some old ruins near Ostia and the mouth of the Tiber. Eyes and hands are raised to Heaven in gratitude for his deliverance, whilst the soldiers are forcing the prisoners to prostrate themselves before the Head of the Church. On the right two Saracens are leaving a vessel, their conquerors seizing them by the hair and beard; others, captive and bound, lie upon the ground, and a body of Christians, preceded by a cross, are advancing to offer their congratulations to the Pope, behind whom stand Giulio de' Medici and Cardinal Bibiena. In the distance the battle is still raging.

Owing to its close proximity to a fireplace, this painting has suffered more than the others in the same room.

It has been engraved by Dorigny, Gerard Audran, and others.

118.

Paintings on the Socles in the Stanza della Borgia.

We have already stated that the figures beneath the large frescoes were really the work of Carlo Maratti; we will therefore merely enumerate the names of the persons represented:—Constantine the Great, Charlemagne, Godfrey de Bouillon, Astulf or Ethelwolf, Ferdinand the Catholic, and the Emperor Lothaire; all of whom were at different times protectors of the Roman church.

119.

SMALL PAINTINGS IN THE EMBRASURES OF THE WINDOWS IN THE STANZA DELLA TORRE BORGIA.

Painted in yellow cameo on brown.

(*a.*) Christ appearing to his apostles after his resurrection, and ordering them to cast their net on the right side of the ship. The four apostles and St. Peter are in the boat, and Christ is standing on the left. This little picture has been engraved by Pietro Santo Bartoli.

(*b.*) " Feed my lambs." Christ on the left is pointing with his right hand to some sheep; Saint Peter kneels near him with clasped hands holding the keys. On the right are the eleven apostles. Engraved by the Master of the Die and Pietro Santo Bartoli.

(*c.*) Simon the Magician and St. Peter before Nero. (See Baronius' "Annals.") Nero is seated on the left, with a young man and a soldier beside him; St. Peter is standing before him. In the centre we see St. Peter again with the keys, and on the right Simon the Magician is floating on a shining cloud, to the astonishment of two warriors looking up at him. Engraved by Pietro Santo Bartoli.

(*d.*) *Domine, quo vadis.* When St. Peter was fleeing from Rome for his life Christ appeared to him, bearing his cross and going towards the town. The apostle said to him, " Lord, whither goest thou?" " To Rome, to be crucified afresh." Then St. Peter turned back and went to suffer martyrdom (St. Ambrosius in Baronius, An. 69). Engraved by G. Bonasone, Pietro Santo Bartoli, and others.

120.

CHRIST AND THE APOSTLES.

Mural paintings in the Sala Vecchia de' Palafrenieri.

We have already stated that nothing remains of the original figures in this room; the frieze, also executed by Giovanni da Udine, has entirely disappeared, but over the entrance-door there is a St. John the Baptist as a child, in grisaille, with a parrot perched on either side, which may have formed part of the painting by one of Raphael's pupils.

It is the same with the figures of the apostles painted in fresco on the pillars of the church of SS. Vincenzo ed Anastasio outside the walls of Rome, near the basilica of St. Paul. They are so completely spoiled that it is difficult to believe that they once represented the same subjects as thirteen fine engravings by Marc Antonio. All description of them is therefore impossible.

The Loggie of the Vatican.

This fine gallery, which is a kind of corridor leading from the staircase of the second story to the Sala di Constantino and the Stanze, consists of thirteen compartments or loggie with small cupolas. On the key-stone of the central division are the arms of Leo X.; and the other twelve have each a Victory or a spirit with a yoke on the shoulders, which emblem was assumed by the Pope in 1512 when he was reinstated in the government of Florence; it bears reference to Christ's words, "My yoke is easy and my burden is light." Four square paintings in fresco adorn each cupola. Forty-eight of the subjects are taken from the Old Testament, and four from the New; they are often called the Bible of Raphael. The paintings are framed in rich coloured and stucco ornaments, and the pilasters are decorated in the same style. The windows are wreathed with flowers and fruits in fresco, and beneath them other biblical subjects, connected with those in the cupolas, are painted in a gilt bronze colour to imitate bas-reliefs. Raphael made sketches for all these pictures and ornaments, and they were executed under his superintendence. For the Loggie paintings, however, he merely made small sketches in sepia, leaving the work to be carried out by his pupils under Giulio Romano. The latter drew all the cartoons, and painted the first cupola as a model for the rest; but we do not know with any certainty how the labour was subsequently portioned out. Raphael confided the execution of the coloured and stucco ornaments to Giovanni da Udine, who had been exceptionally successful in imitating antique plaster work, and Vasari attributes the twelve bronze-coloured paintings to Pierino del Vaga.

Unfortunately, all the socle pictures in this room have been much spoiled by visitors scratching their names on them, and in many cases it would be impossible to judge of what they were without the aid of Bartoli's engravings. For a long list of etchings and other reproductions of the paintings of the Loggie we refer our readers to Passavant's "Life of Raphael," vol. ii. p. 168 to 173 (French Edition); we cannot do more than mention the most famous prints after separate subjects in the course of our descriptions.

The fifty-two Paintings in the Cupolas of the Loggie.

First Arcade.

121.

GOD DIVIDING THE LIGHT FROM THE DARKNESS.

The Almighty is separating dense masses of glowing clouds. His attitude in this and the following pictures reminds us of the type introduced by Michael Angelo.

122.

GOD CREATING THE DRY LAND.

The Eternal Father is represented hovering above the terrestrial globe, which is already covered with forests.

123.

THE CREATION OF THE SUN AND MOON.

God the Father, with arms extended, is bringing into existence the two great lights.

124.

THE CREATION OF ANIMALS.

The Almighty, walking on the earth with a lion beside him, is calling into life animals of every description.

This, and the preceding paintings, betray the hand of Giulio Romano.

Second Arcade.

125.

THE CREATION OF EVE.

God is leading Adam to his companion, and he recognises her to be "flesh of his flesh." According to Vasari this picture is also by Giulio Romano, but his style is not so clearly seen in it as in the paintings of the first arcade.

126.

THE FALL.

Eve, seen in profile, is standing, offering a fig to Adam, who is seated near a tree, round which the serpent, with a woman's head, is coiled. The figure of Eve has been attributed to Raphael himself, but the drawing and colouring are alike unworthy of the great master.

127.

THE EXILE FROM EDEN.

An angel with a flaming sword is driving Adam and Eve from Paradise. Eve, in her shame, is striving to conceal her nakedness, and Adam hides his face. It is said that these two figures are taken from a fresco by Masaccio in the Carmelite church at Florence. The same subject is represented in the stucco ornaments of this arcade.

128.

THE CONSEQUENCE OF THE FALL.

Adam is tilling the ground, whilst Eve spins with Cain and Abel near her. The former is showing his mother some fruits which he has probably stolen from his brother, who appears to be about to complain of the theft.

Third Arcade.

129.

THE BUILDING OF THE ARK.

Noah, with the features of an old man, is standing giving orders to his sons, who are preparing the materials for the construction of the ark, the framework of which is seen in the distance. Vasari attributes the execution of this fresco to Giulio Romano, but we think it is more in the style of Francesco Penni.

130.

THE DELUGE.

In the foreground a man holding a child is trying to save a drowning woman; a youth near is gazing with horror at a woman expiring in his arms; behind him is a horseman, and in the background we see the ark.

131.

THE COMING FORTH FROM THE ARK.

The animals are leaving the ark in pairs, and Noah and his wife, with one of their sons and two daughters-in-law, are looking with gestures of regret at the ravages made by the flood.

132.

NOAH'S SACRIFICE.

Noah stands praying before an altar, whilst one of his sons is slaying a ram; another son is bringing a second ram, and two men with bulls are seen in the distance.

Engraved by Marco da Ravenna and others.

Fourth Arcade.

133.

ABRAHAM AND MELCHIZEDEK.

Melchizedek, King of Salem, is bringing Abraham bread in two baskets and wine in two pitchers. A warrior stands near the patriarch.

134.

THE COVENANT OF GOD WITH ABRAHAM.

Jehovah, resting on clouds supported by two angels, is promising Abraham a numerous seed. The patriarch is kneeling with his back to the spectator.

135.

ABRAHAM AND THE THREE ANGELS.

Three young men are standing before Abraham, who is prostrating himself at their feet; Sarah is hiding behind the door of the house.

This fresco and the two following are attributed to Fr. Penni. It has been engraved by A. M. Zanetti and others.

136.

LOT'S FLIGHT FROM SODOM.

Lot, leading his two daughters, is fleeing from the burning town; his wife, who looked behind her, is changed into a pillar of salt. Engraved by A. M. Zanetti and others.

Fifth Arcade.

137.

GOD APPEARING TO ISAAC.

Jehovah, with his back to the spectator, is appearing to Isaac, who kneels before him, and forbidding him to go to Egypt. Rebecca is seated under a tree on the left.

This fresco has been engraved by Marco da Ravenna, Zanetti, and others.

138.

ISAAC EMBRACING REBECCA.

Abimelech, King of the Philistines, is looking from a window at Isaac embracing Rebecca. By Fr. Penni.

139.

ISAAC BLESSING JACOB.

The old patriarch, lying on a bed, is blessing Jacob who kneels before him. Rebecca stands behind her son, and in the background we see Esau coming in at the door carrying game. Engraved by Agostino Veneziano.

140.

ESAU CLAIMING THE BLESSING.

Esau, returned from the chase, is standing before Isaac, who is lying on his couch, and Rebecca and Jacob are looking on from the distance. Engraved by Zanetti.

Sixth Arcade.

141.

JACOB'S LADDER.

Jacob, asleep in the foreground, turns his head towards the celestial ladder on which six angels are ascending and descending. Jehovah, with arms outspread, appears above in a glory. This painting and the four following are attributed to Pellegrino da Modena. Jacob's Ladder has been engraved by Hugo da Carpi and others.

142.

JACOB AT THE FOUNTAIN.

Rachel, accompanied by a servant, is standing talking with Jacob near a well from which sheep are drinking. A beautiful landscape forms the background. Engraved by Zanetti.

143.

JACOB ASKING FOR RACHEL'S HAND.

Jacob is promising to serve seven years for Rachel, who stands beside him. whilst Leah, with downcast eyes and a sad expression, is drawing back.

144.

JACOB RETURNS TO THE LAND OF CANAAN.

The patriarch, mounted on an ass, and accompanied by his wife and children riding on camels, is returning to his native land with all his goods and cattle.

Seventh Arcade.

145.

JOSEPH TELLING HIS DREAM TO HIS BROTHERS.

The young Joseph is telling a dream to seven of his brothers who are seated on a rising ground. Three others are near him on the right. The different scenes of the vision are symbolically represented in the clouds.

146.

JOSEPH SOLD BY HIS BRETHREN.

Joseph is weeping whilst his brothers conclude their bargain with the merchants. Three camels stand near the group.

The sketch for this fresco was engraved by the celebrated "Master of the Die."

147.

JOSEPH AND POTIPHAR'S WIFE.

Joseph is hurrying away from Potiphar's wife, who is seated on a couch grasping his mantle. Engraved by Marc Antonio, Giovanni Valesio and others.

148.

JOSEPH BEFORE PHARAOH.

Pharaoh is seated on the left and Joseph stands before him interpreting his dreams, which are symbolically represented in the air in two luminous circles. Four figures behind Joseph and one behind Pharaoh complete the group.

Eighth Arcade.

149.

THE FINDING OF MOSES.

Pharaoh's daughter with seven attendants near her, is contemplating the deserted child with a face full of compassion. It is uncertain who is the author of this fresco, it has been engraved by Andrea Meldolla and many others.

150.

THE BURNING BUSH.

Moses, kneeling before the Burning Bush, covers his face with his hands.

151.

THE PASSAGE OF THE RED SEA.

Moses is stretching out his rod over the sea, in which Pharaoh and his host are engulfed; whilst the Israelites, men, women, and children are hurrying away, carrying their goods. Engraved by Zanetti.

152.

MOSES STRIKING THE ROCK.

Above the rock which Moses is smiting with his rod we see Jehovah in a cloud, the right hand raised in benediction. Six men are gazing in astonishment at the water gushing forth.

Ninth Arcade.

153.

MOSES RECEIVING THE TABLES OF THE LAW.

God is giving the law to Moses on the summit of Mount Sinai. The Almighty is seated half hidden by clouds and surrounded by angels, two of whom are blowing trumpets. In the distance on the right we see the encampment of the children of Israel, and in the foreground are four men, but why Raphael placed them there it is difficult to understand.

154.

THE WORSHIP OF THE GOLDEN CALF.

Some of the Israelites are on their knees before the golden calf, and others are dancing round it. In the distance we see Moses, with Joshua near him, coming down the mountain and breaking the Tables of the Law.

155.

MOSES KNEELING BEFORE THE PILLAR OF CLOUD.

Jehovah is speaking to Moses from out of the pillar of cloud, and the Israelites are standing at the doors of their tents.

156.

MOSES GIVING THE LAW TO THE PEOPLE.

Moses is standing on a slight eminence, holding the Tables of the Law and presenting them to the people.

Tenth Arcade.

157.

THE CROSSING OF THE JORDAN.

The waters of the Jordan are rolling back so as to form an arch, beneath which the children of Israel pass with dry feet.

158.

THE FALL OF JERICHO.

The walls and towers of the besieged town are falling down as the ark is carried round accompanied by two men beating cymbals. Several soldiers protecting themselves with their shields, are advancing towards the breach. It is a pity that Raphael has departed from the text of the Bible in this fresco; the seven Levites blowing the trumpets would have added grandeur to the scene.

159.

JOSHUA'S VICTORY OVER THE AMORITES.

Joshua is raising his arms and ordering the sun and the moon to stand still, whilst the Israelites avenge themselves on their enemies. Engraved by A. P. Tardieu.

160.

THE DIVISION BY LOT OF THE PROMISED LAND.

Joshua wearing a crown and Eleazar in a bishop's mitre, are seated near two urns; a child is drawing a lot which he gives to the head of his tribe.

Eleventh Arcade.

161.

David anointed King of Israel.

Samuel is preparing to anoint David in the presence of his elder brothers. The sacrificial altar is on the left.

162.

David and Goliath.

The Philistine, struck by the stone from the sling, is stretched on the ground, and David, resting one knee on the giant's chest, is about to cut off his head. The Philistines are fleeing in terror before the pursuing Israelites.

The original sketch for this fresco has been engraved by Marc Antonio and the painting itself by Hugo da Carpi and others.

163.

David's Victory over the Syrians.

The conqueror, like a triumphant Roman, is standing in a chariot drawn by a pair of horses. He holds a harp in his right hand, a prisoner walks beside him, and his trophies are carried in front.

164.

David sees Bathsheba for the first time.

David, seated at a window watching his troops go forth to do battle with the Amorites, sees Bathsheba robing herself on a balcony.

Twelfth Arcade.

165.

The Consecration of Solomon.

The high priest Zadok is anointing Solomon King of Israel in the presence of the people. In the foreground reclines a river god with a tiger near him. This figure, generally typical of the Tigris, here represents the Jordan.

166.

The Judgment of Solomon.

The King, seated on his throne, is ordering the soldier holding the child to put his sword back in the scabbard, and proceeds to pass judgment. Admiring attendants stand on the right.

167.

The Queen of Sheba.

The Queen is coming to do homage to the wisest of kings, and bringing him rich presents. Solomon, surrounded by his officers of state, is rising from his throne to receive her. Engraved by Tardieu and others.

168.

THE BUILDING OF THE TEMPLE.

Solomon is standing in the background on the foundations of the Temple, examining the plans presented to him by the architect. In the foreground four workmen are cutting stones, and a fifth is sawing a plank. Engraved by Tardieu.

Thirteenth Arcade.

169.

THE ADORATION OF THE SHEPHERDS.

The Virgin kneels near the infant Jesus, and two angels flying above are throwing flowers over him. Two shepherds are coming from the left, one of them carrying a sheep, and on the right St. Joseph is inviting a kneeling shepherd to approach nearer to the holy Child.

This is perhaps the only design in which St. Joseph is represented in action, he is generally merely a passive spectator.

170.

THE ADORATION OF THE MAGI.

The Virgin, with Jesus on her knees, occupies the centre of the picture. The most venerable of the three kings is prostrating himself before them, and holds the infant's leg; the two other Magi, with their numerous suite, kneel further back, and St. Joseph, standing on the left, is looking into a box which the wise men of the East have offered to the new-born king.

171.

THE BAPTISM OF CHRIST.

Christ, with hands clasped, is standing on the borders of the Jordan, and St. John is pouring water on His head. On the right two kneeling angels hold the garments of Jesus and two more fly above. On the left behind Christ, several men are preparing to receive baptism.

172.

THE LAST SUPPER.

Christ is seated, facing the spectator, at the upper end of a table, and the apostles, who appear greatly excited, are grouped round Him on benches.

173.

TEN TAPESTRIES WITH OLD TESTAMENT SUBJECTS.

Some beautiful tapestries, after designs by Raphael, are alluded to by Félibien in his "Entretiens" (vol. i. p. 324); they were presented to the Cathedral of Chartres by M. de Thon, bishop of that town, but they are unfortunately lost, and we know nothing of their fate.

Twelve subjects imitating bas-reliefs on the socles of the Loggie.

These pictures, painted in cameo to imitate copper, on the socle running beneath the windows of the loggie, were, according to Vasari, executed by

Pierino del Vaga, but they are now almost entirely destroyed by the scribbling of ignorant visitors.

They have, however, been preserved to us in twelve etchings by Pietro Santo Bartoli, and with their aid we will briefly describe them.

First Arcade.

174.

GOD BLESSING THE SEVENTH DAY.

The Creator is seated in clouds raising His hand in benediction, and surrounded by choirs of adoring angels.

Second Arcade.

175.

THE OFFERINGS OF CAIN AND ABEL.

The two brothers are kneeling on the left before their altars, and God the Father is hovering above turning towards Abel. On the right Cain is slaying his brother.

Third Arcade.

176.

THE RAINBOW.

God in clouds, surrounded by angels, is showing the rainbow, the token of the Covenant, to Noah and his three sons.

Fourth Arcade.

177.

ABRAHAM'S SACRIFICE.

Abraham is about to slay his son, when his arm is arrested by an angel. On the right another angel is bringing a ram for sacrifice. Engraved by Agostino Veneziano.

Fifth Arcade.

178.

ISAAC BLESSING JACOB.

Isaac, seated on a bed, is blessing his younger son. On the left we see Rachel before the door giving her instructions to Jacob. It was doubtless through some mistake that this subject was executed twice after designs by Raphael in this same arcade.

Sixth Arcade.

179.

JACOB WRESTLING WITH THE LORD.

The patriarch is wrestling with an angel; on the left women are sleeping in tents, and on the right we see shepherds with their flocks.

Seventh Arcade.

180.

THE RECOGNITION BETWEEN JOSEPH AND HIS BRETHREN.

Joseph, with arms extended, is rising from his throne and making himself known to his brothers, who are kneeling before him. Near the door we see asses laden with corn.

181.

THE GATHERING OF THE MANNA.

Moses and Aaron stand on the right, and before them kneels a girl who is raising a basket with the aid of a young man. In the centre two men are collecting manna in vases, and further back a young girl is trying to place a basket on the head of an old woman kneeling before her. On the left a young man holds a dish of manna, and a girl near him is raising her arms to heaven in gratitude.

Ninth Arcade.

182.

A FEW FIGURES.

Bartoli's print (No. 10) is known as the Tabernacle, because a door occupies the centre with figures on either side. But this is a real door opening into the Sala Vecchia dei Palafrenieri, and we neither know whom the figures represent, nor the real name of the picture.

Tenth Arcade.

183.

JOSHUA SPEAKING TO THE PEOPLE OF ISRAEL.

As all the paintings of the cupolas of this arcade represent subjects taken from the Book of Joshua, it is a mistake to call Bartoli's etching (No. 9) the "Propagation of the Gospel;" it is in reality Joshua ordering the officers of the people to prepare for the passage of the Jordan. It has also been engraved by Andrea Andreani.

184.

BATHSHEBA BEFORE DAVID.

David, when on his death-bed, sent for Bathsheba and promised to nominate her son Solomon his successor. Near him stand Nathan the prophet, and the high priest Zadok with Benaiah; the young man coming in is probably Solomon himself. Behind the bed we see Abishag, the Shunammite, who ministered to the king in his last hours.

Twelfth Arcade.

185.

THE RESURRECTION OF CHRIST.

In the centre of the picture Christ is leaving the tomb, holding the triumphal banner; on the left four guards are huddled together, and two more are running away; on the right the three Maries are advancing.

Catherine II. of Russia had all these Loggie paintings copied on canvas under the direction of the painter Huntersberg, and placed them in a gallery expressly constructed for them, after the pattern of that in the Vatican, in the Hermitage Palace at St. Petersburg. This gallery cost 70,000 silver roubles or 300,000 pounds.

Raphael's Tapestries.

First Series taken from the History of the Apostles.

Michael Angelo, who was at first entrusted with the superintendence of the paintings of the Sistine Chapel, decorated the ceiling with six subjects taken from the history of the creation of mankind; and beside these grand scriptural scenes placed the prophets and sibyls who foresaw the advent of the Messiah. In the narrow space above the windows he represented the waiting in hope of the ancestors of Christ, and in the corners of the ceiling the miraculous deliverance of the people of Israel. When Raphael therefore received orders to carry out Angelo's great conception in cartoons to be reproduced in tapestry, he determined to represent the foundation of the Catholic Church, and to fill the lower part of the lateral walls with ten subjects taken from the lives of the apostles Peter and Paul and from that of St. Stephen, the first Christian martyr.

For the decoration of the altar he proposed to paint the "Coronation of the Virgin," as a symbol of human perfection. Later Michael Angelo completed his vast historic poem by the grand fresco of the Last Judgment.

The cartoons for the Sistine tapestries were executed by Raphael in 1515 and 1516; and, according to Vasari, he was assisted in his work by Francesco Penni and Giovanni da Udine. The cartoons were sent to Arras in the Low Countries and copied in tapestry under the superintendence of Bernard Van Orley. In 1518, the tapestries arrived in Rome, and in the following year they were exhibited in the Sistine chapel. They have undergone various vicissitudes and have unfortunately suffered considerably. After the pillage of Rome by the troops of Charles V. in 1527, they were carried off as spoils of war, and for a time were hidden at Lyons and offered for sale in that town in 1530. Later they became the property of Constable Montmorency, who had them restored, and in 1555 returned them to Pope Julius III., as being the property of the Holy See; they were not, however, again placed in the Sistine Chapel but were exhibited annually on the day of the Feast of Corpus Christi. They were once more stolen, together with Raphael's other tapestries, in the Revolution of 1789, and passed into the hands of some Jews, who are said to have proposed burning them for the sake of the gold in them; but as the experiment they tried with one, the "Deliverance from Hell," was unsuccessful, they sold the rest to some merchants of Genoa. In 1808, Pius VII. bought them, and in 1814 they were placed in the Vatican, where they now are.

186.

THE MIRACULOUS DRAUGHT OF FISHES.

This tapestry was placed on the left of the altar beneath the "Finding of Moses," which was afterwards destroyed to make room for Michael Angelo's "Last Judgment."

Jesus is seated in a boat addressing Peter, who kneels before him; behind the Saviour stands another apostle, and in a second boat two more disciples are drawing in the nets, whilst a third holds the helm. At the edge of the water are three cranes; and in the distance, near a town, we see crowds of people.

The drawings and the cartoon for this subject, as well as the tapestry itself, have been many times engraved; by Meldolla, Hugo da Carpi, Andrea Andreani, amongst others.

The Socle Pictures.

These pictures, woven on to the lower part of the large tapestries in imitation of architectural socles in relief, are executed in metallic yellow, with the lights heightened with pure gold. Beneath the miraculous draught of fishes on the left Giovanni de Medici is represented on his way to Rome to assist at the conclave held after the death of Julius II.; the allegorical figure of the town extends one hand in welcome, and on the right we see the same Giovanni receiving the homage of the cardinals on his election as Pope in 1513, under the name of Leo X.

Decoration of the pilaster.

The arabesque woven down one side of the tapestry contains the arms of the Medici in a medallion, besides several small figures and ornaments in the grotesque style, executed in various colours on a white ground.

187.

Christ's Charge to Peter.

Christ, standing on the right, is pointing with his left hand to a flock of sheep, and with the right to St. Peter, who kneels before him, holding the keys which he has just received. The other ten apostles stand behind their master, and a landscape with a fishing-boat on the beach forms the background of the scene. The rich border of golden stars round the white mantle of the Saviour is so very effective, that we do not hesitate to attribute it, as well as ornaments of the same kind in other tapestries, to Raphael's own invention, although no trace of them remains in the cartoons. This composition has been engraved by Giulio Bonasone, P. Soutman, Gerard Audran, Nic. Dorigny, B. Lepicié, and many others. The socle pictures represent Giovanni de' Medici flying from Florence in the dress of a monk, and the pillage of the Medici palace in 1494.

Decoration of the pilasters.

This tapestry has an arabesque on either side; one representing the Parcæ, and the other the Four Seasons. Nothing could surpass the beauty and grace of these designs; they are the finest works of the kind known.

188.

The Martyrdom of Saint Stephen.

The saint is kneeling, turning to the right, and gazing with loving ecstasy at God the Father and Christ who appear to him in a glory composed of three angels, who are putting back the clouds. Behind the martyr a man is flinging a heavy stone at him, five others further off are similarly employed, and in the foreground on the left a man is picking up stones. Saul, seated on the right, is keeping the garments of the executioners. This tapestry is smaller than the others, as it was intended to fill the space of the wall near which the Pope's throne is placed.

The socle pictures:

Represent the entrance of Cardinal Giovanni de' Medici into Florence in the capacity of Papal legate.

189.

THE HEALING OF THE LAME MAN.

The lame man is lying beneath the peristyle of the Temple, and St. Peter and St. John, surrounded by people, are approaching him. St. Peter is in the act of saying, "Rise up and walk." On the left another cripple is dragging himself towards the apostles; amongst the crowd we notice a woman with her nursling, and on the right are two women carrying naked babies, one of which holds two doves tied to the end of a small stick. The wreathed and richly decorated columns of the peristyle appear to have been copied from those still in the Basilica of St. Peter, which from the earliest times were supposed to have belonged to the Temple of Jerusalem.

The drawings for this tapestry have been engraved by Baptista Franco, and Parmegiano, the cartoon by Nic. Dorigny, B. Lepicié and others, and the tapestry itself by several artists, but by none of the great masters.

The Socle pictures.

On the right Cardinal Giovanni de' Medici is surrendering himself a prisoner at the battle of Ravenna to Captain Federico Gonzaga da Bozzolo, who was serving in the French army. On the left his escape from prison in 1512 is represented. The recumbent female is supposed to be a naid, and the satyrs amongst the reeds and in the little house, have evidently some reference to the danger incurred by the Cardinal when Usimbardo kept him shut up in a dove house in order to give him up to his enemies. The two subjects are separated by an arabesque, composed of two lions and some laurel branches, with the words "Leo X. Pont. Max." They have been engraved by Pietro Santo Bartoli.

190.

THE DEATH OF ANANIAS.

Nine apostles are standing on a terrace; St. Peter is pronouncing judgment on Ananias, who is expiring in convulsions; on the right a young man and his wife are kneeling, overwhelmed with dismay; and on the left two men are bending forward in horror towards the man struck by the hand of God. In the distance on the left a man and his wife are carrying clothes, and Sapphira is seen counting over the money she is about to offer, all unconscious of the doom which has overtaken her husband and awaits herself. In the background on the right St. John and some other apostles are distributing alms to the poor.

Agostino Veneziano completed an engraving, after the drawings for this tapestry, which was commenced by Marc Antonio; Hugo da Carpi and G. Audran have also reproduced them, and the cartoon has been engraved by Nic. Dorigny and others.

The Socle pictures.

On the right we have the address of the gonfaloniere Ridolfi to the inhabitants of Florence, and, on the left the entrance of Giovanni de' Medici into that town in 1512. An arabesque, similar to that described above, divides the two subjects. The whole has been engraved by Pietro Santo Bartoli.

Decoration of the pilaster.

On one side of the tapestry is an arabesque representing Faith, Hope, and Charity.

191.

THE CONVERSION OF ST. PAUL.

This tapestry was placed beneath the Nativity on the wall now occupied by Michael Angelo's "Last Judgment."

St. Paul, who has fallen from his horse, is looking up at Christ, who appears to him in the sky, surrounded by three small angels. The companions of the future apostle are running away in terror and a servant is holding and soothing his master's horse.

The cartoon for the "Conversion of St. Paul" is now lost, but it was in the collection of Cardinal Grimani in 1521.

The Socle pictures

Both represent the "Persecution of the Christians by Saul," (Acts viii.) and they have been engraved by Pietro Santo Bartoli under the erroneous titles of the "Massacre by the Spanish soldiers after the taking of Prato, in 1512," and the "Heads of the conspiracy against the Medici before their judges at Florence."

192.

ELYMAS STRUCK WITH BLINDNESS.

The proconsul Sergius on the judgment-seat, is looking with astonishment at the sorcerer suddenly struck blind at the word of St. Paul; an attendant is gazing with horror into the blind man's face, and eight other figures behind him appear more or less agitated. Two lictors stand at the left hand of Sergius. The upper part only of this tapestry still exists, and there was formerly a pilaster ornament on the right of which nothing remains but a clothed female figure, resembling a statue in a niche.

The drawings for this work have been engraved by Agostino Veneziano and Hugo da Carpi, and the cartoon itself by Nicolas Dorigny and many others.

193.

PAUL AND BARNABAS AT LYSTRA.

The apostles, standing under a portico, are looking with dismay at the people of Lystra bringing sacrifices to them; St. Paul is rending his clothes and addressing a man who is offering him a ram. On the left others are leading bulls, and the priest is about to strike one down, when his arm is arrested by a young man. In the foreground the cripple who has recovered the use of his limbs is joining his hands in gratitude, whilst an old man is looking at him with surprise. In the back ground we see a forum with temples, and in the distance, on the right, a statue of the god Mercurius, for whom the people mistook St. Paul.

The cartoon for this work has been engraved by N. Dorigny, B. Lepicié and others, and the tapestry itself by G. Audran.

The Socle pictures.

One represents St. John leaving Antioch; the apostle is embracing one brother, and two others are wishing him good speed. On the left six apostles are standing near St. Paul (Acts xiii.). In the other we see St. Paul teaching in a synagogue (Acts xiii. xiv.); he stands on the left explaining the Scriptures. An arabesque divides the two groups; it is composed of two lions, in reference to the name of Leo X., and the device of the Medici family; a ring with three diamonds and three feathers. Engraved by Pietro Santo Bartoli.

The Decoration of the Pilaster.

The upper part of the coloured arabesques, woven on to one side of the large tapestry, represents the Medici coat of arms, and the lower part is a grotesque ornament with several small figures.

194.

St. Paul Preaching at Athens.

St. Paul, standing on some steps in the Areopagus, is preaching the word of God to the Athenians. Philosophers of different sects stand behind him, and before him are seated several sophists and men of the people arguing together. On the left we see Dionysius, the Areopagite, and his wife Damaris coming up the steps, with faces full of earnest faith; and in the distance, on the same side, is the statue of Mars in front of a round temple, which resembles in shape the chapel erected by Bramante in the cloister of St. Pietro in Montorio at Rome.

The drawings for this tapestry have been engraved by Marc Antonio; and the cartoon by N. Dorigny, G. Audran, and others less celebrated.

The Socle Pictures.

There are four designs, separated by Hermes, beneath the tapestry above described; they are much spoilt, and represent—

(*a.*) The apostle Paul working at tent making (Acts xviii. 3).

(*b.*) Saint Paul, at Corinth, ridiculed by the Jews (Acts xviii. 6).

(*c.*) Saint Paul laying his hands on the Corinthian converts (Acts xviii. 8).

(*d.*) Saint Paul before Gallio.

Pietro Santo Bartoli has produced etchings after all these subjects, but has affixed wrong titles to all but one.

The Decoration of the Pilaster.

The coloured arabesques woven on to the large tapestry represent—on the left, Hercules bearing the celestial globe; and, on the right, the Hours of the day or Apollo, and the figure of the moon, with a clock which marks the twenty-four hours.

195.

Saint Paul in Prison.

The apostle is praying in his prison at Philippi, whilst the foundations are shaken by an earthquake, symbolically represented by the half-length figure of a gigantic man raising the building with his arms and shoulders. The gaoler and the soldier on guard are panic stricken.

This tapestry, which was hung beside the singers' gallery, is only 44¾ inches broad.

The Socle Picture

Represents a man kneeling before a seated warrior or traveller with his staff.

The Seven Cartoons.

We have already stated that the ten tapestries arrived in Rome in 1518, but the original cartoons remained neglected in the manufactory at Arras, where, with the exception of three, they were kept until 1630; when, having been seen by Rubens and by him described to Charles I., they were bought by that king and placed in his Whitehall Palace. On his death they were to have been sold by auction with his other art treasures, but Cromwell interposed and bought them for the nation for £300. A little later, however, Charles II. would have sold them to Louis XIV. had not Lord Danby interposed in their behalf. They remained for a long time in the state in which they left Arras, that is, intersected by narrow bands and riddled with needle prickings following the outlines. William III. had them joined together and affixed to canvas and placed them in Hampton Court Palace, in a room erected on purpose to receive them by Sir Christopher Wren. A few years ago Queen Victoria allowed them to be removed to the South Kensington Museum, where they have become so well known that we shall not trouble our readers with more than a few remarks on each one. They are all drawn with chalk and coloured in distemper.

THE MIRACULOUS DRAUGHT OF FISHES.[1]

The greater part of this cartoon appears to be from Raphael's own hand; it is a masterpiece of drawing, and, with some slight exceptions, is in excellent preservation. Christ's mantle, for instance, was once red, and the reflection of it in the water is still that colour; but it is now a finely executed white mantle. The fishes in the boat and the cranes on the bank are by Giovanni da Udine.

CHRIST'S CHARGE TO PETER.

The figure of the Saviour is the only part of this cartoon by Raphael himself; the colouring of the draperies betrays the style of Francesco Penni, who aided his master in the execution of these designs.

ST. PETER AND ST. JOHN HEALING THE LAME MAN.

This cartoon has suffered much, both from decay and injudicious restoration. We believe that a great part of it is by Giulio Romano; the head of the second cripple dragging himself along, however, is from Raphael's own hand.

---

[1] The subjects have already been described in treating of the tapestries.

The Death of Ananias.

This is one of the most remarkable of the cartoons; indeed, it is impossible to doubt that many of the heads are by the great master himself, we fancy that the greater part of the design must have been sketched by Penni, and finished by Raphael.

Elymas the Sorcerer struck Blind.

This work has suffered more than any of the others; its colours have faded, it has been almost entirely repainted, and is covered with stains, but, for all this, we still recognise the master's hand in many of the heads.

Paul and Barnabas at Lystra.

This cartoon was somewhat spoilt when affixed to canvas, especially on the right side. We recognize Raphael's hand in retouches and corrections, but the actual execution appears to belong to Penni.

Paul preaching at Athens.

Raphael worked a great deal at this cartoon, and it is one of the finest of the series; the architecture in the background is especially beautiful.

A list of engravings and copies after the seven cartoons is given in Passavant's "Life of Raphael," vol. ii. pp. 208-211 (French ed.) Amongst other well known names we find Dorigny, Lepicié, Holloway, &c.

196.

The Coronation of the Virgin.

Tapestry for the Altar of the Sistine Chapel.

The Virgin, with hands clasped in adoration, is seated on a high throne near her divine Son, who is placing a crown on his mother's head with the right hand. God the Father, in a glory surrounded by angels, is blessing the Holy Virgin, and the Holy Spirit, in the form of a dove encircled with golden rays, hovers above the throne. Two angels on either side of the throne are raising a curtain; and lower down on the left John the Baptist stands pointing to Christ; and on the right St. Jerome, in adoration, with his lion at his feet.

Two small angels in front of the throne are singing *gloria in excelsis*, written on a parchment scroll. This design is, as it were, the last canto of a mystic poem, ending with the glorification of the Holy Trinity. The fate of this tapestry is unknown; it has been engraved by the celebrated Master of the Die.

Repetitions of the famous Sistine tapestries are very numerous, but it would be beyond the scope of our present work to enumerate them here. The curious will find full particulars on the subject in Passavant's "Life of Raphael," vol. ii. pp. 212-215 (French ed.)

Raphael's Tapestries.

Second Series. With subjects taken from the Life of Christ.

According to Cancellieri, the twelve tapestries of the "Life of Christ," together with a thirteenth representing allegorical figures, were a present made by Francis I.

to the Pope on the canonization of St. Francis de Paula; but we ourselves are of opinion that they were only promised at that time, as they were certainly not at Rome in 1519, when the canonization took place. Different drawings still in existence prove that Raphael made sketches for the series, but death cut short his career before he had finished his work, which was completed by Giulio Romano and some of his fellow pupils.

These tapestries are all longer than those of the "Acts of the Apostles," but they are of varying sizes; they also differ from the first series by having a large border of flowers and other ornaments. The officers of the Vatican call them *Arazzi della scuola nuova* to distinguish them from the *Arazzi della scuola vecchia* by which title the Sistine tapestries are known.

According to Fea these tapestries were for a long time the ornament of that part of the Basilica of St. Peter, which was destroyed in the pontificate of Paul V., and later, on high festival days, they were hung beneath the peristyle of St. Peter's. Both series are now constantly exhibited in the rooms of the Vatican called the Stanze of Pio V.

197.

THE MASSACRE OF THE INNOCENTS.

Three narrow tapestries.

The subjects represented in these three tapestries were evidently originally one composition, which was divided by Raphael's pupils to suit the requirements of the wall to be covered. Drawings for the three parts are preserved at Haarlem, Berlin, and in the British Museum, but the originals by Raphael are certainly not amongst them. We will briefly describe the three subjects.

(*a.*) In the foreground, on the left, a soldier bending forwards, is seizing a child by the leg, whilst its mother, who has fallen on the ground, still struggles to defend it. Behind her a bearded man is plunging his dagger into an infant's throat, and further back two men are arresting the flight of three women with their children. This massacre is taking place near a handsome building with columns and niches. In the distance we see a rotunda resembling the Pantheon of Agrippa.

A large fragment of the cartoon for this tapestry was in the possession of the late Prince Hoare, Secretary to the Royal Academy. It embraced the whole of the lower portion; but in the time of Richardson,[1] it had been entirely painted over in oil, so that in 1831 it was difficult to recognise it for a cartoon of the school of Raphael. According to Dodsley (London and its environs, vol. iii. p. 160) it was pledged in England, and the pawnbroker, wishing to keep it, covered it with oil colours and a law suit was the result, &c. We give this anecdote for what it is worth; but whether it be true or false, the cartoon, which is the property of the National Gallery, is now scarcely recognisable; it has been varnished and put under glass.

---

[1] See his "Treatise on Painting," vol. iii. p. 459.

(*b.*) In the foreground a woman is seated lamenting over the dead body of her son lying on her knees. Behind her a man is seizing a child, whose mother holds him under one arm, whilst she strives to protect him with the other. In the distance three women are running away, pursued by a man armed with a dagger. We also see a group of men and women on a staircase, who are given up to the wildest grief, and a young girl ascending the steps.

According to Fernow (Romische Studien), the cartoons for the "Massacre of the Innocents," were cut into different pieces, in order to be divided between the heirs of their owner. It is certain that Richardson acquired as many as fifty, one after the other. In speaking of these fragments, he says that most of them are unfinished, being merely sketched in black lead pencil; and the colours of some of them having been partly effaced, he noticed that the drawing had not always been scrupulously followed by the painter. Unfortunately, two only of these fragments are still preserved; one, the head of the woman mounting the staircase, which belongs to Earl Spencer, and is preserved at Althorpe; and the other, the head of the woman with the dead boy on her knees, which is in the Christ Church Collection at Oxford.

(*c.*) On the right a man is bending down to stab a child who has fallen to the ground; near him another executioner holds an infant under his arm, and turns towards a mother struggling to take her child from a soldier. Two other women are escaping with gestures of despair. For background we have the gate of a town and a landscape with some buildings. This tapestry is rather larger than the other two, which are very narrow.

198.

THE ADORATION OF THE SHEPHERDS.

The Virgin is bending down to caress the Infant Jesus in his cradle. Further back in the stable are an ox and an ass; on the left St. Joseph is pointing out the new-born child to four shepherds, one of whom kneels to present a gift of eggs, whilst another plays the bagpipe—a custom still observed at Rome, where the *pifferari* perform before the Madonnas at Advent. On the right, at the entrance to the stable, two more shepherds are arriving, one carrying a lamb and the other holding a large dog in a leash. Above the group, on either side, fly four small angels. This is one of the best of this series of tapestries, it is evidently by Giulio Romano. A fragment of the original cartoon, representing the head of a shepherd, belonged to Richardson and was sold for five guineas at his death.

199.

THE ADORATION OF THE MAGI.

The Virgin is seated in front of a little cottage, with Jesus on her knees; above them shines a star. The Holy Child holds a small golden vase which the most venerable of the kings, who kneels before him, has just presented. The youngest of the Magi stands near, bending forwards, and on the right the third is kneeling, raising the cover of a vase which he is offering to the new-born king; St. Joseph, standing behind the Virgin, looks on in admiration. On either side we see the retinue of the Magi, and behind these groups, horses, camels, and elephants, caparisoned in the Oriental style.

The style of Giulio Romano is easily recognised in the heads and attitudes of the figures in this work. A bistre sketch for it was bought by Mr. Woodburn of the King of Holland for one hundred florins; and it has been engraved by the celebrated Pietro Santo Bartoli.

200.

The Presentation in the Temple.

The high priest, accompanied by a young Levite, is standing beneath the peristyle of the Temple, receiving the Virgin and the Infant Jesus. Behind her are St. Joseph and three women, one of whom carries a basket with pigeons. The arrangement and the drawing of this composition are alike feeble.

201.

The Resurrection of Christ.

Christ, in the attitude of benediction and with the triumphal banner in His left hand, is leaving the sepulchre and stepping on the stone which closed the entrance. On either side guards are struggling together in confusion, or running away. We see Jerusalem in the fine landscape of the background, and the three holy women hurrying to the tomb.

Raphael's own sketch for this composition is in the Oxford collection, but the cartoon appears to have been executed by one of his feeblest pupils. The weaver of the tapestry has allowed himself great latitude in working out his pattern as the landscape in the background is quite in the Dutch style.

202.

Christ appearing to Mary Magdalene.

The Saviour, looking like a gardener, is appearing to Mary Magdalene, who holds a vase of perfumes in her left hand. Behind a rose-bush we see the open sepulchre, and part of the town of Jerusalem. The arrangement of this composition is feeble and the figures are clumsy.

203.

Christ in Hades.

The Saviour, holding a triumphal banner, is standing at the entrance of a cave offering his hand to one of the patriarchs. Adam and Eve, with the young Abel before them, are kneeling near to Christ, and on the left is St. John in adoration. This tapestry was burnt in 1798, report says by the Jews, for the sake of gold threads, and is known to us only by the engravings of Nic. Beatrizet, M. Sorello, and L. Sommerau, but the design is so extremely beautiful that we are tempted to believe the original drawing to have been by Raphael himself.

204.

Christ at Emmaus.

The Saviour is seated at table under a vine, with his disciples near Him, who are watching the blessing of the bread with great emotion. In the foreground a dog is gnawing a bone, which a cat eyes enviously. This inappropriate group may be considered a Dutch addition. A bistre drawing for this tapestry is in the Oxford collection, and the composition has been several times engraved but by none of the great masters.

205.

THE ASCENSION.

Christ is ascending to Heaven, and two foreshortened angels are descending on either side; on the ground we see eleven kneeling apostles. The execution of this tapestry is very inferior.

206.

THE DESCENT OF THE HOLY GHOST.

The Virgin is placed between St. Peter and St. John, with the other apostles grouped around, and two holy women standing behind her. Above we see the Holy Spirit diffusing brightness over all, and lighting up a tongue of fire on each head. The execution of this tapestry is very feeble, and the design is too stiff to be attributed to Raphael. Richardson however, alludes to a drawing for it, which he believes to be from the great master's own hand.

207.

THE ALLEGORICAL SUBJECT.

This allegory, which has reference to the Papacy, represents Religion seated on a rainbow, with a small angel holding an open book. At the feet of Religion is a large crystal globe in which scenes of war and fire are reflected. The figure of Justice is seated on the left and that of Charity on the right. In the landscape below are two lions, each holding a flag, on which the Pontifical canopy and the keys of the Holy See are embroidered. Near the crystal globe are the words, *Candor illæsus*, the motto adopted by Clement VII. when he was a Cardinal under Adrian VI., and in the arabesque beneath are woven the arms of the Medici. This tapestry has a border similar to that round each of the twelve subjects from the "Life of Christ," and we may therefore conclude that it belongs to the same series. There is nothing very noteworthy in this allegorical composition, it is evidently by one of Raphael's pupils; it was restored under Pius VI. with the companion tapestries.

A work appeared in London in 1838, called "The Book of the Cartoons," containing twenty engravings by Sommerau, with explanatory text by Cattermole; and P. Marchetti of Rome began to publish a series of engravings after the tapestries, but was unable to carry out his design; we have not heard of its being resumed by any one else.

Tapestries with Cupids at Play.

Five tapestries with Cupids or winged children have often been attributed to Raphael, and on this account we will briefly describe them, although we do not think that they ought to be included amongst his works.

(*a.*) A crowned Cupid holding a sceptre and some keys, to whom two other children are offering pieces of gold on a plate.

(*b.*) A Cupid mounted on an ostrich, with another Cupid holding the bird's claw, and a third pulling out its feathers.

(*c.*) Two Cupids trying to get back a little child who has just been carried off by a monkey.

(*d.*) A Cupid struggling with a child whom two other Cupids are striking with their bows and arrows.

(*e.*) Eight Cupids playing in a wood.

This design is of such extreme beauty that we may without hesitation attribute it to Raphael himself. The arrangement differs entirely from that of the others, and it probably does not belong to the same series. The inscription on the engraving by the *Master of the Die* however, leads us to suppose it to have been reproduced in tapestry.

The Chapel of the Pope's Hunting Castle, called La Magliana.

This chateau was the favourite residence of Julius II.; it now belongs to the Convent of St. Cecilia at Transtevere, and is famous for some beautiful frescoes by Raphael and others.

208.

THE MARTYRDOM OF SAINT CECILIA.[1]

The part of this painting which still exists corresponds exactly with the engraving by Marc Antonio, known under the erroneous title of the "Martyrdom of St. Felicia," but a great portion of the picture was destroyed, when a large hole was made in the wall in order to open a gallery. The remaining figures are: the judge, seated with eight persons standing near him; on the right the statue of Jupiter and the group round it with three women and the child. We also see part of the recumbent man blowing the fire, but the whole centre of the subject is gone, having been removed in 1830 to suit the convenience of the farmer Vitelli, who wished to erect a gallery, from which he could hear mass without being mixed up with his servants. This act of Vandalism is the more to be regretted, as the rest of the painting is in perfect preservation, and was evidently executed by one of Raphael's best pupils and towards the end of the great master's life; indeed some artists are of opinion that it is from his own hand.

The Bath-Room of Cardinal da Bibiena in the Vatican.

This room is entirely decorated in the antique style; it contains seven principal pictures framed in light grotesque or architectural designs, and with victorious Cupids on the socles beneath. Each wall has two paintings, except that with the door, which of course only required one. The ceiling is divided into twenty-one small compartments of different sizes and colours, framed in gold, and containing symbolical figures of every variety.

---

[1] The legend of St. Cecilia runs thus: After her husband and brother-in-law had been beheaded, outside the town, near the statue of Jupiter; she was thrown into a tub of boiling water, and as she remained unhurt, her head was cut off.

The seven large wall pictures have figures about sixteen inches high, and represent the following subjects :—

209.

THE BIRTH OF VENUS.

In fresco; height $25\frac{1}{2}$ inches, width 16 inches.

Aphrodite Anadyomene is issuing from the foam of the sea; her back is half turned to the spectator; she rests her left foot in a shell, and gazes out upon the vast expanse of water, holding her long hair in her left hand. In the clouds above we see Saturn and Uranus. This beautiful composition has been engraved by Marco da Ravenna, and, it is said, by Marc Antonio himself. A print bearing his monogram was at Dresden in 1836. Raphael's sketch for the figure of Venus is in the Royal collection at Munich.

210.

VENUS AND CUPID SEATED ON DOLPHINS.

Venus, by some called Thetis, or Galatea, is seated on a dolphin, her back to the spectator, but looking over her shoulder. Near her Cupid rides on another dolphin, urging it on with a switch. The sea forms the background, and the whole scene is full of indescribable charm. Engraved by Marco da Ravenna and several others.

211.

VENUS WOUNDED AND COMPLAINING TO CUPID.

Venus, seated under a tree, leans with her right arm against Cupid, and presses her hand, with a gesture of suffering, on a wound on her breast. Cupid, with crossed legs, and holding his bow and arrows, appears to pay little attention to her troubles. The graceful beauty of this pleasing subject is enhanced by its admirable treatment. It has been engraved by Agostino Veneziano and many others.

212.

JUPITER AND ANTIOPE.

This fresco has also been called "Pan and Syrinx." The nymph is seated under the shade of some trees; she has just been bathing in the limpid water which flows at her feet, and is combing her long hair. She turns her head towards the left, and the god Pan is watching her from the foliage near. We believe this composition to be by Giulio Romano. It was in excellent preservation in 1835, and has been engraved by Marc Antonio and others.

213.

VENUS DRAWING A THORN FROM HER FOOT.

Venus, seated beneath a tree, with a dove perched behind her, is drawing a thorn from her right foot, and, according to an old fable, the blood which flowed from the wound turned the white rose red. This design is of the greatest beauty, and was evidently invented by Raphael. It was removed from the bath room long ago; and we can only judge of what it was from the copy in the Villa Palatina. We have also engravings after it by Marc Antonio, Marco da Ravenna, and others.

214.

VENUS AND ADONIS.

This fresco is also called "Ariadne and Bacchus." It is by Giulio Romano, and represents a young man seated under some trees, with his beloved lying at his feet, and resting her head on his knees. The original drawing is in the Albertine collection at Vienna, and the painting has been engraved by Marc Antonio, Agostino Veneziano, and others.

215.

VULCAN AND PALLAS.

Minerva is struggling with a bearded man; a landscape forms the background. Both design and execution are so inferior that we are compelled to ascribe this little picture to one of Raphael's feeblest pupils.

216.

SIX VICTORIOUS CUPIDS

There were formerly seven Cupids, one under each picture, but one of them is entirely rubbed out, and the others have also suffered considerably. These figures are painted in colours on a black ground; the outlines are very beautiful, but the execution is inferior. The designs were probably supplied by Raphael; they are intended to typify the power of love in every realm of nature, and the six which remain may be described as follows:—

1. Cupid standing on a shell which forms a car, holding an arrow in the right hand, and some threads, which serve as a bridle to two butterflies, in the left.

2. Cupid standing on a car drawn by two dolphins, and guiding them with a trident.

3. Cupid standing in a car and striking with his switch the two swans yoked to it.

4. Cupid floating on the sea in an open shell, and pricking the two tortoises which draw it with his javelin.

5. Cupid standing in a little tub on wheels pulled along by two serpents, which he controls with a palm-branch, the symbol of peace.

6. Cupid standing in a small chariot with a seat, guides with reins two snails which pull it slowly along.

217.

CUPID AND PAN.

The rustic god is wrestling playfully with the good-natured child, who has hung his quiver full of arrows on a tree near. A hilly landscape, with a few houses, forms the background. This is the only one of the four ceiling paintings of this room which it is possible to make out; the others having suffered very much from smoke and damp.

The Loggie of the Villa Palatina contain five frescoes borrowed from those in the bath room just described. We mention them here on that account, although Raphael did not assist at them in any way. And we will now pass on to the

Villa Raphael, famous for Michael Angelo's painting of the "Passions aiming at a Target," and the "Marriage of Alexander and Roxana," after Raphael, which latter is the only composition we need here examine.

218.

THE MARRIAGE OF ALEXANDER AND ROXANA.

Roxana is seated on the edge of a bed with curtains all round it; one cupid is removing her veil, and another her sandals, whilst a third leads Alexander, who has laid aside his armour, to his bride. The hero, conquered by his captive, offers her a crown. Behind him are Ephestion, bearing a torch, and Hymen. On the right cupids are playing with the weapons the warrior has just laid aside; six of them carrying one of their number seated on the shield, whilst another holds the javelin, and a ninth hides in the cuirass. Raphael borrowed this design from the description of an antique painting by Ætion, and it was executed in fresco by Pierino del Vaga, with the delicacy peculiar to him. Lucian relates that Ætion gained the prize for his painting of the "Marriage of Alexander and Roxana;" and Proxenides, president of the Olympian games at the time, was so pleased with it that he gave him his daughter in marriage.

Raphael's original drawing for this composition is in the Albertine Collection at Vienna; both it and the fresco have been many times engraved, and also reproduced in other ways.

219.

PORTRAIT OF ANTONIO TEBALDEO.

Born at Ferrara in 1463, died in 1537.

This painting is lost, but it is alluded to in a letter from Pietro Bembo lo Bernardo da Bibiena, dated April 19th, 1516, in the following terms: "Raphael has painted our friend Tebaldeo with so much truth, that he does not resemble himself more than his portrait. For myself, I have never seen a more striking likeness," &c. Vasari tells us that Raphael painted Tebaldeo's portrait amongst the group of poets in the Parnassus; and the man with the beard, on the right of the muse, may represent him, but we cannot speak with any certainty on the subject.

220.

PORTRAITS OF ANDREA NAVAGERO AND AGOSTINO BEAZZANO.

Raphael painted bust portraits of these two Venetian writers on a wide panel for their mutual friend, Pietro Bembo. Navagero, who was born in 1483, and died in 1528, is represented with his head turned to the right, looking at the spectator. His expression is very masculine, almost harsh; his face is full of refinement and intelligence, and he wears a short, curly beard. On his head is a large cap, rather like a turban. Beazzano, on the contrary, is remarkable for the sweetness and calmness of his expression; his broad and florid face is full alike of good nature and intellect. His well-developed forehead, and the refined lines of his mouth, betray a man of large powers and profound learning. He wears a black cap, and his hair, parted on the forehead, falls round his neck. A black doublet, and a full white shirt fastened at the throat, complete his costume. These likenesses are unfortunately lost, but a good copy of them is preserved in the Doria Gallery at Rome, where they pass for portraits of Bartolo and Baldo, two lawyers of the fourteenth century.

221.

The Madonna della Sedia.

On wood; round, 30 inches diameter. Figure to the knees.

The Virgin encircles the Holy Child, who is seated on her knees, with both arms, and leans her head against his. Both look at the spectator; the mother with an expression of indescribable sweetness, the Infant Saviour with child-like placidity. On her head the Virgin wears a striped drapery, which falls gracefully on to her neck, and her shoulders are covered with a rich fringed scarf. On the right, the child prophet, John the Baptist, is looking up in adoration, his rustic cross in his arms, and his small hands reverently clasped. This picture takes its name from the chair which forms the background. It is now in the Pitti Gallery at Florence, and two small sketches for it are in the Wicar collection at Lille. We believe it to have been executed when Raphael was engaged on his greatest works; it is, indeed, a master-piece, and no copy or engraving, however superior, can give a true idea of its indescribable charm. Passavant relates that, having been allowed to examine it closely on an easel, he was surprised to find that the different tints were not blended together, but laid side by side with such consummate knowledge of chiaroscuro, that at a little distance they appear to melt into each other without break or transition.

It would be impossible to enumerate all the engravings after this celebrated and favourite work. Raphael Morghen has reproduced it more than once; A. B. Desnoyers, J. G. Muller, F. Bartolozzi, and many others, have struggled to render it faithfully in every variety of style, and the ancient copies of it are no less numerous.

222.

The Madonna della Tenda.

On wood; height 31 inches, width 21¼ inches.

This is a similar composition to that of the "Madonna della Sedia." The Virgin, seen in profile, is seated on the left; her right arm is round the Holy Child, who is seated on her knees, turning his head slightly round, as though to listen to the words of St. John, who stands behind him in adoration. The mother's head is covered with rich drapery, and she looks lovingly down upon her son. This painting takes its name from the curtain which forms the background.

There are many copies of this beautiful picture, and which really is the original was for a time a disputed point. We believe it to be in the Pinacothek of Munich; and, in any case, the painting there exhibited, under the title of the "Madonna della Tenda," is certainly from Raphael's studio. The Duke of Devonshire possesses a first sketch for this Madonna at his seat at Chatsworth, and the entire work has been many times engraved; by Paolo Toschi, amongst others.

223.

The Madonna with the Candelabra.[1]

Round picture, 25½ inches diameter.

The Virgin, with Jesus on her knees, turns her head to the right, so that her full face is seen; her eyes are downcast. The pose of her head is noble and dignified, and her whole appearance extremely beautiful. The child's figure, also, is admirably drawn, and full of life and action. The angels on either side of this group, with candelabra in their hands, are evidently additions, and the principal figures have been a good deal restored. The "Madonna with the Candelabra" is in the possession of Mr. Munro of London; it has been several times engraved and copied.

224.

Christ Bearing His Cross.

Painted on wood, and afterwards transferred to canvas; height 127 inches, width 91¾ inches.

This painting is also called "Lo Spasimo di Cecilia," because it was once in the church of S. Maria dello Spasimo at Palermo.

Christ, sinking to the ground beneath the weight of his cross, turns to the weeping women who follow Him, amongst whom we recognise His mother, overwhelmed with grief, and supported by St. John, and Mary Magdalene with arms outstretched towards her divine son. In the foreground kneels a woman raising the Virgin's veil, and behind her is another clasping her hands in anguish. Simon of Cyrene grasps the cross to carry it himself; a soldier raises his spear to strike the Saviour, and compel Him to advance, whilst another tries to drag Him up with a cord. A horseman bearing a standard opens the procession, and from the gates of the town issue the Roman judges, the soldiers, and the people. In the background we see the two thieves on their way to execution.

This picture is in every respect a master-piece; the arrangement is perfect—there is not one superfluous figure; the heads are all admirably true to nature, and nothing could exceed the beauty of the Saviour's figure. The divine majesty of suffering, the noble courage to endure, the human weakness and shrinking from pain, combined with heavenly resignation to His Father's will, which were united in the great ideal of Christendom, are expressed in a manner worthy of the subject; and, although "Lo Spasimo" was intended for the altar of a large church, and would only be seen at a distance, the treatment of the details and the delicacy of colouring are no less remarkable; note, for instance, the hand of Christ which rests on the ground, the drawing and execution are alike faultless, and it is besides of ideal truth and beauty; or, again, see how the frail and attenuated figure of the Saviour contrasts with the strength and energy of Simon of Cyrene, or with the coarse health of the executioner, and how well the drooping figures of the weeping women harmonize with the deep pathos of the central group.

---

[1] The custom of representing the Madonna with angels holding candelabra is very ancient, and admirably expresses the idea of Christ being the "Light of the world."

We have already noticed the strange anecdote relating to this picture; how, after the wreck of the vessel taking it to Palermo, it floated into the port of Genoa, and was there detained for some time, and we will only add that it is now in the Museum of Madrid, having been transferred to canvas at Paris under the superintendence of Bonnemain, and at the suggestion of the Duke of Wellington; by whose instrumentality, also, it was restored to its rightful owners, after having figured for a time in the Musée Napoleon. It has been engraved by Agostino Veneziano, Dom Cunego, Paolo Toschi, and many others, and copies of it are also very numerous.

225.

THE VISITATION.

Painted on wood, and transferred to canvas; height 79 inches, width 57 inches.

Saint Elizabeth advances from the left to meet the Holy Virgin, and clasps her hand with great affection. Mary appears slightly embarrassed. In the background we see the baptism of Christ, with God the Father blessing him from the clouds above, and this scene is supposed to have reference to the name of the donor of the picture, Giovanni-Battista Branconio of Aquila, who presented it to the church of San Silvestro at Aquila in the Abruzzi, where it was held in such high esteem that a law was passed on the 2nd of April, 1520, declaring that no copy of Raphael's "Visitation" should ever be made on any account whatever. Nevertheless Giovanni Andrea Urbini of Urbino, obtained permission to copy it for the high altar of the Compagnia dell'Umilta. The original was bought by Philip IV. of Spain in 1665 for the Escurial Palace at Madrid; it was carried off by the French in 1813, transferred to canvas in Paris, restored to Spain in 1822, and is now in the royal museum at Madrid.

Raphael executed the greater part of this painting himself; the head of St. Elizabeth is of extraordinary beauty, but the Virgin's is wanting in the delicate refinement common to the great master's Madonnas; the landscape in the background is treated in a broad and masterly style. The "Visitation" has been engraved by A. B. Desnoyers and several others.

226.

THE HOLY FAMILY UNDER THE OAK TREE.

The Virgin, seated under an oak, holds Jesus on her knees, the latter looks lovingly up into his mother's face, and at the same time bends forward to put his arm round St. John, who is standing near him offering him a parchment scroll inscribed with the words: *Ecce Agnus Dei.* Each child rests one foot on a cradle, on which is written Raphael Pinx. St. Joseph stands on the right resting his arm on a fragment of antique architecture with a bas-relief.

As a whole, this composition is stiff, and the general style leads us to suppose it to have been painted by Francesco Penni after a drawing by Raphael, we do not know for what place it was originally executed, but it is now in the Royal Museum at Madrid. It has been engraved by Giulio Bonasone, and many others, and copies of it are distributed in different European galleries.

227.

THE HOLY FAMILY, CALLED THE PEARL.

On wood; height 36¼ inches, width 46 inches.

The Virgin is seated near a cradle holding Jesus on her knees with the right hand. The Holy Child stretches out his arms towards St. John, who, wrapped in a sheep's-skin, is offering fruits to his divine companion. The Virgin watches the graceful movements of the children with a loving expression, and leans against St. Elizabeth, who kneels on the right with her left arm round her cousin's shoulders. In the background on the left we see St. Joseph in a ruin, and in the landscape on the right are a few small figures. This picture was evidently painted by Giulio Romano, but Raphael added finishing touches in several parts.

The Holy Family now under review, was amongst the pictures bought by Charles I. of the Duke of Mantua. After his death in 1649, the Spanish ambassador acquired it, in the name of Philip IV. for £2,000, and it was sent to Madrid with other art objects. When the King of Spain saw it for the first time he exclaimed, "That is my pearl," hence its present title. It was carried off to France in 1813 and sent back to Spain in 1822, after having been restored and transferred to new canvas. It is now in the Royal Madrid Museum. Several sketches for it are preserved in different collections, and it has been engraved by Giov. Bap. Franco, Lucas Vorsterman and many others. A list of imitations of the "Pearl" is given in Passavant's "Life of Raphael," vol. ii. pp. 252-254 (French ed.)

228.

THE ARCHANGEL MICHAEL.

Painted on wood and transferred to canvas; height 82 inches, width 41½ inches.

St. Michael, flying rapidly down from Heaven, just touches the prostrate lord of hell with his foot. Satan, completely overpowered, no longer offers any resistance to the divine messenger. The winged archangel raises his lance with both hands to strike the demon, he wears a tunic reaching to the knees, a breastplate composed of scales of gold and a waistbelt with a sword; his legs are bare and his feet are shod with buskins leaving the toes uncovered. Red and blueish flames shoot up from the crevices of the ground, and a rugged landscape with the sea in the distance forms the background.

In St. Michael, Raphael appears to have intended to embody an ideal of youth and beauty, for in him are united the gracefulness of youth with the vigour of full grown manhood; the rosy hue of the flesh tints is symbolical of the angelic nature, and the whole figure forms a striking contrast to that of the fallen angel, whose degraded condition as a mere demon, is shadowed forth in the dark brownish colouring of the flesh.

Faithful to his just conception of the requirements of art, Raphael has avoided bringing the prostrate Satan into undue prominence, but by judicious foreshortening of his figure, has made the supernatural power of the archangel the

THE ARCHANGEL MICHAEL.

In the Louvre.

first thing to strike the spectator, the hideousness of the demon serving only to heighten the majestic beauty of his conqueror.

On the border of the archangel's blue garment is written, "Raphael Urbinas Pingebat. MD.XVIII.," and according to Vasari, Raphael painted this picture for Francis I., but this is a mistake; it and another were ordered by Lorenzo de' Medici, who wished to present them to the king, in the hope of gaining his support in his unjust pretensions to the Duchy of Urbino. The paintings were finished in May, 1518, and sent on mules under the charge of a servant to Fontainebleau, where Lorenzo was staying at the time. They appear to have suffered considerably on the journey, and to have been neglected in France, for in the accounts for 1533-1546, we find the item of "£11 to Francesco of Bologna, painter, for superintending the washing and cleaning with varnish of four large paintings by Raphael of Urbino, belonging to the king, viz., Saint Michael, Saint Margaret, Saint Anne, and the portrait of the Regent of Naples." In 1773, the first-named was transferred to canvas by Picault, who again restored it in 1776. Picault the younger cleaned it a second time in 1800, and in our own day much of the repainting was carefully removed by Haquin, and it has become once more possible to recognise the great master's touch, but we can easily understand that all this cleaning and restoring have done the picture a great deal of harm.

It has been engraved by N. Beatrizet, Nic. de Larmessin, Louis Surugue, Alexander Tardieu, and many others. Ancient copies are also very numerous.

229.

THE LARGE HOLY FAMILY.

Painted on wood and transferred to canvas; height 82 inches, width $54\frac{1}{2}$ inches.

The Virgin is bending forward raising Jesus from the cradle. On the left kneel St. Elizabeth and St. John, the former joining the child prophet's hands together as though to teach him to adore the infant Saviour. On the right, behind the Virgin, stands St. Joseph in an attitude of contemplation, and on the other side are two angels, one with arms crossed on her breast, and the other scattering flowers. The wall of the room, with a green curtain, forms the background, and on the left we see a small piece of sky.

From a passage in Vasari's "Life of Giulio Romano," we gather that this artist executed the greater part of the painting now under notice, which would account for the sober flesh colouring of the children and of St. Elizabeth, whilst the heads of the Virgin and St. Joseph are in Raphael's own masterly style.

The "Holy Family" of 1518 was the second picture ordered by Lorenzo de' Medici. Usteri relates that it was at first placed over a fire-place at Versailles and was rescued from its smoky position by Wille (the engraver of Königsberg at Paris), and placed in an antechamber. As the panel on which it was painted had suffered considerably, it was transferred to canvas, and is now in a very satisfactory condition, except for its brownish tone, which probably arises from the lampblack used by Giulio Romano for the sketch.

It has been engraved by G. Edelinck, Virgilius Solis, and many others; several studies for it are preserved in different collections, and copies of it of various kinds are numerous. See the French edition of Passavant's "Life of Raphael," vol. ii. pp. 259, 260.

230.

SAINT MARGARET.

On wood; height 72½ inches, width 50 inches.

St. Margaret, who resisted the temptations of the world by the power of faith, is always represented subduing a dragon. In this picture also we see a noble maiden of extreme beauty treading on a fearful dragon, which is rolling at her feet. In her right hand she holds a palm-branch, and in the left the mantle which covers her shoulders.

We believe this painting to have been almost entirely executed by Giulio Romano, but we recognise the genius of Raphael in the innocence and purity of the Saint's expression and in the arrangement of the draperies. Vasari tells us that the "Saint Margaret" was sent by Raphael to the King of France. It was one of those cleaned by Primatticcio in 1530, and is now in the Louvre, having been transferred to canvas. It has unfortunately been so much cleaned and restored, that it is only in parts that it retains its original beauty. It has been engraved by L. Surugue, A. B. Desnoyers, and others.

231.

THE ST. MARGARET OF THE VIENNA GALLERY.

On wood; height 64 inches, width 49 inches.

This is a remarkable repetition of the picture described above, with certain important changes. The Saint is here represented leaving the cavern holding a small crucifix in the left hand and raising the red drapery which falls from her left shoulder with the right. Here she does not look at the spectator, but at the dragon rolling in fearful contortions at her feet. As its name implies, this composition is in the Vienna collection. It was probably executed by Giulio Romano after a drawing by Raphael.

232.

THE SMALL HOLY FAMILY OF THE LOUVRE.

On wood; height 15 inches, width 11½ inches.

Jesus, standing up in his cradle, leans across his mother's knees, and caresses the cheeks of the child St. John with both hands. St. Elizabeth kneels beside her son, and holds him with the right hand. Ruins covered with shrubs and plants, with a rich landscape on either side, form the background.

This small painting is treated in a delicate but spirited and masterly style; it is, however, impossible to deny that the Virgin's head is rather large, and her feet are rather small compared to the rest of her figure. The warm colouring and the execution of the landscape lead us to suppose that this Holy Family was painted by Giulio Romano after a drawing by his master. According to Félibien it was given by Raphael to Adrian Gouffier, papal legate in France in 1519. In any case it belonged to him, and it was protected from injury by a small wooden shutter, still preserved in the Louvre, with a figure of Plenty painted on it in grisaille by Francesco Penni, after a sketch by Raphael himself.

The "Holy Family of the Louvre" has been engraved by Fr. Poilly, F. Massard, A. B. Desnoyers and many others.

233.

Portrait of Joan of Aragon.

To the knees. On wood, height 47½ inches; width 38½ inches.

The young princess is seated, seen three-quarters face, and turning to the left. Her face is of a pure oval shape, and her beautiful light hair falls in masses round her throat. Blue eyes, arched eyebrows, an open forehead, a delicate nose, a small and pretty mouth, a round and dimpled chin, together make up a most pleasing countenance. On her head is a red velvet cap, adorned with pearls and precious stones; and her amaranth-coloured velvet dress has wide sleeves of yellow silk with under sleeves of gauze. With her right hand she grasps a fur pushed back from her neck, and the left rests on her knees. For background we have a room looking out upon a garden across a richly decorated *loggia*.

We believe that Lorenzo de' Medici had this portrait painted as a present for Francis I., who, as is well known, was a great admirer of the fair sex. It was placed in the Apollo gallery of portraits in the Louvre by Henry IV.; and, having by some means escaped when the gallery was destroyed by fire in 1660, is still one of the ornaments of the National Gallery of France. Raphael executed the principal part of this famous picture himself, G. Romano adding the accessories. There is a good copy of it in Warwick Castle, and it has been engraved by Raphael Morghen.

A few words on the history of the celebrated subject of this portrait may possibly be of interest to our readers, and for the verdict of her cotemporaries on her charms, we refer the admirers of her likeness to Passavant's "Life of Raphael," vol. ii. pp. 266-269. (French ed.)

Joan of Aragon was the daughter of Ferdinand, Duke of Montalto, and married Ascanio Colonna, Prince of Tagliacozzo, Duke of Palliano and Constable of Naples. She was one of the most famous of the female wits and beauties of the sixteenth century, and retained her celebrity to a very advanced age; she shared the adverse fortunes of her husband when Paul IV. confiscated all the possessions of the Colonna family in the States of the Church, was detained a prisoner in her palace at Rome, and would have been poisoned, had she not managed to elude the vigilance of the Caraffas in 1556, escaping on horseback with her two daughters, just in time to aid the cause of her son, Marc Antonio Colonna, the hero of Lepanto. She was joyfully received by the Duke of Alba, when Viceroy of Naples, who likened her to the famous Cloelia who fled from the Etruscan camp and swam across the Tiber to Rome. Joan's husband was at this time in prison at Naples, where he died on the 24th of March, 1557, after three years' detention, on account of an alleged attempt on the life of the king. His wife survived him a few months only, and died in October, 1557.

234.

PORTRAIT OF LEO X. (BORN 1475, DIED 1521) WITH CARDINALS GIULIO DE' MEDICI AND LUDOVICO DE' ROSSI.

On wood; height $54\frac{1}{2}$ inches, width $44\frac{3}{4}$ inches.

The Pope, turning to the left, is seated in an arm-chair, near a table with a red cloth, on which is a richly chased silver bell and a breviary adorned with miniatures. He holds an eye-glass in his hand, and would seem to be speaking to some one opposite to him after looking at the pictures in the breviary. On his left stands Giulio de' Medici, and on the right Ludovico de' Rossi with his hands resting on the back of the chair. Some architecture, with an open arcade on the right, forms the background. The Pope wears a red velvet cap, a collar of the same colour, and a loose white robe with wide sleeves trimmed with fur. The presence of Ludovico de' Rossi, who was created cardinal in 1517 and died in 1519, proves that this painting was executed about 1518. It is one of Raphael's greatest masterpieces, and has raised him above all other portrait painters. The figure of the Pope is not only treated in a masterly style, but is also finished with the greatest care, and it exactly corresponds with the description of Leo X. in contemporary authors. At a glance we take in his character, his manner of address; in a word, his likeness brings him before us as he was in life. We cannot speak quite so highly of the other portraits, although they are both admirable; that of Giulio was more rapidly executed than the Pope's, and Ludovico has a somewhat worried expression.

In 1589 this painting was hung above the entrance door of the Florence Tribune, in 1797 it was carried off to Paris, where it was injudiciously cleaned, and after the peace of 1815 it was restored to Florence and placed in the Pitti Gallery. A study of the drapery is in the Oxford collection, and a list of copies of it is given in Passavant's "Life of Raphael," vol. ii. p. 273. (French ed.)

235.

PORTRAIT OF LORENZO DE' MEDICI, DUKE OF URBINO (BORN 1492, DIED 1519.)

Lorenzo de' Medici, son of Piero de' Medici and father of the famous Catherine, wife of Henry II. of France, is represented half length, three-quarters face and turning to the left. He has the characteristic features of the Medici family, and his hair and beard are cut short. He wears a cap with a medal, a white shirt, a doublet with red sleeves stitched with gold, and a fur-trimmed cloak. He holds the pommel of a dagger in his right hand and lets the left fall behind him.

This portrait was painted in 1518, and was at Florence in the time of Vasari, but we do not know what became of it afterwards. The copy from which we have taken our description is in the Fabre collection at Montpellier and is shown as the original, but it is impossible to accept it as such.

236.

PORTRAIT OF A VIOLINIST (1518).

This is a bust portrait of a youth about twenty years old; we have no positive information as to his name, but we believe him to be Andrea Maorone, an impro-

visatore of Brescia, who was rising into fame in the time of Leo X. Raphael evidently painted this likeness with real pleasure; the finely-shaped head, the noble brow, the eyes full of genius, and the intellectual expression of the whole face, are rendered in the great master's best manner, and it is difficult to understand how he could paint two characters so totally different as Leo X. and the young musician almost at the same time with equal success.

Marone, as we venture to call him, is represented three-quarters face, turning his head towards the right shoulder. He wears a black cap, and his brown hair cut straight, falls round his throat; his green mantle, with a fur collar, is trimmed with black velvet, and he holds a violin bow and a few laurel leaves and immortelles in his left hand. The background is grey and on a railing in the foreground, we decipher the date MD.XVIII.

This valuable portrait is in the Sciarra Colonna palace at Rome, it has unfortunately been unnecessarily cleaned lately, and the result is considerable deterioration.

237.

Raphael's Mistress.

On canvas. Half-length figure.

This remarkable portrait, preserved in the Pitti Gallery, Florence, represents a beautiful Roman maiden, seen three-quarters face, and turning to the left. Her hair is parted on the forehead and put back behind her ears, leaving the perfect oval of her face completely visible. Her lustrous black eyes are full of life and fire, her complexion is pale, her nose rather short, and her well-formed lips are parted by a pleasing smile. A veil, fastened behind her head, falls gracefully on either side, completely covering the right arm, a necklace of black stones encircles her throat, her shoulders are covered with a white chemise, of which even the small plaits are distinctly visible, and a bodice trimmed with gold, with a sleeve of white damask, completes her costume.

The first thing which strikes us in looking at this portrait is its singular resemblance to the "Madonna di San Sisto," at Dresden; of course it is understood that this is a likeness from nature, and the Madonna an ideal creation, but at the same time it is evident that the woman here represented was Raphael's model for the Virgin in his famous work.

The celebrated Ludwig Grüner has engraved this portrait of Raphael's Mistress, and a good copy of it has been reproduced by Wenceslas Hollar.

238.

The Madonna di San Sisto.

On canvas; height 118½ inches, width 89½ inches.

The Virgin is seen between two green curtains drawn back on either side of the picture; she stands on a mass of clouds with Jesus in her arms, and looks out of the picture with an expression of celestial repose. A glory, composed of innumerable cherub's heads, surrounds her on every side. Pope Sixtus, in a white tunic and gold coloured pallium turned back with purple, kneels in supplication on the left, and appears to be pointing to his flock, which is invisible to us; near him, but a little below, is his tiara; and opposite, on the other side of the Virgin, kneels St. Barbara, her hands folded on her breast, looking down with eyes full of love at the faithful wrapt in adoration below. We also see two small angels leaning on a balustrade which finishes the lower part of the picture. One of them looks up, and the other at the spectator with a charming expression.

This painting exceeds in value all others produced in Raphael's later years, because it is evidently entirely from his own hand, he appears to have sketched it off in a moment of divine inspiration, finishing the heads with the aid of earthly models.

The "Madonna di San Sisto" was seen by Vasari in the church of the San Sisto Monastery at Placentia about the middle of the sixteenth century, and was bought by Augustus III., Elector of Saxony, for 10,000 sequins or 60,000 florins in 1754. It was received at Dresden with great pomp, and a few years later, was carefully cleaned and revarnished by Palmaroli, the celebrated picture restorer of Rome. The colours, however, having become very dry, the picture soon appeared to be covered with stains, and it was feared that Palmaroli had cleaned it too much. It was only in our own day that the true state of the case was discovered, the back of the canvas was carefully bathed with some volatile oil, and the very next day the famous masterpiece reappeared in all its primitive beauty.

239.

The Loggie of the Farnesina.

These famous frescoes were ordered by Agostino Chigi, but their execution was long delayed on account of the many great works undertaken by Raphael. In the end the great master drew cartoons for the ceiling paintings, representing the history of Cupid and Psyche, leaving his pupils Giulio Romano, Francesco Penni and Giovanni da Udine to complete his work. One female figure, however, in the group of the Three Graces, to whom Cupid is presenting Psyche, is from the great master's own hand, and is remarkable alike for masterly execution, beautiful colouring, and fine drawing, the other figures are rather wanting in delicacy, and the flesh tints are coarse. It is, however, difficult to judge of the original appearance of these paintings, so much have they suffered from decay. Carlo Maratti, who undertook to restore them was obliged to have them fastened to the roof by 850 brass pins, and to repaint the sky entirely. He has been greatly blamed for the harm he did by injudicious restoration, but as we are indebted to him for being able to look at these beautiful creations of genius at all, we should in common justice refrain from hasty criticism.

The Pendentives, or triangular Pictures:

(1.) Venus seated on clouds pointing to Psyche and urging Cupid, who stands beside her, to avenge her on her rival. The God of Love looks with a smile in the direction indicated, and holds an arrow ready in his hand.

(2.) Cupid showing Psyche to the Three Graces, who are seated on clouds.

The sketch for this group is in the royal collection at Windsor, and it has been engraved by Marc Antonio.

(3.) Juno and Ceres interceding with Venus, who is hurrying away, in behalf of Psyche. Engraved by Marco da Ravenna.

(4.) Venus in her car, drawn by two pairs of doves, hastening to Olympus to invoke the interference of Jupiter.

(5.) Venus before Jupiter, praying for vengeance on Psyche, and urging the lord of heaven to send Mercury in search of her. Jupiter holds the thunderbolt in his hand, and his eagle is at his feet.

(6.) Mercury holding a trumpet, and hurrying through the air to fulfil his mission. Engraved by Marc Antonio.

(7.) Psyche, upheld by three genii, joyfully bringing a vase of the water of the Styx, to appease the anger of Venus.

(8.) Psyche presenting the vase sent by Proserpine to the astonished Venus.

(9.) Jupiter embracing Cupid, and giving his consent to his marriage with Psyche. The eagle, with the thunderbolt in his beak, is near his master. Engraved by Marc Antonio.

(10.) Mercury carrying Psyche to Olympus, there to be married to Cupid, according to Jupiter's orders. Engraved by Jacopo Caraglio.

The two large Ceiling Pictures:

(11.) "The Assemblage of the Gods." Juno, Pallas, and Diana, are nearest to Jupiter; and further back on the right we see Mars, Apollo, Bacchus, Vertumnus, and Janus, with two sea gods. Cupid stands before Jupiter, and defends himself from the accusations brought against him by his mother Venus, whilst Mercury offers Psyche a cup containing the ambrosia which is to confer immortality upon her. Engraved by Jacopo Caraglio.

(12.) "The Marriage of Cupid and Psyche." The gods are all half-reclining round a magnificent table. Cupid and Psyche occupy the seat of honour, and the Three Graces, standing behind them, pour perfumes over the bride. Jupiter, seated near, is taking a cup of nectar from the hand of Ganymede; whilst Bacchus, attended by genii, fills the flagons of the other guests. The Hours are scattering flowers over the assembly, and on the left Apollo is singing and playing the lyre; whilst Venus, crowned with roses, joyfully prepares to dance. Engraved by the Master of the Die, and others.

The fourteen Cupids in the Lunettes:

(13.) Cupid, with a face full of fun and frolic, is floating about in the air, proudly showing his arrows. In the clouds, on the right, we see another little spirit.

(14.) Cupid holding Jupiter's thunderbolt, with the eagle flying beside him.

(15.) Cupid, with his back to the spectator, flying away with Neptune's trident.

(16.) Cupid running off with Pluto's staff, whilst another spirit holds back Cerberus. Bats are flying near.

(17.) Cupid flying through the air with the shield and sword of Mars, surrounded by hawks and other birds. Engraved by Ag. Veneziano.

(18.) Cupid, as the conqueror of Apollo, flying away with his bow and quiver held above his head, and the griffin beside him.

(19.) Cupid, whose figure is foreshortened, and who is seen full face, is gaily displaying the caduceus and winged cap of Mercury.

(20.) Cupid, with the thyrsus staff of Bacchus, balancing himself in the air, and looking at the panther following him.

(21.) Cupid, looking very mischievous, flying about with Pan's flute in his hand. Near him is an owl tormented by birds.

(22.) Cupid carrying off the helmet of Pallas and the shield of an Amazon. According to Bellori, these are the arms of Alexander the Great.

(23.) Cupid, holding a round shield and a helmet, rejoicing at his victory over Mars. An engraving of this group by Agostino Veneziano has been copied by Marco da Ravenna.

(24.) Two cupids carrying Hercules' club, with a harpy flying beside them.

(25.) Cupid flying away with the hammer and fork of Vulcan, and a crocodile on the other side of the picture.

(26.) Cupid subduing a lion and a sea-horse, in token of his dominion over all living creatures.

240.

Saint John the Baptist.

On wood; height 69½ inches, width 62 inches.

The Forerunner is here represented as a youth of about fifteen. He is seated on a moss-covered stone in a rugged desert, his only covering being a panther's skin flung over the left shoulder, and half hiding the right thigh. With his right hand he points to the rays which stream from the top of a little rustic cross, and symbolize the Passion of our Saviour; and in the left he holds a parchment scroll, with an inscription, of which the word "DEI" is all we can make out.

According to Vasari, Raphael painted this picture for Cardinal Colonna, who presented it to his doctor, Jacopo da Carpi, after his recovery from a dangerous illness. It is now in the Florence Gallery, where it may be compared with the original study. It is difficult to believe it to be by Raphael himself, as it is wanting in the chief characteristics of his style: parts of it, however, leave no doubt that he aided in the execution; the torso, for instance, is admirably outlined and full of life. The truth would appear to be that it was finished after his death by Giulio Romano, or some other of his pupils.

The study for "John the Baptist" has been engraved by Ugo da Carpi, and the painting itself by C. Bervic and others. Copies of it are also very numerous, and a fine one may be seen at Tintern Abbey, near Chepstow, the seat of Lord Clifford.

241.

The Transfiguration.

On wood; height 160½ inches, width 111½ inches.

This was Raphael's last and finest oil-painting, and was ordered by Cardinal Giulio de' Medici for the cathedral of Narbonne; it was not quite finished when the great master's career was cut short by death at the early age of thirty-seven, and it was carried in his funeral almost before the colours were dry. For several years it was preserved in the church of S. Pietro in Montorio, its owner being unwilling to remove it from Rome after the unexpected death of the great master. The French, who were less scrupulous, carried it to Paris with other art treasures; and on its return to Italy, in 1815, it was placed in the Vatican, where it still remains.

The "Transfiguration" consists of two distinct parts: in the upper, Christ, accompanied by Moses and Elijah, is lifted up in glory above Mount Tabor, on which the three apostles have prostrated themselves, overwhelmed by the brightness which emanates from the Saviour's figure. The two ecclesiastics, who kneel in adoration at the extremity of the mount, and appear to us to be rather out of place, are Saints Julian and Lawrence, and were probably introduced at the request of Giulio de' Medici, in honour of his father Giulio and his uncle Lorenzo. At the foot of Mount Tabor is a touching picture of human suffering, forming a striking contrast with the glory of the transfiguration above. An afflicted father, followed by a crowd of people, is bringing his demoniac boy to the apostles, who await their Master's return. The disciples confess their powerlessness, and point upwards to the only One who can cast out devils. The combination of these two scenes of light and darkness, of heavenly glory and earthly humiliation, has been much and unjustly criticised; but when the meaning is once grasped, the beautiful harmony of the whole is evident. It has also been said that Raphael copied his "Transfiguration" from a fresco in the church of S. Miniato a Monte, near Florence; and although there is no foundation for this assertion, it is impossible to deny that he followed a traditional type in the arrangement of the upper part of the picture, but this does not in the least detract from the marvellous beauty of the execution and colouring, or from the deep meaning of the composition as a whole. In this work Raphael appears to have endeavoured to show his complete mastery of chiaroscuro, and he succeeded admirably, but unfortunately much of the effect of his judicious distribution of light and shade is now lost, owing to the use of lamp-black in finishing the work after his death. This difficult task was confided to Giulio Romano, and to him was paid the remainder of the sum due, at the request of Count Castiglione.

Different studies for the "Transfiguration" are distributed throughout Europe, and several are preserved in the Oxford collection. Ancient and modern reproductions of it are alike numerous; a copy in black chalk by Casanova hangs between two of the cartoons in the South Kensington Museum: the whole work has been engraved by Nicolas Dorigny, A. P. Tardieu, Raphael Morghen, and others; and parts of it by G. Bonasone, Raphael Morghen, and many less celebrated artists.

The Sala di Constantino.

Following the example of Sebastiano del Piombo, Raphael proposed to decorate the walls of this hall with oil paintings; and, having prepared a general drawing of the whole composition, he had the figures of Justice and Meekness, on either side of the "Battle of Constantine," painted in by Giulio Bonasone and Francesco Penni, under his own superintendence. But here death cut short his career, and his two pupils, aided by Rafaelle del Colle and Giovanni da Lione, leaving untouched the finished figures, removed the prepared coating from the rest of the wall, and completed the design in fresco.

Four large paintings intended to imitate tapestry, with subjects taken from the life of Constantine, adorn the walls of this hall: by the side of each picture a pope is seated in a niche, surrounded by genii and allegorical spirits; above smaller figures are represented, on pilasters—Apollo, the moon, boys and maidens with the yoke emblematical of Leo X.; and below, caryatides with the diamond ring and other symbols of the Medici surround compartments of various sizes, containing subjects from the life of Constantine, painted in yellow to imitate bronze.

242.

The Address of Constantine to his Troops.

The Emperor, standing on a platform on the left, with a Roman captain beside him, is relating his vision to four standard-bearers, who appear filled with enthusiasm at the recital. In the foreground is a guard, and at the feet of the Emperor are two young pages holding his weapons. In the distance we see the apparition of the shining cross with the inscription, "EN TOUTO NIKA" ("By this sign thou wilt conquer"). Beneath it are the tents of the army, and the soldiers hurrying to tell of the marvellous sight. Further back flows the Tiber, and we distinguish several well-known monuments on its banks. The deformed dwarf on the right in the foreground, was added by Giulio Romano, at the request of Hippolyte de' Medici, to whom the unfortunate creature belonged. The pages at the Emperor's feet are also additions.

243.

The Battle of Constantine.

Height 93½ inches, width 213½ inches.

The scene is laid on the left bank of the Tiber, the chain of the Monte Mario hills, with Mount Janiculum and the Ponte Molle on the right, form the background. In the centre of the picture Constantine is dashing across the battlefield on a powerful white horse, with his spear levelled at Maxentius, who, with his army, is driven back into the Tiber. Three angels with flaming swords hover above the Emperor's head, and proclaim the victory which God has given him. Meanwhile the struggle is desperately maintained, although the troops of Maxentius are falling back in confusion before the cavalry of Constantine, and fugitives are already hurrying across the bridge.

This wonderful composition, entirely designed by Raphael and executed by Giulio Romano, is the largest historical subject ever painted, and is remarkable alike for the number and variety of the episodes depicted, and for the life and spirit of the whole design. The great master has managed to avoid everything repulsive in the bloody struggle, whilst truly representing all the rage and hatred of the combatants; he has given us many a touching incident—the old soldier raising the dead body of the young standard-bearer, for instance, and has relieved the horror of the overthrow by the gallant bearing of the vanquished.

The colouring of this painting is rather cold, but the drawing is correct, bold, and masterly, and it is impossible to speak too highly of the truth with which the ancient costumes and weapons are rendered.

There are several drawings for the "Battle of Constantine" in the Oxford and Royal collections, and it has often been engraved, but by none of the great masters.

244.

THE BAPTISM OF CONSTANTINE.

The ceremony took place in the baptistery of the Lateran, which still exists in Rome, and is accurately copied in this fresco. Pope Sylvester, with the features of Clement VII., stands on the lower steps of the font, and pours water over Constantine, who kneels before him, his royal robes laid aside, and his right hand resting on a book held open by a priest. Near the Pope is a deacon with the consecrated oils, and behind the emperor a church official is waiting with a towel. A noble page is seated on the steps on the right, keeping his master's garments and weapons; in the background we see the cross-bearer and two children with candelabra; near the font a man, accompanied by his children, is ready to receive baptism, and in the foreground, in Roman costume and wearing the royal crown, stands Crispus, the son of Constantine, who, according to tradition, was baptised at the same time as his father.

This is the feeblest of the paintings in this hall, it was executed by Francesco Penni, who made many deviations from Raphael's design.

245.

CONSTANTINE'S DONATION OF ROME TO THE POPE.

In this picture the scene is laid in the interior of the ancient church of St. Peter. St. Sylvester, seated on a throne in the background, is blessing the emperor, who kneels before him, offering him a golden allegorical figure of the town of Rome. Several prelates stand near the Pope, and amongst the kneeling figures behind the emperor, Bellori recognises a member of the Flavi family, who was at that time Grand Master of the order of St. Gregory, which Constantine is said to have founded; Swiss guards, in the costume still worn in Rome, guard the interior of the church and keep back the crowd. Between the columns on the right we recognize portraits of Giulio Romano, of the poets Pontano and Murello, and on the left that of Count Castiglione. The beautiful nude figure of a boy riding on his dog, in complete unconcern of the imposing ceremony taking place near, and several picturesque groups, were added by Giulio Romano, and much as we admire them, we cannot but consider them somewhat out of place.

The execution of this painting is attributed, we believe with justice, to Raffaelle del Colle. It has been engraved by J. Battista Franco and others.

246.

THE EIGHT POPES WITH THE ALLEGORICAL FIGURES.

(*a.*) The Apostle Peter in pontifical robes, with the keys in his left hand, and two small angels near, holding back the curtains of the canopy. Above him on the right is seated the allegorical figure of the Church, pointing to a small temple on her knees, as though repeating the words of Christ: "Thou art Peter, and on this rock will I build my Church." Opposite to the "Church" sits the figure of "Eternity" holding a book, an inkstand, and a pen, and by her side is the phœnix, typifying the everlasting duration of the Church.

(*b.*) Pope Clement I., who lived under Domitian, Nerva, and Trajan, is represented in the same attitude as Peter, with two angels holding back the canopy. On the left is "Moderation" with a bridle in each hand, and on the right "Meekness" with a lamb at her feet. This group has been engraved by Robert Strange, and the figure of "Meekness" is one of the two executed in oil under Raphael's own eye.

(*c.*) Alexander I.—erroneously called Pope Sylvester in the inscription—lived in the time of Hadrian, and died a martyr to his faith. He is represented with a book in his hand, looking up to heaven in ecstasy; on one side sits "Faith" holding a chalice, and on the other "Religion," with two tablets, one bearing the inscription: "*Liber generationis Jesu Christi filii David.*"

(*d.*) Urban I. was Pope under the Emperor Alexander Severus in the third century. He is represented with angels holding back his pontifical mantle, and his figure is full of majesty and dignity. On one side is "Justice"—the second of the oil paintings—with a pair of scales in the left hand, and the right resting on the head of an ostrich, sometimes used as a symbol of uprightness of dealing; and on the other "Charity" is seated with two children on her knees, and a third standing at her right hand, looking up into her face.

(*e.*) Pope Damasus I. was the thirty-eighth bishop of Rome, and flourished about the beginning of the fourth century. He is represented looking up to heaven, with his head uncovered and his hands clasped in devotion. "Prudence," dressed as Minerva, is seated on the left, looking at herself in a round mirror, and opposite to her is "Peace," with an olive branch in her hand.

(*f.*) Pope Leo I., surnamed the Great, lived about the middle of the fifteenth century, and successfully opposed the doctrines of the Nestorians and the Manichees. He is represented seated, surrounded by three angels, one of whom appears about to kiss his foot. "Prudence," with a dove as symbol, is on the left, and on the right sits "Truth," throwing back her veil.

(*g.*) Pope Felix III., by some mistake called Sylvester in the inscription, who opposed the Emperor Zeno and the Patriarch of Constantinople with so much ability and perseverance, is represented reading, and surrounded by four angels. The mail-clad figure of "Force," with a lion at her feet, is on one side, and on the other a window.

(*h.*) Pope Gregory VII., who defended the rights of the Church so energetically, is writing in a book, and surrounded by four small angels. The figure on the right, with a thunder-bolt in the right hand, and a book in the left, may be looked upon as an impersonation of spiritual power.

These eight figures have been attributed to Giulio Romano, and some of them, that of Urban I., for instance, are undoubtedly from his hand; but it is difficult to speak positively of all.

The Socle Pictures in the Sala di Constantino.

Beneath the allegorical figures caryatides are placed two and two on a marble ground, with different emblems of the Medici family; and between them, under the large pictures and the figures of the popes, are compartments of various sizes containing subjects mostly taken from the life of Constantine. We believe them to have been executed after drawings by Francesco Penni.

Under "Constantine's Address to his Troops:" in the centre, the "Fortification of a Camp;" on one side, "The victorious Emperor riding into a Town," and, on the other, a "Horse led in the Emperor's retinue."

Under the "Battle of Constantine" three pictures in the centre: "The Roman Camp;" "Constantine after a Victory, giving audience to prisoners, with a figure of Victory behind him, and the dead body of Maxentius floating down the river near;" and the "Assault of a Town." On one side, the "Departure of the Camp;" and, on the other, "A Vessel filled with Roman warriors, carrying away the head of Maxentius."

Under the "Baptism" two pictures only: "Constantine ordering the burning of the edicts against the Christians;" and the "Erection of the Church of St. Peter by Constantine," in which Pope Sylvester is represented, with the features of Clement VII.

Under the "Donation of the Town of Rome" three pictures: "The Empress Helena finding the True Cross;" Constantine on his knees before the Pope, who has cured him of his leprosy;" and the Apostles Peter and Paul appearing in a dream to Constantine, when the latter was laid up with leprosy."

In the embrasures of the windows are two wide compartments with allegorical subjects: "The Encouragement of Agriculture and Road-making between Rome and Florence;" and the "Encouragement of the Arts and Sciences." With four small pictures: the "Pagan Converts to Christianity destroying Idols;" "Saint Sylvester chaining a Dragon;" "Constantine saluting his mother Helena on her return from Jerusalem;" and "Saint Gregory, inspired by the Holy Spirit, composing his homilies."

Fourteen of the seventeen subjects of the socles and embrasures of the Sala di Constantino have been engraved by Pietro Santo Bartoli.

248.

THE CORONATION OF THE VIRGIN.

On wood; height 126 inches, width $91\frac{3}{4}$ inches.

In the upper part of this picture the Virgin is seated on clouds by the side of her divine Son, who is placing the crown on her head; on either side are two angels, one scattering flowers and the other in adoration. Beneath this group, and separated from it by a thick cloud, the twelve apostles are standing round the deserted tomb, which is full of flowers. In the background we see a town near a cascade.

Raphael promised to paint a picture for the high altar of the convent of Monte Luce as early as 1505, but he was unable to redeem his word. In 1516 a new contract was entered into, and he made sketches for the "Coronation of the Virgin;" but numerous engagements again interrupted his work, and at his death the drawing on the panel was scarcely finished. Four years later Giulio Romano and Francesco Penni undertook to complete the painting, and on the 21st June, 1525, it was at last placed on the altar for which it was originally intended, remaining there until 1797, when it was removed to the Napoleon Museum; in 1815 it was restored to the States of the Church, and is now in the Vatican.

SUPPLEMENT TO THE CATALOGUE OF RAPHAEL'S PAINTINGS.

BESIDES the pictures already enumerated, there are some which we cannot include in our chronological table, as we have no documents relating to them; and others to which Raphael only added a few finishing touches, the actual execution being by his pupils. To make our work complete, we have decided briefly to notice these paintings in a supplement, together with the most interesting of those falsely attributed to the great master.

249.
ADAM AND EVE.

Baseggio, a Roman dealer in art objects, bought a small panel in London in 1835, representing Adam and Eve, which had formerly belonged to a picture with three subjects. The landscape is rich, but the colouring cold, and the head of the woman reminds us of the style of Mariotto Albertinelli, to whom the painting may reasonably be attributed.

250.
THE SACRIFICE OF CAIN AND ABEL.

A stone altar, on which the brothers are offering sacrifice to God, forms the centre of the picture; on the right kneels Abel, his hands clasped, and his eyes raised to heaven in gratitude, for he has seen the celestial fire consuming his offering, and the spiral flames ascending from it. Cain, on the contrary, is standing on the right, grasping the altar with both hands, and struggling in vain to blow alight his neglected gifts. At his feet are a club and some drapery, and a landscape with a few flowers forms the background. The execution of this painting reminds us of Raphael's earlier works, and the originality and power of the conception justify us in assigning it to him. It has unfortunately suffered greatly.

251.

NOAH'S ENTRANCE INTO THE ARK.

(A coloured cartoon.)

This picture is in the Manfrini palace at Venice, and is exhibited as one of Raphael's works; but we are of opinion that it is by a Dutch artist who had studied at Rome, and intended it for a tapestry pattern.

252.

ELISHA RAISING THREE YOUNG MEN FROM THE DEAD.

On wood; height 19¼ inches, width 12¾ inches.

A small painting, representing the prophet restoring three young men to life, erroneously attributed to Raphael. We believe it is really by Pinturicchio, of the school of Perugino.

253.

JUDITH.

On wood; height 51¼ inches, width 32½ inches.

The heroine is standing leaning against a wall, and holding a large sword in her right hand. Her right foot rests on the head of Holofernes, and a landscape with the sea forms the background.

This beautiful picture has been attributed, with apparent justice, to Alessandro Bonvicino, surnamed Il Moretto; it is now in the Hermitage Palace at St. Petersburg.

254.

THE ANNUNCIATION.

This picture is lost; but it is familiar to us in engravings by Marco da Ravenna, Villamena, and others; there is little doubt that it was by Raphael himself. It represented the Virgin on her knees, with the angel standing on the left, raising the right hand in benediction.

255.

THE NATIVITY.

A round picture, 34 inches in diameter, by Lorenzo di Credi, in the Rospigliosi Palace, Rome; at one time attributed to Raphael. The Holy Child is lying on the ground, with the Virgin and St. Joseph kneeling in adoration on either side.

256.

THE ADORATION OF THE MAGI.

(*Of the Ancajani Family.*)

On canvas; 98¾ inches square.

Although this painting has for a long time been attributed to Raphael, we are inclined to believe that it is in reality by Spagna, one of Perugino's best pupils, and a most successful imitator of Raphael's style. The subject is treated in the traditional manner; the infant Jesus lies on a blue cushion, the Virgin kneels in adoration on the left, with St. Joseph near her. The eldest of the Magi is kneeling before the Holy Child, and the others are waiting behind him with their gifts and attendants.

257.

The Last Supper.

A convex semi-circle; height 384½ inches, width 204 inches.

This fresco is in the refectory of the old convent of S. Onofrio, at Florence; it remained unnoticed by art critics until 1845, when it was discovered by Carlo della Porta and Zotti, who at once attributed it to Raphael. It was then much spoilt by smoke, for the room containing it was occupied by a carriage varnisher; a careful restoration, however, soon remedied the evil, and the inscription "Rap. Ur. Anno MDV." on the border of the garment of St. Thomas appeared to confirm the opinion of the two artists as to its author; and the old building, with the painting, were bought by the Tuscan government for the sum of 700 and 12,000 scudi respectively. We ourselves, however, can find nothing to confirm this decision; we believe the fresco to have been executed by Spagna, after a design by Perugino, in the style of Raphael. Two engravings in the Gotha collection, which appear to have been executed after Perugino's original composition, exactly resemble the fresco in its principal parts, and we have already stated with what success Spagna imitated the manner of his illustrious fellow-pupil.

The arrangement of this fresco is similar to that of the old bas-reliefs of the twelfth century, representing the Last Supper. Christ is seated at a long table surrounded by his apostles, and is in the act of raising his hand, and saying, "One of you shall betray me." St. John leans against the Saviour, who embraces him with the left arm. The other apostles, in various attitudes, express their astonishment with animated gestures. Judas Iscariot, seated opposite to the Saviour, turns away his head, with an uneasy and terrified expression. His treacherous face contrasts well with the honest indignation written in that of James the Less, and the characteristics of the other apostles are no less accurately rendered. The head of the Saviour is extremely beautiful, and his face is full of patient suffering. In the distance we see the Mount of Olives, with Christ in agony, and the three apostles asleep near.

258.

Christ on the Mount of Olives.

A single figure. On wood; height 14½ inches, width 5¾ inches.

The Saviour kneels in supplication, with hands clasped and eyes raised to heaven; an angel is descending with the cup of suffering in the left hand, and one foot resting on a cloud. This small picture, which is of a pure and delicate execution, reminds us of Raphael's style in 1505; two small panels, subsequently added, represent the instruments of the Passion painted in grisaille.

259.

The Baptism of Christ and the Resurrection.

Two small pictures in the Pinacothek of Munich.

Two small subjects painted on wood, which appear to have formerly served as the predella of an altar-piece by Perugino. Although Raphael's name is inscribed on the shield of one of the soldiers, we cannot look upon these pictures as anything more than pleasing works of the school of Perugino.

260.
Two Small Pictures.

Formerly in the church of S. Pietro Maggiore, at Florence.

One of these paintings represented the Virgin with Jesus and a few angels; the other the dead Christ mourned over by the holy women. They were carried to France with other works of art, and their subsequent fate is unknown, as they were not returned to Italy after the treaty of 1815. They have both been attributed to Raphael, but with what degree of justice it is of course impossible to decide.

261.
A small Picture in Raphael's Paternal Home.

In the "Morgenblatt," No. 141, published in 1811, allusion is made to a small painting in Raphael's old home at Urbino, supposed to be a youthful attempt of the future master; but we have no further information on the subject except that it was carried away by the French.

262.
Jesus Christ in Prayer.

This is a figure of the size of life, with the hands folded on the breast. It is, apparently, by one of Perugino's pupils, and has been attributed to Raphael. It is now at Frankfort-on-Main.

263.
The Funeral of the Holy Virgin.

In an inventory of Carlo Maratti's pictures, published in Rome in 1712, a painting on wood, by Raphael of Urbino, is valued at a thousand scudi. It is now lost, but it represented the Virgin carried to the tomb by the Apostles, and accompanied by Mary Magdalene and other women. Above, two angels were presenting the soul of the Virgin to God the Father and God the Son.

264.
The Assumption.

A picture at Wilton House, the seat of the Earl of Pembroke, representing the Virgin standing on a cloud surrounded by angels, has been erroneously attributed to Raphael; it really belongs to a much later date.

265.
The Last Judgment.

According to Gerard Hoet, the Count of Plettenberg possessed a "Last Judgment" by Raphael in 1738, which was sold for ten thousand florins. This is all the information we have on the subject.

266.

THE MARTYRS.

A painting representing the martyrdom of several saints was bought by W. Young Ottley in 1801 for £115. It was supposed to have been executed by Raphael when very young, but we are unable either to test or to accept its authenticity.

Holy Families and Madonnas.

267.

THE MADONNA DELL' IMPANNATA.

On wood. To the knees. Figures nearly the size of life.

The Virgin standing on the right is about to receive the Holy Child from the arms of St. Elizabeth. A woman, Mary Magdalene probably, touches Jesus with her finger, and he turns his head towards her with a smile, but embraces His mother. On the right, John the Baptist, who appears to be about ten years old, is seated on a panther's skin, pointing to the Saviour. This picture takes its name from the sun-blind (*impannata*) in the background. There is little doubt that it is by Raphael, who painted it for Bindo Alloviti of Florence. St. John the Baptist being the patron saint of that city, it was necessary to bring his figure into prominence, and he is therefore represented much older than Christ. The "Madonna dell' Impannata" is now in the Pitti Gallery, Florence. It has been engraved by Villamena and many others.

268.

THE REPOSE IN EGYPT.

On wood; height 62 inches, width 46 inches.

The Virgin, in a recumbent position, holds Jesus towards the kneeling St. John, who is offering the Holy Child some fruits in a corner of his sheep's skin. St. Joseph is approaching, leading an ass by the bridle, and caressing St. John. The landscape in the background is lit up by the setting sun.

An old engraving by Giulio Bonasone proves that this fine picture, which is in the Belvidere of Vienna, was painted by one of Raphael's best pupils, after a design by him; but certain grave faults in the arrangement of the figures justify us in supposing it to have been executed without his personal superintendence.

269.

THE MADONNA DEL PASSEGGIO.

Full length figure, half the size of life.

This picture is lost, but numerous copies of it have rendered it familiar to us; one of the best is in the Bridgwater Gallery, and was bought by the Duke of Bridgwater in 1798 for 3,000*l*.

The Virgin is standing pressing Jesus against her with her left hand, whilst she places the right on the head of St. John, who, approaching from the left, is about to embrace his divine companion. Behind a bush near a tree we see St. Joseph, and a rich landscape forms the background.

270.

THE VIRGIN IN THE RUINS.

On wood; height 43½ inches, width 30 inches.

A painting of this name, formerly in the sacristy of the Escurial, but now at Kingston Hall, Devonshire, has been atributed to Raphael, but it was probably only executed under his superintendence.

The Virgin, bending slightly forward, is holding Jesus on a fragment of a cornice, and St. John is kneeling, offering the Holy Child his rustic cross. In the background St. Joseph with a torch is wandering about the ruins.

271.

THE VIRGIN WITH THE ROSE.

Figure to the knees; painted on wood and transferred to canvas; height 44 inches, width 36 inches (Spanish measure).

A Holy Family, with the figures half the size of life, (passed from the sacristy of the Escurial to the Royal Madrid Museum,) in which the Virgin is seated with Jesus upon her knees, Saint Joseph behind her in an attitude of contemplation, and John the Baptist standing on the left, offering the Holy Child a parchment scroll with the words: *Ecce Agnus Dei*. In 1852 this picture was so thickly covered with dust that it was impossible to decide on its author, but it has since been cleaned, and its authenticity proved beyond a doubt. When it was restored a rose was added in the lower part, and it received the name of the "Sacra Familia de la Rosa."

272.

THE MADONNA OF THE DIOTALEVI FAMILY.

On wood; height 27½ inches, width 19¼ inches.

The Virgin, with Jesus seated on her left knee, looking down at St. John, who is half visible on the left.

This painting is in Raphael's first manner, and reminds us a little of the Madonna of the Solly collection; for a long time it belonged to the Marchese Diotalevi of Rimini, but was subsequently bought by Dr. Waagen for the Berlin Museum.

273.

THE MADONNA OF COUNT BISENZO.

On wood; height 31½ inches, width 21¾ inches; figures to the knees.

The Virgin holds Jesus lying across her knees, and supports him with the right arm. The Holy Child looks towards the spectator, whilst his Mother gazes anxiously at him. In the upper corners of the picture are two small angels, and in the centre of the background some falling drapery, with a landscape in the style of Pinturicchio on either side. It is doubtful whether this painting is by Raphael or not; if it be, it was probably painted about 1504; it is now at Frankfort-on-Main.

274.

THE VIRGIN GIVING FLOWERS TO THE INFANT JESUS.

Figures to the knees.

The Virgin holds Jesus seated on her knees, and offers him flowers with her right hand. The Holy Child stretches out his arms to receive them, and turns his head towards his mother. In one hand he holds a half open book.

The design alone of this picture is by Raphael himself, but there are many good paintings after it in different collections; one of the best is that in the Tribune of Florence.

275.

THE VIRGIN IN THE MEADOW.

The Virgin is seated with her body turned to the left and her head to the right, looking at St. John, who is kneeling holding his rustic cross and offering a parchment scroll to the Holy Child, seated on his mother's right knee. A rich meadow forms the setting of this picture, which in its general style reminds us of the "Virgin in the Meadow" of the Vienna collection, although the details are different.

The best copy of this composition is that in the St. Petersburg Gallery, but we do not know what has become of the original.

A long list of "Madonnas," which have at various times been erroneously attributed to Raphael, is given in Passavant's "Life of Raphael," vol. ii. p. 337 to 345. (French edition.)

Religious Subjects.

276.

THE VIRGIN WITH SAINTS.

On wood, 83¼ inches square.

The Virgin, seated on clouds, is carried to heaven by cherubims, four saints stand round her tomb, which is filled with flowers. On the left St. Philip and St. John look up at the Virgin with faces full of enthusiasm, and on the right St. Paul stands beside the kneeling St. Francis.

There is little doubt that this painting is really by Raphael, it probably remained unfinished in 1508, when the great master was called to Rome, but was completed by one of his friends. It is now at Warwick Castle.

277.

THE FIVE SAINTS.

On wood; height 49 inches, width 39½ inches.

The Saviour, seated in a glory, in the midst of clouds filled with cherubim's heads, raises his arms as though to invite all men to come unto him. The Virgin is on the right and John the Baptist on the left. In the lower part of the picture, on the left, stands St. Paul, a sword in his hand, and on the right, near a fragment of a wheel, kneels St. Catherine, holding the palm of martyrdom. A landscape forms the background.

The design for this picture, engraved by Marc Antonio, is certainly by Raphael, but we think the painting itself was executed by one of his best pupils, by Giulio Romano perhaps. It is now in the Academy of Parma.

278.

St. Luke painting the Portrait of the Virgin.

On wood; figures the size of life.

St. Luke, with one knee resting on a stool near an easel, is painting the likeness of the Virgin, who, with the child Jesus in her arms, appears to him in the midst of clouds. Raphael, who is represented as a young man without a beard, stands behind the artist and attentively watches his work. Near at hand we see the head and shoulders of an ox, which is the symbol of the patron saint of painters. The head and arm of St. Luke appear to be all that Raphael himself painted of this picture, the rest was evidently done by several different artists. The whole work has suffered considerably both from decay and injudicious restoration; it is now in the Academy at Rome.

279.

St. Jerome.

This painting is lost, but a study for a kneeling figure which may have served for St. Jerome, is preserved in the British Museum.

280.

St. John the Evangelist.

On wood; height 34 inches, width $65\frac{1}{4}$ inches.

A picture representing St. John seated on his eagle, and supported in the air on a cloud, with a tablet in his left hand, on which he is about to write the Revelation, has been erroneously attributed to Raphael. It formerly belonged to Louis XV., and is now in the Marseilles Museum. A better painting with the same subject is in the Berlin collection.

281.

The Apostles Peter and Paul.

When Fra Bartolommeo was compelled to quit Rome, he left two pictures of Saints Peter and Paul to be finished by Raphael; the great master faithfully accomplished his task, and we easily recognize his style in the head and hands of St. Peter. The paintings are now in the Quirinal Palace.

Raphael also completed another of Bartolommeo's works, representing Saint Catherine of Sienna and Saint Catherine of Alexandria, which was executed for the lateral altar of the Church of S. Romano at Lucca.

282.

Mary Magdalene.

All trace of this painting is lost, and we have no copy, engraving, or drawing of it to refer to; but it is alluded to in "Pungileoni," p. 42, and in "Dennistoun's Memoirs of the Dukes of Urbino," vol. iii. p. 441, published in London in 1851.

Mythological and Allegorical Subjects.

283.

CHARITY AND HOPE.

Two small pictures, formerly at Rome, but now, we believe, in London, representing Charity as a woman with children in her arms, and Hope as a young girl with a flower in her right hand, have been attributed to Raphael, but were, we think, executed by Franc. Penni.

284.

PEACE.

A nude female figure with wings of peacock's feathers, standing on the sea shore, holding an olive branch in her right hand, and gazing up at a bright ray of light above her head. This is a painting of the school of Francia, which has been falsely ascribed to Raphael.

285.

THE HOURS OF THE DAY AND NIGHT.

Twelve isolated female figures on a black ground, with a socle beneath, on which animals and other objects are represented.

286.

APOLLO, THE MOON, FIVE PLANETS, AND FOUR STARS OF THE ZODIAC.

Eleven subjects decorating the roof of the Sala Borgia, in the Vatican, executed by Giovanni da Udine and Pierino del Vaga, under Leo X.

287.

FOUR MYTHOLOGICAL SUBJECTS.

Taken from the vestibule of the Palazzo Madama.

(1) Jupiter and Ganymede; (2) Pluto and Proserpine; (3) Neptune with the Sea-Horses; (4) Juno on a Chariot drawn by Peacocks. Nos. 2 and 3 appear to be by Giulio Romano, and Nos. 1 and 4 by Giovanni da Udine.

288.

ACHILLES AT SCYROS, AND ACHILLES RECOGNIZED BY ULYSSES.

Two mural paintings in the Palazzo Madama at Rome, executed by a feeble pupil of the great master of Urbino.

289.

DIANA AND CALISTO, SATURN, VENUS.

These figures are on a ceiling, painted by Baldassare Peruzzi in the Farnesina, Rome, and have been attributed to Raphael.

290.

Neptune and Amymone.

Amongst a number of pictures sold by the Duke of Devonshire in 1840, there was one representing Neptune embracing Amymone, with Cupid seated in triumph on a dolphin, stealing away the sea-god's trident. It was sold for the small sum of £14 3*s*. 6*d*., but the buyer had it cleaned, and pronounced it to be one of Raphael's finest works. We have not been able to ascertain the truth of this assertion.

291.

Apollo and Marsyas.

Marsyas is seated on the left, playing a flute, and Apollo stands opposite to him, holding a staff in his right hand. His lyre hangs on a tree near, and his quiver and bow are on the ground.

The owner of this picture, Mr. Moore of London, is fully convinced that it is one of Raphael's most valuable works; but we ourselves have no doubt that it is by some painter of the school of Francia, and are inclined to attribute it to Timoteo Viti.

Portraits.

292.

Raphael and his Fencing Master.

On canvas; height 50 inches, width 42½ inches.

A picture in the Louvre bearing this title has given rise to many controversies; it is difficult to decide whom it represents, and who it is by. In the foreground stands a powerful bearded man, resting his hand on his sword whilst he turns to a man standing behind him, and points to some object outside the picture. We are inclined to believe that the younger man represents Raphael himself, as he resembles the fresco portraits of the great master in the Palazzo Lante, but we can pronounce no decision as to the author of this fine work.

293.

Portrait of Federico Carondolet.

On wood; height 48 inches, width 37¼ inches.

Federico Carondolet, Archdeacon of Bitonto, in the kingdom of Naples, was Spanish Chargé d'Affaires at the Papal Court. In this picture he is represented seated, leaning his right arm on a table, and looking at the spectator with an intelligent and thoughtful expression. His secretary is near him, awaiting his master's orders, and in the background on the left we see a bearded man with a paper in his hand. The head of Carondolet is the most remarkable part of this composition, and it was probably drawn and sketched on the panel by Raphael himself. The portrait was presented to Lord Arlington by the Dutch Government, and now belongs to the Duke of Grafton.

294.

Portrait of Monsignore Lorenzo Pucci.

Figure to the knees.

This is really a very remarkable likeness, and was probably painted by Raphael about the same time as the *Saint Cecilia* already noticed (No. 109). Pucci is represented full face, with a white beard; on his head is a black cap, and in his right hand a paper with an illegible inscription. His eyes are turned towards the left, and he appears to be about to address some one invisible to us. Unfortunately this valuable portrait has suffered considerably; it is now in the possession of Lord Aberdeen.

295.

Portrait of Cardinal Borgia.

To the knees.

A picture bearing this title is preserved in the Borghese Palace, Rome, but it is doubtful which Cardinal Borgia it represents. In any case it is a very fine likeness, and the head and hands bear the impress of Raphael's genius, and contrast vividly with the coldness of the execution of the rest of the painting. The cardinal is seated at a table, turning to the right, and looking at the spectator. His face is long and full of character, his head is almost bald, but a few black locks of hair fall on his well-developed brow, and his long black beard and red cap add still more to the dignity of the portrait. A room with bookcases, &c., forms the background.

296.

Portrait of Cardinal Antonio del Monte.

Figure to the knees. On wood; height 34 inches, width 27½ inches.

A likeness of this cardinal was bought at Rome in 1845 by Fabri, and is attributed by him and other connoisseurs to Raphael, but we think the correctness of this opinion more than doubtful, as Del Monte is represented in quite a different style in the fresco of the "Giving of the Decretals." A description of this and other portraits of cardinals, falsely ascribed to the great master of Urbino, is given in the French edition of Passavant's "Life of Raphael," vol. ii. pp. 359 and 360.

297.

Portrait of the Mistress of Raphael.

On wood; height 17 inches, width 12¾ inches.

At Blenheim Palace a portrait is exhibited under the title of "Dorothea, the Mistress of Raphael." It represents a woman of middle age turning to the right, and seen three-quarters face. The head-dress, of white drapery, covers the back of the head only, leaving the oval face, with its setting of black hair, uncovered. This painting is certainly not by Raphael; we are inclined to attribute it rather to Sebastiano del Piombo. We must just notice another portrait of the same woman in the Imperial Gallery of St. Petersburg, which was executed by one of Raphael's pupils. It represents a girl leaving the bath, with a towel thrown across her knees, and the rest of the figure nude. It is not of sufficient excellence to merit further notice, but it has nevertheless been attributed to Raphael.

298.

PORTRAIT OF A YOUNG LADY.

In 1844 Dr. Kestner bought a very fine portrait of a woman for the museum which he founded at Hanover.

It is evidently by a painter of Raphael's school, but we cannot, as other critics have done, attribute it to Raphael. It represents a young girl with refined and pleasing features, wearing white striped drapery about her head, and a narrow gold necklace round her throat. Her dress is white, with large sleeves gracefully arranged, and in her hands she holds a dark brown fur.

299.

PORTRAIT OF GIO. FRANCESCO PENNI, SURNAMED "IL FATTORE."

On canvas; half-length figure.

An interesting portrait by Penni himself, in which he has proved himself a pupil worthy of his great master. It represents a man about thirty, with a grave and reserved expression of face. On the table is a monogram formed of the letters S. and R., but this is evidently a modern addition.

300.

PORTRAIT OF PARMIGIANO.

Valati, a picture dealer of Rome, sold this likeness to an Englishman, giving it out to be that of Parmigiano, by Raphael. It is a half-length figure of a man with a sheet of music and a book in his hand, and rings on every finger. It may be considered a good painting of the school of the master of Urbino.

301.

PORTRAIT OF GIOVANNI DELLA CASA.

On wood. Figure to the knees.

A half-length figure of a prelate about forty years old, with a short brown beard. Although attributed to him, this likeness cannot have been painted by Raphael, for Della Casa was only twenty when the great master died. It is more likely by Francesco Salviati.

302.

PORTRAITS OF CÆSAR BORGIA.

Two paintings, said to be likenesses by Raphael of the notorious son of Alexander VI., are exhibited in the Borghese Palace, Rome, and in the collection of Count Castelbarco, at Milan; but a moment's thought will prove how great a mistake this is, as Raphael was still working under Perugino when Cæsar Borgia escaped from Ostia, and met his death before the castle of Vianoa in Spain.

303.

PORTRAITS OF JACOPO SANAZZARO, SURNAMED ACTIUS SINCERUS.

Born in 1458, died in 1530.

The Cavaliere Lancellotti of Naples possesses a portrait of the poet Sanazzaro which is attributed to Raphael, but was really painted by an earlier master. Another likeness of the same man, incontestably by Raphael himself, is preserved in the St. Petersburgh collection. It is of remarkable beauty, but it has suffered so much, both from decay and restoration, that it is difficult to imagine what it was like at first.

304.

PORTRAIT OF A CARTHUSIAN MONK.

On wood; height $10\frac{1}{2}$ inches, width $7\frac{3}{4}$ inches.

This precious little picture belongs to Dr. Spicker of Berlin. It is a half-length profile figure of a friar gazing up to heaven. The head is treated in much the same style as in the distemper portraits of two monks already described (No. 43), and we conclude that Raphael painted this likeness about 1505. The ear, nose and eyes are beautifully drawn, and the shadows of the flesh-tints are warm, but the light parts of the cheek and chin are executed in a less satisfactory style.

305.

PORTRAIT OF A YOUNG MAN.

In the Louvre; height $23\frac{1}{2}$ inches, width 17 inches.

A half-length portrait of a young man of a melancholy disposition, turning to the left, and looking at the spectator, which has been attributed to Raphael, but is more likely by Ridolfo Ghirlandajo.

306.

PORTRAIT OF A MAN IN A RED MANTLE.

To the knees—on wood; height 34 inches, width $25\frac{1}{2}$ inches.

A portrait was publicly sold in Paris on the 30th March, 1827, as a likeness by Raphael of one of the Medici, but after enjoying a brief notoriety it returned to its original obscurity.

307.

PORTRAIT OF A YOUNG MAN.

In the Fabre collection, Montpellier.

On wood; height $65\frac{1}{4}$ inches, width $54\frac{1}{2}$ inches.

A young man, with an incipient beard, seen three-quarters face, and turning to the left. He wears a black cap, and his light brown hair falls on his shoulders. His head and face are very beautiful, and their charm is increased by his earnest and melancholy expression. The colouring reminds us of Raphael's Florentine manner, but the painstaking execution is altogether different from his easy and spirited touch. We have little doubt that this likeness was really painted by Ridolfo Ghirlandajo.

308.

PORTRAIT OF A YOUNG MAN.

A portrait of a man in the Duke of Alva's collection at Madrid has been attributed to the master of Urbino, but it appears to us to belong rather to the Venetian school.

309.

PORTRAIT OF A WOMAN.

In the German translation by Volkmann of the "Life of the Painters of Argenville," a beautiful portrait, belonging to the collection at Modena, is alluded to as an authentic work by Raphael, but this is all the information we have on the subject.

310.

PORTRAITS OF MARC ANTONIO RAIMONDI.

M. Parade de l'Estang of Aix has a very fine portrait of the celebrated engraver of Bologna, and Signor G. Villardi of Milan has another of the same person. Both are attributed to Raphael, but with what degree of truth we are unable to decide.

311.

PORTRAIT OF RAPHAEL'S MOTHER.

A portrait painted on wood is exhibited in the Museum of Naples, as a likeness by the great master of his mother, but as she died when he was only eight years old, we need not pause to criticise either the paintings or the opinions concerning it.

312.

PORTRAIT OF A YOUNG GENTLEMAN.

This is a half-length figure of a young man said to be the portrait of Antonio Tebaldeo by Raphael, but it neither represents him, nor is it by the great master of Urbino.

313.

PORTRAIT OF RAPHAEL'S APOTHECARY.

A bust portrait of a man about thirty-five years old is exhibited under this title at Copenhagen. We doubt whether it is really by Raphael, but in any case it is a very fine painting.

314.

PORTRAIT OF A YOUNG MAN.

Sir Thomas Baring of Stratton possesses a fine portrait of a young man said to be Lorenzo de' Medici, which was probably painted by Andrea del Sarto, or by one of Raphael's pupils.

We should never finish if we were to enumerate all the portraits which have at various times been attributed to Raphael, but we have said enough to show on what slight grounds many assertions of authenticity are made, and in conclusion we would urge our readers to weigh well the evidence on both sides before pronouncing a decision in doubtful cases.

TABLE OF RAPHAEL'S PAINTINGS,

CLASSED ACCORDING TO THEIR SUBJECTS.

Frescoes and Oil Paintings in the Vatican.

The Stanza della Segnatura.

The Stanza d'Eliodoro, in the Vatican.

The Stanza of the Incendio del Borgo, or di Torre Borgia, in the Vatican.

The Sala di Constantino, in the Vatican.

[1] The numbers refer to the Chronological Catalogue.

The Loggie of the Vatican.

52 Frescoes in the cupolas; 48 subjects from the Old and 4 from the New Testament, executed by Raphael's pupils after his small sepia sketches, under the superintendence of G. Romano, 121-172.

12 Subjects in cameo, imitating copper in relief, executed by Pierino del Vaga, 174-185.

Subjects from the Bible.

The Frescoes of the Loggie, from the Creation of the World to the Resurrection of Christ, 121-172.

Church Banner: The Holy Trinity and the Creation of Eve, at Citta di Castello, 4.

Original Sin; on the Ceiling of the Stanza della Segnatura, in the Vatican, 67.

Moses with the Tables of the Law, on the Socle of the Stanza della Segnatura, in the Vatican, 74 (*i*).

The Judgment of Solomon, on the ceiling of the Stanza della Segnatura, 70.

God appearing to Noah, fresco on the ceiling of the Stanza d' Eliodoro, in the Vatican, 94.

The Sacrifice of Isaac, fresco on the ceiling of the Stanza d' Eliodoro, 95.

Jacob's Dream, fresco on the ceiling of the Stanza d' Eliodoro, 96.

Moses prostrate before the Burning Bush, fresco on the ceiling of the Stanza d'Eliodoro, 97.

Joseph before Pharaoh; the Red Sea; Moses receiving the Tables of the Law, small pictures in the embrasures of the windows of the Stanza d'Eliodoro, 103.

The Prophets, frescoes in S. Maria della Pace, at Rome, Daniel and David, Jonah and Hosea, 105.

The Prophet Isaiah, fresco in the Church of St. Agostino, at Rome, 85.

The Vision of Ezekiel, Pitti Palace, Florence, 110.

Subjects relating to Christ.

The Birth of Christ (lost), 111.

The Adoration of the Shepherds, formerly at Bologna, 36.

The Infant Jesus with St. John the Baptist, at Perugia, 1.

Raphael's Tapestries, in the Vatican, second series, taken from the Life of Christ, 12 subjects and a thirteenth representing allegorical figures (the greater part after Giulio Romano and other pupils of Raphael), 197-207.

Raphael's Tapestries, first series, 10 subjects from the Lives of the Apostles, 186-195.

Raphael's Seven Cartoons, in the South Kensington Museum, pp. 261, 262.

Christ and the Apostles, fresco in the Sala Vecchia de' Palafrenieri at Rome, repainted by Taddeo Zucchero, 120.

Christ and the Apostles, in the embrasure of a window in the Stanza della Segnatura, 73.

Christ on the Mount of Olives; in the Maitland Collection at Stanstead, Sussex, 17.

Christ bearing his Cross (Lo Spasimo di Sicilia), Madrid Museum, 224.

Christ on the Cross, with four Saints; in Lord Ward's Collection, 6.

The Entombment, Borghese Palace, Rome, 48.

Three small round pictures: Christ seated on a sarcophagus, St. Lodovicus and Herculanus; in the Berlin Museum, 20.

The Resurrection of Christ, in the Vatican, 2.

Pax Vobis, in the Tosi Collection at Brescia, 27.

The Transfiguration, in the Vatican, 241.

Subjects relating to Christ, in the embrasures of the windows of the Stanza della Torre Borgo, in the Vatican, 119.

Holy Families and Madonnas.

The Holy Family of Naples, in the Museum of Naples, 91.

The Holy Family called the Pearl, in the Madrid Museum, 227.

The Holy Family under the Oak, in the Madrid Museum, 226.

The Holy Family with Jesus seated on a Lamb, in the Madrid Museum, 46.

The Large Holy Family of 1518, in the Louvre, 229.

The Small Holy Family in the Louvre, 232.

The Holy Family of the Canigiani Family, in the Museum of Munich, 45.

The Holy Family with St. Joseph without a beard, in the Hermitage Palace, St. Petersburg, 38.

The Holy Family under the Palm, in the Bridgewater Gallery, London, 33.

The Madonna di Fuligno, in the Vatican, 84.

The Madonna della Sedia, Pitti Gallery, Florence, 221.

Subjects relating to the Virgin.

Saints.

Mary Magdalene and Saint Catherine, in the Camuccini Collection, in 1845, at Rome, 8.
Saint Margaret, in the Louvre, 230.
The Saint Margaret of the Vienna Gallery, a repetition of that in the Louvre, 231.

Mythological and Allegorical Subjects.

The Parnassus, fresco in the Stanza della Segnatura, in the Vatican, 58.
Apollo flaying Marsyas, on the ceiling of the Stanza della Segnatura, 68.
Allegorical Figure of Poetry, on the ceiling of the Stanza della Segnatura, 64.
Allegorical Figure of Theology, on the ceiling of the Stanza della Segnatura, 63
Allegorical Figure of Philosophy, on the ceiling of the Stanza della Segnatura, 65.
Allegorical Figure of Jurisprudence, on the ceiling of the Stanza della Segnatura, 66.
The three Allegorical Figures, Prudence, Force, and Moderation, fresco in the Stanza della Segnatura, 60.
Astronomy, or the Contemplation of the Heavenly Bodies, on the ceiling of the Stanza della Segnatura, 69.
Speculative Philosophy, on the socle of the Stanza del Incendio Borgo, 74 (*c*).
The Knowledge of Divine Things, on the socle of the Stanza della Segnatura, 74 (*a*).
Twelve allegorical Figures, and twelve small symbolical compositions, on the socles of the Stanza d' Eliodoro, 102.
The Bath Room of Cardinal da Bibiena, in the Vatican; seven mythological subjects in fresco, 209-215.
And in the same room, six Victorious Cupids, beneath the principal frescoes, 216.
On the ceiling, Cupid and Pan, 217.
Galatea, fresco in the Farnesina, Rome, 106.
Loggie of the Farnesina, subjects taken from the fable of Cupid and Psyche, 239.
The Three Graces, in Lord Ward's Collection, London, 42.
Tapestries, with Cupids at play, five subjects now lost, pp. 266, 267.
The Vision of a Knight, in the National Gallery, 13.

Antique Subjects.

The Sibyls, frescoes in S. Maria della Pace, at Rome; the Cumæan, Persian, Phrygian, and Tiburtine, 105.
The Sibyl of Tibur, on the socle of the Stanza della Segnatura, 74 (*b*).
The Marriage of Alexander and Roxana, in the Raphael Villa, Rome, 218.
Alexander the Great placing the poems of Homer in the tomb of Achilles, grisaille picture under the Parnassus, in the Stanza della Segnatura, in the Vatican, 71.
The Siege of Syracuse, on the socle of the Stanza della Segnatura, 74 (*g*).
The Death of Archimedes, on the socle of the Stanza della Segnatura, 74 (*h*).
The School of Athens, fresco in the Stanza della Segnatura, 59.
The Emperor Augustus forbidding the burning of Virgil's Æneid, grisaille picture under the Parnassus, in the Stanza della Segnatura, 72.
A Heathen Sacrifice, on the socle of the Stanza della Segnatura, 74 (*d*).
Oriental Scholars and Magicians, on the socle of the Stanza della Segnatura, 74 (*f*).

Subjects relating to the Church.

Theology, or the Dispute of the Holy Sacrament, fresco in the Stanza della Segnatura, 57.
Heliodorus driven from the Temple, fresco in the Stanza d' Eliodoro, in the Vatican, 98.
The Miracle of Bolsena, fresco in the Stanza d' Eliodoro, in the Vatican, 99.
The Baptism of Constantine, in the Sala di Constantino, in the Vatican, 244.
Constantine's Address to his Troops, in the Sala di Constantino, 242.
The Donation of Rome to the Pope, embrasure of a window in the Stanza d' Eliodoro, 103.
Subjects from the History of Constantine, socle pictures in the Sala di Constantino, in the Vatican, 247.
The Coronation of Charlemagne, fresco in the Stanza of the Incendio del Borgo, in the Vatican, 115.
Gregory IX. giving the Decretals, fresco in the Stanza della Segnatura, 62.
The Oath of Leo III., fresco in the Stanza of the Incendio del Borgo, 114.
The Incendio del Borgo, fresco in the Stanza of the same name, 116.

Battles.

Portraits.

Ornaments, &c.

PICTURES ATTRIBUTED TO RAPHAEL.

Subjects taken from the Sacred History.

Holy Families and Madonnas.

Religious Subjects.

Mythological and Allegorical Subjects.

Portraits.

ALPHABETICAL INDEX.

CHISWICK PRESS

PRINTED BY WHITTINGHAM AND WILKINS,
TOOKS COURT, CHANCERY LANE.

CPSIA information can be obtained
at www.ICGtesting.com
Printed in the USA
LVHW031257060423
743358LV00019B/76

9 783382 133399